I'LL TAKE THE FIRE

by the same author

Lullaby
Adèle
Sex and Lies
The Country of Others
Watch Us Dance

LEÏLA SLIMANI

I'll Take the Fire

*Translated from the French
by Sam Taylor*

VOLUME THREE

faber

First published in the UK in 2026
by Faber & Faber Ltd
The Bindery, 51 Hatton Garden
London, EC1N 8HN

First published in France in 2025 by Éditions Gallimard
under the title *J'emporterai le feu*

Typeset by Typo•glyphix, Burton-on-Trent DE14 3HE
Printed and bound by CPI Group (UK) Ltd, Croydon CR0 4YY

All rights reserved
© Éditions Gallimard, Paris, 2025
Translation © Sam Taylor, 2026

The right of Leïla Slimani to be identified as author of this work
has been asserted in accordance with Section 77 of the
Copyright, Designs and Patents Act 1988

A CIP record for this book
is available from the British Library

ISBN 978–0–571–39534–7

Printed and bound in the UK on FSC® certified paper in line with our continuing
commitment to ethical business practices, sustainability and the environment.
For further information see faber.co.uk/environmental-policy

Our authorised representative in the EU for product safety is
Easy Access System Europe, Mustamäe tee 50, 10621 Tallinn, Estonia
gpsr.requests@easproject.com

2 4 6 8 10 9 7 5 3 1

To my sisters, May and Hind, the clan.

To Hakima, the best of friends.

To the #Horslaloi

Q: If your house was burning down, what would you take with you?
A: I'd take the fire.

Jean Cocteau

Anyone who believes that nostalgia for our origins sings within us is mistaken; it is lost, and anyone who leaves is expelled, struck off the list, their civil status revoked. We have no rights, no role, no memory. And if we travel to this place that we left before, we cannot use any form of the verb 'to return'. There is no return for us [. . .]
He who leaves the South becomes a deserter.

Erri De Luca,
quoted in *Frescoes* by Giuseppe Caccavale

Dramatis Personae

Mathilde Belhaj: Born in Alsace in 1926, she met Amine Belhaj in 1944 while his regiment was stationed in her village. She married him in 1945 and, one year later, joined him in Meknes, Morocco. After three years at the family house in the medina, they moved to a remote farm where Mathilde gave birth to two children, first Aïcha and then Selim. While her husband worked furiously to make the farm a success, she turned her home into a clinic to care for the health of the peasants from the surrounding area. She learned the Arabic and Berber languages and, despite many difficulties and her opposition to certain traditions, particularly those concerning the status of women, she grew to love Morocco.

Amine Belhaj: Born in 1917, the eldest son of Kadour Belhaj, an interpreter in the colonial army, and Mouilala, Amine became head of the family after his father's death in 1939. He inherited Kadour's lands but, when the Second World War broke out, chose to enrol in a Spahi regiment. Along with his aide-de-camp, Mourad, he was sent to a POW camp in Germany, but managed to escape. In 1944 he met Mathilde, and they were married at a church in Alsace in 1945. In the 1950s, while Morocco was in turmoil, he devoted himself to the farm, which he dreamed of turning into a prosperous, modern business. He developed new varieties of olive and citrus fruit trees and, after years of setbacks, his partnership with the Hungarian doctor Dragan Palosi finally enabled him to start making a profit and to become part of the bourgeoisie in Meknes.

Aïcha Belhaj: Born in 1947, Aïcha is Mathilde and Amine's only daughter. She attended a convent school, where she finished top of the class. In the late 1960s she went to Strasbourg to study medicine before returning, in the following decade, to live in Rabat, where she became a gynaecologist. She married Mehdi Daoud, a brilliant economist and senior civil servant.

Selim Belhaj: Born in 1951, Selim is Mathilde and Amine's only son. Spoiled by his mother, he went to a colonial school. In the summer of 1968 he joined a hippie community in Essaouira. After spending time in Ibiza, he moved to New York City in 1973 and became a professional photographer.

Selma Belhaj: Born in 1937, Selma is the sister of Amine and Omar. Cosseted by her mother, this radiantly beautiful girl was jealously watched by her brothers. An inattentive student, she frequently played truant from school, and in the spring of 1955 she met the young French pilot Alain Crozières and became pregnant by him. To avoid scandal and dishonour, Amine forced her to marry his former aide-de-camp, Mourad. In 1956 she gave birth to her daughter, Sabah. In the late 1960s she had a relationship with her nephew Selim, and her husband died in an accident. She then decided to move to Rabat.

Mehdi Daoud: Born in Fes in 1945, he was the son of Mohamed Daoud, who worked for French people, and of Farida, a violent morphine addict. After a brilliant academic career at the colonial school, he finished top in the national exams for financial inspection. He then moved to Rabat, turning his back on his family and his childhood. A committed communist as a young man, he earned the nickname Karl Marx, but ended up accepting a position at the Ministry of Industry in the early 1970s. In 1972 he married Aïcha Belhaj.

Mia Daoud: Born in 1974, she is the eldest daughter of Mehdi and Aïcha.

Prologue

One night in November 2021, I lost my sense of taste and smell. There was a woman sleeping in my bed. I licked her shoulder, buried my nose in her neck. I moved my face down between her legs. I couldn't taste anything. The woman began to stir. She pulled me towards her, murmuring my name: 'Mia.' She wanted to make love, but I was terrified. I turned my back on her. I closed my eyes and pulled the sheet over my face. The sheet didn't smell of anything either.

Next came the fever. I lay in my bed shaking, as if I had malaria. Nothing seemed able to warm me up. I covered myself with duvets and blankets, but my teeth wouldn't stop chattering. I lay there, bedridden, for days, alone in my apartment. Nobody came to see me and I didn't answer the phone. The few people who called me must have assumed I was busy writing. I kept coughing, and one night I thought I was going to die. I felt like I couldn't suck enough air into my lungs. Around three in the morning I thought about calling an ambulance, but shame held me back. The shame of opening the door to them in my filthy pyjamas, of letting them into an apartment that had not been cleaned or aired for days. I didn't die. The fever abated. I ended up calling back the people who had left me messages. My editor. My mother. 'What's wrong with you?' they asked. I told them it was nothing. 'Just tired, that's all.'

In the days that followed, I tried to start work again. I would wake at dawn and sit at my desk. And wait. I could stay there for hours without doing anything, staring at the open Word document. I found it impossible to concentrate on my novel. Sometimes I would take a deep breath, slap myself on the cheek and try to focus on the chapter I'd been working on. But soon my mind would start to wander, my thoughts growing blurry. Images would appear one after another, vague ideas bubbling up before vanishing with a pop. I couldn't gather my thoughts, or rather I didn't have any thoughts to gather. I would read the same page five or six times without being able to retain a word of it. As if it were written in a foreign language: the alphabet was familiar, but the vocabulary meant nothing to me. I felt lost, overwhelmed.

I'm the kind of person who always makes lists, but during this period it became an obsession. I would write to-do lists on a notepad in an attempt to clear my head, to simplify my life, but it just made things worse. I would stare at the list and start crying. I didn't know where to start: what book to read, what chapter to write. I was paralysed with indecision – should I do my laundry or clean the apartment? – and ended up just lying in my dirty sheets for days on end. I stopped going to the supermarket because I would freeze in front of every shelf, unable to choose. I felt like I was drowning. Sometimes I would realise that a whole day had passed without me managing to decide to get undressed and take a shower.

Everything seemed insurmountable. I would watch TV for hours, the shutters closed, my phone turned off. I couldn't follow the plots of the shows I watched, but it passed the time and distracted me from my anxiety. I would roll joints in the middle of the afternoon and eat standing up in the kitchen: bland ready-meals that I covered with mustard or Tabasco. There was a metallic taste in my mouth that reminded me of licking out certain women, although I couldn't recall their names or their faces. I slept, but not the way I used to sleep. It was like I'd been smoking opium: I was simultaneously comatose and agitated, and every time I woke up I felt even more exhausted.

I avoided going out. But I couldn't stop people worrying about me. I would leave their messages unanswered, but they didn't give up. Finally, at Christmas, I agreed to eat dinner at my sister Inès's apartment. It was a nightmare. I tried so hard to be cheerful. I drank champagne and – for a moment – I even felt happy to be there, to watch the children tear open their presents with their little hands and squeal with joy at the sight of a doll or a plastic lorry. And then I felt myself disappearing. As if I'd been dragged to the depths of a pond by a crocodile who was going to let me rot in the mire before devouring me. I couldn't follow the conversations around me. It's like there was a delay between the words emerging from people's mouths and reaching my ears, and all I could manage by way of an answer was a goofy smile. It must be like this when you're very old. The others sit you in an armchair in the corner of the room and the party goes on around you: people laugh, they argue, and from time to time someone wipes the drool from your lips. 'She's tired,' my mother said, and I nodded. Just tired, that's all.

After that, I stayed at home. The outside world ceased to exist. This was not an unfamiliar feeling to me. I often isolate myself like that when I'm writing a novel – in my apartment or a house in the country – and I lose all notion of time. But I wasn't writing. I couldn't find the words. I just stared at the blank page as if petrified. I had suffered from writer's block before; my inspiration had dried up and I'd been through fits of rage and despair. But this was different. The words churned around my head: I could think them, choose between them, but I couldn't write them down or speak them aloud. One night, I woke with a start. I'd had an idea for my novel. I grabbed a blank page and a pen from my bedside table and scribbled down ideas for a scene. Mehdi in prison and a bar of chocolate. The next morning, when I woke, I looked for my notes. The sheet was lying at the foot of my bed. I tried to read what I'd written, but it made no sense. They weren't even letters, just a mess of random lines, some vertical, some horizontal. I burst out laughing. I was going mad.

In March 2022, I decided to call a doctor. The woman who answered was a secretary. She was eating as she spoke. She offered me a choice of different dates and times, and I panicked. I couldn't understand what she was saying. I asked her to repeat it. My forehead was damp with sweat. I felt as if the woman could see me and was going to make fun of me. I hung up. I tried again a couple of times, then finally managed to book an appointment online with a GP in my neighbourhood. The doctor's office was on the first floor of an apartment building on Rue d'Amsterdam. I'd noted down the entry code for the door on the palm of my hand, and I stared at it throughout the journey there. It was all that mattered to me. I climbed the stairs. The door was half-open. I pushed it and went inside. Three people were seated in the waiting room, all wearing masks. I sat by the wall, to the right of the bathroom. Across from me, a woman with very beautiful eyes was looking at a poster about the dangers of smoking. I wanted to pull her mask down, to see her face. Through years of observation, I have noticed that people are always uglier than you imagine them to be. You can't trust the beauty of a pair of eyes.

A woman about five feet tall came out of the office, holding a prescription to her chest. I heard my name. 'Mia Daoud?' A very tall man came along the corridor. He signalled for me to follow him and I stared anxiously at his massive back, his grimy white coat. My mother would never have worn a coat like that, with a torn pocket. He sat behind his desk and told me to take a seat. He never glanced at me for more than half a second at a time, and I started to imagine that there was something about me that disturbed him. He wrote down my date of birth and my address, then asked what I did for a living.

I'm a writer.

He turned from his screen to look at me.

'Ah, yes, I thought I recognised your name. Didn't you win a prize?'

I nodded. I was sweating inside my winter jacket, but didn't want to take it off.

'So what brings you here?'

I tried to explain. I kept repeating the word 'tired'. I told him about crying in the supermarket and about the day when I forgot the code to my own apartment building. He didn't seem worried. He was probably the kind of person who thinks all artists are a bit crazy.

'You're depressed.'

I couldn't argue with that. Of course I was depressed, but not to the point of losing my memory or my sense of direction. He advised me to book an appointment with a psychologist he knew.

'He's very quick and effective. A miracle-worker.'

The psychologist worked remotely. One Monday morning, I saw his face appear on the screen of my phone. Several times, during the hours before this appointment, I had thought about cancelling it. But now I was here, lying on my bed, staring at the face of a stranger on a screen. I had spent a long time debating what to tell him, but in the end I didn't say much at all. I mentioned my novel, the difficulties I was experiencing with writing, my faltering memory, my father's death, and he started to nod. 'Let me stop you there for a second.' He tried to explain something to me about dissociation and repression. He compared me to those fruits you sometimes find on cakes, those little round fruits whose name I can't remember. 'It's very important that you continue to see me.' He seemed so sure of himself. I booked an appointment for the following week. I had to pay in advance: a hundred and forty euros. I made the bank transfer, but I didn't keep the appointment. I blocked his number.

Back then, I was watching a TV series about a man with a brain tumour. I became convinced that this was what was wrong with me. The GP had made a very serious mistake. The psychologist had completely missed the point. I talked to my best friend Hakim about this on the phone. I never hide anything from him. I knew he wouldn't make fun of me. He gave me the number of a man who had taught him neurology when he was a student in Paris. 'He's a brilliant doctor and a very good teacher too.'

I liked him straight away. The moment I first saw him in the hospital corridor, I knew I could trust him. He was looking around like a lost child at a fairground. I have often noticed this kind of behaviour among people with extremely sharp minds. They play at being lost, as if they are right there in front of you and at the same time miles away. I sat down in his light-filled office and he stared at me. His eyes were beautiful and distant, as blue as the sky in my homeland. He struck me as honest and humane. He listened attentively while I spoke, glancing down to take notes then looking up at me again with those blue eyes of his. I really liked the way he showed interest in me: sometimes he would repeat the ends of my sentences – 'being there without being there' – and sometimes he would start them. He asked me questions.

'Do you take drugs?'

I told him I smoked joints occasionally. He didn't look up from his notepad.

'That's all?'

I didn't want to tell him the truth. I had only known him for a few minutes, yet I hated the idea of disappointing him.

'I took cocaine for a few years.'

'It destroys the neurons. Did you know that?'

Then he went through a questionnaire. He wanted to know if I remembered what I'd eaten the previous night, what I'd watched on television. He asked me if I was having language problems.

'Do you sometimes get mixed up between words? Are there times when you can't think of a particular word? And, if so, do you tend to forget common nouns or proper nouns?'

He listened to my heart.

While he was examining me, I felt compelled to make conversation. I was afraid he would think I was a lunatic or a hypochondriac. I really wanted him to take me seriously. I told him that my mother was a doctor, that it was a profession I admired.

'There's nothing worse for a writer, you know . . . If I lose my memory, if I lose my language, I'm finished.'

He smiled and sat down behind his desk.

'A few days ago I saw a patient who was a glass-blower. He had the same symptoms as you. Difficulties with language and attention. For him, though, a second's inattention would leave him with third-degree burns on his hand or his whole workshop on fire.' He fixed me with his beautiful blue eyes. 'Have you ever heard of brain fog?'

I shook my head. And yet I felt immediately that those two words described perfectly what I had been experiencing. Often, during the previous months, I had felt as if I was walking through the same thick mist that we used to get in Rabat, those mornings when my mother would turn on the car's headlights and we would see, in the middle of a roundabout, the ghostly figures of white wax policemen.

'I saw my first cases in July 2020,' the doctor went on. 'Patients who were in despair because they no longer recognised themselves. I treated engineers who suddenly couldn't tie their laces any more. Politicians and doctors who fell to pieces whenever they had to make a decision. Imagine that each personality is a sort of harmonious ball,' he said, tracing a circle in the air with his hands. 'Suddenly the ball shatters into a thousand pieces and the patient can't put them back together again. It's as if they're running after themselves, never able to catch up, overwhelmed by everything that's going on around them.'

With a piece of paper and a pen, the neurologist explained how the Covid virus attacks the human brain. Whenever he used a difficult word, he would apologise and attempt to translate it into layman's language. Some of his images were so clear and poetic that they made me envious. I tried to draw him into what for me was more familiar terrain: emotions, literature. This man studied the brain – memory, language – the very stuff of my own work. I wanted to talk with him about Proust and Perec, and when I did, he smiled.

'Ah, yes, but that's something else. You know the brain is a highly complex machine.'

He asked me about my medical history.

'On your mother's side of the family?'

'Blindness, madness, dementia.'

'And on your father's?'

'Cancer.'

That was all I knew. My family tree was obscure, its branches hidden. The doctor prescribed a PET scan of my brain and advised me to be patient.

'But what if I've lost all my memories?'

'No, no, your memories are there, buried somewhere. From observation, I would say that the more you use your brain, the more you deluge it with information, the more difficult it becomes to access your memories. It's emotion that will help you rediscover them. Fear, for example, is a very powerful marker.' As I stood in the corridor outside his office, he put his hand on my shoulder and, in a voice that suddenly sounded shy, hesitant, he added: 'You mentioned Proust earlier. If I could give you one piece of advice, mademoiselle, it would be this: find your madeleine.'

I

At five o'clock, Mehdi stood up. He placed some files in his bag, put on his coat and left his office. He walked through the corridor, paying no attention to the astonished faces of his colleagues. Najat, one of his senior managers, caught up with him as he was about to leave the building. She was holding an accounts book and she waved it in front of Mehdi's face.

'Monsieur le Président, you—'

Mehdi cut her off. 'See you on Monday, Najat.'

'See you on Monday, Président.'

He hurtled down the stairs – the lift was still out of order – and found himself on Rue de Reims. Shivering with cold, he shoved his hands into his coat pockets. He had no idea where he'd left his car. He tried to concentrate, but all that came to mind were columns of figures, green-and-blue graphs, names of clients. The street watchman came running; he wore faded overalls and a baseball cap pulled down over his forehead. 'The R12?' he asked. Mehdi nodded, and the man escorted him to his car. 'I washed it, Président,' he said, holding out his hand. Mehdi slipped him some cash, then sat behind the wheel. The car smelled of rotten fruit and stale tobacco. He rummaged through the pile of papers that covered the passenger seat and found an orange covered with mould. He picked up a copy of Le Monde dated 8 March 1980. A headline on the front page read: 'Arabs Attacked'. Somewhere in France a group of racists had ambushed some students outside a secondary school. The eighth of March. So it had been six days since he had last gone home. Working constantly, locked in his office, he had lost all track of time. For six days he had been surviving on tuna sandwiches and croissants. For six nights he had been sleeping on the short, narrow divan under the window. One night, frustrated by these cramped, uncomfortable sleeping arrangements, he had kicked out at the armrest and broken it.

He tried to start the engine, but it just made coughing noises. The watchman knocked on the window. 'It needs to warm up,' he explained, and Mehdi had to force himself to calm down to avoid yelling at the man that he didn't need his idiotic advice, thank you very much. Miraculously, though, the car started and he set off towards Rabat. There were trucks coming from the port, and he could see smoke pouring from the factory chimneys up ahead. Some schoolgirls in uniform crossed the road, laughing, and one of them waved at him. He let himself drift into thoughts of her smile as the traffic grew ever more congested. Although he had been working in Casablanca for more than six months, this city remained a mystery to him. Sometimes he felt afraid that he would get lost in its vast labyrinth of streets, that he would never find his way again. At a red light, two teenage boys appeared out of nowhere and poured soapy water all over the windscreen. 'Go away!' Mehdi shouted, but the boys, grinning, started wiping the glass with yellow cloths. Behind him, other drivers honked their horns impatiently. Some overtook him. Mehdi handed over the last coins he could find in his car.

Yes, this city frightened him. Casablanca and its two million inhabitants. The foreigners had left: the Spaniards from

Maârif, the Italians from Belvédère, even the French aid workers who'd believed in the future of young Moroccans. Every day peasant families would arrive at the bus station. Casablanca, where the French word for slum – *bidonville* – had originated, was growing so fast that it seemed as if a new alley full of shanties appeared every night, and gangs of beggars accumulated around the doorways of the city's clubs and restaurants. Carriages drawn by emaciated horses creaked past luxury apartment buildings. Young women with bloodshot eyes, high on hashish, were stabbed by the beach in La Corniche. The buildings could never be high or white or modern enough to conceal the city's poverty. There were so many patches of wasteland in Casablanca that Mehdi couldn't tell if the city was eating into the countryside or if the countryside was colonising the city. Gaunt cows wandered between skyscrapers, and a cockerel strode proudly in the backyard of an upmarket clinic, waking the patients at dawn every morning. Further off, in the neighbourhoods where police cars patrolled with their headlights off, boys with thick curly hair composed forbidden songs. Cassette tapes were passed from hand to hand, full of fiery sermons or rock songs. The city resisted, like a living organism fighting off a disease. It resisted the silence, the repression, the orderliness that the people at the top wished to impose on it, as if they were strapping a woman's torso into a corset. The white city thrilled and disturbed Mehdi in equal measure. He was sickened by the smells of iodine and refuse that lingered constantly in the air, by the way even the wind here seemed slimy and dirty, and yet at the same time he could no longer live without it. Sometimes he thought that all it would take was a single spark and the whole place would explode into riots, as it had in 1965. All the ingredients were present: drought, inflation, the costly Saharan war. The country was on its knees, worn down by poverty and unkept promises. The time of utopias and optimism seemed impossibly distant now. The Marxists – the real ones – were in prison, while politicians of all stripes called for realism, pragmatism, compromise.

At another red light, Mehdi got the attention of a taxi driver. 'I'm trying to find the motorway to Rabat . . .'

'It's right in front of you!' shouted the taxi driver, before laughing his head off.

At the top of the next hill, Mehdi merged onto the motorway, pushing his old R12 as fast as it would go. This was the country's first motorway, and the bourgeoisie saw it as a sign that Morocco had finally entered the modern world. Mehdi had argued about this with a former colleague at the Ministry of Industry – a man with oily skin and a constantly half-open mouth who kept repeating in his nasal voice what he had read in palace-funded newspapers: 'We must invest in infrastructure.' Mehdi had retorted that education was the priority. 'Eighty per cent of our population is illiterate. You want motorways all over the country, I want people to be able to read the road signs.' Maybe he shouldn't have spoken to the man like that, in the peremptory tone he took whenever he was annoyed. Aïcha often warned him about it. 'You talk too much, Mehdi. You hurt people's feelings, and it will come back to bite you one day.'

The sky was darkening and purple clouds were massing above the ocean. Night would fall soon, and Mehdi was sleepy. He yawned, forced his eyes wide open, slapped his own cheeks. He was in a strange state, simultaneously exhausted by lack of sleep and overexcited by all the work he'd accomplished and the ambition that was devouring him. He would go to bed as soon as the match was over. He'd have a few beers with his friends, but he wouldn't invite them to stay for dinner. His desires at that moment were simple: to take a long shower, to sleep in clean sheets, and to drink coffee that did not taste burned.

The motorway didn't go all the way to the capital, so he had to join the coastal road. Mehdi turned on the radio. As he'd expected, the journalists were debating the Africa Cup match between Morocco's team, the Atlas Lions, and Algeria's Fennec Foxes. Three months ago, in December 1979, Morocco had suffered a humiliating 5–1 defeat to Algeria at the Stade de Casablanca, sending the fifty thousand supporters in the stands mad with rage and disappointment. People had protested in the streets afterwards, carrying a coffin bearing the epitaph: 'Here lies football'. On the radio, the commentators were calling for vengeance. Tonight, the Morocco team had to save the nation's honour. They needed to win, not only for the glory and joy of their supporters, but for the country, which was fighting, in the south, for its territory in the Sahara. 'What a bunch of idiots,' cursed Mehdi. The journalists repeated hollow phrases that they had learned by heart, fanning the flames of hate against the opposing team. Mehdi found such behaviour disgusting: whipping crowds into a frenzy, expecting athletes to act like soldiers, to play as if they were going to war. He couldn't stand those fanatical football supporters who regarded their opponents as the enemy. Besides, the journalists omitted to mention that, the day after that disastrous match in

1979, the Algerian footballers had visited Casablanca's medina to buy souvenirs for their families, and the vendors had greeted them warmly, refusing to take their money.

There was nothing nationalistic about Mehdi's passion for football. Of course he loved his team and tonight he would pray for Zaki's Lions, but he also loved Zico's Brazil, and he had wept real tears when Cruyff's Dutch team had lost in the 1974 World Cup final. Football made him want to travel the world, and in his wildest dreams he imagined himself singing along with the fans in the Bombonera or the Maracanã. Ultimately, what mattered to him was not the nationality of the team or the name of the club, but the quality of the football. He loved *el jogo bonito*, and he felt a childlike joy when a player – almost any player – started running across the pitch, the ball glued to his foot, when he swerved and danced, when the whole stadium swelled with pride as if it were one man's chest. Mehdi believed absolutely in the great football legends – in those stories of little boys raised in the muddy streets of a *bidonville,* a *favela* or a *barrio* – and sometimes he would imagine himself in their place, playing the game with their genius. The crowd roared for him. It chanted his name: 'Mehdi! Mehdi!' And in his dreams, he dribbled like a god. On a football pitch the script was never written in advance. Anything could happen. It could all change in a second, and nothing was over until the final whistle. Football – which he would sometimes pronounce like a Brazilian: *futebol* – was the sport of the poor, of the Third World, the only place where hysterical crowds would lovingly shout out the name of a Black man or a lower-class man.

It was dark when he reached the centre of Rabat. The cafés were starting to fill with excited supporters, and on Avenue

Mohammed V little boys were selling cigarettes and roasted peanuts. When Mehdi got home, he found Aïcha and Fatima folding curtains and placing them inside crates. The two women were standing opposite each other, holding the corners of the fabric in their hands, and they advanced, folded, then retreated, as if they were performing some old-fashioned dance, a sort of minuet. 'Why don't you let her take care of it?' Mehdi said to his wife. 'You're eight months pregnant – you should be resting.'

He placed his hand on the back of Aïcha's neck and leaned down to kiss her, but she turned away irritably. 'Not in front of the maid.' Mehdi jumped over a box and tried to execute a dance step to make her laugh, but she seemed not to notice. He draped his coat over the back of a chair and went down to the basement, where the television was.

Aïcha was angry with him, and her coldness towards Mehdi, her rejection of his attempts at tenderness, had nothing to do with the presence of Fatima. She resented his long absences while she was kept under house arrest by her pregnancy. She had begged her department head to let her keep working, but he had laughed in her face: 'You can't help women give birth when you're seven months pregnant yourself!' So Aïcha had been forced to accept her situation: stuck at home with her six-year-old daughter and with Fatima, whose belief in superstitions and old wives' tales she found deeply irritating. In the past two days, Aïcha had embarked upon a major clean-up of the house, to keep her mind occupied. She'd had the master bedroom, where the infant's crib would be set up, cleaned from top to bottom. She'd emptied the kitchen cupboards, rearranged the books in the library in alphabetical order, and today she'd been overcome by an urge to take down and wash the curtains, stained yellow by tobacco smoke and dust. 'You know what this means?' Fatima said, picking up a crate. 'You're going to give birth soon. You're making your nest, you see. I know you're highly educated and all that, but I'm telling you: when a woman starts tidying, it means the baby's coming.'

Aïcha sighed. 'I'm going to Mia's room.' And she went upstairs.

Mehdi closed the living room door. He took off his jacket, his tie, his burgundy Church's, and lay on the sofa. Aïcha's tantrums were starting to get on his nerves. It was hardly his fault that women were the ones who got pregnant, was it? Besides, hadn't he spent two years running round in circles, with never a word of complaint? His friends called that time his 'wilderness years'. After leaving his post as chief of staff at the Ministry of Industry, and managing the Football Federation until 1976, Mehdi had found himself unemployed. For weeks he had waited to be assigned a position befitting of his intelligence, his political knowledge and his capacity for hard work. But nothing happened. He could have asked his influential friends in government circles for help, but Mehdi was proud of his refusal to play the old feudalism game. He wanted to be given a job purely for his own qualities. And miraculously, in the summer of 1979, without Mehdi ever being able to guess who might have spoken up on his behalf to the king, His Majesty had made him the president of the Crédit Commercial du Maroc, an obscure credit organisation specialising in real estate and tourism. That July, brimming with enthusiasm, he had turned up to his new offices in Casablanca. At first, parking his car outside a building on Rue de Reims, he thought he must have got the wrong address. 'A hovel,' he told his wife later. The offices occupied two floors that had previously belonged to some French families. In the entrance hall, which smelled of cooking oil and bleach, Mehdi was greeted by Farid, a tubby man sent by the palace to assist him in his new post. Farid had very dark skin and a boxer's face. He looked as if someone had smashed his nose into the shape of a pear before using a blunt instrument to slice his upper lip in half. From the rumours that circulated and from Farid's own insinuations, Mehdi understood that his new assistant had grown up at the royal palace, a child running through the corridors of power. Some claimed his mother was a cook there, and his father a prince's chauffeur. Mehdi didn't want to know the details. He was suspicious of this mysterious, affable man, who struck him as far shrewder than he appeared. He had a courtier's intelligence, moulded by form and custom, capable of taking into account not only the ancestral laws of the Makhzen but also the tastes, habits and moods of men in power. 'I am here to help you,' he said to Mehdi, who heard: 'I am here to spy on you.'

Farid gave him a tour of the property. He introduced Mehdi to the managing director, Hicham Benomar, then took him upstairs to the president's office. Mehdi struggled to conceal his disappointment. He stood in the doorway, brow furrowed, mouth slightly twisted, staring at the portrait of the king that hung from a nail on the piss-yellow wall. Behind the desk, two windows overlooked a noisy interior courtyard where housewives beat their rugs and the air smelled of cooking. How could he be expected to concentrate in a place like this? He turned to Farid and examined his expression, trying to work out whether this was a practical joke or, worse, a deliberate attempt to humiliate him. How could they treat him like this, after he had finished first in the financial inspection exams? All his classmates from that year were now directors of banks or prestigious institutions, and he imagined them in vast offices with magnificent views, pretty secretaries, a chauffeur in livery. Farid, though, remained impassive. They're testing me, Mehdi thought. And, as always when he felt himself challenged, his chest swelled with pride, energy, rage. He was eight years old again, in his too-large glasses, with his bulging forehead, the only Moroccan boy at the colonial school. He was eight years old and determined to be the best pupil in his class. The other managers' offices were on the same floor. 'And what's in this room?' Mehdi asked. Farid opened the door and for a few seconds Mehdi observed the large, empty room: the dust balls on the floor and, on the window, the smear of a smashed fly. It was here that he decided to summon the fifteen employees of CCM for their first meeting. They came in slowly and gathered in front of their new boss, who stood with his back to the far wall. Benomar kept sneezing and eventually asked if someone could open the window. They all eyed Mehdi with a mixture of suspicion and boredom. Who was this man, with his thick beard and his sweat-drenched short-sleeved shirt?

Traffic noise rose from the street below. In the distance Mehdi could hear children shouting happily in a playground. He cleared his throat, pressed his hands together in front of his mouth and took a deep breath. When he started to speak, a shiver ran through the assembled employees; instinctively they recoiled. The president's voice, his cavernous voice, came as a shock. They were like children lost in a dark wood, petrified by the booming timbre of an ogre. Mehdi used sport metaphors – 'We are a team' – that made Hicham and certain others want to applaud. Together, they were going to 'work up a sweat', building a bright future for this country. Of course, he knew that times were hard. The International Monetary Fund had put in place a plan for economic stability, but debt and poverty were rising fast. 'But we are not obliged to submit,' he said, making a little movement with his hips, as though dribbling past an opponent on a football pitch. 'We are not doomed to depend on rain or migrants or international charity.' The new president of this small credit company wanted to give Morocco back its pride, to make it a modern nation, to cure it of its inferiority complex. He had long been convinced that his country could be a paradise, and not only for the tourists who came here to enjoy its miles of sun-soaked coastline, its majestic mountains and the legendary hospitality of its inhabitants. 'We may not have oil, but we have tourism!' he repeated several times, and Farid smiled delightedly. This was the purpose of CCM: to fund tomorrow's great projects, the hotels with swimming pools, the golf courses and holiday clubs, but also the social housing programmes for people living in slums. In a country where access to property was reserved for the elite, Mehdi dreamed of the emergence of a middle class who would buy their own home and car, who would educate their children in schools worthy of the name. 'Be bold!' he bellowed, and Farid looked over his own shoulder. 'Stop being docile!' he roared, and Farid applauded.

Once again, the room was plunged into silence. The employees were lost for words, their heads spinning. Some of them half-heartedly clapped, while others just nodded. Mehdi observed the surprised expressions on their faces, as if they were trying to understand whether all this was real or just so many words – words that some of them found a little too complicated to grasp. Najat Goumine, the only woman on the management team, took a step forward and raised her hand, like a polite student. She asked if this meant she wouldn't be able to take the holiday she'd asked for yesterday. She had promised her children she would take them to the south of Morocco. A man in a shirt so transparent that his dark nipples were visible through the fabric asked the president about wages. Mehdi stiffened. 'We'll talk about that later.'

In the days that followed, he locked himself in his office and barely spoke to the others. Folders piled up on his desk. The floor was carpeted with sheets of paper. He had croissants and coffee delivered in the morning, and he smoked so much that his tongue was soon covered with a yellowish film. Then one afternoon he left his office, his eyes red from fatigue and cigarette smoke, and he gathered his employees in the large room again. He paced around silently as they watched in alarm. Then he told them what he had discovered. His voice was hoarse, his throat sore. 'I carefully read every file. I went through everything I could find on the client accounts, and it's clear to me that – to say the least – this company has been mismanaged for years.' Some people tensed up, braced for a reprimand. Others nodded or smiled, ready to call out: 'I've been saying that for ages!' But Mehdi went on: 'The clients aren't paying on time, and credit has been granted without any guarantees. If we go on like this, the company will be bankrupt in six months.' He placed his hand against the wall and slapped it three times. 'That's why we're going to turn this into a computer room.' The employees were speechless. Some of them, including Najat, thought they were doomed. This fanatical new president wanted to invest in machines so he could get rid of people, so he could fire them all as soon as possible.

In January 1980, a team from IBM came to install mainframes in the room on the third floor, and all CCM's employees had to take classes to learn how to use them. Mehdi hired eager young executives from all over Morocco. 'The management teams of other banks are made up solely of bourgeois types from Fes,' he told Hicham Benomar. 'I want people from every class and region. I want our team here to mirror Moroccan society.' He swiftly promoted Najat, who had a knack for working with computers. Every employee was given the task of digitising their clients' credit files. This was time-consuming, painstaking work. Sometimes a computer would spend the whole night crunching numbers to determine whether a client's account was up to date. Once that was done, Mehdi told each manager to meet with their clients and remind them of their obligations. He advised them based on his experience working in the tax office. 'The first thing they'll do is tell you about all their friends in high places. If that doesn't work, they'll start crying over some sick mother or a kid in a private school or whatever. And if you still haven't given in, they'll try to slip you an envelope. And I'm warning you now: accepting bribes is a sackable offence.'

That winter, the team united around Mehdi. Unlike their previous boss, who used to turn up at eleven in the morning and often didn't reappear after lunch, Mehdi was an extremely hard worker. He seemed to live for his job. He would often spend fourteen hours a day in his office or in the computer room. He was polite to everyone, and although he never spoke about his private life he knew the names and the family situations of all his employees. He could be harsh sometimes, but he knew how to light a fire under his employees, how to get the best out of them. 'You know, I think he might actually do it,' Hicham said to Najat one day. 'He might actually make CCM the top credit bank in the country.'

Fatima opened the door. She was carrying a tray with bottles of beer, bowls of black olives and steaming briouats. 'Thank you, Fatima. Morocco are going to win tonight – just you wait and see!' The maid nodded, as if Mehdi had given her an order or told her the kind of fact that only an educated man would know. Who was she to argue?

At eight o'clock, Mehdi's friends arrived: Abdellah, who still taught at the university in Rabat; Rachid, who worked with Aïcha at the hospital; and Hicham Benomar, CCM's managing director.

From Mia's bedroom, where she was sorting through a pile of clothes, Aïcha could hear them laughing and talking. Her daughter lay on the bed, watching her. Aïcha picked up a pair of OshKosh dungarees that Mehdi had brought back from one of his business trips. 'They're too small for me,' said Mia, who at six was by far the tallest child in her class. 'Are you going to give this stuff to the poor?'

'No, we're going to keep it for your little brother or little sister,' she said, softly stroking her belly.

Until this point, Mia hadn't believed it was actually true. People kept telling her that she would soon have a brother or a sister, and her mother had explained that a baby was growing inside her belly, but Mia hadn't taken it seriously. Last night, though, Aïcha had unbuttoned her blouse and taken Mia's hand in hers. Then she had placed it on the distended skin of her belly, pressed it down lightly and said: 'There, that's the foot. Can you feel it? This baby seems really keen to meet you.' Mia had quickly pulled her hand away. There was something inside her mother. A creature was growing there, a creature that only her mother could feel and with whom she already appeared to have a unique and tender relationship. Many times Mia had caught her mother talking to herself, and now she realised that it was to this baby that she had been speaking in that gentle voice, a peaceful smile upon her lips. Mia felt a sudden urge to start ripping up the pile of clothes on the bed. She didn't want anybody else to wear them. She didn't want this eager little baby to come into the world. Perhaps Aïcha sensed her daughter's agitation, because she asked her to budge up against the wall so she could lie down beside her. The girl buried her face in her mother's chest. Those soft, swollen breasts – as big as her grandmother Mathilde's – were the only things she liked about this pregnancy. She breathed in her mother's smell and the thought crossed her mind that, if she squeezed her mother hard enough, if she prayed with all her strength, she might be able to slip inside her again and kick out that other child. After a few minutes, though, Aïcha stood up. She put her hands on her belly, and as she looked down a terrifying grimace deformed her face.

'Mummy, are you okay?'

'Yes, sweetie, don't worry. It's nothing.'

It must be the baby kicking again, thought Mia, with a surge of hate. Her mother kissed her cheek, pulled the pink duvet up to her chin and walked unsteadily to the door of the bedroom, one hand touching her right side. 'Don't come downstairs, Mia, okay? You know your father doesn't like being bothered when he's watching football.'

Aïcha closed the door and stood there in the dark for a few minutes, leaning against the wall. The baby was coming. That damn maid had been right. It was only the thirty-seventh week but Aïcha had been putting herself under too much strain, ignoring the recommendations that she always gave her patients – no lifting heavy objects, get plenty of rest – so it would hardly be surprising if she gave birth early. She went down to the basement. The match had just started. Morocco must already have created a couple of chances, because she'd heard yells of excitement ('Come on, come on!') followed by groans of disappointment ('How did he get caught offside there?'). The men stood up to greet her. Abdellah offered her his spot on the sofa, but she shook her head. 'If I sit down, I'm not sure I'll be able to get up again.' She signalled to Mehdi, who grudgingly got up and asked her what the problem was.

'I'm having contractions. I think it's going to happen tonight.'

'What do you mean?'

'What do you mean, what do I mean? I'm in labour! We need to go to the hospital.'

A bottle of Heineken in his hand, Mehdi turned to look at the television. For a few seconds he seemed completely absorbed by Labied's run and shot, saved by the Algerian goalkeeper.

'Don't you understand what I'm saying?' Aïcha asked.

'Yes, yes, of course. We'll go, don't worry. But you always say yourself that it takes hours, so we can wait a little bit, can't we?' Mehdi turned to his friends. 'Guys, listen . . . Tonight, Morocco are going to win and I am going to have a son.' And he yelled: 'Champagne!'

Almost immediately, Fatima appeared on the stairs, holding a chilled bottle. Mehdi handed a coupe to Aïcha and said: 'One glass can't do any harm.' Soon nobody seemed to remember she was there. Labied was shown a yellow card and the men on the sofa started to argue about the referee's decision. Aïcha gripped the edge of the table, and when she felt the contraction coming she held her breath. Her belly hardened, all her muscles tensed and she had to bite her lip to stop herself crying out in pain. Mehdi was right, after all: labour lasted a long time, and she herself had often sent patients back home. 'Go and walk around a bit,' she would tell them. 'Or go home and get some sleep. It'll be a while yet.'

She shivered at the idea that, a few hours from now, she would be lying with her legs spread in one of those labour wards that she hated so much. She had too much experience to believe the happy myths about childbirth. She had seen and heard too much to think that the joy of having a child could erase the crude horror of it all. She'd seen too many torn uteruses, too many chewed nipples, too much blood splattered on white coats and plastic clogs. It was all so raw in her mind. Babies were not born in roses, and all storks ever did was shit on the windscreen of her car while she was stuck at the hospital for hours on end. The longer she worked there, the greater Aïcha's repugnance grew every time she had to enter the labour ward, where the women – sometimes four or five of them – were separated only by thin curtains. The smell in particular was unbearable, an odour that mingled shit, blood and fetid amniotic fluid. In summer, the temperature in the ward would rise to more than forty-five degrees. Even with the windows open and a small fan whirring the atmosphere was suffocating, and the women, their faces streaming with sweat, would sometimes faint in the middle of labour. The winters were almost worse, though, with their biting cold: Aïcha would have to wear a thick sweater under her white coat, and two pairs of socks. Some of the nurses wore woollen gloves. But what Aïcha found most exhausting, more than the smell or the filth or the lack of privacy, were the women's screams. The moans, the wails, the bellows . . . It sounded like an abattoir in there. Some of them, half-crazed with pain, would call out, 'Oh God, oh God', as though they were about to come. Sometimes, especially at night, the labour ward would tip into madness. One patient bit a nurse, sinking her teeth into the woman's breast. Another time it was a doctor who lost his head: he slapped a patient who had scratched him, before yelling furiously, 'Is that how you cried out while he was fucking you?'

Even amid this chaos, Aïcha always did her best to concentrate on her patients, terrified as she was by the idea of seeing one of them bleed out and die before she had even held her child. Aïcha was not the kind of doctor who liked to minimise the dangers or deny the severity of the pain. She wasn't one of those who sneered: 'What the hell is she complaining about? Nobody *made* her have a fifth kid!' She knew there was nothing she could do to alleviate their suffering, so she simply told them to be brave, reminding them of the millions of women who had given birth before them. Her gentle words never helped, though, any more than her scientific explanations. These women, with their legs wide open, their feet in stirrups, their faces curdled into monstrous expressions, seemed to have lost all sense of restraint, all rationality. They wanted someone to take care of them and were outraged whenever the doctor dared leave them for a moment to look after another patient.

Aïcha poured herself a second glass of champagne. I don't want to go to hospital, she thought. She imagined herself dead, ripped open from vagina to anus. She saw puddles of blood on the lino floor and that viscous cord that connected all women back into the mists of time. Perhaps she could avoid this ordeal, find another way of bringing her child into the world? The alcohol was going to her head. She felt like talking but was too afraid. Mehdi would get angry if she interrupted them. Or, even worse, if she pretended to be interested in the match.

At half-time Fatima came to take away the empty beer bottles and the overflowing ashtrays. She brought in another bottle of champagne and Mehdi served his guests glasses of whisky. Rachid offered to examine Aïcha. They went up to the master bedroom, where Aïcha lay down and Rachid inserted his finger into her vagina. 'A couple of centimetres. How long between contractions?'

'Twenty minutes, maybe less.'

'We've got time, then. Come on, the match is about to start again. I'm not as optimistic as your husband, I'm afraid. The Lions are too keyed up. I have a bad feeling about this . . .'

As Rachid went down to join the others, Aïcha picked up the phone to call Selma. Please let her be home. Please don't let her be drunk, she prayed, and miraculously her aunt answered. 'Is this a bad time?' Aïcha asked. She could hear women laughing, Arab music. Selma was renowned for organising the best parties in the city at her apartment on Avenue de Témara. 'Could you come here now? I need you to stay with Mia. We'll be going to the hospital soon.' The next second, she heard Selma cry out in a high-pitched voice: 'The party's over, people. Everybody out!'

Aïcha went back to the basement. She sat in front of the television and asked for more champagne. She drank two or three coupes and smoked a few cigarettes. Time seemed to slow and she felt strangely calm. The room was blurry with smoke. From time to time Mehdi would look at her, and she would flash him a reassuring smile. He was convinced that the baby would be a boy, and the idea of having someone to watch football matches with made him so happy. He pretended to worry about the downsides of having a son – 'They're so much more boisterous than girls' – but it was obvious that he dreamed of producing an heir.

The Algerians clamoured for a penalty. All the men in the room leapt to their feet, arms out wide, yelling at the referee on the screen. Aïcha would never have dared say this, but she was hoping for a Morocco defeat. If they won, people would go out into the streets. The sound of car horns would fill the air. There would perhaps even be a celebrating crowd in their neighbourhood. She didn't want her child to be born amid such agitation. She grabbed the bottle of champagne and poured the last drops into her glass. Please let them lose, she prayed. Please let them lose. And in the champagne-induced haze, she thought it would only be fair if her husband was disappointed, if he suffered too, as much as she was going to suffer.

Aïcha's forehead was slick with sweat. She couldn't relax her hands. The contractions were coming closer together, growing more intense. She shivered, and then a memory came to her: the freezing chapel where she had prayed as a child, on her knees, her arms crossed. 'Blessed art thou among women, and blessed is the fruit of thy womb.' She was about to call out to Rachid, but he was yelling, completely drunk, his face in his hands. Mehdi kicked the table.

'What's the matter?' Aïcha asked weakly.

'What, are you blind? The Algerians just scored. In stoppage time – can you believe it?'

Just then, Selma appeared on the stairs.

'Why aren't you at the hospital? Don't tell me they made you wait until the match was over!'

When her mother came back from the hospital, Mia announced: 'This is the worst day of my life.' Aïcha stood in the entrance hall, pale and smiling, the baby in her arms. Mia didn't want to look at it. Aïcha insisted. She said Mia should sit on the sofa and hold her sister in her arms, but Mia refused. 'It's a monster. I don't want to touch it.'

In the days that followed, she refused to sleep or eat. Whenever her mother breastfed Inès, Mia clung to her legs and wept. She kept repeating, between sobs, that she didn't have a mummy any more, that this baby, this monster, had stolen everything from her. Mia lay on the floor, her body twisted in pain. She swore that she was sick, that she wanted to throw up, and her mother made her drink spoonfuls of Vogalene. Fatima tried to console her. 'It could have been worse,' she kept saying. 'You could have had a brother.'

Nobody took her seriously. Mia was only six, and the adults mocked her as a drama queen. Selma burst out laughing when, in a sudden fit of rage, the little girl threw Aïcha's driver's licence and car keys into the toilet, along with the butterfly-shaped earrings that Mehdi had given her for Christmas. And as if to rub salt in her wounds, Inès turned out to be a perfect little baby.

The birth had gone smoothly, almost painlessly. Whereas Aïcha's memory of the birth of her first child was horrific, Inès's entrance into the world was haloed with sweetness. The infant that was placed in her arms was calm, the round little body curled up against hers, absolutely trusting. Inès fed at regular intervals, she laughed when they gave her a lukewarm bath and she never cried. She was so silent, in fact, that Amine, during a visit to Rabat in the spring of 1980, became worried. 'Is it normal that she never screams?' As the weeks passed, Mia's worst fears came true. That baby had kicked her out of the paradise where she had lived for six years, happy and loved. Inès had stolen her life.

It was during this visit that something terrible happened. They were drinking aperitifs on the terrace, in the shade of the medlar tree, its branches sagging under the weight of fruit. Ever since arriving in Rabat, Mathilde had not been able to stop criticising the house. She made remarks about the noise from the street, the lack of privacy. She claimed that the woman next door was spying on them and that it wasn't normal to live like this, all packed in so close together. At the farm, Mia could swim in a real pool instead of paddling in a plastic bowl, watched by the maid. 'Don't you think, Amine?' Aïcha bit her lip. She was afraid that her husband would get angry. Mehdi was always arguing with his mother-in-law. He said she took up too much space, that she talked constantly despite having nothing to say. He insisted that she was racist because she had dared to criticise Moroccan music and because she had once said that she was disgusted by Eid al-Adha. He had even threatened not to let her take Mia to the farm any more: Mathilde was a bad driver and she taught her granddaughter rude words that no six-year-old should know.

Amine shrugged. What bothered him were the girls' names. When Mia was born, he had made his displeasure plain, asking why they couldn't give her a real Moroccan name like Hind or Latifa. 'But Inès? What even is that?' Aïcha explained that Mia and Inès were names that were easy to pronounce in any language, something that would help the girls later in life. 'Are you ashamed of being Arabs or something? You're raising them to become foreigners, and one day they'll turn their backs on you!' he told his son-in-law. Amine had had too much to drink – the rosé went straight to his head – and, besides, everyone knew what was really bothering him. His son, Selim, had moved to New York – 'a city of criminals and whores' – and now wanted to be called Sam. At thirty years old, he still didn't have a proper job – 'Taking photographs is a hobby, not work!' – or a wife or any children, and he had never shown the slightest interest in taking over the farm.

Aïcha stood up. 'I'm going to make dinner.' She walked past the kitchen, where Fatima was working, and went upstairs. She wanted to lie down next to her baby. She would take Inès out of her cradle and lay her on the bed, their faces close together. She would breathe in the infant's smell, which intoxicated her more than any man's ever had. She knew now that nothing really mattered – nothing but the love she felt for her children. That love was so vast, so all-consuming, that it had amazed even her. Since becoming a mother her mind had been filled with her daughters, and she found it surprising that so much had been written about romantic love, about sex, that there were so many stories about men and women, when she was convinced that only one true form of love existed. She wished she could build a house without windows for her children, a house with walls as high and thick as possible. Walls that no one could ever scale or break, behind which her daughters would grow, safe from all harm, in a place where they could be themselves. Mehdi called her a she-wolf, a mother bear. He made fun of her, of the way she loved her children, the way they were always clinging to her. 'They'll eat you alive.'

Aïcha went into the bedroom, dimly illuminated by a night light in the shape of a cat, and she put her hands to her mouth to stifle the cry that was rising up her throat. She ran out of the room, went back to the terrace and shot Mehdi a look of such terror that he instantly leapt to his feet, knocking over the bottle of rosé. 'What is it?' he demanded 'Tell me – what's wrong?' Aïcha, dumbstruck, gestured towards the corridor and Mehdi rushed into it. In the bedroom, he stood and looked at the cradle. The baby's body could not be seen. It was buried under a pile of cushions and folded blankets.

Mehdi turned to his wife. He couldn't understand why she had run away like that, why she had been such a coward. Why had she – the mother, the doctor – left it to him to find out if their baby was still alive? Mehdi grabbed the cushions, the duvet, the blankets, and tossed them out of the cradle. Inès appeared. He put his hand to the child's chest and he could have wept with relief when he felt her breathe. She didn't even seem to have noticed what had happened to her, and apparently she had not suffered, let alone suffocated. Her skin was cool and she was sleeping peacefully.

Aïcha, who had been standing in the doorway, went into the room, and for a few minutes they both stood there, leaning over the cradle, admiring their baby. Then Aïcha put three fingers to the infant's neck and took her pulse. All thoughts fled her mind. She felt Inès's blood beat against her skin, and in the end Mehdi had to gently pull her away, whispering, 'You'll wake her', before she would leave the bedroom.

They went back to the terrace. Mathilde was standing, hands pressed together, waiting for them. And it was when she saw her mother's anxious face that anger took possession of Aïcha. Mia was a murderer. Mia had tried to kill her sister. She had picked up everything she could find – cushions, duvet, blankets – and she had tried to smother Inès. Try as they might to remind Aïcha that her daughter was only six, try as they might to convince her that she hadn't known what she was doing, she remained certain: Mia had wanted her sister dead.

Fatima arrived with a mop. She cleaned up the puddle of rosé. 'Where's Mia?' Mehdi asked her. 'She's sleeping,' replied the maid, and as he headed for her bedroom Fatima grabbed his arm. 'Please, Sidi, in God's name, she's just a little girl. Forgive her as God forgives us.' But Mehdi wasn't listening, and he shoved the maid against the wall. That night, Mia was dragged from her bed by Mehdi. And for the next five days her father's handprint remained imprinted on her bottom, changing colour from purple to yellow before fading away.

Mia's hate, though, refused to fade, and she did not learn the lesson of that night. To her, it seemed that the more she hated her sister, the more the world gave her good reason to hate her. Over the years, Inès grew into a little girl of startling beauty. Everyone felt sorry for poor Mia, whose hair, at the time, was so frizzy that her parents kept it cut very short. Mia had inherited Mathilde's tall stature and her broad shoulders, but her skin was as dark as the bark of the olive trees on the farm. With her slanting eyes and her aquiline nose, she looked like one of those Native American chiefs photographed by their white conquerors. Inès, by contrast, had softly curled hair, caramel skin and slender, muscular legs. But it was her eyes that sent people into raptures. They were bright, intelligent eyes, with ink-dark irises and long, long lashes. 'Look at those eyes!' everyone would say – friends, family, strangers in the street – before turning in confusion towards her older sister, who stood staring down at the ground. The kindest or the stupidest among them would, in an attempt to make her smile, pinch Mia's cheek and say: 'Your little sister is very pretty, isn't she?' Yes, Inès was pretty. As pretty as the dolls with porcelain faces that Mathilde had given them one day, before saying that they weren't allowed to play with them.

Nothing could soften Mia's feelings towards her sister. She remained impassive when Inès started babbling and her first word was not 'Mama' but 'Mia'. Inès would look up at her big sister through eyes transfixed with love, and you would have sworn that she was silently pleading to be forgiven. As soon as she was old enough to speak, she would always defend her sister. She didn't denounce her when Mia abandoned her on a deserted road, miles from the farm, in the hope that she would get lost. She didn't complain when her sister put black beetles on her plate or kicked her under the table. Inès said it was her own fault if she swallowed mouthfuls of water in the swimming pool, despite Mia's attempts to drown her. 'We were just playing,' she always said. Whenever their father scolded her sister, Inès would throw herself in the way, shouting 'Leave her alone!' And Mehdi, furious, would snarl at Mia: 'You don't deserve to have such a good lawyer on your side.' At the same time, he blamed Inès for her weakness, lamenting: 'Even dogs learn to avoid people who don't love them.'

Aïcha thought it was out of contempt for her sister that Mia started acting like a boy. From about ten years old, she flatly refused to wear skirts or let her hair grow long. Inès can wear dresses, she thought. *She* can have bows in her hair and frilly skirts. *She* can twirl around and make Mum and Granny smile.

Inès knew all the songs from *The Sound of Music* by heart and was taking ballet classes at the Russian Cultural Institute on Avenue de la Victoire. Inès wanted so desperately to be like her mother that she would borrow her stilettoes and stuff clementines down the front of her dress and smear make-up all over her face. For Christmas in 1984 she asked for a doll, a carry cot and a table on which she could change the doll's nappies. Mia, on the other hand, was proud of looking exactly like her father: she had the same bulging forehead, the same brown skin, the same long and slender fingers. She did everything she could to distance herself from the world of women. She despised the way they acted, the sound of their laughter, the things they liked. Their preoccupations struck her as banal – 'Can you believe how much a kilo of potatoes costs now? Four dirhams! And it's three for a kilo of carrots . . .' – and their high-pitched voices pursued her through the house. She despised them for spending so much time in the kitchen, backs bent over counter-tops, their hair smelling of saffron. Mia preferred to watch football matches, sitting nuzzled next to Mehdi, and she concentrated hard to memorise the names of players and technical terms. At home, she was the only one to show any interest in the car that her father had just bought – a Jeep Cherokee, with a dog barrier at the back – and she asked him if one day he would take her hunting and show her how to fire a rifle. Mia wanted to console Mehdi. She nurtured the secret, unspeakable hope that she might eventually become her father's son. She was hurt when she heard her parents' friends say things like: 'It's a shame you only have girls. You should try for a boy!' The idea that her mother would give birth to a male heir terrified her more than anything.

Aïcha and Mehdi often argued about their daughters' education. Aïcha criticised him for spending so much time at work. 'Why did you bother having a family if your career is all that matters to you?' She begged her husband to do things with the children, to show more enthusiasm. But Mehdi didn't like to play. He hated cards and board games. He never went with them on picnics because he thought it was ridiculous to sit on the grass to eat when you could be so much more comfortable at the dining table, being waited on by servants. In 1985, towards the end of summer, they spent their holidays at the farm and he agreed to teach Inès to swim. He tied a rope around the little girl's waist and told her to dive into the pool. 'Move your arms!' he shouted while she thrashed around in the freezing water. 'Kick your legs!' as she did her best not to drown. When Inès reached the middle of the pool, where the water was deepest, she turned and saw that her father had let go of the rope and was sitting in an orange deckchair smoking a cigarette.

In December 1985, a few days before Christmas, the Crédit Commercial du Maroc opened its new headquarters on the prestigious Avenue Hassan II in the centre of Casablanca. In five years, CCM had become a respected organisation with a rate of growth – between ten and fifteen per cent every year – that was the envy of its competitors. Mehdi Daoud had done it. For the past three years Najat Goumine had not been able to take a single holiday, but she'd been given raise after raise and now made enough to send her children to private schools. Mehdi was regarded as a bold and brilliant leader, the archetype of the modern, tech-savvy boss. A visionary, in short. In only a few months he had fully automated credit approval for individual clients. The era of endless debates, tearful pleas and bribes was over; now, it was the computer that took care of everything, producing contracts that the company's managers were not permitted to alter. What used to take several weeks was now done in a few days. He created a life insurance policy to reassure men with families and launched a major ad campaign targeting the middle classes. Within CCM, he fought for the right of each employee to be granted favourable credit terms, enabling them to buy an apartment or a new car. Mehdi gave his blue R12 to Selma and bought himself a Mercedes with brown buckskin seats. Mustapha, the street watchman, became his chauffeur, swapping his blue coat for a smart suit.

And one night in February 1986, a little tipsy after a few aperitifs, Mehdi asked his eldest daughter: 'Would you like to see where Daddy works?'

It was a Wednesday morning and Mia didn't have school. She was wearing beige corduroy trousers and a denim shirt with sleeves that came down over her hands. She got into the back of her father's car and watched as he took a pile of folders from his bag, which smelled of new leather. Mia admired him because he was able to read in the car without getting travel-sick. He had told her that she should practise this too. She was almost twelve, and she was in secondary school now: imagine the time she would save if she could read wherever she went. She held the copy of Jean Giono's *The Horseman on the Roof* that her father had given her, but she was afraid to open it. If she vomited on his buckskin seats, he would get angry and the day would be ruined.

Mia was always slightly nervous around her father. She worried about doing or saying the wrong thing, not meeting his expectations. When he looked at her she sometimes had the painful feeling that he was hiding his disgust or disappointment. He didn't treat her like a father would normally treat his little girl, with tender smiles and indulgence. No, he was strict, demanding. She was supposed to know when to keep quiet and when to speak. They were heading towards the coastal road. Mia didn't dare ask what he had planned for the day. Would he take her to a restaurant? Would he introduce her to his colleagues? And what was Casablanca like?

For the first time in her life, Mia was in a car on the motorway. She felt a surge of fear when Mustapha accelerated into the flow of traffic. She looked at the folder beside her on the back seat, and read the words on the front: 'Construction of a Hispano-African tunnel under the Strait of Gibraltar / Morocco EEC Application'. Black smoke was pouring from the exhaust pipe of the van in front. Mustapha smoothly overtook it.

Mia stroked the folder's cardboard cover and asked her father: 'What is this?'

'Ah, that's an extraordinary project. Like something out of a Jules Verne novel.' Mehdi handed her a sheet of paper showing an illustration of the plans. She turned the page in every possible direction, but she couldn't make head nor tail of it.

'According to the Japanese engineers, we now have the ultra-sophisticated techniques necessary to build a floating tunnel between Africa and Europe. If we manage to convince international opinion, and if bankers like me can attract foreign investors, in the year 2000 we'll be able to travel from Casablanca to Madrid in only a few hours.'

'So you build tunnels?'

'No, not exactly. I find money and I give it to the people who need it. To build houses, hotels. So that people can have better lives and Morocco can grow as a country, you understand?'

She nodded.

To their right, the usually green landscape was looking sad and grey. The country was going through an endless season that was neither summer nor winter, and that, for Morocco's farmers, represented the ultimate nightmare. The mornings were freezing cold, burning the flowers and buds, and the afternoons were swelteringly hot, drying up the valleys and the plains. It hadn't rained for three years and the ground was so hard that the fellahs had put away their ploughs, having given up the idea of ever sowing new seeds. On Fridays, in mosques all over Morocco, people prayed for a breath of wind, a few clouds. But the rain didn't come, and under the small stone bridge that the car passed over, the Oued Cherrat river was nothing but a dry bed. The trees were covered with a thick layer of whitish dust. In the distance Mia could see a dozen emaciated cows. They were wandering across the plain in search of a blade of grass. If this drought continued, whole herds of cattle would have to be slaughtered. And if they weren't killed by a bolt to the head, they would end up choking to death on one of those discarded black plastic bags that hung like flags from the tree branches.

She turned to face the other way and watched as a train roared past. Then they drove past a high wall with gaps in it. It was impossible to know whether construction had been stopped or whether farmers had opened these breaches to drive their cattle through. Mustapha was driving very fast and, her nose to the glass, Mia was only able to glimpse through the gaps a few shanties, some muddy streets, a donkey. A little girl in a blue dress, with a scarf tied around her head, holding a chubby baby in her arms. A man sitting at the back of a cart filled with oranges and onions, wearing plastic sandals on his feet. Some kids standing on top of the wall, giving the finger to the motorists who honked as they sped past.

Mia didn't leave the house very often. To her, Morocco was an unknown land. Most of the time, she and her sister were alone at the house, except for the servants. Aïcha spent long hours at the hospital and would sometimes disappear in the middle of a meal or on a Sunday afternoon. 'This baby's not going to wait until tomorrow to be born.' The girls were growing up like indoor pets, like zoo animals who have lost the instinct for roaring or leaping.

'Happy is the mother whose child is afraid.' Aïcha had absorbed this adage and did her best to warn her daughters against the dangers of the world. They might fall, or choke, or get beaten up; they might drown or get lost in some crowded place where a predator would come and kidnap them. She inoculated them with fear as if injecting them with a vaccine. And every stage of life brought new reasons to worry: men, pregnancy, car crashes. She taught them to speak quietly, never to offer their opinion, always to be careful, to be wary of everyone they encountered because police informers were everywhere and in the blink of an eye you could be arrested and dumped in a dark cell where no one would ever find you. Aïcha hoped that these threats would get through to them, that they would develop an aversion to risk. She wanted cowardly children who would never even think about getting angry or rebelling or talking too loud. She wanted docile children who would kowtow to authority, little Scheherazades who would be able to charm tyrants and live to see another day.

But Mia was an intelligent, lively, observant child, curious about the lives of others. Sometimes, on Sunday mornings, she would accompany her mother to the central market where she did the weekly shopping. Mia would walk behind her, through shaded alleys where the air smelled of rubbish bins and warm bread. She would hear people complaining: the oranges were dry, they didn't give any juice. The man at the dairy shop had run out of milk. Children her own age ran up, offering to carry their parcels. Aïcha refused. She asked: 'Do you go to school?' And a boy with long blond eyelashes stared at her and laughed. Mia understood that this was poverty. All these children, roaming the streets, hunted by police patrols who would hit them with truncheons as if they were adults. Children from rural villages whose parents had lost them. Little girls sold as maids, and babies rented as props for begging on the avenues of the city centre. Shoe-shiners, delivery boys, apprentices sitting cross-legged in attics. Mia knew that there were children who never went to school, who didn't own a doll. Children without childhoods. At the entrance to Souk Sebat, outside the old mosque, beggars sat on the ground. A blind man with white eyes shook some coins in his copper bowl. An ageless man showed off his deformed body, his legs as thin as wooden sticks. 'He has chorea,' Aïcha explained. 'It's a very serious disease.' Europeans would sometimes say: 'Morocco is beautiful, but it's too poor.'

Amine, her grandfather, liked to tell her scary stories about Bolsheviks and revolution, peasant revolts and violent riots. He told her about the countryside, where the wells were dry and wheat so expensive that people were starving to death. He shook his head at all the douars that ceased to exist as their inhabitants migrated to cities or to Europe. 'It's not as if there's more employment in cities, but at least there they can always find something to eat in a rubbish bin.' This image was engraved in Mia's mind. The image of these people rummaging through waste, and the image of the police who would raid the lobbies of apartment buildings where they took refuge. She became infused with a sense of threat, a sense of injustice. The newspapers were filled with anxious articles about cholera – the disease of dirty hands – which was spreading through the slums due to the lack of hygiene. Amine's conclusion, invariably, was: 'Do you realise how lucky you are?'

Fatima said that too. She would tell Mia all day long: 'You should thank your parents for giving you an education.' The maid would sit next to Mia when she was doing her homework and ask: 'What does that say?' And Mia would read: 'When Robinson regained consciousness, he was lying with his face in the sand.' Fatima laughed. She understood French better than she let on and she used her fingers, covered in burns and damaged by bleach, to trace the curve of a B or a G. The girls would watch television in the basement with Fatima when their parents were at work. They were mad about *Dallas*, and the maid said that one day Inès would be as beautiful as Sue Ellen. Every programme began with a reading from the Quran, followed by the national anthem played over images of Hassan II. The king was ubiquitous and the children were fascinated by him. There he was, inaugurating a dam, cutting a ribbon, opening the Friday prayers. There he was, in a European suit, in a golf outfit, in a djellaba. There he was, walking on a red carpet in a small coastal town or getting out of his Rolls-Royce to be greeted by leaders from all over the world. Fatima was proud of this king, so respected in the West. She claimed there was a fragment of hyena skull in the signet ring he wore, and that this was why he was able to mesmerise his audiences. Mia was afraid of the king, whose portrait was on display everywhere, even above the vegetable stall in the central market or at the Berber corner shop in Meknes.

Two years before this, in January 1984, rising prices had led to violent protests in Marrakech and the north of Morocco. Mia had sat in the maid's lap and watched Hassan II give a speech. The king had been disappointed in his people. He had brandished pamphlets with photographs of the Ayatollah Khomeini and accused the mob of being manipulated by Marxists and Zionists. 'Have you all become children?' he'd demanded. He had denounced the protesters as thugs, and Fatima had applauded. The king was right. The king was right. The maid would never dare say that the king was wrong. In fact, she wouldn't even dare think it, so certain was she that he had ways of seeing into her heart. Fatima knew all about corruption and poverty, about the violence inflicted daily by village headmen, petty officials and the police. 'They're thugs,' she repeated, staring into space. 'That's what they are.'

When their parents were home and they invited friends over, Mia would leave Inès sitting in front of the television so she could go upstairs and spy on the adults. She was good at making herself invisible. She would listen, frowning, as they talked about the Iranian revolution, the Moroccan exception, the condition of women. She got used to hearing the word 'Palestine' ('Resist the oppression of your enemies, oh beloved Palestine'), the names François Mitterrand and Luchino Visconti. She had to concentrate to memorise the words they used. Words that she would sometimes find in the books she read so avidly, an experience that left her with a strange feeling. As if books weren't that remote from life after all. As if they echoed and reflected it. As if, in their pages, she might find answers to the thousands of questions that tormented her. Whenever Aïcha caught her spying, she would point to the door and snap: 'Out!' And then the adults would start whispering. Her mother would hiss at Mehdi: 'Don't talk about that in front of the children! What if they repeat it?' Her father would grow indignant at this, especially if he'd had a few drinks. He loathed the idea of talking to children as if they were stupid. 'They are blessed with reason,' he repeated. 'They're perfectly capable of arguing their case or receiving criticism.' He couldn't stand it when one of the girls burst into tears if he told her that what she was saying was stupid.

He was willing to answer Mia's questions, even the most metaphysical ones. Why do we die? Why are there poor people and rich people? But as soon as she asked about him, about his life, he fell silent. One day, when they were coming home from a holiday at the farm, Mia asked Mehdi why she had never met her grandparents on his side of the family. She wanted to know if she had uncles and aunts, if she had dozens of cousins she could play with, like her friends at school. Did he have any photographs of his family? Did she look like them? Mehdi stood up, went to his library and came back with a copy of *Martin Eden*. 'This is my story,' he told her. Now, whenever she grew curious or tried to talk about the past, he would hand her a book. 'Stop asking questions and read this.'

Her father remained elusive. He was a man of whims and urges, who ruled his house in waves, when he was feeling especially angry or happy. He might go into a rage because the children weren't disciplined enough, then suddenly decide that they didn't need to go to bed early, even if they had school the next day. He would play a Paul Anka record at top volume and teach them to dance, then he would grow distant again and hardly even listen when Mia told him about her day at school and the compliment that her teacher had paid her. Whenever she tried to hug him, she would feel his body stiffen with embarrassment and he would push her away. 'Go and play,' he would tell her. 'I want to smoke.' Who was her father? On the console table in the living room there was a photograph of him as a young man, with long hair and a thick beard, wearing flares. But her father no longer looked anything like that man. His beard was neatly groomed now, and his hair, cut very short, was turning white. He wore Italian suits and never loosened his tie until dinner.

Whenever he had guests, he would resemble an actor seeking to impress his audience. He would tell stories about his travels in Russia, where he'd dined on caviar and vodka with the women of the Bolshoi Ballet. He would talk about how, as a child, he had almost lost his sight, or how he had killed a dog for no reason by throwing it in a ditch. Sometimes, when he was drunk or in a good mood, he would dwell at length on his childhood. He would claim that he had been a brilliant musician, playing the guitar or the trumpet, and that this was why he had a voice like Louis Armstrong. He would tell his listeners that he had travelled across Europe with ten francs in his pocket and slept under the stars on Spanish beaches. He said he had been one of those young people who wanted to change the world and had almost taken part in a revolution. Mia knew her father was from Fes, but she also knew that he collected *grand cru* wines – exclusively Bordeaux. Sometimes he would put on a Jacques Brel record and sing at the top of his voice: 'The bourgeoisie are like pigs / The older they get, the dumber they grow . . .' He would often contradict himself, not only in his anecdotes but in the image of himself that he portrayed. Liberal, then abruptly authoritarian; revolted by injustice, then calling for patience; feminist, yet sickened by women. He was the exact opposite of Aïcha, who was so easy to read, so inflexible, who always kept her promises. Mia struggled to make sense of the lessons her father tried to teach her. He spoke about freedom of expression, equality for women, the right of each person to lead their own life. Then he would frown sternly and add: 'But that's not how it works here.'

They entered Casablanca. Mia was expecting a dirty, chaotic city, teeming with people. A city like the London of Dickens novels, populated by sooty-faced factory workers and women walking the streets with screaming babies in their arms. What struck her first was the light. The intense, radiant light that seemed to come from the ocean and to be reflected from the walls of the tall, white, art deco buildings. They drove past United Nations Square, the old clocktower, the Arab League Park. A succession of avenues flashed past. She saw restaurants next to foreign shops or one of those private clubs where rich people go to relax and bathe. Casablanca radiated an impression of freedom that Mia had never felt in Rabat. She noticed restaurants with American names: in Rabat you would eat lunch at La Bourgogne or Le Café de France, but in Casablanca you would go for a drink at Rick's or The Sun or The Oklahoma.

They reached the business district. Opposite the bank, Mia spotted the entrance to an ice cream shop with an Italian name. She saw men in suits leaving a luxury hotel, each carrying a briefcase. Mehdi got out of the car and held out his hand. They walked into the building together. In the lobby, a strange dance began. Behind the reception desk, the women fell silent. One of them touched her hair, then stood to attention. Two young men pressed themselves against the wall to let Mehdi pass, along with the young girl who was with him. They got into the lift. On the third floor, the doors opened to reveal two men in grey suits, who lowered their faces and came inside, shoulders slumped, as though they'd been caught doing something bad. 'Monsieur le Président,' they muttered reverentially. For the first time, Mia was seeing her father away from the house. She was in his world now. The outside world in which he was the president.

Mehdi's office was on the tenth floor. His secretary rushed towards him as soon as she saw him, asking if he would like a coffee and handing him a stack of notes. She placed her hands on Mia's shoulders and looked into her eyes, as if they were long-lost friends. 'You must be Mia. I've been looking forward to meeting you.' Wafa was a beautiful woman, with permed, blonde-dyed hair. The lipstick she wore was dark brown, with a sticky texture that made Mia feel sick. She followed her father into his vast office. It was bigger than their living room in Rabat. To the left was an imposing desk of pale wood, on top of which lay piles of folders with coloured covers. There was a brown leather pot full of fountain pens and a sheet of headed notepaper on which was elegantly handwritten, in the top right corner, in sky-blue ink, the words: 'Le Président-Directeur Général'. Across the room, four leather armchairs were positioned around a small glass table on which Wafa placed the tray of coffee. But what fascinated Mia, who fixed it in her memory forever, was the view of Casablanca. Her father signalled to her to go over to the window and together they looked down at the ballet of cars that, at this altitude, appeared as small as children's toys. Never before had she viewed the world from so high up. The street was pastel-coloured – pale orange, aqua green – and she had the impression that what she was seeing was not a real city but a film set, created just for her. 'I have learned to love this city,' Mehdi said, taking a sip of coffee. 'It's unique, you know? In Fes or Meknes, strangers always ask you who your father is. Here, your father can be a complete nobody, it doesn't matter. Casablanca is a city without a memory, an El Dorado for ambitious bastards and orphans. Like in Balzac. You've read Balzac, right?'

Mia shook her head.

'Remind me to give you one of his books. Anyway, I need to work now. Wafa!'

Mia left the office, closing the door behind her. Was this her father's secret? That *his* father had been a complete nobody? The secretary opened a drawer and took out of a sheaf of white pages and some coloured felt-tip pens. 'Would you like to draw?' Mia stared at her, and Wafa must have felt a bit ridiculous, standing in front of this twelve-year-old girl who was nearly as tall as her. 'I've got my book, thanks.' Mia fell into a chair and lay with her legs touching her chest. The two of them stayed there all morning, facing each other, not talking. The book was difficult and Mia used a pencil to underline the words she didn't understand. People went in and out of her father's office, folders under their arms. Several times, Mehdi called for more coffee. When Wafa answered the phone, she took off her gold-plated earring and used it to clean her fingernails. Later, Mia would learn that it was Wafa who had bought birthday presents for her, Inès and Aïcha. It was Wafa who remembered Mother's Day, who had the best pastries delivered for Ramadan, who called the house to warn them when Mehdi would be late coming home.

'What are you reading?' Mia looked up. Wafa was leaning over her; she had put her coat on and was holding her handbag to her abdomen. Mia showed her the cover of *The Horseman on the Roof* and the secretary shrugged. 'Ready to go?' Mia didn't dare ask what her father was doing or why he hadn't reappeared. She followed Wafa through the streets of the business district and they sat at the terrace of a restaurant to eat grilled chicken and chips. Wafa, no doubt hoping that her words would be repeated, was full of praise for Monsieur le Président. She told Mia how grateful she was for all he had done for her. He had believed in her, fought to make sure she got a promotion, and when her husband had abandoned her and their two children, he had helped her. He'd been so angry with that 'irresponsible' man, that 'coward' who had not taken his role as husband and father seriously, and Wafa had almost died with happiness when she heard him say those words. Besides, she added, he was not like the other men she'd worked with in the past. 'You'll understand what I mean when you're older.' She leaned close to Mia and, in a soft voice, told her how one of the company's managers had been found mistreating a female employee. 'He was bothering her, if you know what I mean. When Monsieur le Président found out, he was furious. It was the first time I ever saw him like that: red-faced with rage. He summoned the manager to his office, and do you know what he said to him?' Mia chewed the straw that she had stuck into her Raibi Jamila. 'He said: "As long as I am president, this company will not recognise the *droit de seigneur*."' Wafa burst out laughing and wiped her greasy hands on a paper napkin. 'The *droit de seigneur*! Your father talks like someone from a book.' She signalled to the waiter to bring them the bill, then added: 'He's not like other Moroccan men. Actually, your mother is French, isn't she?'

After lunch, they went for a walk in La Corniche, then on the beach, although Wafa refused to sit on the sand because she didn't want to get her skirt dirty. Mia played football with some boys, who were bare-chested despite the cold. She thanked the secretary for buying her a balloon filled with grains of rice and a pack of Bongo sweets. Later that afternoon, Wafa took her back to the office and she fell asleep in a leather chair. When her father woke her, it was night-time. Through the window she saw, as in a dream, the lights of the city shining brightly through thick fog. She followed her father into the lift and the same ritual happened again: men lowered their heads and women fluttered their eyelashes. One of the men stroked Mia's chin. 'So, my boy, your daddy brought you to see his office?' Then he said something in Arabic and Mia, still half-asleep, looked up at her father and asked: 'What did he say?'

A heavy silence filled the car as it took them back to Rabat. Her father was annoyed, but Mia was too afraid to say anything. It was too dark to read, so she leaned her head against the window. Through the mist she could barely see the palm trees swaying by the roadside or the ochre walls of the kasbah on a hill overlooking the sea. The landscape seemed as unreal to her as the fairy tales that her mother read to Inès at bedtime. She would have liked to hear the story of that kasbah and to know more about the ocean, so close she could hear the sound of the waves crashing against rocks. She wondered what she would remember of this day, what impressions would remain engraved in her mind. Mehdi lit a cigarette and said: 'Do you know why Angelo doesn't catch cholera?' Mia turned to look at him. She tried to think as quickly as possible so she could give him the right answer, but instead she just panicked. She felt sure that she had failed to understand the book he had given her, that he would be disappointed in her. He would raise his eyebrows and say: 'Oh, you're too young to understand.' And then he wouldn't give her any more books. But instead Mehdi smiled and in a soft voice told her: 'It's because he's innocent.'

'Innocent of what?' the child asked.

Mehdi blew a puff of smoke from his mouth, stubbed out the cigarette in the overflowing ashtray and put a hand to his daughter's cheek. 'You know, the first people I ever loved were people in books.' And Mia wondered how much he loved her, since she didn't live in a novel.

That night, in the upstairs room that they shared, Mia told Inès about her day with Monsieur le Président. She talked in the dark, the sheet pulled up to her chin. She couldn't see her sister's face, which was frustrating because she felt certain that the six-year-old Inès must be staring at her with wide eyes and a gaping mouth. She told her that their father looked after money. He found money, everywhere he could, and gave it to the people who needed it. And she had seen him, with her very own eyes, counting thick wads of banknotes behind his enormous desk. She told Inès about Wafa, who in her telling became as blonde as the actresses in the Hollywood musicals they both loved. The secretary had taken her to an amusement park and had given her all the sweets she wanted – sweets that Inès had never tasted because they only existed in Casablanca. And she'd eaten an ice cream, unimaginably different from the one-dirham ice creams that their mother bought them at the Agdal. This ice cream had come straight from Italy, and Mia added: 'Daddy promised that he'd bring one back for you one day, so you'll be able to taste it too.' Excited by her own story, she got up and sat on the edge of her sister's bed. She turned on the night light that sat on the bedside table and put her hand on Inès's shoulder. 'Daddy's like a sort of king,' she whispered. 'Honestly, when we got in the lift, all the men bowed to him, like this . . .' And she lowered her head to show her sister.

She was used to hating Inès. But just as time erodes love, it takes the edge off hate. Part of her – a part whose existence she would never have admitted and against which she struggled – was attached to this little girl with her cowlike eyes who believed everything she said and treated her like an idol. Of course, Mia liked to wind her up. She was cunning and she enjoyed making Inès angry. Even Aïcha would laugh hysterically when Inès had a tantrum. She would pick up her youngest daughter and smile at Mia while Inès, crimson-faced, kicked her legs in a fury and screamed: 'Stop laughing!'

But in the shared solitude in which they were often left, Inès was a docile, obliging playmate. Their parents would rent films from the Souissi video club and the girls spent hours in front of the television. They watched *Sissi* so many times that the videocassette stopped working. From that film they learned the word 'etiquette' and noted that unhappy women often fainted. They loved musicals, especially ones starring Cyd Charisse, Audrey Hepburn or Marilyn Monroe. Inès could never follow the stories, but she remembered the words to all the songs. Mia often wondered if those Hollywood stars, when they had been little girls, used to worry about their eyebrows being too thick, or the down on their upper lips, or the long dark hairs that covered their legs. One day, she stole a razor from Mehdi and locked herself in the bathroom where, resting her foot on the white enamel bidet, she tried to shave her legs. Mia and Inès would put on shows together and perform them for their parents' friends. Mia was a tyrannical director. She forced Inès to learn several songs from *Starmania* by heart and to sing 'Le Blues du Businessman' for the adults. Mehdi had tears in his eyes when he heard that.

One day soon, perhaps, they would play 'giving away money like Daddy', but for now it was Aïcha's job that fascinated them. Their mother brought babies into the world and saw inside women's bodies. Mia was the casting director, so Inès always played the patient. Sometimes Mia would stuff a cuddly toy under her sister's dress to make it look like she was pregnant. Other times she made her lie down, lift up her skirt and spread her legs. Once, Mia borrowed a white coat from Fatima and told her sister to stretch out on the bed and not to move. She palpated her throat, her arms, her chest. 'You are very ill,' she announced in a solemn voice. From her pocket she took an orange tee that she had stolen from her father's golf bag. She inserted it slowly into her sister's vagina. 'Does that hurt?' she asked.

'No,' replied Inès. 'I can't feel anything.'

From their bedroom, the girls could not hear their parents fighting. Mehdi was furious. Mia had humiliated him and it was all Aïcha's fault.

'Why do you cut her hair so short? Everyone thinks she's a boy. She's twelve now – you need to let her hair grow long.'

'It's her choice. I'm not going to force her to have long hair.'

'And is Mia . . . I mean, is she . . .'

'Is she what?'

'Has she reached puberty?'

Aïcha scoffed. 'Does it really disgust you that much? No, as it happens, your daughter has not yet had her first period. But she's twelve, so—'

'All right, all right, I don't want to know.'

Mehdi used the glowing stub of his cigarette to light a new one and went on: 'Don't you understand how I felt? Not only did people think she was a boy, but she couldn't even answer one of my colleagues when he blessed her in Arabic. That's your mother's fault.'

And he launched into his usual speech. The same one he'd delivered in the car on the way back from Meknes after Christmas. He'd been revolted by the Tino Rossi record, the oysters, the salmon, and poor Amine dressed up as Father Christmas, sitting on top of a donkey that refused to budge. He accused Mathilde of vulgar excess, with the Berber maid in a frilly apron and the obscene mountain of presents on which the children had thrown themselves, squealing. There was a perpetual war being fought between Mathilde and Mehdi. The girls' grandmother liked to feed them sausages during Ramadan. She lambasted men for their contempt and violence towards women. 'Better to live alone than die a slave,' she liked to repeat, and Mehdi was convinced that it was her fault that Mia was the way she was. Unlike him, Mathilde was fond of talking about herself and her past and especially about Alsace, a place that, in the girls' imagination, had the fantastical beauty of a scene inside a snow globe. She would tell her granddaughters about her childhood, the afternoons spent picnicking in the cemetery with her sister, eating cervelats and damsons. The children were fascinated by this tall blonde woman who had lived through wartime and could recite Goethe's poetry in German. Next to her, Mehdi felt diminished, and he could see that the girls were drawn to this Alsatian matriarch, that they would end up like little white Europeans despite their frizzy hair, dark skin and long black eyelashes.

Yes, of course, he told Aïcha, he was proud to have a wife like her: ambitious, modern, independent. And he was convinced that his children would benefit from their mastery of the French language and French culture because France was a great country and one day they would go to university there. Didn't the king himself boast that he had been raised in a double culture, and that this had given him a better understanding of the world? 'But not if it means denying who you are or where you're from.' Mehdi bit his lip, as if he wished that he could suck those words back into his mouth.

Aïcha rolled her eyes. Her husband's hypocrisy got on her nerves. It wasn't Mathilde's fault that he was incapable of reading classical Arabic! Besides, Fes was only an hour and a half from Meknes: if he really wanted to show his children who he was and where he was from, all he had to do was take them there. He could show them round his family home, introduce them to his brothers and sisters. He could talk to them in Arabic, tell them stories of his childhood, take them to a mosque on the Night of Power and buy a sheep for Eid al-Adha.

'I'm going to hire someone to teach her Arabic!' Mehdi exclaimed, slamming his palm against the arm of the sofa.

'As you wish. I'll tell you one thing, though: I'm not going to take care of it. I have enough on my plate already.'

It was Aïcha who found the teacher. She couldn't stand listening to Mehdi complain about Mia any more, so she asked the receptionists at the hospital, then talked to a patient whose husband was the headmaster of a primary school. One night in March 1986, the doorbell rang and Fatima called out: 'Mia, your Arabic teacher's here. Go up to your room now!' Mia was furious. She had been hoping until the very last moment that she would be saved, that the dreaded teacher would not actually turn up. She had prayed that he would have an accident, fall sick, die. She wanted to stay in front of the television with her sister and watch *How to Steal a Million* for the hundredth time.

At the French school everyone hated learning Arabic. The students made fun of their teachers for their unfashionable clothes, for their accents when they spoke French and for their outdated teaching methods. Every afternoon the children would drag their feet as they went into the ground-floor classrooms, and many of them fell asleep at their desks or doodled in their notebooks. The teachers would write their names on the blackboard – from right to left – and, to a gale of laughter, point at someone randomly to ask them a question. Every year the students had to memorise Quran verses. They would recite them in a drone, not understanding a word they were saying, trying to outdo each other with the speed of their delivery. Like her classmates, Mia had been traumatised in Year 4 by

Madame Doukkali, an almost bald and very small woman who had nonetheless terrified them all. One day, she had told them that only Muslims went to heaven. 'What about Christians?' Mia had asked. 'They will go to hell,' the teacher had said. When Mia started sobbing, instead of consoling her, Madame Doukkali had pinched her ear and dragged her out of the classroom. When she got home, Mia had told her parents this story. They'd been horrified. Mehdi had uncorked a bottle of Bordeaux and angrily denounced this fanatical teacher and the school that had hired her. Why weren't they teaching the children history instead of religion? He'd told Aïcha to go to the school and give Madame Doukkali a piece of her mind. Aïcha did go the next day, but – faced with this tiny woman, whose enormous glasses made her eyes appear to bulge out of her head – she could do nothing but mumble apologetically. Mia was a sensitive child; please don't hold it against her. By the time she started her second year of secondary school, Mia could barely recite the alphabet in Arabic or write her name.

Fatima escorted Professor Slimane to Mia's bedroom. He was wearing a beige suit and pointed leather shoes. He was an immaculately groomed man, his hair neatly combed, his moustache neatly trimmed, and in his hand he carried a leather satchel full of books. The maid was very respectful towards him; she called him 'Professor', took his coat and asked if he would like anything to eat or drink. The teacher hesitated, then in a mellifluous voice, clearly articulating every syllable, he asked for some warm milk and honey.

Mia and her teacher stood side by side in the doorway, both of them motionless. On the windowsill, Inès's Barbies were sitting naked, their legs spread, their beautiful blonde hair spilling over their shoulders. The teacher looked away, then saw, on the wall, a portrait of Marilyn Monroe and a shelf full of books, all of them in French. 'You only have one chair?' he asked, gesturing at Mia's little desk. He asked the question in Moroccan Arabic and the girl shrugged. Then, turning to the door, she shouted – also in Darija – 'Fatima, bring another chair!'

Fatima returned with the glass of milk, a cup and the chair. 'Be a good girl, benti,' she said before leaving. Mia watched as the teacher slowly poured honey into his glass. He drank the hot liquid noisily. She thought it was weird, an adult drinking warm milk.

Professor Slimane took some duplicated pages from his satchel and asked Mia what class she was in.

'Year Eight. I'm at the French school.'

He grunted, then stroked the stack of pages.

'But you're learning Arabic, aren't you? You can read classical Arabic?'

'A bit,' she said. 'It's difficult.'

'And in the other subjects, how do you get on?'

'In the other subjects, I'm always top of the class.'

Professor Slimane came every Thursday. Mia was a polite, obedient pupil, but her progress in Arabic was painfully slow. She had a sharp mind, no doubt about that, but she didn't work and only completed her grammar exercises at the last minute. He knew she would never have done that with a history essay or a French writing assignment. Her parents would have told her off if she'd shown a slapdash attitude towards her maths homework, because maths was so important for her future. Professor Slimane had spent a few years teaching at a French

Catholic school and he knew the contempt that such people felt for the Arabic language. The children there did not learn about Morocco's history or geography. The other teachers always used to talk about the 'Christmas holidays' or 'Easter break', and one day a history teacher became very angry when he had to return earlier than expected from his weekend in Oualidia because of a Muslim holiday. 'It's ridiculous that we have to sit in front of the TV to find out if the moon has appeared or not. There must be ways of calculating that, surely? We're not in the Middle Ages any more!' In the teachers' common room, the Moroccans always sat together. None of the French people made any effort to get to know them, apart from the odd young idealist, freshly arrived and eager to learn the local language. It never took them long to lose their enthusiasm, however. 'Arabic is badly taught,' they complained. 'And, really, what's the point in learning it when everyone speaks French anyway?' As for the parents, they never came to the meetings he arranged and clearly couldn't care less if their child was failing Arabic as long as they were doing well in the other subjects. 'Classical Arabic?' they all said. 'Why would anyone need to know that?'

So Professor Slimane had returned to the public sector, but to make ends meet he also gave private classes to students in chic neighbourhoods. He enjoyed this, and when he got home he kept a record in a spiral notebook of the things he had seen or heard in those houses in Souissi or on the Route des Zaërs. The books on the shelves, the piano in the corner, the maid who was sometimes even younger than the child he was teaching. He would do something with all these details one day: a novel or a short story. He felt like he was entering an unknown world, a place whose codes he didn't understand but which he found intriguing. He was not motivated by any unhealthy desire, and he did not feel any envy or resentment; it was more the strange impression that this country was comprised of discrete blocs, separate little worlds, each with their own jealously guarded secrets.

One Thursday night, he announced to Mia that they were going to take a break from learning grammar this week. He had brought a book with him that smelled of mildew. He began to tell her, in Darija, the story of King Idris I – the flight from Arabia, the murder ordered by Harun al-Rashid – and for once Mia dared to ask questions. She noted down vocabulary words, and the following week, miraculously, she remembered them. For three weeks he taught her about the corsairs of Salé, occasionally using French words so as not to lose her attention. He liked the way she looked at him when she was absorbed by the narrative, and in those moments he felt like he wielded great power over her. From time to time they would go back to conjugations and grammar, and he would feel himself become again, in Mia's eyes, the grey, boring man who slowly twirled his spoon around his cup of milk and got cream stuck to his moustache. But when he left behind the dry academic lessons, when he started telling her about legends and historical events, her face lit up. He would allow himself to take his jacket off and sometimes he would laugh at his own jokes.

One night, he gave Mia a conjugation exercise and while she was working on it, her face leaning close to her notebook, he watched her. He had been touched to notice that she too now asked for a glass of warm milk and added two spoonfuls of honey to it.

'Did you know that Morocco will soon have the tallest mosque in the world?'

'Yes, I know,' replied Mia. 'Daddy says it's not normal that Moroccans should be obliged to pay for it. He says we'd be better off building schools and dealing with poverty.'

'Yes, yes, I see. Your father is not entirely wrong. But, you know, there were poor people in Paris when they built the Notre-Dame cathedral.'

He had been surprised by how freely the child had answered him, and he'd had to bite his tongue to avoid telling her that she ought to be more careful. But the next time, he questioned her again.

'Tell me, is your mother French?'

'Yes. Well, actually, it's my grandmother who's from Alsace. And she's Christian too,' she said firmly, staring at him.

'Yes, yes, I see. All the people of the book are children of God, and Moroccans have always lived in harmony with them. No witches were ever burned here, you know.'

He smiled. His student, he thought, was trying to shock him or make him angry. Perhaps she was hoping he would quit, so she would have Thursday evenings to herself once again.

But in fact, the reason Mia was insolent towards her teacher, the reason she did her best to perturb him, was to conceal her shame. She was trying to create a diversion, to buy time, because she felt guilty at her inability to remember words, expressions, conjugations. She felt nauseated every time her teacher asked her to write a few lines on subjects as simple as 'a memory of a holiday' or 'describe your family'. She would stammer, chewing her pen until the ink stained her lips blue. The Arabic language refused to let her in. No matter how hard she tried, it seemed to her that this language – this language that should have been hers – left no impression on her brain. A part of herself was slipping through her fingers and that made her angry. More than anything, she wanted to belong, to be 'from here' in the way some of her classmates were. Like them, she would have liked to have cousins in many different Moroccan cities. She would have liked to go to weddings where the women wore kaftans and the men djellabas. She would have liked to laugh at jokes and wordplay in Arabic, to know the words to the songs that everyone sang. What her teacher saw as pride and impudence was something closer to sadness.

Professor Slimane never lost his cool. When Ramadan began, he came earlier in the afternoon. As the month wore on, he started to look paler. Purple bags deepened under his eyes and he seemed exhausted. Once or twice he bumped into Mehdi in the corridor. Mia's father asked him, in his booming voice, how the classes were going, and Professor Slimane, out of loyalty to his student, said that he was very satisfied with her progress. The holy month gave them the opportunity to discuss the five pillars of Islam. Fasting. Charity. Faith. Prayer. The pilgrimage to Mecca. 'A Muslim must go to Mecca at least once in his life.' Mia said that her grandfather had gone, and Mathilde too, and that they'd come back with Zamzam water in little bottles and some fragrant wood. As for prayer, she had never learned how. She didn't even know if her father believed in God. 'I've only ever seen him pray during football matches,' she admitted. 'He says that Maradona is a god.'

The one time she'd attended mosque had been with Selma, on the twenty-seventh night. The Night of Power. The two of them had walked in the forecourt, surrounded by crowds of people. She'd been given a new outfit, but not a dress because she hated dresses. Professor Slimane explained that the kind of clothing she wore was of no importance. Ramadan was the opposite of pride, and the reason people fasted was to put themselves in the place of those who could not afford to eat.

'But you're still young, so you don't have to do it. One day, though, you will fast during Ramadan too. When you're a woman.'

Mia laughed. 'Me? I'll never be a woman.'

Selma didn't believe in the evil eye. She didn't believe in destiny either, not any more. Perhaps she'd thought differently before, when she was still young and naive, when Alain Crozières used to stroke her hips and tell her about the thrill of flying a plane, when she had a destiny worth believing in. It would have killed her to admit it, but Mathilde, her sister-in-law, had been right when she'd said that a person's destiny was not something that was decreed but something they had to build for themselves with sweat and hard work. Yes, Selma had sinned out of laziness, and now, at almost fifty, her adolescent dreams were all dust, Alain Crozières's promises nothing more than ashes. The pilot was dead.

She was in her kitchen when she found out, one night in May 1986, a night when she'd sworn to be good, to eat lentils in tomato sauce in front of the television. She was peeling red onions, rubbing with her sleeve at the tears that rolled down her cheeks, when she saw her former lover's name in the newspaper that she was using to catch the peelings. 'We have been asked to inform you that Colonel Alain Crozières has been called to God. He leaves behind a wife and three children. A mass will be held at the Sainte-Eugénie Church in Biarritz on 13 May.' A wife and three children. A church by the seaside. A colonel. In that moment, it was not grief that Selma felt. Not even a faint nostalgia. No, she was overcome by anger and jealousy. She hated Crozières for having built a life of his own, for having married another woman and had a family with her. Alone in her kitchen, knife in hand, she spoke to him: 'And what about the girl you left in my belly? She wasn't invited to your funeral, was she?' She felt an irresistible need to know. What did Madame Crozières look like? Were the children girls or boys? How old were they, and had they loved their father? She wanted to know how much money he'd had, where he'd lived, and she had the strange but undeniable feeling that her life had been stolen from her. She would have been perfect playing the role of the tearful widow. She could see herself now, in a black fur coat, a veil over her face, weeping for her beloved husband. She threw the peelings in the bin and smoothed the newspaper with the back of her hand, trying to rub away the purple smears left behind by the onion. She didn't know what she was going to do with the obituary. She felt an urge to show it to someone. Mathilde? No, her sister-in-law would pretend not to understand; she would say something stupid and annoying like: 'Don't stir up the ghosts of the past.' Her daughter, Sabah, perhaps? She could call her in France, tell her the name of her real father and ask her to go to the family's house and tell them who she was. Who knows, maybe *she* would have a destiny? After all, what was so shameful about claiming your rightful inheritance? But no, Sabah was too volatile. If only she wasn't an overweight drunk . . . She had followed some loser to Amiens, a lazy, mediocre guy she didn't even want to marry. 'I'm not saying you should do it out of love, but at least for the papers,' Selma had said, trying to convince her daughter. Sabah and the guy lived with the guy's parents. Neither of them had a job. All they had was a dog with a blue tongue. The guy's parents had called Selma once. 'We know our son is mad, we're not denying that, but please come and get your daughter,' they had begged her. 'They're not good for each other.'

Selma stood in the middle of the living room holding the onion-scented newspaper. Her apartment was like a mausoleum. Everything in it had aged. In the chipped mother-of-pearl pot her collection of matchbooks was gathering dust, and the blue fabric of the benches had faded. On the shelves of the bookcase, on the walls and behind the benches, framed portraits of her seemed to tell visitors: Look how beautiful I used to be. There was a photograph of her taken in Venice, at the Piazza San Marco, with Selma laughing at the pigeons perched on her head and her arms. She had travelled the world – on the arms of men who saw her as a source of entertainment. She remembered forced smiles on the terrace of one of those luxury hotels where nothing unexpected ever happened, the mirror on the ceiling of a room, and the urge she'd felt, at times, to run away, not to go back. And then there were the photographs of New York that Selim would send her occasionally and which she pinned to the corkboard above the telephone. The portrait of a laughing prostitute, straddling a bench. A view of the Hudson at nightfall and the spectral silhouette of a bridge seen through mist. She dreamed of going to America, to that country from which no one ever returned. Over there she wouldn't be a nobody, a poor, lowly peasant like the European 'zmagris'. There would be an ocean between her and her ghosts, and she would be able to reinvent her life. Selim had promised to help her, to find her a room and organise a visa. She had been saving for months now, and soon she would have enough money to pay for a one-way trip to New York.

She put on an Asmahan record and went back to the kitchen. She tossed the onions and tomatoes into a saucepan and chopped up a bunch of coriander. The telephone started to ring. Later, she would often wonder what might have happened if she hadn't answered it. If she had just kept listening to Asmahan's melancholy voice and stirring the onions to stop them sticking to the bottom of the pan. What might have happened if for once she had been able to stay where she was, if she'd listened to her instinct and taken a bath before going to bed. Instead of which, she turned off the gas under the saucepan and picked up the receiver. It was her friend Narjiss, calling from the television studio where she had recently started working. She invited Selma to a party. 'There'll be a band.' A band? thought Selma. So what? She knew all the hits by heart; she could have recited the lyrics in her sleep. She had danced to all those songs, surrounded by a circle of admirers, never missing a beat, and she had even learned to spin around without losing her balance. No, she couldn't care less about the band. She had Asmahan all to herself at home, so why go out? She had seen and heard everything Rabat had to offer; nothing here could surprise her now. She would have given her most precious belongings for a surprise – a real surprise. Her jewels, her rabbit-fur coat, even her favourite grey leather handbag . . .

But Narjiss didn't give her time to refuse before adding: 'There'll be French guys too.' In recent months, Morocco's national television channel had been going through a revolution. To celebrate the twenty-fifth anniversary of Hassan II's reign, the powerful minister of the interior, Driss Basri, had been disguising the usual state propaganda with a modern, attractive veneer – fuelling the cult of the king while making Morocco look like an open-minded country, so different from the other Arab states, a country whose monarch would play golf with the sport's champions and explain the mysteries of the Muslim world to Reagan and Gorbachev. With money no object, Basri had managed to entice French TV professionals to freshen up the opening credits, dust off the programmes and fire all the old journalists. Narjiss was still merely an assistant, so she wasn't travelling on private jets or going shopping in Paris like some of the channel's star presenters. But she had been promised that she could audition as a weather girl. 'You've got a big future,' one of her colleagues had told her.

Selma looked at the newspaper article on the pedestal table, and the name Crozières looked back at her. Well, you never know what destiny has in store for you, she thought. To her friend she said: 'Pick me up in half an hour.' She put on a blue-and-white polka-dot dress and tied her hair into a chignon to expose the nape of her neck. When she went down to Avenue de Témara, Narjiss honked the car horn and waved at her. The young woman was wearing a black dress with shoulder pads and an enormous golden brooch above her breast. They left the city centre and drove along the almost deserted Route des Zaërs. Near the Dar Es Salam golf course they spotted a long line of cars parked outside a white building. From the street they could hear the band playing a mix of Moroccan folk songs and American pop hits. 'Are you sure this isn't a wedding?' Selma joked. When they went inside, black-jacketed waiters greeted them and offered them champagne. A red velvet carpet had been unfurled across the tiled floor. The party was taking place in the garden, where a crowd of people was gathered in front of the stage. Women were dancing, blowing kisses at the musicians. Selma watched them, hips swaying in skintight dresses, and she felt a sudden urge to go home. No, it was actually more like a sense of foreboding, and she saw herself standing in the living room again, the telephone receiver pressed to her ear, the smell of coriander on her fingertips. At that moment, she could have been lying on her sofa, the orange blanket covering her legs, slowly drifting into sleep. But Narjiss pulled her by the arm and they joined a group of men sitting in a booth. Her friend introduced her to them. They were all French, and they seemed to be enjoying their time in Morocco. Selma smiled and nodded as they talked: Oh, the light here is beautiful, and the people are so friendly, Moroccan hospitality is no myth, and as for the cuisine . . . You can live like a king here, that's for sure, it's better than any of the other Arab countries. One of them, a man in his forties with thick grey hair, was looking around in every direction. Where was their host? He wanted to thank him. 'What a party!' Never in his life had he seen a buffet like this one. 'And, believe me, I've been to my share of parties,' he said to Selma. 'Apparently, they've even used chemicals to kill all the mosquitoes here so the legs of the pretty ladies will be protected.' Selma smiled and the man, whose name was Thibault, put his arm around her waist and laughed.

They drank champagne. Then ice-cold gin with lemon. Narjiss was waiting for her lover, but he was late, and when he did finally arrive – a short, pot-bellied man with a handsome face and an impish smile – he barely paid attention to her. Like the other guests, he seemed to be on the lookout for something. The rumour was that a princess was going to arrive, or maybe a cousin of the king – someone from the palace anyway, someone important – and that would completely change the atmosphere of the party. Hours passed. The singer, having run out of material, launched into an Otis Redding hit for the second time that night. Nobody from the palace came, and Selma and Narjiss kept drinking. The younger woman was fuming now, half-sprawled over a bench, her heels digging into the grass. She was furious with her lover, who was flirting with a young woman, tracing his index finger over her chin. No, she wasn't even a woman, just a girl, a whore . . . Selma told Narjiss to stop shouting. 'You're drunk.' And she dragged her into the house.

The living room was so dark, the ceiling so low, that they felt like they were entering a cave. They got lost in the corridors before finally finding the bathroom. Narjiss looked at herself in the mirror: she was pale, her eyes red, and she spat her chewing gum into the sink. She splashed water onto her face. Selma rummaged through drawers and stole a perfume sample and a nail file. 'That bastard,' whined Narjiss.

Selma grew irritated: 'Oh, give it a rest. That guy's a piece of shit, so what do you care? Come on, let's go home. You've had too much to drink, and so have I.'

Narjiss took off her shoes and walked barefoot to the entrance hall. The waiters handed them their jackets and they were about to leave when Narjiss suddenly turned back. 'Just a second. I want to look that bastard in the eyes.'

But the bastard had disappeared and so had the girl with the adorable chin. Like a Fury with muddy feet, Narjiss shoved her way through the crowd of guests. The Frenchmen watched her, smirking – Women, eh? Wherever you go, they're always the same – and it turned them on a little bit, seeing this girl cast off the last shreds of her dignity. She ran to the car. 'El kelb!'* she yelled, and years later Selma would still wonder how Narjiss had managed to open the door and start the engine and, above all, why she had got in with her.

A watchman on the street spotted them and started laughing. He put his hand on Narjiss's shoulder. 'All right, my dear, calm down. I'll call you a taxi on the avenue. Just smoke a cigarette while you wait for me, okay?'

Narjiss pushed his hand away. 'Go fuck yourself! You men are all the same!'

She had trouble driving the car at first: it stalled twice as the watchman observed her anxiously. Sitting next to her, Selma tried to talk her down. 'Come on, what's the point of this? Where do you think you're going?'

'I'm going to follow him. I know where he's taken her. I swear to God, Selma, I don't give a shit. I'm going to kill that son of a bitch.'

Narjiss was slurring her words, and for a second or two Selma thought her friend was about to vomit all over the steering wheel. But she managed to steer the car onto Route des Zaërs and ran two red lights. The car swerved wildly from side to side, then Narjiss lost control of the vehicle. Selma heard a noise – a car horn, maybe, or the squeal of tyres on tarmac. She put her hands over her ears and shut her eyes. Later, she would be told that the car had flipped over several times and she would have a vague memory of that – her head banging against the side panel, darkness pouring in, the sensation of falling.

* 'The dog!'

For a long time she was unconscious, the car on the roadside, her legs trapped under the glove compartment. A sound reached her from far away: something jingling, or perhaps the ticking of an old clock. Something was close to her ear and it took a huge effort of will to open her eyes. At first she thought her eyelids were stuck together. With blood, perhaps. It was as dark as if they were in the middle of the countryside, and for an instant she thought she was underneath the car, that she would have to crawl along the ground. Squinting, she perceived a dim light, and when she turned her head towards the window she saw something. A figure. Someone knocking on the glass. The vague shape of a man and a beam of torchlight. She felt afraid then. The fear was so intense, so rarely felt, that she told herself: I must be dreaming. You only feel scared like this in nightmares. The man signalled for her to wait. He disappeared, the light faded, and Selma found herself in darkness again. Had she closed her eyes? She tried to cry out, but no sound emerged from her mouth. Her lungs were hurting, as if something heavy was crushing her chest. The man came back. He wasn't alone this time. A woman in a headscarf was holding the torch, lighting up the man as he tried to open the car door. The stranger had a long brown beard and wore a small crocheted cap. In her confusion, it crossed Selma's mind that she was in heaven and these were fellow Muslims. Blood was beating in her temples, the way it does when you hold your breath underwater for too long, playing dead. Then her anxiety evaporated and Selma had the gentle, comforting feeling that she was slipping away, moving far far away from this car, this avenue, this city, and had she been more aware she might have thought that Rabat had managed to surprise her after all. The man started to pray, hands joined in front of his crotch, face leaning down. He prayed as if at a graveside, murmuring rapidly, swallowing the syllables. Soon the police turned up, then an ambulance. It took them several hours to get the bodies out of the car. Narjiss had died instantly. Someone had stolen her brooch.

Two days later, Selma woke up in a bed at the Avicenne Hospital. A dim light came through the window and she didn't know if it was the first glimmers of dawn or the last remnants of daylight. If someone would soon come into the room or if she would have to face the endless solitude of night. Slowly, she turned her face to her neighbour: an obese woman who was moaning softly, her arm hanging out of the bed. Her cheeks were streaming with tears as she called out to God and her mother. Selma was in pain, such terrible pain, and she wanted to cry out, to ask for help, but her face felt paralysed. She couldn't move her right arm either: it was entirely covered in a plaster cast. Her body was just a mass of pain now and even the smallest movement made it worse. With every breath she felt as if small needles were being pressed into her chest and throat. Snot ran from her nose and she was too weak to sniff it back inside. One of the windowpanes was cracked and an icy draught of air penetrated the room, burning her face. Selma realised that this was why the fat woman in the next bed was whining: she was freezing under the coarse hospital sheets.

Selma felt submerged by a vast wave of sadness, the kind of sadness that only children and old people feel. A helplessness, a sense of shame at being alive, a primal fear. When a nurse came into the room, she found Selma sobbing. 'Now, now, you should thank God that you're alive,' the nurse told her. 'There's no point crying now.' For a few minutes the nurse moved about the room; Selma had no idea what she was doing. Lying in bed, she felt terribly vulnerable. She could hear the sound of a toilet flushing and a cart with squeaky wheels. The nurse treated her roughly and Selma sensed that this was not simply because the woman was tired or unhappy with her working conditions. She didn't speak to her so harshly or grip her wrist so firmly just because she was stuck in a dirty, poorly insulated hospital lacking in basic equipment, forced to send poor people home to die on a regular basis. No, there was something else that seemed to give her the right to be brusque with Selma, to mock her sadness and ignore her pain. The nurse leaned over her. She examined Selma's face, then frowned as she announced: 'They want to see you.' Selma heard people in the corridor talking about her. Two men in uniform, deep in conversation, came into the room. The doctor, in his frayed, greyish coat, stood to the right of the bed. On the other side was a detective, cap tucked under his arm.

It was the first thing Amine saw when, at his wife's urging, he decided to visit his sister. A policeman, on guard duty outside the door to the hospital room, holding an unlit cigarette between his fingers. It had been the police, not the hospital, who had informed him about the accident. 'They were drunk, hachak*,' explained the policeman on the telephone, and he prayed that God would help the patient find the right path again. For the other woman – the one who'd been driving –

---

* An Arabic term used when inappropriate actions or words are performed/ spoken in front of someone.

God could do nothing now except welcome her among the sinners and forgive her. The cop was quite friendly. He had recognised Selma's surname: 'Belhaj, like the chief of police?' Amine wished everything could have been dealt with that way, easily and remotely, by telephone. He wished he hadn't been forced to face this wretched sight.

'What a dreadful humiliation,' cursed Amine, standing under bare bulbs that cast a gloomy light through the hospital corridor. 'My poor mother must be turning in her grave.' Mathilde had brought a thick woollen blanket, towels, bread rolls and hard-boiled eggs. She had also brought a few things for Selma's roommate, to avert the risk of theft or arguments. Mathilde walked up to the bed and placed her hand on her sister-in-law's forehead. 'It's cold in here. Do they just leave you like this?' She spread the blanket over Selma's body and stared at her swollen face, her unseeing eyes. In her mind, she saw once again the eight-year-old girl who used to graze her knees in the alleys of the medina and who had once fallen down the stairs at home, bloodying her forehead and the bridge of her nose. Back then, Mouilala had blamed her daughter's misfortune on her beauty: 'She's too pretty. People are giving her the evil eye.' Now, in Arabic, her hand still resting on Selma's face, Mathilde told her: 'You're too pretty. People are giving you the evil eye.'

The doctor and the detective observed this tall, confident blonde woman. They exchanged a look of surprise when they heard her speak Arabic with a Germanic accent and the doctor bowed respectfully when she addressed him. 'How bad is it?' asked Mathilde, and abruptly he regained his self-importance, shoving his hands into the pockets of his coat and, in perfect

French, delivering his diagnosis. In addition to a few broken ribs and the bruises and lacerations on her face, Selma had an open fracture of the femur that had required a long and complex operation. If she was brave, she would one day learn to walk again. 'She's brave,' said Mathilde. 'Eh, aren't you?'

The detective kept his eyes on Amine. He had met the police chief, Omar Belhaj, only once, at the very start of this career, and he was now trying to find some resemblance between that man and this one. Amine did not react. 'Can we talk?' he asked, and all three men went out into the corridor.

Mathilde, still sitting on the edge of the bed, stroked Selma's bare arm. 'They'll make you all better again, just you wait and see.' The woman in the next bed was asleep. Mathilde put a kesra, a carton of milk and an old copy of *Paris Match* on her bedside table. When Amine returned, Mathilde grabbed her handbag and stood up. 'I need to go and buy some medicine before the pharmacy closes. I also need to go to the butcher's. I'll be back soon.' And, without giving her husband time to respond, she went.

Brother and sister were left alone in the dark room, the cold night air whistling through the broken window. Embarrassed and angry, Amine paced the room, skirting around Selma's bed as if it contained a wild animal, possibly dangerous, but one that he was nevertheless determined to confront. Finally he stood in front of her.

Selma still couldn't speak or even fully open her eyes, but she could perceive Amine's presence, and she could almost feel the weight of his shadow on her own body.

He examined Selma's face, the purple lacerations on her right cheek and the scabs on her lips. And at that moment he wondered: Did I do this to her? He looked over his shoulder and saw the back of the policeman standing guard in the corridor. Anxiety gripped him: he felt sure he had done something bad, that he had punched a woman in the face, had felt bones cracking under his knuckles. The woman lying here in front of him . . . Who was she? At first he thought: I'm her father, and he reproached himself for not taking better care of her. He bit his lip. His hands were freezing and he knew, deep down, that all he could do was wait. Stare at his shoes, breathe, not make any rash decisions, and wait. He felt as if he was late for something, and someone was going to come in, he was sure of that, he would have time to gather his thoughts, but before he could do that he felt himself slipping, whirled around endlessly. Was the cop guarding the door because of him? Did they know about his rages, about the red mist that would descend upon him and make him deaf to a woman's pleas and screams? Amine looked at the cracked windowpane and he wanted to laugh, like a child or an idiot, as he imagined escaping through that window and jumping down onto the yellowed lawn outside the hospital. The woman moaned, startling him. She was trying to move her hand. He put his hand on her arm. Tears pricked his eyes, he couldn't stop them, and for the first time in years he felt warm liquid on his cheeks, the taste of salt in his mouth. He struggled desperately to remember, to calm down. No, he didn't know who she was, but slowly, slowly, another truth was rising to the surface. He loved her. He loved this woman. He leaned close to her then and, in a soft voice, murmured into her ear: 'I'm sorry. I didn't mean to hurt you. I don't know what got into me. You know how I am.' He wanted to kiss her cheeks and to hold her tightly, so close he could swallow her. But Mathilde opened the door.

She stared at him for a moment. She recognised the invisible veil that sometimes seemed to cover his eyes, the veil that had been falling over them more and more often in recent months. She took some boxes of medicine from a plastic bag, shook two pills into her palm and turned to her husband. 'Can you help me?' They slowly lifted Selma up from the bed and, like a good little girl, she swallowed her medicine.

Aïcha, too, came to the hospital. She had picked up Inès from her piano lesson and Mia from her friend Hakim's house. 'I'll just be a minute. You can wait for me in the car.' But the girls refused. 'It's too dark, I can't read,' Mia complained. 'I'm scared,' said Inès. So they walked across the car park together and Aïcha, used to similar surroundings, failed to consider the effect such a place might have on the girls. She didn't notice the smell of ammonia and dirty water in the reception area. A stretcher had been wedged into the mouth of the lift, and an old man, his head thrown back, his lips white, appeared to be asleep. In the waiting room, a woman in a brown djellaba was weeping softly while under her chair a cat was suckling her babies on the linoleum floor.

Inès pulled at Aïcha's arm. 'I want to stroke the kittens.' But her mother shook her head. 'You must never touch babies that have just been born. Otherwise their mother won't recognise their odour and she'll kill them.' Inès's heart tightened with horror and she pressed herself against Aïcha's leg. She was holding the drawing she had made for her great-aunt – a house with a pointed roof, an orange sun and some flying flowers.

They went into the room. Selma's face – that beautiful face that she had always admired – was covered by something thick and red. Inès stared at her fingernails, perfectly rounded, painted with mother-of-pearl varnish. She loved these little details that made Selma a woman, a real woman, not like Mathilde whose hair was always drenched with sweat, or Aïcha whose shoes were often splattered with blood – even those black ones with white polka dots that she dreamed of inheriting when she was older. Selma kept her cigarettes in a leopard-skin case and collected matchbooks from bars all over the world. She always wore lipstick and she kept a pot of rose-petal hand cream in her purse.

'That's disgusting!' cried Mia. 'Why is there a steak on her face?'

'To stop the swelling. Although it's a bit of an old wives' tale. Your grandmother must have done that.'

Aïcha picked up the slab of meat and dropped it into a plastic bag. She leaned close to Selma, put her hand on her aunt's arm and kissed her forehead.

'It's because I'm too pretty,' mumbled Selma. 'It's the evil eye.'

First I have to buy flowers. Mum always had flowers on the tables when she had people coming over. Yes, I should buy flowers, but it's November – not ideal for flowers. I'll have to buy them at the last minute. On the morning of the party. I'll have to get up early, before Fatima, Mehdi or the children are awake. I'll have to get up early and go to the flower market to see what they have. Anyway, I prefer being alone when I'm shopping. When the children are with me I tend to rush and I often forget something. And there's always one of them whining or throwing a tantrum. Do they think I like having to think of everything? So of course I end up giving in. I really have to stop that, I need to be firmer with them. Will they have roses in November? I can't see anything with all this rain. And that idiot who hasn't even turned his headlights on. He looks like he's about to crash into the back of me. Hey, dickhead! I knew the day would be ruined. When I woke at four in the morning, I knew I wouldn't be able to fall back asleep. I shouldn't have stayed in bed. Every time I do that I just toss and turn and all it does is make me worry even more. I should have got up, grabbed a pen and paper, and written my to-do list. Now I can't even get it straight in my head. The day's barely started and I'm already sleepy. And I can't even tell Mehdi that I'm sleeping badly, since I'm not sharing a bed with him any more. I told him it was because he snored, and it's true, he does snore: hardly surprising with all the cigarettes he smokes and the whisky. I've told him, but he doesn't care. Sometimes I want to scratch his face when I see him sucking on those cigarettes like they were his mother's breasts. I want to tell him: If you can't quit for me, do it for the girls, because you're not invincible, Mehdi – even CEOs get cancer, you know. But it does no good. It's the same thing when I tell him to watch his tongue. You talk too much, Mehdi, you're not careful enough. What does he think he's doing, talking about the Oufkirs' escape in front of the girls? If the children repeat that, we'll be in serious trouble. You really think people aren't informing on you for the jokes you make about powerful people? And when you brag about being the most intelligent and incorruptible man in Morocco? It makes your friends laugh, but you'll see: he who laughs last laughs longest. I've told you before: nobody ever regretted not running their big mouth. Sometimes staying silent is a way of resisting, a way of refusing to compromise yourself. Yeah, yeah, I know, me and my peasant mentality, my country paranoia, yeah, I'm just like my father, but so what? That's nothing to be ashamed of. No, but this time I really am going to tell him. It's my birthday and I don't want any scenes. I don't want you talking to my friends as if they were morons, just because you reckon doctors are shameless and backward-thinking. You know the truth? You get annoyed because we talk about things you don't understand. But you've made no effort with them for fifteen years. You think they don't notice when you roll your eyes and sulk like some kid who's been excluded from the adults' conversation? You can't stand not being able to give your opinion, and it gets on your nerves that we have the power to save people's lives, and no matter how important you think you are, you know that nobody will ever come and kiss your shoulder like they do to me or Rachid because you will never save anybody's life. It's because of you that Oumaïma almost didn't come to my party. I had to beg her, I had to tell Rachid to talk to his wife because he was upset too, and if he does come it's only for me, out of friendship for me. How could you call her 'mad as a box of frogs'? Just because she didn't agree with you! Mad as a box of frogs – what would you say if someone said that to your daughter? I have to buy flowers and I don't have enough tablecloths. I should call Mum – she has more tablecloths than she knows what to do with – but if I do, she'll start questioning me, she'll tell me I'm doing it all wrong, she'll criticise the menu because she doesn't like Moroccan cuisine, supposedly because she finds it hard to digest. I'll never get through that puddle. For months they prayed for rain, and when it finally came the streets flooded and now they're complaining because their car's stuck in a pond. Just let me past, let me past, thank you, monsieur, I didn't want to organise this birthday party, I don't know what got into me, I can't even remember who it was that said 'but it's your fortieth – you have to celebrate that' . . . just someone else who wants to have fun at my expense, but I should have just stayed at home with the girls, we could have watched a film and that would have been fine with me, but instead I said yes and now it's up to me to buy the flowers, organise the menu and make sure we have enough tablecloths because even though Fatima always says she knows how to do everything, that she's the one who keeps the house clean and that annoys Mehdi, ah yes, *that* annoys him, he accuses me of losing control of my own home, of letting her run things and raise my children, but he doesn't know what the hell he's talking about, and besides, I'm forty years old, it's about time I stopped being so afraid of my mother and my husband, it's about time I stopped caring when Mum comes into our house and stares in silence at the new furniture we've bought. I didn't want to move to a new house anyway. It was Mehdi who insisted after that disastrous dinner with his management team. Farid was inspecting our living room and I had to explain to him that the noise in the chimney was made by a nest of mice, and he told Mehdi: 'That's not possible, Monsieur le Président.' After that, it became an obsession. Moving to the Ambassadors district. Oh, he loves saying that, the Ambassadors, because everyone understands what it means, 'I live in the Ambassadors', and the houses don't even have numbers, 'we live in the Ambassadors at Kilometre 5', and people know we must have a big house and that our neighbour is a Polish ambassador or an American and I knew I would be the one who'd have to deal with it all. Of course Mehdi found the architect, and everyone in Rabat knows that he studied in the United States and that we have a 'Californian-style' house. If he says that one more time, I swear I'll scratch his eyes out, except he hasn't come to a single construction meeting, and it's been me, yes, me, who had to badger the architect and the contractor while Mehdi just insisted that we have separate wings for the parents and the children. 'And I want an enormous office, with cedar bookshelves, an office far away from the children.' Women should live in tiny houses. We should live in nests. Won't this damn traffic light ever turn green? I've never liked driving, and since we started living in the Ambassadors it's taken me, what, at least half an hour to drive to the clinic. But *he* doesn't care that I have to drive at night, on this deserted Route des Zaërs, whenever there's an emergency, and even though I lock the car doors, even though I drive as fast as I can, it scares me, maybe it reminds me of the old days, the farm at night and Mum's cries, but I don't want to think about that, if I hadn't slept so badly I wouldn't be thinking about it. Ah, finally, we're moving forward, come on, get going or it'll turn red again, but there's no point getting worked up, what's done is done and the party will be perfect, and it'll be a housewarming too, and I'll put the flowers on the sideboard. I need to book an appointment at the hairdresser's, that's the problem with this style, I should never have listened to him, everyone swears by Jean-Marie, 'the best hairdresser in the city', yeah, so they say, and they always add 'even if he's queer', that makes them laugh, but it's always the same thing with me, I'm forty years old and I'm afraid of hairdressers, it's always the same, I'm forty and I'm a doctor but put me in front of a hairdresser and I'm like a little kid again, I can't get the words out. I didn't want this stupid Lady Di haircut. He said, 'let's show off the back of your neck', and I almost wept when I saw those long strands of hair falling onto the tiled floor. I know Mehdi doesn't like women with short hair and I knew he was going to yell at me, but I wasn't expecting Inès to start crying as if I'd been disfigured for life. I mean, it's not that bad, really, it's not that bad, it's just that it needs so much upkeep, which is probably why Jean-Marie suggested it to me, so I have to go back to the salon once or twice every week to get it blow-dried and I smile like an idiot while he goes on about how dense my hair is – 'You have very thick hair, you know.' I bet Lady Di doesn't have this kind of problem, and I know it's stupid but I feel kind of ashamed, going to the patisserie myself. I'll go to the Little Duchess and she'll say 'Who's it for?' and I'll say 'It's for me' and she'll write my name and 16 November 1987 on my cake and I'll have to buy the candles too and Mehdi will probably be too drunk by the time we get to the dessert so I'll have to turn off the lights too . . . Seriously, it makes me ashamed, and I could have done without this, I'm tired on Saturdays. If I don't order the shoulder of lamb today, there's no guarantee I'll have it for Saturday and, shit, if someone's taken my parking spot again I'm going to get annoyed, everyone thinks 'oh Aïcha she's so nice, she won't get angry', but I don't see why I should be obliged to drive around the neighbourhood when I've got a reserved spot outside the clinic and nobody ever takes Rachid's spot or the one belonging to Mokhtar the anaesthetist. Mehdi always says that I don't assert myself: you can't say no, not to your daughters or to your patients or to anyone. The way he said: 'Honestly, did you have to agree to that midwife training course in Marrakech?' And if he calls me 'Aïcha the martyr' one more time I'll rip out his eyeballs, I can see that it's getting into Mia's head. That's why she dresses like a boy – she thinks she can escape the curse of girls and mothers, who always end up acting like martyrs. No, of course I didn't have to agree to it and, damn it, it's true that I can't say no and that's going to be my birthday resolution, now that I'm turning forty, I'm going to start saying no, asserting myself, and I won't fall to pieces when I have to tell him that I'm going to be spending ten days a month in Paris this winter for a breast cancer training course. He'll laugh and tell me that I'm mad, then make jokes about Fatima, then he'll shout: 'Well, I don't want your mother here, so find someone else to look after the children.' I already talked to Selma – he likes Selma – and since the accident she's not the same as she used to be, she's . . . I don't know, more serious, different. She observes Ramadan and practises sadaqah for the dead. The girls like her too. They'll see how they manage without me. They'll see.

* * *

Aïcha parked outside the clinic. She grabbed her handbag from the passenger seat, her navy jacket, and just as she was about to close the car door she heard the sound of laughter. Inès and Mia were sitting in the back seat, giggling. 'I don't believe it! Why didn't you say anything? You're going to be late now!' She turned on the ignition and sped away. The rain was falling even harder than before and she felt like she was being crushed under a wave of weariness. 'Don't tell Daddy.' It wasn't the first time she'd forgotten to drop the girls at school. Sometimes she was so absorbed by thoughts of work, by her endless to-do list, that she automatically followed the route to the clinic. A few days after they had moved into their big new house on the Route des Zaërs, she had forgotten the girls at the supermarket. Inès had taken advantage of the situation to steal a pack of chewing gum. Mia had told on her and the owner of the supermarket, embarrassed, had assured Aïcha that it wasn't a big deal. 'They're just children, Doctor.'

Aïcha dropped Mia outside the secondary school, but when she got to the primary school she had to park the car, take Inès by the hand and run to the gate to beg them to open it. 'It won't happen again, I promise.' Raindrops were running down the back of her neck and she felt like crying. When she arrived at the clinic, it was past nine and the secretaries jumped up as soon as they saw her. Two women were insisting on being seen without an appointment. They said they knew Aïcha and the secretaries didn't know what to do. Aïcha put on her white coat and sighed. 'Okay, let's try to fit them in.'

She washed her hands for a long time with soap and hot water. She would go to the butcher's during her lunch break to order the shoulder of lamb. Then tomorrow at dawn she would go to the central market for the flowers and the fish. She was thinking about fresh sea bream, gleaming calamari and a prawn-and-tomato salad when the first patient entered. 'Get undressed,' Aïcha told her, and while the woman – who must have been in her mid-twenties – took off her clothes behind the screen, she wrote down her menu ideas on a prescription note. 'Lie down.' The patient had a very nice body. Aïcha continued to notice this kind of thing and, strangely, she took a certain pleasure in examining women whose physical attributes she admired. This one had beautiful breasts, firm and golden, a soft and rounded belly that seemed to invite you to place your cheek against it, and thighs covered with a faint down of soft brown hairs. 'You have to open your legs.' The patient was tense and Aïcha realised it must be her first appointment with a gynaecologist. 'Relax.' She rubbed her hands together to warm them up, then put them on the young woman's thighs. Aïcha respected her patients' modesty, but it worried her too. If you were too ashamed to spread your legs or expose your breasts, if you were too ashamed to talk about how it felt when you had sex or urinated, you ran the risk of not knowing that you were ill or that you had an unwanted pregnancy. 'Hchouma'. Here, dying of shame was not merely an expression. Even language was stained by it: with lowered eyes and blushing cheeks, these women felt obliged to say 'hachak' every time they mentioned an intimate part of their body. My breasts, hachak. My vagina, hachak. They never pronounced the word 'cancer' and nervously shook their heads when Aïcha dared to deliver an ominous diagnosis. The shameful disease that devoured their ovaries, their vulva or their breasts and caused their husbands to leave them.

Aïcha questioned the young woman. 'When was your last period? Are you sexually active? Do you know your family medical history?' The patient got dressed again and Aïcha thought that, for dessert, she might make a hazelnut cake and a strawberry pavlova. For the main courses she would stick to Moroccan dishes. Lentils with khlii. A tagine of onions and tomatoes that would take hours to cook. A confit of shoulder of lamb. The second patient came in. Aïcha greeted her warmly. She had been treating Rokia for years: she called her by her first name and knew the first names of her children too. She spotted her patient's husband in the waiting room, his face hidden behind an old magazine. He always came with his wife to her appointments, and afterwards he would approach Aïcha, his eyes overflowing with gratitude, and say: 'Thank you, Doctor, God bless you.' Less than a year ago, Aïcha had diagnosed Rokia with breast cancer and had referred her to the best surgeon in Rabat, who had performed a mastectomy with lymph node dissection. The surgery had been horrifically painful and left her mutilated, but the young woman had accepted these side effects with admirable courage. Rokia lay down on the examining table. She had lost a lot of weight, but her arms had swollen since the operation and her skin had coarsened. 'Is it painful?' Aïcha asked.

'Not really. I just feel like my clothes are too small and sometimes, at the end of the day, I don't have enough strength to lift my arms. What bothers me is not being able to pick up my children any more.'

The patients came and went. In the top-right corner of each folder, Aïcha had written a few letters – in a code that only she knew. 'H' for hypochondriac. 'VH' for violent husband. 'C' for chatty. 'TC' for too chatty. These coded letters designated anxious patients, tearful patients, shy patients, quirky patients. Patients who were left in a deep depression after giving birth – 'I want to love him but I just can't' – and the cranks, who believed in the power of the moon or placing heated lead close to their vaginas. Mehdi would say: 'You bring home all their germs and their sadness.' He didn't like her talking about her work in front of the children. He hated it when she mentioned disgusting details at the dinner table, and he wouldn't even crack a smile when she told amusing anecdotes, like the time she had pulled a small cucumber out of a woman's vagina. Nobody wants to hear about vaginas when they're eating, he told her.

In Rabat and even beyond, everyone knew that Dr Daoud was not interested in money. She took care of people, irrespective of their income or social status, and at the time this was enough to massively expand her patient list. Prostitutes, maids, labourers, market vendors and dressmakers from Takaddoum, even peasant farmers from the hinterland, people who lived near beaches, on the periphery of the city. Her partner, Rachid, and the clinic's secretaries did not know what to make of this influx of poor people, or the smells of henna and dried thyme that pervaded the air of the waiting room, or the women who offered to pay their bill with a live rabbit or some freshly laid eggs. They were torn between their admiration for Aïcha ('Aïcha the saint') and a certain irritation ('Aïcha the martyr'). They feared that the clinic would lose its standing, and the bourgeois patients from the city centre would be shocked to hear people complaining in Berber.

Aïcha did not treat men, but she recognised the imprint they left on women's bodies: a bruise on a cheek or a hip, a love bite on a neck, lesions on the vaginal wall. Unintentionally, she often informed her patients about their husbands' infidelities. The reason you can't urinate is that you have a disease that he has transmitted to you. Aïcha entered these women's beds and their innermost thoughts. She listened with delight to a woman driven into half-crazed ecstasies by a lover and shared her anxieties about secret meetings, letters slipped into handbags, the ache of absence that gnawed away at body and soul. She shared their sadness, sympathised with their disgust. 'Couldn't I just have a period all the time? That way, he'd never touch me.'

She was in the middle of an examination when the telephone rang. 'Excuse me,' she said before picking up the receiver. It was Mia. 'I need some double copy pages with large squares. And not the Moroccan stuff – it's like blotting paper. I need French pages.'

'Couldn't you have told me this before?' whispered her mother.

'I forgot.'

No matter how many times Aïcha explained to her daughters that it was not okay for them to call her at work like this, they took no notice. Inès would call her in the afternoons especially: 'Are you almost finished? When are you coming home?' The girls had realised that their mother was entirely devoted to them, that she was capable of crossing oceans in a single bound if one of her children needed her. Inès was a worrier, and Mia was as self-centred as Mehdi. At thirteen, she seemed to believe that the whole world revolved around her and her desires. And, just like her father, she had a talent for surrounding herself with people whose only ambition was to make sure that she was always happy.

At four thirty, the telephone rang again. 'What is it now? Sorry, Jamila, I meant to ask who is it.'

'It's the school, Doctor. About the little one, I think.'

Aïcha turned pale and for a few moments she stood petrified, staring at the door. She instantly imagined the worst. Inès had choked on her food, she had fallen from a tree, one of the other children had strangled her, she was vomiting blood, she had broken a leg or cracked her skull. Aïcha always imagined the worst. When one of her daughters had a headache, she would rack her brains to remember what she'd learned in university about cases of cancer in children. She would make them have an X-ray or get their blood taken for the smallest pain or sniffle.

'Ask them what's wrong! Ask them!' she yelled into the receiver, as the frightened patient put one hand over her crotch and the other over a breast to preserve her modesty.

The secretary said reassuringly: 'They say you have a meeting with the teacher at four thirty. She's waiting for you.'

At five thirty, Aïcha arrived outside the empty school. She was glad that she was late and did not have to see the other mothers, carrying paper bags from the bakery covered in hand-shaped grease stains. A childhood instinct took hold of her and she felt a sudden urge to run, the way she used to run up and down the hills around the farm. A school monitor led her to the Year 4B classroom. The teacher was standing in front of the door, holding Inès's hand. 'Wait for us there,' she told the little girl, pointing to a bench in the corridor, before signalling for Aïcha to follow her. In the classroom, some logs were burning in an old stove and children's paintings were drying on a piece of string. Aïcha started to look for her daughter's artwork, but the teacher asked her to sit down in the chair facing the desk. She was wearing a denim jacket with sleeves too short for her arms, and her hair – grey with yellow highlights – fell over her shoulders. She had large hands, which she laid flat on the desktop. A man's hands, thought Aïcha.

'Were you looking for Inès's drawing? It's here,' she said, gesturing at a sheet completely covered with colours, although it was impossible to guess what the shapes meant. 'It's a butterfly,' the teacher explained. 'She says you eat butterflies at home. Amusing, isn't it?' She stared at Aïcha with her green, almost liquid eyes, and Aïcha smiled shyly, thinking of farfalle pasta in tomato sauce. 'So, Madame Daoud, I wanted to talk to you about Inès. Perhaps you're aware that we had the medical visit a few days ago. Oh no, don't worry, Inès is in good health. That's not what I want to talk about. I only mention it because, for practical reasons, we divided the girls and boys into separate groups. The girls got undressed here, in my classroom, and the boys in Monsieur Caroube's classroom. I was very busy trying to calm down some of the girls who were terrified of getting a shot and didn't want to take off their sweaters. I'm sure you know how frightened children are of doctors, how they imagine things . . . Anyway, I suddenly realised that Inès had disappeared. I thought she must have been scared too, that she'd hidden somewhere. I looked everywhere for her – under the desks, in the bathroom – but it wasn't until I walked across the playground that I saw her. Barefoot, in a vest top, standing outside Monsieur Caroube's door.' She paused for a second, as if expecting a reaction, but Aïcha remained silent. 'She was standing on tiptoes, looking through the half-open door. I came up behind her, but she didn't seem surprised. I asked her what she was doing there. She said: "I'm looking." I asked her what she was looking at, and she laughed and said: "The boys." To be perfectly honest with you, Madame Daoud, I didn't know how to react. I should probably have told her off, at least for leaving the classroom without telling me and making me worry about her. But she was just standing there, smiling at me, in her white vest. You know what she's like: with those big dark eyes and that angelic face, it's hard to think badly of her. So I took her by the hand and led her back to my classroom. And just before we went in to join the others, I asked her: "Why did you want to look at the boys?"'

Aïcha swallowed. The teacher opened her hands wide, drawing out the suspense.

'And what did she say?' asked Aïcha, who felt humiliated by this whole conversation.

'You won't believe this. She said: "Because I can feel my heart in my thingy." And then she put her hand . . . Well, you know. Down there.'

Inès was not afraid of doctors, shots or even pain. When her first milk teeth started to loosen, she decided to pull them out herself so she could get the promised reward more quickly. She stood in front of the bathroom mirror, picked up a ball of cotton wool and wiggled her tiny tooth back and forth. She could feel it coming loose from the gum and she watched as the cotton wool became soaked with blood. She was being very brave, she told herself. When the tooth came out, she swallowed her metallic saliva and ran, trophy in hand, to the living room. 'Guess who's coming to my room tonight? The tooth fairy!'

It was Inès who insisted on visiting Selma every weekend. Each time, she brought a stack of blank pages and put them on the coffee table so she could draw while the adults talked among themselves and Selma rested. Soon her drawings were all over the apartment. On the photograph from Venice, Selma stuck Inès's drawing of the house with the pointed roof and the big orange sun. The images of New York disappeared behind the little girl's scrawlings and Selma gave up her dreams of escape. Now, since the recent rule changes, she would need a visa even for Europe. Inès drew Selma's hands and the bouquet of flowers that stood on the little plastic table. Once, she tried to copy the long scar that ran down Selma's thigh and looked like a constellation.

Selma asked her: 'Will you draw my portrait one day?'
But Inès shook her head. 'I don't like drawing faces.'

One Saturday, Inès helped Selma dye her hair because a long streak of white had appeared in it. She filed her nails, learned to varnish them without going over the edges, and even used a black pencil to cover up the scar in the middle of her right eyebrow. Since the accident, Selma's face had changed. She wasn't disfigured, but it was as if her features had grown harsher. Her lips were thinner and her eyes, which used to invite you to get to know her better, now kept you at a distance. She had lost a lot of weight and her leg was extremely painful. For Christmas 1987, Mathilde gave her a cane that she'd found at the flea market and that dated 'back to the time of the French'. It was made from dark wood and had a round pommel decorated with a stone so polished that it was like a mirror.

When she did her stretches and the pain brought tears to her eyes, Selma would wonder if her brother really had come to the hospital and talked to her or if she had simply dreamed it. She could not have said if he had been tender or cruel. Maybe both, in the same way that a man could kiss you and hit you at the same time. After a few weeks she started walking again and her limp was like a stylish accessory. Selma resembled the actresses in the noir crime films that Mehdi made them watch. Lauren Bacall, with a cane and a cigarette-holder. Inès could not have put this into words, but she sensed in her great-aunt a strange combination of power and independence (because she lived alone and free) and sadness and desperation (because she lived alone and free). Inès admired her. She wanted to be her, or rather she wished she could mend Selma's destiny, be a better version of her. She wanted to complete her. Selma sensed this in the little girl of eight and drew strength from the reflection she saw in her eyes. It was stronger – oh, far stronger – than the love of men that she had often felt like a gust of hot or cold air. Stronger, too, than what she had felt for Sabah. Her own daughter, Sabah. Selma had never taught anybody anything, never passed on an ounce of wisdom or even a recipe. She had never given any of her clothes to Sabah, whose hips were wider and whose feet were smaller than hers. She observed Inès and knew that the child possessed the science of seduction, which was impossible to teach, an art that could not be foolishly reduced to acting or manipulation.

During the winter of 1988, while Aïcha was attending her breast cancer training course in Paris, Selma went to pick up Inès every Saturday to take her to dance class. The little girl would jump for joy when she saw her great-aunt appear in the changing rooms that smelled of sweat and mouldy linoleum. Selma was more beautiful than all the other mothers. She wore mohair sweaters, transparent leopard-print blouses, plum-coloured leather skirts and often a pair of cowboy boots or square-heeled pumps. The young dancers were all intrigued by the woman with the gleaming cane who held hands with Inès as they walked up Avenue de la Victoire. Selma would say: 'Let's go for a ride on Fifth Avenue.' She would pretend that her car – Mehdi's old R12 – was a limousine and her crumbling apartment building 'a mansion'. But what Inès liked best was the boutique where Selma worked: a shop behind Place Pietri that Amine rented to her, where she sold clothes and accessories. 'At least this way she'll have a respectable occupation.'

One Saturday in February, they were walking along Avenue de la Victoire under the flame trees, which trembled in the gusting wind. The morning's rain had left large puddles in the pavement, with cigarette stubs floating on the surface of the water. Selma rubbed Inès's back to warm her up. 'You shouldn't have kept your dance shoes on,' she told the girl. 'They'll get damaged.' She handed Inès a pain au chocolat and bit into a sandwich. 'I didn't have time for breakfast.' As they went past St Peter's Cathedral, some teenage boys shouted obscene compliments at Selma. 'One-track minds, the lot of them. They don't care that I'm old and I walk with a limp. They'd screw anything with tits and an arse.'

Selma opened the door to the boutique and Inès went and sat behind the counter. Almost immediately she saw a waiter come out of the café across the road, carrying a teapot and two small blue glasses on a tray. He poured the foaming liquid slowly into the cups. 'Compliments of the boss,' he said, before going back to work. The boutique was one long, narrow room with hanging rails running along either side and, in the centre, a wooden display case filled with costume jewellery. For Inès, this was the most extraordinary playground imaginable. She could try on dresses in the dusty cubicle, and she could help Selma fold clothes, put on price tags and empty boxes of new supplies. She loved the feel of tissue paper and the leather smell of new shoes and the way they felt when she slipped her plump little feet into them. Sometimes she would sit behind the counter and tap her fingers rapidly on a calculator. 'That will be one hundred dirhams,' she would say to an imaginary customer.

Inès was just finishing her cup of tea when a customer – a real one – came into the shop. The woman looked shy and her fingers gripped tightly to her leather handbag. She leaned down to look at the jewellery in its display case. It was the third time she had been here this week. 'So, you still can't decide?' asked Selma, taking a thick gold chain and pendant from its setting.

She stood behind the customer, who pulled her hair up and, looking in the mirror, hand on heart and earnest-eyed, said: 'No, honestly, I just don't know.'

'What's holding you back?' Selma asked. 'You love this necklace, don't you?'

The customer looked down again at the price on the tag.

'You couldn't lower it a little bit?'

Selma was already unfastening the chain. 'We don't haggle here.'

Selma would much rather have been dealing with the whims and vulgar desires of men than sitting here waiting for the hours to pass. She hated this boutique and this neighbourhood, and she couldn't stop thinking about her shattered dreams of New York. She would constantly make mistakes in the accounts and forget to update the columns of sales and expenses in the big spiral notebook. She would give dresses to her friends for free: 'Of course, you should take it – it looks so good on you.' Once, Inès saw her have an argument with a customer: a woman with dark frizzy hair insisted on seeing the black dress displayed in the shop window. She spoke French with a slight accent. Selma was in a bad mood. Staring at the floor, she repeated like a stubborn child: 'It's not for sale.' 'Then why is it in the window?' the customer asked, surprised. Selma said nothing. She had already decided to keep it for herself.

In the hours that followed, the boutique remained empty. Selma paced up and down the street. She smoked cigarettes and Inès admired the way she wasn't afraid of what people might say about her. Selma was very different from the other Belhajes. She didn't care about people who claimed only immoral women smoked in public; sometimes she would even sit on one of those café terraces on Avenue Mohammed V that were usually filled only with men. She would tell Inès family secrets. It was through Selma that Inès found out about the existence of Jalil, her mad old great-uncle who had died of hunger. Selma showed her photographs of Omar, a tall thin man in thick glasses, who had blown his brains out on the beach at Skhirat in 1978. That was what Selma said, and the little girl would never forget that expression: 'he blew his brains out'. 'In this family, everyone ends up losing their marbles. Me too – one day I'll be drooling and I won't know who you are.' Selma liked to boast about the old days, when she was so beautiful that men would go crazy for her. 'I had hair like this and eyebrows like this,' she would say, making expansive movements with her arms. Selma was a language, a manner of speaking. Talking about Aïcha, she said: 'Your mother is a *lady*.' She said the last word in English, but Inès didn't speak English, so what she heard was *laide*. Ugly.

The little girl went up to the jewellery display case. 'Do you like that necklace?' Selma put it around her neck, and Inès couldn't stop smiling and touching it. She felt like she was wearing a river of diamonds. A woman from the neighbourhood poked her head through the door. She said hello and promised she would drop by later. 'She won't come back.' Selma was bored. She had thrown her sandwich in the bin and now the shop smelled of onions and sardines. 'Come here,' she told Inès. She went to fetch a rattan stool from the changing cubicle and used it as a step-stool to climb into the shop window. There, she put her arms around the white, armless mannequin in a red cotton dress with a chestnut wig on its faceless head, and carried it away. In its place she put the rattan stool. She told Inès to sit on it, then took a lipstick from her handbag. She gave a fake smile, which the child imitated, and Selma rubbed the scarlet, scented gloss against her lips. With a brush, she spread some pink blush across Inès's cheeks, and she drew around her eyes with black eyeliner. 'That doesn't hurt, does it?' The two of them burst out laughing, as if they'd just had a brilliant idea or as if they were doing something very naughty. Inès's little feet swung from the stool. She could see her reflection in the window. She stared at a shoe shop across the street and deciphered the letters emblazoned above it: Bata. Soon, passers-by were stopping to look at her, surprised or amused, and some of them waved at her to see if she was actually alive or just a very pretty mannequin. Some children pointed at her as if she was a panther or a tapir at the zoo.

All afternoon, customers poured in. Women from the neighbourhood, whom Selma had never spoken to before, came to introduce themselves. Where had she found such an adorable little girl? Her hair was so beautiful, golden and curly like a European girl's. And those eyes! So big and dark and soulful. 'She's going to be a heartbreaker.' Some of the customers pretended that Inès was actually for sale. 'How much for the little girl?' they asked. And if they bought a dress or some jewellery, would Selma give them a discount?

Inès did not let herself be distracted by any of this. Despite the discomfort, she sat in the window all afternoon, straight-backed and straight-faced. Now and then she would allow herself to smile or wave when someone spoke to her. 'How old are you?' a fat lady with bright-pink eyelids asked her. 'Almost eight.' That day, she felt like the heroine of *Lady and the Tramp*: the pretty cocker spaniel puppy with a red bow in her hair. A beautiful, docile little creature loved by everyone.

Another customer came into the shop, but she did not appear so enchanted by the window display. 'You should be ashamed of yourself, exposing a little girl to the evil eye like that!'

'I don't give a shit about the evil eye,' Selma replied.

In September 1989, Mia started at the Lycée Descartes. The locals, who all knew that imposing white building in the heart of the Agdal neighbourhood, called it 'Lycée dial flouss', the 'money school'. Formerly known as the Lycée Gouraud and founded in 1963, it boasted a long list of former students who had gone on to become ministers, wealthy businessmen, famous artists or high-level athletes, and even more who had been accepted at the most prestigious universities in Paris. The school spread over several streets, between the Avenue des Nations Unies and the gloomy Forêt Hilton, where eucalyptus trees grew, their trunks peeling. At the foot of the building there was a car park for the teachers (with the French cars distinguished by their yellow number plates) and the chauffeurs who drove the children to school (and sometimes carried their bags). On the square in front of the impressive black gate, a vendor sold sweets including Indian-head liquorice and sugar-coated spearmint dough. In spring, silkworm merchants would set up their stalls there, the ground covered with boxes full of insects and mulberry leaves. Walk through the door of the school, some said, and you entered France, that secular land where people had rights (real ones) and the Moroccan police were not allowed to set foot.

The students were hand-picked and the school offered them the best of everything. There were football pitches and basketball courts, and an athletics stadium where students could train for the hundred metres and cross-country races. Behind the language classrooms there was a swimming pool, and rumour had it that the students could cool off there between exams when the heat became unbearable. The teachers were all French and highly qualified, delighted to have been chosen to teach at this prestigious institution, this symbol of Franco-Moroccan friendship. The children – because they *were* children – had the reputation of being studious, docile and ambitious. The Lycée Descartes was a place dedicated to the pursuit of excellence, particularly in mathematics, the one subject that parents considered more important than any other. But there was also a drama club and several groups of musicians, including one that played cover versions of Rita Mitsouko hits. For teachers freshly arrived from France, the school and its surroundings could produce a strange impression, an illusion of familiarity. Certain Moroccan parents liked to show off their love for France and its values. They claimed to adore Brassens, Aznavour and secularism. They all followed the famous 'headscarf affair' at Creil and they were loudly in disagreement with those 'Arabs of France' who brought shame on them and with whom they had nothing in common. 'Thankfully, the king made those girls' families see reason. In Morocco, girls that age don't have to wear a headscarf. They have completely misunderstood our religion, which is open and tolerant.'

But, as the months passed, the teachers could feel the weight of fear and propaganda pressing down on them with growing force. They learned, sometimes to their cost, that there were certain things they were not supposed to talk about. It was not a good idea to show an interest in politics or women or money.

There was always one teacher – older, more experienced – who would point out to them the lines that should not be crossed: religion, the king, the Sahara. Not to mention Palestine and the Intifada. The more seasoned among them knew that the Lycée Descartes was modelled on the famous Lycée Lyautey in Casablanca: an enclave where an elite class raised with foreign values, speaking a foreign language, could reproduce itself and, completely dissociated from the country in which it lived, could dominate that country without suffering from a guilty conscience. The Descartes students lived on a sort of island, partly cut off from the world. They wondered what their place was and how others saw them. They had no idea who they were. Were they beautiful or ugly? From here or from there? Did they matter?

Back then, it was said that the king had a powerful transmitter at the palace that enabled him to tune in to all foreign channels, and that certain inhabitants of Rabat were able to access this too. When he left the city, the king took the transmitter with him, and then it was the turn of the people of Fes or Marrakech to watch foreign shows. Mia never knew if it was thanks to the king that she was able to watch French television, but in the summer of 1989 the Daouds had a satellite dish installed on the roof of their house. There were growing numbers of these white and grey half-moons appearing all over the city; you could see them on terraces and balconies. And those who could not afford to buy this magical device on the black market found some extravagant ways to mimic its appearance, like a couscous steamer or a black plastic bag attached to an aerial. They would also place a filter in front of the screen to turn the black-and-white images into colour. Some people said: 'A television without a satellite dish is like a car without wheels.' Every afternoon, naked women would enter people's apartments: blondes with bee-stung lips, infidels with names like Kelly or Susan. They had enormous and very white teeth. Housewives talked about this in kitchens, at markets, in government offices. They made remarks about the way these women dressed; they railed at an adulterous lover named Rick. They knew the theme music to all these shows. And the women who appeared in them, these American girls, lived by an immense ocean, under a sky that was permanently blue. They drove their cars and men fell in love with them. Morocco's defenders of morality were deeply offended by this. They wrote articles against the 'diabolical dishes' on the city's rooftops and declared war on the demons that were perverting the country's youth, threatening the modesty of its women.

A new era was beginning. So said Mehdi. One night in November 1989, Mia was sitting on the rug, at her father's feet, and they were watching a news report on the fall of the Berlin Wall. Mehdi gasped with joy. He called out to Aïcha, who was in the kitchen: 'Come and watch! Surely you can see that this is more important than whatever we're having for dinner?' Hundreds of people were gathered in front of the Wall. Some of them, mostly young people, had climbed it and were waving their arms as if trying to be seen from a great distance. People came and went in front of the camera. A girl with blonde curly hair smiled into the lens and made the peace sign. The reporter questioned a boy in a denim jacket. His voice was hoarse from yelling. He seemed happy, on the verge of tears. That night, Mehdi furtively ran his hand through his fifteen-year-old daughter's short hair. 'Freedom always triumphs in the end,' he told her. 'Now that the Wall has fallen, we just have to wait. Soon it will be Poland, then Hungary and the Soviet Union.' He predicted that peace would conquer the world and democracy would spread across every continent. 'No wall can withstand the dreams of youth.' That night, Mia thought again about the tunnel that her father had once wanted to build under the Strait of Gibraltar. And she imagined a world where there would be no more walls, only tunnels.

At fifteen, Mia was for the first time aware of having her own ambitions, her own unique desires, which nobody else could understand. Until this point, everything she had known about herself had been told to her by other people. As if she was nothing but the sum of a series of anecdotes repeated year after year by her parents, her grandparents, her sister, changing a word or a detail here and there. Of course, there had been the time when she'd tried to kill Inès. The day when, at eight years old, she had started a tractor engine on her own and ploughed a field. Aïcha liked to remind her of the remark that her Year 5 teacher had written on her end-of-year report: 'Mia will go far.' Sometimes she would hear people talking about her. Her parents were thrilled to have such a serious, studious daughter. An intelligent girl who had never been any trouble and who spent most of her time reading novels. Mehdi and Aïcha rejoiced at seeing her, year after year, inside that bubble of fiction. What a good girl she was! And what a prodigious memory she had, capable of reciting passages from Camus or Zweig! One day she would be a writer herself. It was Mehdi who declared this during a family meal, and nobody raised a word of protest. Her parents believed, naively, that books were a sort of invisibility cloak that would protect their daughter from danger and misfortune. They had not understood that Mia was looking for something else, that novels had nurtured within her an immense yearning for freedom and a bitterness towards her dreary, nondescript life, here at the periphery of the world.

Until now, Mia had never given much thought to the people who wrote the books she read. Or rather, these writers were for her as unreal as the characters they created. Baudelaire strolling through the mist of Parisian boulevards. Tolstoy managing his estate in his white coat. Balzac drinking cup after cup of coffee in an attic room. But one night during the autumn of 1989, as she was doing her homework on the living room table, she saw for the first time, on television, the face of Salman Rushdie. A fatwa had been declared against him, and in the streets of Pakistan fanatics with red-dyed beards were burning his book. Mia didn't know what the word 'fatwa' meant, but at fifteen she wondered if she would ever be willing to die for her ideas.

She sensed that something was tearing her, slowly, from the comfortable, lukewarm cocoon of family life. It was no longer enough for her to be Mia, her parents' daughter. She wanted a life of her own, with friends and secrets. At school she had picked up new preoccupations. The girls had started to develop breasts and the boys were growing downy hairs on their upper lips. She watched, slightly stunned, as the world changed around her. Half of her classmates smoked Kents or Camels. The girls were now divided between those who did it and those who didn't. Someone had told her that Afafe – who had been in Mia's class in Year 4 and who used to fall asleep on her ink-smeared notebooks – had had an abortion. There were stories, too, of girls so thin that they had ended up in hospital. Nobody swapped marbles or Panini cards any more. Nobody argued over bars of chocolate. Nowadays they suffered from heartbreak or ruined reputations.

It took Mia months of patient observation to figure out the school's social hierarchy. At the back of the playground, near the cafeteria, was where the tough kids hung out, the ones who smoked cigarettes at eight in the morning and rolled joints after lunch. Most of them were the class dunces, for whom their teachers foresaw a dark future and whose freedom Mia envied. Some of them had even been given official warnings by the headmaster or been suspended from school. They were known by their nicknames (The Flame, Criss-Cross) or by their surnames (Kamouta, Drissi). They would force themselves to laugh when the teachers handed back their essays with a muttered 'Pathetic'. They often skipped classes, and Mia – in one of the overheated classrooms on the first floor – would sometimes look up from her maths notebook and watch the dunces and their girlfriends through the window. She liked the way they put their hands in the small of the girls' backs, just above the swell of their buttocks, and the kisses that went on forever, heads tilted sideways, tongues twisting, caressing, intertwining. It was disgusting and wonderful all at the same time.

Between the two chestnut trees, around the stone table, were the children of the French volunteers, whose parents taught at the Lycée Descartes or at the primary school on the other side of the street. They didn't mix with the Moroccans, and in truth nobody wondered why. They had another way of life, another way of thinking and dressing. Most of them lived in the Agdal – the neighbourhood known as 'Little France' – and they would walk to school every morning because their homes were in the streets nearby. Their parents did their shopping at Madame Cochon, the charcuterie, and pinned small ads on the cork noticeboard: 'Maid wanted – serious applicants only' or 'Litter of European-bred kittens for sale'. Unlike the city's Muslims, they were permitted to buy alcohol during Ramadan. On the weekends, they would organise picnics at the beach or cultural visits to the medinas in Fes or Tangier. Mathilde complained that these people were so ignorant about the country in which they lived that they would walk around the medina in shorts and haggle over a few centimes. In winter, the girls wore fleeces and black or green Kickers. From France, they brought Clairefontaine exercise books, packs of Toblerone and copies of teen magazines like *Jeune et Jolie*. They would say: 'There's nothing here.'

Each person's place in this hierarchy depended on elements that seemed superficial or stereotyped: your results in class, your physical appearance, the neighbourhood where you lived. 'It sounds simple,' Mia explained one day to her little sister, 'but in fact it's very complicated.' So many different factors came into play. Was your family religious? Did they have a garden? Did one of your parents have a different nationality? Did you have acne or some other repulsive physical flaw? Did you eat local products (Aiguebelle chocolate, La Cigogne lemonade, Henry's biscuits) or imported products? There were some who spoke Arabic, and not only with their maids or their chauffeur; some could read the newspaper and even follow the king's speech on television. And then there were the binationals, whose mothers were French, German, Russian, even Vietnamese or Japanese. It was always the mother who was a foreigner. The men were from here; they just preferred imported women to local ones. Several times Mia had seen the Japanese woman at the central market, where she bought fresh fish to make dishes that reminded her of her homeland. Mathilde was friends with the German women who gathered on Saturday afternoons to eat cream cakes and organise proper Christmas festivities. These children had another passport, another country, and while they still had to learn Arabic, it was only as a second language. Their parents would tell them: 'Don't worry, it's not important. Nobody speaks classical Arabic.' There were diplomats' children who didn't stay long, didn't bother making friends, and for that reason were highly desirable. There was Aïssatou, the daughter of the Senegalese ambassador, whom all the boys thought beautiful but they didn't dare admit it because you weren't supposed to like Black girls. There was Gilles, the son of the Belgian ambassador, a tall blond boy with an unpronounceable surname, who had lived in America and listened to heavy metal music. And then there were the Jews who had names like Ronit, Mike and David, and who were Moroccan but not in the same way. There were poor kids too, and everyone wondered what they were even doing here. How had that girl from Kenitra managed to get into the school, when she had henna on the soles of her feet and her notebooks were all cheap Moroccan crap?

Nobody ever questioned this social order. The students put up with the injustice of it, here as in the outside world. Mia wasn't at the bottom of the hierarchy, in limbo, with the ugly ones, the uncool ones, the boring ones. With Bayane, mocked by everyone because the clothes she wore were too small for her, or with that group of spotty boys who had sweat stains in their polo-neck jumpers and who had never been abroad. But nor was she part of the highest circle of students: the coolest of the cool. She was too well behaved for that, too studious and obedient. Mia had started smoking (although she still didn't inhale), but she wasn't allowed to go out at night and had never done anything wild enough to make people remember her. She could never have claimed a place on the stairs – the famous staircase that led down to the sports fields and on which, in accordance with some semi-sacred law, only the trendiest students could sit. Every day Mia observed the chosen few. On the lower steps sat the pretty girls who would, every morning before the first bell, stand in front of the bathroom mirrors to put on mascara and strawberry lip gloss. These girls had long, varnished fingernails, and a word from them could make or break your reputation. At the top of the steps were the handsome boys, the ones who played an instrument and drove their fathers' cars even though they didn't have a licence. These were the oldest boys, generally, and they had all the things that Mia desperately wanted: a sex life, a gang of friends, popularity.

Her first few months at the school were a nightmare. In October 1989, Mia's face and back were suddenly covered with acne. The spots were huge, with yellowish tips, and she felt a constant urge to scratch or squeeze them to see the viscous liquid pour out. But her mother had warned her about the risk of scars, so Mia resisted this temptation, praying that the outbreak would clear up as quickly as possible. A few weeks later she got an unpleasant surprise when she looked down at her seat in the middle of a maths lesson and saw a bloodstain. She raised her arm: 'Can I go to the nurse's office?' Blushing furiously, she tied her blue sweatshirt around her waist before walking out of the classroom. She could feel the liquid running down between her legs, soaking into her jeans. It was so unjust, she thought. Why did she have to go through this? For two or three years she had been hearing girls bragging that they were now women. They seemed ridiculously proud as they described their cramps or took packs of sanitary pads from their bags – never tampons, because those could tear the hymen. (Not that Mia cared about her hymen.)

That cold December day she walked to the corner shop near the roundabout. In the queue before her, a Frenchwoman was buying vegetables. 'Give me some tomatoes, would you?' she said to the Berber shopkeeper in a voice dripping with condescension.

The shop smelled of sawdust and soap. A young man from Sous asked Mia what she wanted, but she didn't know how to say 'sanitary pad' in Arabic. She grabbed a pack of chewing gum and some Henry's biscuits from the counter and, while the shopkeeper was adding up the cost, she added: 'And some Always.' This was the name of the brand that her mother used.

The boy picked up a ladder and took it to a shelf at the back of the shop, where he selected a pink-and-blue packet. 'How many?' he asked. And he smiled sarcastically, as if hardly able to believe that a girl like this – a girl who looked more like a boy, with her short hair and her baseball cap – could possibly have her period.

Mia shrugged. 'I don't know. Three?' The boy took three thick pads out of the packet, wrapped them in newspaper, then shoved them into a black plastic bag, as if sanitary pads were something to be hidden, like a bottle of alcohol or a gun. Mia flashed a proud smile at him, then headed back to school. In the bathroom she cleaned her jeans with some soap and water, then stuck a pad into her knickers. It was so thick that Mia felt like she was wearing a nappy. Now she understood why girls would sometimes turn to look at their own backsides and ask their friends: 'Does it show?'

Yes, she was a girl, even if she tended to forget that sometimes. Her friends, who were all boys, also seemed blind to this reality. They saw her as a mate: she was a good forward when she played football, and on Mondays they liked hearing her talk about the previous day's matches on television. They probably thought that, like them, she had a dick and balls between her legs, and that she wore two pairs of boxer shorts to stop herself getting a hard-on. She was five feet nine, and from behind you might easily get her mixed up with Yassine or Ismaël. She never took off her (black or grey) baseball cap during class. Mia was not the kind of girl who talked about clothes or make-up. She dressed like they did, or rather the way they wished they could. Mia wore Levi's jeans, which Mehdi brought her back from the USA, and high-top Reeboks with a red-and-blue stripe. Her friends, on the other hand, had to make do with counterfeits bought at the kissaria: jeans that faded after a few washes, and fake Nike trainers that started to stink after a week of being worn. And although they took the piss out of her for being a teacher's pet, she knew that they were impressed by her results in school, and that they respected her intelligence. Her friend Hakim would sometimes beat her, but only in mathematics. He was the son of her father's oldest friend, Abdellah, the only one among all their friends who had remained true to his Marxist convictions. Mia had known Hakim for as long as she could remember, and there had always been a fierce competitiveness between them.

The boys weren't embarrassed to tell jokes in front of her, not even the dirtiest ones they knew. They told stories about girls who'd been licked out by their dog, or of maids with an expertise in tagines and fellatio. One day, their friend Adil said he'd gone to Tiflet during the holidays, and that he and his brother had shared a whore. He described in great detail how they'd laid her down on the back seat of a car, the noises the girl had made, and the fact that she had been the one who'd chosen to do it doggy style. Adil, as always, could not help exaggerating for effect. 'Liar!' yelled Badr when Adil started banging on about his prowess as a lover, even swearing that the girl had come to his house the next day to ask for more. By the end of that first year at Lycée Descartes, Mia had the impression that everything revolved around sex. It was the most basic and essential rite of passage, and if you wanted to call yourself an adult you had to have done it at least once. Thanks to her mother, Mia had a scientific, anatomical vision of sex. She knew how women got pregnant, and Aïcha had also warned her that she should protect herself against AIDS. And yet she always made Mia close her eyes when there was a love scene on the television.

There was an encyclopaedia of sex that did the rounds in the school playground, with the boys using it to help them perfect the art of masturbation. One day, Mia and her friends watched a pornographic film – *DallaX* – for the first time, in the basement of Badr's house. His parents were away and Mia suggested they roll a joint. She had been practising for days and had now mastered the technique. She took two small cigarette papers from the orange Zig-Zag packet and, with a quick lick, stuck them together. On the screen, a woman was being fucked in a barn. Staring at the woman's breasts, Mia slowly crumbled a bit of hashish that she had bought on her way out of school. On the sofa, the boys sniggered. Adil put his hand on his dick, and Hakim, who found all this stuff disgusting, said he would rather go home. 'Poofter!' Adil called out, and Mia lit the joint. She took a big drag that made her cough and continued to watch the screen, where a man was sitting behind the wheel of his Mercedes, which another woman had just climbed into. Mia started laughing too. Under the blanket, Adil was wanking.

Mia liked joints, and she liked even more the taste of beer, or vodka and orange juice. To celebrate the end of the school year and her excellent results, Mia was allowed to go to a party. At first, when she had asked Mehdi for permission – 'I am almost sixteen, after all' – he'd said no. Then, seeing his daughter's face fall, he'd added: 'Ask your mother.' After that, it had been easy. Aïcha had brought back a miracle cure for acne from her most recent trip to France, and Mia had been using it for a few weeks now. To start with, the effects were horrific and she even begged her mother to let her skip school. 'I can't show up like this!' The skin of her face and her hands was so dry that she sometimes feared it was about to crack and crumble to dust. Even her tongue seemed to be peeling. But, after a few weeks, the zits had vanished and her skin was as smooth as it had been before.

The party took place at Amnesia, the only decent nightclub in the city centre. Mehdi and Aïcha had danced there in the old days. It was said that the crown prince went there, as well as some students from the Royal College. On the pavement, a dwarf in a Charlie Chaplin costume was selling red roses. A woman in a grey djellaba, with a baby strapped to her back, held out her hand to Mia. 'Get out of here!' the doorman shouted at her, but Mia took some money from her pocket and gave it to the woman. Aïcha had warned her against the dangers of the night – don't get in a car with anyone who's been drinking, watch out for children sniffing glue, don't take your money out in front of other people – but Mia wasn't afraid. As she was queuing to get into the club, she thought: I don't want to be innocent any more. She was thirsty for danger, and a memory from *The Horseman on the Roof* came back to her: the letter that Angelo's mother had written to him. 'I am afraid that you won't do anything reckless.'

They walked down the steps into darkness, passed the cloakroom and sat at the far end of the dancefloor, looking up at the enormous bus hanging from the ceiling. Badr and Adil were wearing shirts and belts. Fake Armani or Calvin Klein. Hakim was the handsomest one. He had Abdellah's green eyes and his mother's white skin. His features were so fine, so delicate, that as a child he had often been mistaken for a girl. His thick black hair was swept back with gel, like Andy Garcia in *The Untouchables*. And all the girls dreamed of running their hands through his petrified hair. Mia didn't stray far from the bar. People kept walking past and she bought drinks for girls, making them laugh out loud. She drank vodka and orange juice, and she didn't dance. She liked everything about the night. The vibrations of the speakers and the deafening music. The cigarette smoke that stung her eyes. She even liked the red velvet carpet and the black leatherette chairs, into which boys would slump, glassy-eyed. The waiters ran in all directions, a bucket of ice cubes in one hand and a stack of glasses in the other.

After an hour or so, the teenagers were all drunk. The girls squealed: 'I love this song!' and two of them climbed onto podiums to wiggle their hips like women in films and make the boys drool. Mia refused to be dragged onto the dancefloor, even when the DJ was playing Michael Jackson or 'Lambada'. As the opening notes of a Bee Gees song were played, Mia heard someone call out her name. She spotted Selma, sitting in the VIP area, where Mia and her friends would never dare go. Her great-aunt, one hand gripping the pommel of her cane, beckoned her over, and – watched by her envious classmates – Mia went to join her. Selma introduced her friends, but Mia did not remember any of their names. Still, what did it matter? 'What are you drinking?' Selma asked her, and without waiting for an answer poured her a glass of the best vodka. 'Bring your friends over if you like, I don't mind.'

The VIP area was on one side, with a special entrance from the street to protect the famous from prying eyes. From here, you could see without being seen and Mia, increasingly intoxicated, admired the crowd that was freaking out to a Donna Summer hit. She felt loved and a feeling of pure joy rushed through her. She was ready to abandon herself, to reveal her secrets. She turned to Selma, who smiled and raised her glass. Mia thought blurrily: We are both of the night. Nothing matters at night.

Mia looked at girls and girls looked at her. They came up to her and sometimes Mia held them by their shoulders and whispered sweet and tender compliments to them. Unlike the compliments of boys, Mia's words didn't scare them. Mia loved them, these girls who talked about clothes and make-up. She thought the strawberry lip gloss they wore was pretty. She admired their tanned bellies, the navels that some of them had had pierced without their fathers' knowledge. She glimpsed a flash of fuchsia knickers under the miniskirt of a dancing girl. She waved at the girl and the girl waved back, thrilled to have drawn the attention of the great Mia. Soon, she felt sure, she would be able to take her place on the stairs.

During the winter of 1945, when he was in Germany under the command of General de Lattre de Tassigny, Amine had found himself on the front line with some American soldiers. He'd been impressed by these men, who had let him help himself to their stores, without which he would not have survived that freezing winter. One day, in Mannheim, a shopkeeper from Wyoming – or maybe Montana? He couldn't remember any more – had offered to take a photograph of Amine and his men standing on their Tiger tank. Afterwards they'd had a conversation, and this boy – who could not have been more than twenty – had told them in bad French that he would soon be going back home, where his parents had a farm and some horses. '*Un vrai cow-boy,*' he had repeated, tapping his chest proudly. The American had explained that the reason men had been able to tame horses was that the horses saw men as much bigger than they really were. 'Their eyes,' the cowboy said, putting his hands on the sides of his head. There was something wrong with their eyes that gave them a distorted view of reality.

Amine had been thinking about the war a lot lately. When he walked along the paths lined with olive trees on the farm, or at night when he couldn't sleep, or during the interminable meals when he felt bored of Mathilde's company, he would dive back into his memories. There was a delight in immersing himself in the past, not because he wanted to flee the present but because he felt convinced that he no longer had a future. At seventy-three, he was still a vigorous man, capable of walking several miles and of reading without glasses. But he felt useless. Nobody needs me any more, he kept telling himself, and nostalgia beckoned him. How he missed those days when they had struggled against humiliation, when they had been totally focused on building a future for their children. He would have given anything, and especially his tranquillity, for a battle he could fight, some challenges to overcome. It revolted him, the way Mathilde talked about wanting to 'enjoy life'. He felt ashamed to live in a house cluttered with knick-knacks, to sit in one of those soft velvet armchairs whose tassels he wanted to rip off. He felt like a wild beast trapped in a box of chocolates. 'I miss the war,' he kept muttering to himself. 'I miss the war.' War was this country's DNA, its identity. For centuries it had given meaning to men's lives, while deciding the order of the world. Then the French had come. They had disarmed the men of the tribes, who had been left idle, bereft of any work or purpose. They had survived, true, but to what end? And now, mused Amine, there are too many of us. Far too many.

Mathilde tugged at his sleeve. 'Keep moving,' she told him. 'You're blocking the way.' He advanced through the narrow aisle of the aeroplane, towards the front, and let Mathilde sit by the window. As a young man Amine had been fascinated by America. The country of pioneers and brave men. He had dreamed of turning his farm into a little California, and imagined himself as Cary Grant or Burt Lancaster, with a woman as beautiful as Deborah Kerr on his arm. But ever since

Selim had moved to New York, his feelings had changed. Amine had started to hate the United States, the lies of Hollywood, and he had become convinced that, like a horse, he had seen the Americans as bigger than they truly were. Mathilde took off her shoes and put on her compression socks. The pilot made an announcement. They would land in New York after an eight-hour flight. The weather at their destination was warm and sunny.

This was the first time Amine had been to visit his son. Until now, he had always found an excuse not to go. Work, of course. The olives, or the almonds, or the oranges had to be harvested. The fertiliser had to be spread. The irrigation system had to be set up. 'He'll come back in the end, anyway.' But Selim didn't come back, and Mathilde wouldn't stop talking about it. At one point Amine had mentioned his fear of flying. He couldn't possibly get on a plane: the very idea of flying over an ocean made him feel nauseated. She had pointed out that it didn't bother him to fly to the Middle East when he was seeking new markets, now that Spain and Portugal had joined the European Community and exports of citrus fruit had fallen dramatically. The Middle East? Well, exactly. And Amine had given his wife a lesson in international geopolitics. 'The Americans don't like Arabs, except for the ones that have oil. I'll never set foot on American soil.' But Mathilde had begged him. What did their son have to do with Bush or US foreign policy? It was hardly Selim's fault that the Americans had bombarded Lebanon and abandoned Palestine.

During the summer of 1990, it was Selim who had taken the initiative. He'd asked to speak to his father on the phone, which he normally did only for his birthday or for Eid al-Adha. He'd explained to him that a fashionable gallery was organising a retrospective of his work and that he couldn't imagine his parents not being there to see that. Selim had sent them two business-class tickets and Amine had not been able to say no. And now, he was afraid. Afraid of seeing his long-lost son again, the tall blond son who had always felt like a stranger to him. What did they have to talk about, after all? What did they have in common? Selim lived in the same apartment building as Thomas Barrett, the man to whom he owed his career as a photographer. Barrett was a financier and art collector, and Selim mentioned him in all his letters. Mathilde was fascinated by him. Amine, on the other hand, had never met this man and had no desire to. His son talked about this Barrett like he was a father, a real father, and he wouldn't stop going on about his qualities, his wealth, his erudition. Amine couldn't help thinking: And what about my wealth? That isn't good enough for you? He raged against his son's ingratitude and judged his way of life to be superficial and decadent.

The flight attendant, in a navy-blue suit and high heels, pressed the brake on her cart. Amine looked at her calves: thick calves in flesh-coloured tights. 'Would you like something to drink?'

Mathilde, overexcited, struck up a conversation with the woman. She told her that her son lived in New York. 'But he's travelled all over the world.' She mentioned his name. 'You've probably heard of him.' The flight attendant, holding a bottle of champagne, was not given time to respond. 'His photographs have even been published in *Paris Match*.' And Mathilde waved a copy of the magazine under the young woman's nose. On the cover was a photograph of Caroline of Monaco. Amine ordered a mineral water, which was served in a plastic cup, and he ate the piece of salmon and damp bread on his tray without pleasure. A little tipsy, Mathilde finally fell asleep, her head resting on her husband's shoulder. Amine picked up the magazine that she had dropped on the floor and looked at his son's photographs. His gaze lingered on the portrait of a woman with blonde hair cut very short, like an infantry soldier. She had blue eyes, as piercing as a wild animal's, and freckles on her nose. She was holding a cigarette in one hand and smoke was pouring from her nostrils. A woman like that could not really exist, he thought, with a surge of arousal. But he didn't get an erection, or not much of one at least, and eventually he fell asleep while imagining the body of that woman with the catlike face.

When they landed in New York, it was evening. Amine had a migraine and Mathilde struggled to get her shoes back on. In the arrivals hall, there was a long line of passengers. While they waited to show their passports to the police, Amine noticed that he was being stared at by a tall, muscular man. The man wore a thick leather jacket, and when their eyes met he slowly unzipped it. Amine tried to look away, but he felt irresistibly drawn to this strange man and, inside the jacket, he saw something gleam. Amine shook his head. He crossed his arms. He wasn't stupid. Maybe these Americans thought that, just because he came from Africa, he must be feeble-minded, easily manipulable. They still imagined they were living in colonial times, when they could subjugate an entire village with a few trinkets and broken mirrors. This guy, this pervert, was trying to sell him some crap. Some fake Rolex, some pimp bracelet. Amine looked away. Let him find some other sucker, he thought, pushing Mathilde forward in the queue. But in the corner of his eye he could see the man coming over. His jaw tensed. 'Now it starts . . .' he hissed.

Mathilde didn't have time to ask him what was starting before the man stood in front of them. He held his jacket slightly open and whispered in English: 'Sir, please would you follow me?'

Amine grabbed Mathilde's arm. In French, he said: 'All right, that's enough. Let us go. We don't want to buy your crap.'

'Sir, please. New York Police. Do you understand?'

Amine looked down then, and saw the gleaming badge on the man's inside pocket. And below it, hanging from his belt, a revolver. He felt scared at first. Scared that this cop would make him pay for his arrogant attitude. He'd seen plenty of American police films and he could already imagine himself lying in a dirty prison cell or handcuffed to a table in a small dark room where at regular intervals men would come to ask him, over and over, the same exhausting questions. But this policeman turned out to be quite friendly. He spoke slowly, smiled, and escorted them through a labyrinth of corridors. In the doorway of a room, he lowered his head and stretched out his arm like a maître d' showing them to their table. He didn't seem to realise that Amine didn't speak a word of English. 'These people think everyone speaks their language,' he would tell Mathilde later.

They were asked to wait in a basement office cluttered with filing cabinets and smelling of stale coffee and cigarettes. The cop had taken their passports and signalled for them to take a seat. Amine pretended to be calm. He put his hands on his knees and tried to think about something else. About the coming almond harvest. About the pond he planned to build at the entrance to the farm. A man in uniform walked past, and Amine asked him if he could go to the bathroom. The man stared at him wide-eyed and uncomprehending, and Amine, blushing, thought: Surely I'm not going to have to mime taking a piss? *'Toilettes,'* he repeated, in French, and the man smiled, then led him to another room. And it was there, seeing his reflection in the bathroom mirror, that Amine understood. This was why he'd been arrested. It was obvious. Amine looked like the bad guy in a Hollywood film. With his black coat, his sun-darkened skin, his frizzy grey hair, he could easily have been an Iranian spy, a Hezbollah terrorist, an exiled Palestinian come to plot a kidnapping or an assassination.

Amine went back to the office where Mathilde, puffy-eyed and pale-lipped, was fighting to stay awake. The man in the leather jacket returned, accompanied by a young woman in uniform whose bottom was so enormous that she could barely manage to walk. Never in his life had Amine seen such a fat woman. She had his passport in her hand. *'Vous parlez français?'* she asked. She examined his passport, turning it over several times, as though it was illegible.

Mathilde put her hand on her husband's thigh. She was afraid he would lose his temper and start yelling: 'What, you don't want me here? Well, I don't want anything to do with your cursed country!' In faltering French, the young woman asked where they would be staying and how long they planned to be in the United States. Did they know anyone here? Mathilde took the magazine from her handbag then and waved it at the policewoman. 'We've come to see our son. He's a famous photographer. He's even been published in *Paris Match*.'

Surely it wasn't this line of argument that won over the border police, but Amine was given his passport back, and the man in the leather jacket patted him on the shoulder and said: 'Have a nice time in America.'

This whole charade had put Amine in a bad mood. While they waited in line for a taxi, he warned Mathilde: 'We're not going to get ripped off. Tell him to put his meter on.' They were lucky: the driver was Lebanese and he spoke to them in Arabic, asking lots of questions about Morocco, a land he had always dreamed of visiting. The journey seemed interminable and, sitting there surrounded by traffic, Amine and Mathilde felt like children lost in a big, strange world. An hour later the taxi came to a stop outside a big black building that looked more like a warehouse or an aircraft hangar than a place where people lived. He took their bags from the car's boot and, after Mathilde had paid him, he waited, eyebrows raised, for the tip. It took her a while to understand what he wanted, but in the end she gave him more money and they found themselves alone on the pavement, breathing in air that smelled of tarmac and fried onions. In the distance they could see the abandoned docks. Three young men walked past, laughing loudly, all dressed provocatively. Mathilde stared helplessly at the piece of paper on which she had noted down her son's address.

'Are you sure this is it?' Amine asked, and she wanted to kill him for asking such a stupid question. Instead, she overcame her exhaustion and anxiety and forced herself to smile at him.

'Yes, this must be the place. It's the right number. I don't understand.' She was about to start crying when she heard her son's voice. She turned around, but he wasn't there.

'Up here, Mom!' Selim was leaning from the second-floor balcony, waving at her.

'Be careful, sweetie! Don't lean over the edge like that, you might fall.'

Inside the apartment, Mathilde held her son tightly in her arms. She told him he looked too thin and that he seemed tired. She stroked his face. 'Everyone sends their love.' And she started listing the names of neighbours, friends from Meknes, the doctor and the dentist that Selim had seen when he was a kid. According to her, they all worried about Selim, and missed him so much. 'Ah, that's nice of them,' he replied, even if the names Amrani, Slimani and Kabbaj no longer rang any bells for him. 'How was your trip?' he asked, and Amine, who did not want to take off his coat, recounted the episode with the policeman in the leather jacket and the taxi driver who wanted a tip despite being unhelpful. 'You must be tired,' Selim said. And, picking up their suitcases, he led them up the broad white staircase without guardrails that ascended from the right side of the living room.

Amine and Mathilde went into the bedroom and looked at each other in horror. The bathroom was separated from the bedroom only by a transparent plastic curtain and the toilet was just to the right of the bed. Did their son really think they were going to pee in front of each other? Did he imagine that Amine was going to take a shower while his wife watched, or that he would want to watch her rub soap all over her body? Mathilde stroked her husband's palm. A brief, tender gesture that meant: Stay calm. She opened her suitcase and began removing the gifts that she had brought for Selim. A bag of oranges from the garden, some gazelle-horn pastries (half of which, she noticed sadly, had broken inside the tin) and a jar of almond honey. She sat on the bed, her back to the toilet, and stared at the wall. 'I'm so tired, I think I'll fall asleep as soon as my head touches the pillow.'

The next day, as they were walking downstairs to have breakfast – Amine had showered in the dark and he hadn't managed to rinse his hair properly, so his scalp itched – they thought they glimpsed a woman in the living room. But she vanished, like an antelope catching the scent of a lion, and they found themselves alone with their son. Selim, standing behind the counter, was pouring boiling water into an Italian coffeemaker. Mathilde couldn't just stand there and watch him make breakfast for them, so she started moving around the small space that her son called a kitchen. Selim kept telling her to sit down, but she opened the fridge, took out a box of huge white eggs and offered to make an omelette. While she was arranging the plates on the counter, Selim asked them what they planned to do with their day. 'I can't be with you today, I'm afraid, because I have to oversee the final details in the gallery to make sure that everything will be perfect tomorrow night.' He squirmed on his barstool and, looking at his father, added: 'So you'll be proud of me, you know.' He had a strange way of speaking French. His phrases were scattered with English words and he sometimes seemed to hesitate before conjugating a verb. Amine wondered if he even had a slight accent. Was it possible to lose your native language? Your mother tongue, which you had heard and spoken from birth, the language in which your parents had first told you that they loved you?

They walked through the city. Mathilde was holding a guidebook: she had a very precise idea of the places she wanted to go. Broadway, Times Square, Fifth Avenue. She had drawn up a list of people she wanted to bring back presents for. Mia, Inès, Aïcha, but also the women who worked at the farm, some friends from Rabat, the dentist who was always so kind to her. Fifth Avenue had a bizarre effect on Mathilde: she started to behave like a drug addict taken into an opium den. She wanted to enter every shop, see everything, try on everything, buy everything. She was shaking with excitement because it was all so beautiful, the saleswomen were all so friendly and the objects on the shelves so desirable. Jeans and shoes, linen dresses baggy enough to conceal her curves, a Ralph Lauren safari jacket, sweatshirts emblazoned with 'I ♡ New York'. As the hours passed, she lost all self-control. In the clothing boutiques, Amine would wait on a chair while she tried on blouses or chose another gift. From time to time she would turn to him and ask: 'What do you think of this? Inès would love it, don't you think?' But she didn't really care what he thought of anything, and she would immediately turn back to the saleswoman and speak English to her with a slight German accent. They ate lunch at a packed pizzeria in Times Square, where they had to line up with their plastic trays between other tourists and students who talked very loudly. Amine didn't like this city. He didn't like the skyscrapers' long shadows or the icy wind that blew through the streets. He thought: For all their tall buildings and big cars, this place is like something from the Third World. America, too, had its poor people. He saw them sprawled on the pavements, pupils dilated, marinating in their own shit.

By the time they made it back to Selim's apartment, their arms full of packages, they were exhausted. Amine had only one ambition: to take off his shoes and lie on the bed. But Selim was waiting for them in the living room. A woman was sitting on the white sofa, and on the coffee table there were four glasses, a bottle of white wine and some raw vegetables cut into bite-size pieces. It's the woman with the catlike face, thought Amine, and he leaned down to shake the hand of Cynthia Barrett. Her wrists were so thin that he feared he might snap them. She was tall – taller than Mathilde – and so slender it was almost surreal.

Mathilde couldn't stop staring at her. She was fascinated by this woman, not only because there seemed to be something going on between her and Selim, but because she came from another world altogether. Mathilde had only ever seen women like her in films or on television. The woman spoke to them in French. 'I adore France. When I was a child, we used to go there every summer.' She looked at the bags that Mathilde was holding and smiled. 'I see you've been shopping.' Mathilde took this as an invitation and began unwrapping all her packages. She couldn't possibly have imagined that Cynthia would, later that day, make fun of her, that she would laugh as she asked Selim: 'Do your parents live behind the Iron Curtain?'

Selim boasted about Cynthia's superb taste: she was the one who had decorated the apartment, and Mathilde nodded as she dipped a piece of cauliflower into a thick sauce. 'Yes, it's very pretty. Very simple.'

Cynthia smiled. 'Minimalist,' she said. 'I hate knick-knacks.'

Mathilde climbed to her feet. She gathered up the things she had bought, which were scattered all over the sofa, and put them back in the bags. 'I hate knick-knacks,' she kept repeating to Amine throughout the evening. She was convinced that Cynthia had said that to hurt her feelings. 'I hate knick-knacks.' And that blonde giraffe presumably thought she had superior taste to Mathilde.

The giraffe didn't eat much at dinner – a few salad leaves at most – but she certainly talked a lot. About her travels, and about her husband, whom she called by his surname, Barrett, and whom she kept describing as a 'genius'. Thomas Barrett had met Selim in Ibiza, where he'd been living with a bunch of hippies. 'Do you know Ibiza?' Cynthia asked. They had a house there, which they'd bought for peanuts. A house that she had decorated. Barrett would have loved to be here tonight, but he was in Trancoso, an old fishing village on the coast of Brazil, where he had just acquired seventy-five acres. Every time she talked about her husband – his possessions, his success, his incredible business acumen – her voice grew high-pitched, as if she'd just sucked on a helium balloon. Mathilde was even more annoyed since Amine was now smiling for the first time today. He kept grinning idiotically at this woman with the catlike face. Barrett had bought this building, on Tenth Avenue between 20th and 21st Streets. He had also acquired some old tailors' workshops in Chelsea so that he could rent them out to artists. Cynthia complained about their neighbourhood. 'Apart from the International Market, which is international only in name, there's nowhere here to buy groceries. I have to walk for miles to find a bakery.' Three months ago, she had been mugged in the lobby. 'By some girls who couldn't have been more than twelve or thirteen. Blacks.' Amine and Mathilde glanced at each other. 'They followed me and when I came into the building one of them aimed a pistol at me. They took my bag, my watch and my engagement ring. I reported it to the police and a few days later they contacted me. They had found my purse at the girls' apartment. They'd spent the money on hamburgers. As for the pistol, apparently it was just a toy.'

That night, while they lay in bed, Mathilde and Amine thought about the young girls with the gun. How could their son live in a place like this? How could he walk through these streets, which were infested with rats from the nearby docks? How could he stand the noise, the continual vibration that emanated from the bars at the end of the street? And then there were those men who paraded past their windows in outfits that Amine would never have been able to imagine, even in his worst nightmares. Had Selim completely forgotten where he came from?

The exhibition took place at a Soho art gallery. Mathilde wore a new dress that flattened her stomach and she swore to herself that she would eat as little as possible. This turned out to be easy, since there was nothing to eat there. The gallery was a narrow space filled with people, and at the back of the room, on a table covered with a white cloth, some waiters were serving coupes of champagne. Amine and Mathilde made their way through the crowd. Enormous women in grey suits chewed pensively at their spectacles. Pairs of slender, long-haired boys went to the bathroom together, arms around each other's shoulders. For the first time in years, Amine held his wife's hand. He squeezed it nervously. What were they doing here? She should have known that it would be humiliating, that they would look like a couple of ignorant peasants. He held her fully responsible for this disaster. 'Let's find Selim and then leave.' Their son appeared. He was surrounded by a dozen people – Cynthia, the gallery owner, various admirers – and when he spotted his parents, he waved them over to join him. Mathilde, who spoke English well, joined in with their conversation. Amine stood there for a few minutes, smiling like an imbecile, then discreetly slipped away. He walked through the gallery again, more slowly this time, paying more attention to the photographs on the walls. He knew nothing about art. He had never taken his children to a museum and he could not have named a single famous photographer. He felt drawn to the portrait of an old man in a grey tunic, with a turban on his head. He moved closer and couldn't help thinking that the old man looked like him. The same brown face, like a clay statue left to dry in the sun. The same sturdy hands and the same faded irises. The caption was in English, but he was able to work out that the photograph had been taken in Egypt, on the banks of the Nile. I bet that guy is a peasant farmer, he thought. Ignorant and uncultured, like me.

Amine had only a vague idea of what beauty was. For him, it was essentially an emotion, a feeling of warmth in his chest, impossible to articulate or explain. He was incapable of judging whether his son had talent, but he did feel that warmth when he looked at this portrait. His head was spinning. He felt hot and he worried that he was going to faint. Was he having another one of those episodes where he seemed to leave his own body? He went outside to breathe the fresh night air. A woman was running across the pedestrian crossing. She had foam curlers in her hair. For the first time since his arrival he found himself enjoying the agitation of this city, where something always seemed to be about to happen.

Selim suddenly appeared in front of him, glass in hand. 'I was looking everywhere for you. Mum was worried. Don't you want to come back inside?'

'I don't understand what anyone's saying. And I needed some air.'

Selim leaned against the wall, beside his father.

'What did you think of the exhibition?'

'It's beautiful. I like the photo of the peasant by the Nile.'

'Yeah. I like that one a lot too.' Selim took a pack of Marlboro from his pocket. He began twirling a cigarette between his thumb and his index finger. At forty, he still feared his father's disapproval. 'It started off as a photo-reportage for a magazine. But it's difficult to sell stuff like that to American newspapers.'

'They don't like Arabs.'

Selim smiled. 'They're not really interested in the rest of the world, that's true. Apart from photographs of the Mamounia Hotel, I've never managed to publish any of my pieces on Morocco.'

He took a drink of champagne.

'Are you going to stay here?' Amine asked.

'I'd like to, but I need to go back inside. All these people came to see me.'

'No, I mean in New York. Are you going to stay here?'

Selim turned to face his father. He looked into his beautiful, sad eyes and for the first time he could sense a shyness, a vulnerability in his father. He was at a loss for words.

'Because there's the farm, you see, and I won't be alive forever. So I was thinking that we need to talk about it . . .'

'Of course, we'll talk about it. Let's go inside. Mum must be wondering where we are.'

But Mathilde hadn't even noticed their absence. She was deep in conversation with a couple – potential buyers – who seemed absorbed by what she was saying. 'There he is,' she said, pointing at her husband. 'The romantic soldier.' And they all laughed.

Amine raised his eyebrows, as if to say: 'Yep, that's me.' And yet he'd warned her not to drink too much champagne because alcohol always went to her head like this. Which was strange, now he thought about it, given how much weight she'd put on. Wasn't fat supposed to absorb alcohol? Mathilde was talking very fast. She kept repeating 'Morocco' and Amine realised that she was describing her arrival in Meknes in 1945.

'It's like a novel!' exclaimed the woman, whose hair was held in place by a garnet-coloured velvet headband. Mathilde translated this line to her husband, grinning as though it was the highest praise imaginable. No, it's not a novel, thought Amine. He hated the way his wife twisted their life whenever she put it into words. Who knew what she had invented this time, what details she had omitted or even added to the narrative. It was always a lie. As soon as she started telling the story, it was already a lie. Mathilde was so romantic. So desperately romantic. Even at her age, at sixty-four, she reacted to life like a starry-eyed girl. That winter, she had wept over the death of one of her friends, heartbroken at the thought of Hamza, the widower, who had lost the love of his life. She felt certain he would not survive the ordeal, and for weeks she had taken him gratin dishes and cream cakes. Then, a month ago, she had spotted Hamza in a restaurant, with a woman younger than Aïcha. It had been a terrible blow to her, and she had told Amine in a bitter voice: 'You'll find consolation quickly too.'

*

That weekend, Selim suggested they could all go to visit the new Museum of Immigration on Ellis Island and the Statue of Liberty. They took the ferry at Battery Park. The weather was beautiful, and with the sun reflecting off the surface of the water this city of concrete and steel appeared softer, more harmonious to Amine. Selim wore a camera on a strap around his neck, and occasionally he would raise it to his face, quickly focus the lens and take a photograph. A group of French tourists was sitting at the front of the ferry. Amine supposed they must be one big family: he thought he could distinguish the grandparents, the two daughters with their respective husbands, and the grandchildren: two teenage boys hunched over their brand-new Game Boys. The grandfather, his belly as swollen as a pregnant woman's, was reading out a leaflet to the rest of the family. From time to time he would raise his voice and shoot a disappointed look at the two boys. When the Statue of Liberty appeared, the family got up and stared, like the rest of the passengers. The teenage boys stopped playing and rose to their feet too. The statue was even bigger and more impressive than Amine had imagined. It stood there like a lighthouse, and on the ferry the tourists whooped enthusiastically. The grandfather repeated what he had read about this 'symbol of America', then added: 'It feels like we're in a film, doesn't it?'

Selim went up to his father. He put one hand on his shoulder and they looked at the statue's face. 'You remember the peasant by the Nile?' he asked. 'Well, apparently Bartholdi, the sculptor, modelled this statue on an Egyptian peasant woman. An Arab. Originally, the statue was supposed to be for the Suez Canal.' Amine smiled and Selim grabbed his camera.

'Don't move, Dad!' And before Amine could say a word, he pressed the button.

They disembarked at Liberty Island. Near the landing stage was a shop selling plastic torches and crown-shaped headbands. 'Do you want to go up to the crown?' asked Selim, but Mathilde laughed and shook her head. 'At least the pedestal, then. There's a beautiful view.' Amine looked around for the French family, and in particular the two teenage boys. He wondered if they'd put their Game Boys away; if they had – like him – surrendered to the magic of the place. What did America mean to a fifteen-year-old French kid?

They climbed up to the pedestal. The grandfather was there, followed by his grandchildren. 'Do you know why the crown has seven spikes?' The teenagers shrugged. 'They represent the seven seas and the seven continents.'

'I thought there were five continents,' said one of the boys with a smirk.

'Wouldn't you like to learn something for a change? Listen to this,' the grandfather said, and he told them about Emma Lazarus's poem, engraved on a bronze plaque at the foot of the statue. He cleared his throat and read the translation from his leaflet: *Donne-moi tes pauvres, tes exténués / Tes masses innombrables aspirant à vivre libres / Le rebut de tes rivages surpeuplés / Envoie-les-moi, les déshérités, que la tempête me les rapporte / Je dresse ma lumière au-dessus de la porte d'or!*

'Okay, whatever.' And the two boys burst out laughing.

Les déshérités? This was how the French leaflet had translated 'the homeless', but Amine didn't know that. To him, it meant 'the deprived' or 'the disinherited'. The word startled him.

Liberty and its flame, New York and its apartment buildings . . . All of this was for desperate people, people who had nothing. But his son? His son was not one of those people. He wasn't seeking asylum from war or famine or poverty or persecution. Amine didn't understand. Why had Selim left his homeland? And why did he feel no desire to return? These people, these poor immigrants, had left behind nothing but desolation. But his child? Amine himself had lived up to his father's legacy. He had done his duty. He had chosen, not to be free, but to be from somewhere. He had ploughed the earth, he had made it fruitful, he had suffered and struggled. This was how the world worked. Everybody wanted to inherit something. That desire was what tore families apart, what pitted brother against sister, what divided grandchildren. One day, perhaps, those two teenage boys would argue over their grandfather's watch, over an old clock or a chest of drawers. What had he done to deserve this? To have created children who didn't care about his legacy?

Amine remained silent throughout the rest of the visit. In his head, he rehearsed the words he would speak to his son before his departure. He was not going to beg him, but simply invite him to shoulder his responsibilities. To behave like a man. It was two o'clock when they got back to Manhattan. 'I'm starving!' exclaimed Mathilde, and Selim said they could eat lunch at the Empire Diner. Amine ordered a steak ('Tell him that I want it well done') and Mathilde bacon and eggs ('You can't get this in Morocco'). They would be flying back to Casablanca the next day, and Amine felt hesitant at the idea of launching into a serious conversation that might ruin their meal. But he had to face reality. He was the first man in his family to live this long. All the others – his father, his brothers – had died in the prime of life, and he alone had been granted Allah's protection. But for how much longer?

'We need to talk about the farm.'

Mathilde poured some ketchup onto her plate, staring at her fried eggs.

'I'd like to get things sorted. You must come to Meknes so I can teach you how to run the business. You never know what might happen. Our country is going through a difficult period. For now we are protected by the king, but he won't live forever either.'

'Yeah, that's the problem with monarchies. You never know what kind of king you'll get next!'

Selim had been trying to make them laugh. Instead of which, his father turned around and his mother frantically waved her arms.

'You mustn't say things like that! What's wrong with you?' she whispered, as if there might be a microphone hidden in the salt-shaker or a spy in the next booth. Selim realised then that his parents were afraid. Their entire being, their every gesture, radiated fear. They didn't know what it was to be free. To say what they thought. Out loud, in public. Freedom, he thought, is a matter of muscle memory. And he remembered the first time he had seen a protest march, in the streets of New York in the early 1970s. He had joined a group of young people who were chanting against the war, and – slowly – he had raised his hand and made a peace sign with his index and middle fingers. And he had not been afraid.

Amine cleared his throat and started again. 'Your mother and I have worked our whole lives to give you this inheritance. I can't accept the idea that, when we die, the farm will be abandoned. You have responsibilities, you see. You can't just do whatever you want in this life. That land must remain Belhaj land.'

Selim picked up the bottle of ketchup and gently shook it. A peasant farmer? Was that how his father saw him? 'Okay, Dad. As soon as the exhibition is over, I'll fly to Morocco.'

Hakim walked across the playground and headed towards the boys' toilets. He leaned against the wall of the language classrooms and spotted Mia, at the top of the stairs that led down to the sports fields. She beckoned him over but he stayed where he was and lit a cigarette. She was his oldest friend, but his feelings for her were conflicted: a mixture of admiration and jealousy, a desire to protect her and to punish her. He liked talking with her about books and politics. She was the only person he knew who cared about literature, who read books for pleasure, not simply to pass her exams. The only one to whom he could show an underlined passage at the end of a chapter. She would look up at him with those shining eyes of hers as if she truly understood what it was about this phrase that moved him. He envied the way she was, simultaneously, a popular girl, invited to all the best parties, and a brilliant student, praised by all her teachers. At parties, Mia was not the type of girl who spent her time on the dancefloor or reapplying her lip gloss in front of the bathroom mirror. You would usually find her at the end of an alley, sitting on the bonnet of a car drinking cans of beer. She never got drunk and could hold her booze better than most of her classmates. She had invented a game that consisted of taking a drag from a large conical joint every time Bob Marley sang 'Jamming' in the song of that name. When it reached the chorus, most of the boys would start coughing their guts up, and Mia would laugh. Hakim envied her self-confidence, even her virility – the way she carried her backpack or sat down, legs spread, cap on backwards. She strutted around like a boy, with an air of dominance and invulnerability. Nobody would ever dare make fun of her the way they did with Yanis, who was called a queer, a fairy, a poofter, and who had even spent a whole morning locked in the school broom cupboard. Girls liked Mia. They weren't wary of her. They would rub themselves against her, and kiss her on the neck, or even – briefly – on the mouth, before giggling and blushing. Hakim had only ever kissed one girl – last summer, on the beach in Bouznika. Her name had been Mouna, and they had French-kissed for a long time: clumsy, sloppy kisses. He had even fondled her breasts between two beach huts, but there had been no chance of going any further than that. Mouna was a good girl, as she emphasised herself, a 'bent nass' who would not lose her virginity before marriage and who believed in the idea of waiting for the love of her life. Good girls would let you kiss them, caress them, lick them, but not penetrate them. And it was because there were all these good girls that boys were obliged to do it with prostitutes or even other boys. Mia, thought Hakim, was the girl without consequences. She was a sort of boy, but a girl could do it with her without risking her hymen or her reputation.

The bell rang. Hakim tapped his wrist. Mia took off her cap, and as she came over towards him he noticed that she still had the face of a child. There was an innocence to her face that seemed incongruous for someone so tall and broad-shouldered, someone who swaggered when she walked. Every time he saw her high cheekbones and her sad, dark eyes, he felt drawn to her, moved. The miniskirted girls stood up and he followed them into the corridors and then the staircases where the first-year students headed docilely up to their classroom like a flock of sheep. The teacher, Monsieur Duchamp, was standing in the corridor, his foot wedged into the half-open fire door that led to the emergency stairs. He was smoking a hand-rolled cigarette and when he saw the class he made an impatient hand gesture – 'Come on, come on, hurry up!' He was wearing his eternal sky-blue cotton trousers and a beige linen shirt with the top few buttons unfastened, revealing a chest covered in red hair.

Monsieur Duchamp was new at the Lycée Descartes. He had arrived in August 1990 to teach history and geography, and his colleagues had warned him about this particular class, which was more rebellious and insolent than most. They were nasty pieces of work, these sixteen-year-olds. Colette Rivière, the French teacher, had told him about the prank played on her the previous year. In one of his essays, Yassine – a mediocre student – had kept quoting the Moroccan writer Abdellah Mouchtachfine. The quotations were pompous and convoluted, and Madame Rivière had strongly suspected Yassine of having made them up. When she handed him his marked essay, with his grade of five out of twenty circled in red, he had grown furious and accused her of being racist because she wasn't interested in Moroccan literature. 'Well, teach me, then,' she'd said, calling his bluff. 'Bring me a book by this Mouchtachfine and I'll be delighted to give you my opinion.'

'I can do better than that,' Yassine had said. 'I know this writer. I'm going to invite him to our class.'

Colette Rivière had felt guilty. She had started to question herself: had she shown a lack of curiosity towards her students, towards this country where she was living? When the famous writer had turned up to her class, she had welcomed him with deference and genuine interest. The novelist did not speak French, so Yassine had offered to translate his words. The students had started laughing, and Madame Rivière had thought this was because of the writer's cheap suit, his dusty shoes, his generally scruffy appearance. It was not until a few days later that she learned that the dazed-looking man who had sat on stage and responded with yes or no answers to all the questions she asked him had, in fact, been Yassine's chauffeur: a poor, illiterate man forced by these rich kids to take part in their wretched prank.

So, Monsieur Duchamp had been expecting the worst, and ever since the start of school he had enforced an iron discipline in his classes. He would punish students for making even the faintest noise, grabbing the brush that he used to erase the blackboard and brandishing it like a weapon, ready to throw it in the face of anyone who questioned his authority. Today, the class was about the Third World, and on several occasions the teacher used Morocco as an example. He cited the illiteracy rate, the poverty statistics, and compared the kingdom's situation to those of so-called developed countries. Staring at the pink-and-green diagrams in their textbooks, the students brooded. They were angry. From the back of the classroom, some of the girls started heckling him. 'Shut up!' the teacher yelled. He told Hakim to change places with Abla, a girl who always sat in the back row, next to the radiator. She would sit beside Mia and they would make a presentation together.

Abla, rolling her eyes and sighing heavily to make her friends laugh, walked reluctantly to the front row. Mia observed her transparent-plastic pencil case, her biros with their chewed caps and the round, regular handwriting that covered the pages of her notebook. Abla was a pretty girl, in Mia's top-three list for the most fuckable students in the class. She had very pale skin, hair as straight as a European girl's and slightly bowed legs. Her brother, Kamel, was a school celebrity. He sat with the dunces in the cafeteria and had failed his baccalauréat exam. He liked to fight, people said, and when he came out of nightclubs he would slip keys between his fingers before punching people in the face. Until now, Mia had never really paid much attention to Abla. She was a well-behaved, slightly dull girl with average grades. One of those girls with overprotective parents who never let her go out at night or hang out with her friends at the beach on Saturdays.

In the days that followed, Mia invited Abla to her house so they could work on their presentation together and she discovered that Abla was very different once she was away from school. Sitting together in the back seat of the car, as the chauffeur drove them along the Route des Zaërs, Abla admitted that she admired Mia for her excellent grades and that she wished she too could be an all-As student. 'Books aren't really my thing,' she admitted, and Mia couldn't help feeling hurt. She didn't like the way that Abla had said 'books'.

At the house, Mia fetched a second chair from the kitchen and positioned it in front of her desk, so the two of them could sit in her bedroom together. It was early October, and the poplar trees in the garden had turned golden-brown. Coco the parrot, perched on a bougainvillea branch, squawked:

'Fatima!' Mia opened her history exercise book and told Abla about René Dumont's *False Start in Africa,* which her father had made her read, and the famine in Ethiopia, for which Michael Jackson had written a song. Abla stared at her as if she was speaking in a foreign language. 'Wow, you know stuff,' she said.

They got a good grade for the presentation. Of course, Mia didn't admit to her the fact that, if she'd written the presentation with Hakim – as she usually did – she would have had an even better grade. But Abla seemed so happy when the teacher handed her back the presentation with '17/20' written in red ink. After that, she often asked Mia to help her with her homework. They lived very close to each other, and Mia's chauffeur brought them back together almost every evening. They listened to Patricia Kaas tapes, and Abla and Inès would sing along at the tops of their voices. Sometimes Mia couldn't help finding Abla a bit stupid and superficial. She had trouble understanding even simple exercises, and although Mia would say things like, 'It's not your fault, I'm just explaining it badly', she didn't believe that for a second. Abla had not read anything, she watched nothing on television but American sitcoms, and she chewed gum with her mouth open. They were polar opposites. Abla lived in a house without central heating, decorated in such a hideous fashion that Aïcha would have been appalled. Shiny organza banquettes, multicoloured blown-glass chandeliers, wide armchairs with golden armrests. The house had no library, but there was a black marble plaque hung on the wall, with a sura from the Quran engraved in gold letters. Abla's parents were very different from hers: they had been to Mecca, did not drink alcohol and had made it perfectly clear that Abla would never marry a non-Muslim. They treated her older brother Kamel like some demigod, and despite all the dreadful grades and warnings about his behaviour, they had given him a car and a surfboard. Mia told her friend about her own family, and Abla seemed to think it was cool, all this stuff about her Alsatian grandmother and Christmases in the countryside. Her eyes widened with shock when Mia told her that her father would sometimes drink champagne.

Mia was prepared to do anything to make her friend happy. She hung out with Abla and her friends in the playground, and one day Hakim asked her what she saw in these seventeen-year-old bimbos whose heads were filled with nothing but gossip and clothes. 'I don't recognise you any more,' he told her, and she was forced to admit that she was no longer herself. Or rather, that the thought of Abla, the presence of Abla, was enough to blur her conception of herself. She felt as if she had been transformed into a sort of ectoplasm, something soft and malleable, with no shape or will of her own. She felt ready to give up everything, to contradict herself, to humiliate herself. One Saturday afternoon, she was in Abla's bedroom with Abla's other friends. They were lying on the bed, drinking Poms and Fanta. There was an old blue teddy bear on the duvet. The room was cold and empty. There were a few childish drawings in felt-tip pen on the off-white walls, and Mia imagined that Abla's parents must have told her off for those. The bed base lay directly on the freezing tiled floor, and to the right of the bed was a dark-blue Sony CD player. The other girls kept giving Mia strange looks, as though they couldn't understand what she was doing there. Mia listened, almost absent-mindedly, as they said mean things about the other students and shared rumours about the cutest boys. Karima talked about her latest diet, which consisted of eating an apple for lunch and steamed green beans for dinner. She lifted up her sweater, exposing her plump belly. 'I've lost four pounds. You can tell, right?'

They listened to Paula Abdul's 'Straight Up' over and over again and tried to imitate the choreography from the video. Abla threw her hair to one side then the other, and attempted to mimic the mix of tap-dancing and flamenco that had made the American star so famous. Mia couldn't take her eyes off her. Abla was a girl. A real girl. The most beautiful of all girls. And what Mia felt for her was what she had felt for Isabelle Adjani when she'd secretly watched *One Deadly Summer*. The way Abla would snap her fingers, the way she would wink at Mia when she managed a perfect spin. She moved her lips – those pink, fleshy lips of hers – as she sang along with her favourite part of the chorus: 'papapapapa'.

Then Abla suggested a makeover. She went to her mother's room and came back with a large eyeshadow palette and some bottles of nail polish. 'I'm going home,' said Mia, and the other girls burst out laughing.

'Come on!' Abla said. 'Trust me. You're so beautiful.' Abla stared at her with those hazelnut eyes and smiled.

Mia was stunned. Nobody had ever told her that she was beautiful before, or at least not like that. With other people – the boys she hung around with, her family – it was as if she had no body, as if they did everything they could to ignore it. There was something about her that bothered them, and she had often caught people staring at her with consternation or contempt. People felt sorry for her parents, that they should have been cursed with a daughter like this. A daughter who was not a real girl. Abla sat Mia down and put her hands on her cheeks. She pulled delicately at one of her eyelids and, with remarkable precision, traced a black line along her eyelashes. 'You have gorgeous eyes.'

Then she applied a crimson lipstick to Mia's chapped lips and the girls squealed: 'Come on, you have to see this! Let's go to the bathroom!'

They grabbed her by the arms and dragged her in front of the mirror. Mia would have liked to shove them away, to run as far as possible, but she stared at her reflection and tears welled in her eyes. I look like a monster, she thought. A clown. A circus freak. She knew it was ridiculous – that this was no reason to cry – and yet she felt submerged beneath a vast wave of sadness. She felt as if she'd had her face slapped, or rubbed in the dirt. She heard Hakim's voice in her head – 'I don't recognise you any more' – and, with the back of her hand, she wiped the lipstick away.

'What the hell are you doing? You're messing it up!'

She left without saying goodbye and by the time she got home she was out of breath. She went in through the garage, then across the kitchen. She would have run straight to the bathroom to clean her face before anyone saw it, but her father was coming along the hallway. He grabbed her by the chin and examined her. 'Are you wearing make-up now?' He thought she was ugly, she knew it.

When she got home after school, Mia would lie on her bed and listen to her Walkman. She would think about Abla. She would listen to Guns N' Roses or Tracy Chapman – 'Oh, you better run, run, run, run' – and Abla's face would hover around her, wherever she looked. Her face was slightly asymmetrical, but the sum of her flaws was magical. Her front teeth were slightly crooked and she had a star-shaped scar in the middle of her cheek. I'll have to ask her where she got that, thought Mia. Every day, Mia awaited their homework sessions with ever more eagerness and excitement. 'And I had a feeling that I belonged, I had a feeling I could be someone, be someone.' She would watch Abla working, copying a physics or mathematics exercise in her round handwriting with hearts above the *is*. Abla would say she was hungry and Mia would run to fetch her a bowl of crisps or pitted olives, which Abla would distractedly devour. Mia stared longingly at her fingers, at the hollow of her waist. She desired Abla, and that desire was like a tidal wave, like the feeling of being hungry after swimming for a long time. She wanted to taste her sweat. She didn't know how to tell Abla the way she felt. How to tell her that she desired her, that she loved her, because, yes, those were the words that came to her, that rose from her guts to her mouth, and it was so hard to stop herself saying them. Mia was afraid that Abla would realise everything that was happening in her head and her heart. Her mind was filled with scenes she had watched in films or read in books. She would hear notes played on an imaginary piano and remember lines of poetry that she felt she was understanding for the first time. She wished she could give them to Abla, could throw them at her feet, and the words were like hands sliding over her skin. She could understand, now, all those girls who spent hours in class writing the name of the boy they loved in the back of their notebook with an imported pen that smelled of apple or blackberry. Her mother said there was nothing worse than a teenage crush: an infatuation like that could ruin a studious girl, kill her ambition.

The day before the Christmas holidays, Abla came to the Daouds' house for a sleepover. Mehdi was on a business trip in the United States and Aïcha had been called to the clinic for an emergency – 'a vaginal prolapse'. The girls ate grilled koftas while they watched *Flashdance*, and Inès fell asleep on the sofa.

'Where do your parents keep the alcohol?'

Mia took Abla by the hand and led her to the kitchen. She opened the cupboard. The wood smelled of damp. 'Let's see,' she said, and took three bottles from a shelf. 'We should mix them together.' And Abla, who knew nothing about alcohol, watched her do this. In two glasses, Mia poured some gin, some vodka and some Malibu. She went to the American fridge and added a few ice cubes. They clinked glasses, laughing, and drank this coconut-flavoured cocktail down in one. Mia coughed. The liquid burned her oesophagus. She could feel it descending to her stomach, warming her innards. She adored that sensation. She made another mix. 'A bit more Malibu this time.' They sat on the kitchen floor, backs against the cupboard, and started to laugh hysterically. They didn't really know why they were laughing – maybe because of Karima, whom they were making fun of, or simply because they were breaking a taboo, in the absence of any maids or parents. Mia started talking fast. Very fast. About how nobody at school understood her, but that was okay because one day she'd show them who she really was, and she'd never told anyone this because she was afraid people would laugh at her but ever since she had been old enough to think for herself she had felt sure that a great destiny awaited her.

'Oh yeah?' smirked Abla. 'And what are you going to do?'

'I'm going to be a world-famous writer.'

'I'll read your books. Do you think you'll ever write about me?'

'Maybe. I don't know.'

The alcohol had made Mia brave or reckless, and she leaned towards Abla and kissed her lingeringly on the cheek.

Abla shivered. She slid down the cupboard until she was lying on the floor. Her head was spinning. Droplets of sweat trickled down the back of her neck and she felt like curling into a ball and falling asleep.

'What's the matter?' asked Mia. 'You're white as a sheet.'

'I'm just sleepy, that's all. Let me close my eyes and I'll be fine.'

'No, no, you need to get up. You can't stay here – my mum will be back soon.'

Mia put the bottles back in the cupboard, rinsed the glasses and helped Abla to her feet. They went through the darkened hallway. Abla lay on the bed, arms by her sides. Mia took off her shoes. 'Do you feel sick? Are you going to throw up?' Abla didn't say anything. 'Let the whirlpool take you. Don't try to fight it – just let yourself fall and you'll be okay.' Mia lay beside her. She put a hand on her forehead and stroked her hair. Abla's breathing gradually slowed. She turned her head to the side and Mia realised that she had fallen asleep. The lights from the garden came into the room through the window. The sound of toads croaking. Mia stroked the small of Abla's back, then pressed her face against the sleeping girl's neck. Abla smelled of Cleopatra soap, the same one that Selma used, and Mia felt an urge to bite her skin, to tear off a little piece of Abla and keep it for herself. She ran her finger along Abla's shoulder, sliding off the strap of her vest top. Abla had breasts, like her. She had a belly, like her, and the same thing between her legs, but her body was nothing like the body of Inès or any other woman. It was nothing like looking at her own body in the mirror. There was nothing more mysterious than this body that resembled hers. She kissed Abla's bony, golden shoulder. The girl still didn't move and Mia whispered words into her ear. 'It'll be okay, just wait and see.' Her friend's hair was soaked with sweat. Mia gently brushed it back over her ear. She was drunk too, but she felt certain she had never seen things this clearly before. Everything had been leading up to this moment. Suddenly, Mia's life – the life that was hers alone – was coming into focus. Her existence was beginning and she felt a sort of euphoria at the idea of having a destiny that would follow its own winding path. Delicately, she pulled at the straps of Abla's vest and her breasts appeared. Small, firm, milk-hued breasts, pointing up at the ceiling. For an instant Mia sat motionless, contemplating them. She wanted to press her face against them, to take them in her mouth, and when her fingertips stroked the right breast, Abla started to moan softly. Mia wanted to cry. She lay on top of her friend's slender body. She was afraid she would crush her, so she leaned on her right arm and, without thinking, without calculating, began to rub herself against the body beneath her. She took off her T-shirt and rested her damp skin against Abla's. Abla kept making little moans. She was halfway between sleep and waking, but she put her hands on Mia's hips, and Mia read that as an invitation. To eat her up. To lose herself in her. To take all the love she could, to deny herself nothing.

While Mia was secretly smoking in her bedroom, Mehdi was asleep, mouth open, head thrown back. Rays of incandescent sunlight shone through the oval window, staining his shirt bright orange, like a little flame of joy. A flight attendant gently touched his shoulder. The aeroplane was beginning its descent and it was time to fasten his seatbelt. Mehdi rested his forehead against the window and saw the coastline of Morocco below. He could make out the golden sand of a beach and the smooth grey surface of the sea. It was a cloudless day, the sky a pure blue. Today was 21 December. The plane leaned to one side. He saw farmed fields – wheat, he thought, or maybe corn – and patches of uncultivated land stretching out into the distance. Mehdi could discern buildings, separated by simple wooden barriers, and rocky slopes where tractors moved, raising clouds of dust. Casablanca was close by, and Mehdi thought that in ten or twenty years these fields would have disappeared. These small farms would be replaced by housing estates, sports fields, schools. Here, near the airport, they could build an aeronautics research facility, then a luxury hotel for travellers who were just passing through. Someone had told him once that to see an island you first had to leave it. You had to sail out to sea, because it was only with a certain distance that you were able to appreciate its outline, its topography, its beauty. From his window seat, Mehdi wondered if seeing it from the sky gave him a better understanding of his homeland.

This was his third flight of the week and he was exhausted. And yet, for many years, he had imagined that a successful life was a life filled with journeys, moving ceaselessly from one side of the planet to the other. In his visions of a glorious future, his passport was covered with stamps from exotic lands and he had an endless supply of anecdotes to tell his envious, sedentary friends. Travel was the sign of success. Or, even better, the proof of privilege. But tonight, he was eager to get home, to unpack his suitcase, to eat a home-made meal. He felt bloated from a constant diet of restaurant food, and his stomach ached. He found it hard to sleep in hotel rooms and spent his nights watching foreign TV shows. His fatigue was not only physical. He felt a sort of moral malaise, a discomfort that he couldn't quite name. A mixture of shame and anger. He felt an urge to be surrounded by faces he knew, to be relieved of the obligation to make conversation. During this long week of travel, he had felt like the main character in that Buñuel film whose title he had forgotten. Yes, he was the ambassador of an imaginary country who goes to a dinner party where he has to endure the other guests' criticisms of his homeland. 'I've heard that there's a lot of corruption'; 'I read that opposition leaders have been locked up'; 'Your country is very poor, isn't it?' The pilot warned them to expect some turbulence. The woman beside Mehdi began to pray, tightly gripping her pale-wood rosary. He opened his mouth wide and yawned. His ears were blocked. He remembered that, in the film, the ambassador – played by the great Fernando Rey – took a pistol out of his pocket and shot the people who had insulted him.

*

The winter in Washington had been cold and harsh. The forecast for Christmas had been minus thirteen degrees, so Mehdi had sent Farid to buy him a scarf and a pair of fur boots before he went to his meeting at the National Bank. In the corridors of that prestigious institution, he had seen the same friends as usual. Brilliant products of the post-independence age who lived in countries with authoritarian regimes and came here to beg for credit or debt restructuring. Here, in this frigid capital city, the fate of a continent at the mercy of the diktats of the International Monetary Fund was decided. A former Gabonese minister, here to plead the cause of his troubled homeland, patted him on the shoulder. 'How are you, brother?'

Mehdi shook his hand. He straightened his tie, buttoned his suit jacket and headed towards the upstairs meeting room. Aïcha thought it was amusing to call him 'The Great Pretender', and not only because they had once kissed to that song. Her nickname was a reference to his talent for convincing people, winning them over, his ability to make others follow his lead. One year earlier, he had obtained a line of credit from the International Bank for Reconstruction and Development, and this meeting was intended to assess the quality of the projects and how well they fit with market demands.

A rectangle of tables had been arranged in the large, overheated room. Mehdi, Farid and Hicham Benomar sat facing the window. Across from them were the World Bank's analysts. They were served tasteless coffee in large white cups and Mehdi watched as the Americans took their seats. They were wearing T-shirts under their shirts and their suits were poorly cut. Through the window, he could see snow falling. I'm in America, he thought. I'm a little Arab in glasses, but I'm the one they're here to listen to. His suit was perfectly tailored and his tortoiseshell glasses had been bought at a trendy New York boutique. His feet were sweating inside his fur boots.

All morning long they discussed the projects that CCM had set up. Social housing in Casablanca and Rabat. A clinic, a kissaria, even a hammam. Film studios in Ouarzazate. A winter tourism resort in Marrakech. A major hotel complex near Agadir, with a golf course modelled on the Aga Khan's club in Sardinia. Around the table, the conversation touched on occupation rates and operating costs, debt ratios and returns on investment. At last, Mehdi announced that CCM had been chosen by the palace to take part in a project known as The Breakthrough, a road connecting the Hassan II Mosque to Casablanca's city centre, modelled on the Via della Conciliazione between Rome and the Vatican. The bank had to finance the rehousing of people evicted from the old medina and planned to repay itself from the real estate projects built in their place. 'It might look good on Lotus, but in reality it will take you decades to make back that money,' interjected Curtis O'Hare, the chief economist.

Mehdi was stopped in his tracks. He patted his pocket. 'Okay if I smoke?'

'Let's take a break in my office. You can smoke through the window.'

Curtis accompanied Mehdi to the end of a long, carpeted corridor. The man was a giant, with curly red hair and chubby cheeks. He liked Mehdi and admired his work.

'I'll open the window. You can stand here.'

Mehdi lit a cigarette. 'I know what you're going to say.'

'Listen, Mehdi, I'm concerned. Circumstances have changed. I don't think this is the right time to be launching into monumental projects. Your debts are going up because of the housing crisis, and this war isn't going to help.' In August 1990, the Iraqi president Saddam Hussein had invaded Kuwait, and the Americans, supported by an international coalition, were preparing to attack. 'Who would want to invest or travel in an Arab country right now?'

'Oh, come on – Morocco isn't Iraq! And let me remind you that King Hassan II is on the same side as the West in this war.'

'Maybe, but most people can't tell the difference. Listen, I'm a numbers guy. I just wanted to warn you. Morocco is very unstable right now and the fundamentals aren't good.'

'And whose fault is that? For six years now we've been stuck with this structural adjustment which is just aggravating inequality. There's no more investment in health or education. You know perfectly well what I think of these stupid neoliberal theories.' He stubbed out his cigarette on the ledge before closing the window. He was freezing. Yes, things were going badly in Morocco. Phosphate prices were falling, the dirham had been devalued and debt was exploding. There were seven million poor people in the kingdom, and on 14 December some youths in Fes had set fire to the Marinid Palace. A few foreign television reporters had tried to interview the rioters but they had simply crossed their hands in front of their mouths: 'We're not allowed to speak.' Others had been less tight-lipped, yelling at the cameras: 'They're robbing us! We want some honesty!' They expressed their hatred for the corrupt, Westernised elite who were making money from the liberalisation that was crushing ordinary people. The government was under the thumb of the IMF and was no longer hiring. Every year the number of unemployed graduates went up. 'We need to create jobs to fight against despair and fundamentalism,' shouted Mehdi. 'We need major projects to help make Morocco a popular tourist destination. Tourism is our oil!'

'Do you want to smoke another cigarette or shall we go back?'

'Let's go.'

The meeting continued. Farid shot Mehdi anxious looks. 'What did he say?' he whispered, but Mehdi just made an irritated gesture. For two hours they went through the columns of figures, compared graphs, made ten- and twenty-year projections. They agreed that a Bird team would carry out on-site inspections. 'We'll take stock of your previous successes and failures, then make our decision,' Curtis concluded.

Mehdi walked along the icy pavement towards the hotel. For several months he'd had the feeling that everyone was trying to warn him about something, to curb his ambitions. Farid in particular kept telling him to be less aggressive, less scathing towards people who claimed to have friends in high places and came to ask for unsecured credit or who were eyeing a piece of land in which CCM had already invested. 'These people will hold a grudge, you know. You don't want them as your enemy.' Mehdi sat at the hotel bar and ordered a whisky. He was very proud of his accent when he spoke English and had convinced himself that he could easily pass for an American. The television on the wall behind the bar was showing a baseball game. How could anyone prefer a boring sport like that to football? He looked around. There was a couple sitting at the bar, drinking beer. And some men – either colleagues or friends – were sitting at a table behind him, talking about the game. He wondered how these people saw him. He was trying to get off the island, to imagine what an American might make of this bespectacled, thickly bearded Arab in his Italian suit. What did the barman think as he took Mehdi's order of a second beer? Although Mehdi often told his daughters that it was a mistake to care too much what others thought of you – that the only thing that mattered was what you were actually like, inside – he knew this was nonsense. We were always what others perceived, the image of ourselves that we projected. The secrets of the heart, the hidden qualities of the soul, a man's good intentions . . . None of these counted for anything in the real world.

In Paris, he went through the whole charade again. Mehdi had lunch with a client at Le Meurice. Jean-Pierre Delambre had created a holiday club in the South of France and was planning to launch another one amid the palm trees of Marrakech. For the past six months, CCM had been helping him locate funding. They ordered a tray of oysters and a beef stew. Mehdi chose the wine: a glass of Riesling for the starter and a bottle of Montrachet to accompany the main course.

'I don't know if I ever told you this, but I was born in Algeria,' Jean-Pierre told him. 'I don't remember much about it – I was only about ten when we had to leave. But I can still recall the scents, the light, the easy living there. So, you see, Morocco is familiar to me.'

'Sure,' said Mehdi. 'Although you know that Morocco and Algeria are very different.'

'I'm glad to hear you say that.'

Mehdi took a cigarette from his pocket. Lunch had been delicious, and he would happily have ordered a digestif or another glass of wine if he weren't so worried about shocking his client.

'It doesn't bother you, does it?' he said, lighting his cigarette.

'No, please, go ahead. So, I'm not going to lie to you: my regular bankers are a little anxious. With everything that's going on in Algeria and Iran, they're concerned that Morocco might be next on the list.'

'What list?' laughed Mehdi.

'The Islamists, Mehdi, the Islamists! How can you sell hotels with swimming pools and access to the beach in a country where women aren't allowed to go out and thieves get their hands cut off?'

'You're joking, right? Come on, let's be serious for a minute: Morocco is not Sudan or Saudi Arabia. It's a peaceful country where Islam is open and tolerant.' And he listened to himself give his lecture for tourists, all about how Morocco was a unique land, with a natural immunity to the dangers of fanaticism.

'Don't get me wrong,' said Jean-Pierre, 'I firmly believe in Morocco's huge potential as a tourism destination. But you only have to turn on the TV these days to hear the mood music. It's the Arabs versus the civilised world, right?'

They said their goodbyes outside the hotel. 'I'll let you know,' promised Jean-Pierre before jumping into a taxi. Mehdi decided to walk. He went up Rue de Rivoli and headed towards the Palais-Royal. He was slightly drunk and very cold. Paris was shrouded in grey – even the faces of passers-by were ashen – and he felt very tired. He had sent Farid to do the shopping for his wife and daughters. They had given him a very precise list: particular brands of jeans and shoes, CDs and videocassettes, medicines and ointments that were not available at home. He stopped outside the Comédie-Française. He looked up and spent a minute or two contemplating the carved stone facade. Then he turned slowly around. He observed the terrace of Le Nemours, the entrance to the metro station, the Hôtel du Louvre, and the Louvre itself. Another few steps and he found himself looking down Avenue de l'Opéra. In the distance was the Tuileries Garden, and if it had been summer he would have walked there, staining his Church's with white dust and taking a nap on one of those reclining green chairs by the pond. He felt tiny.

He wondered what it would be like to live in a city like this. To take the metro to work, to walk in places where nobody would call you 'brother', to drink wine on a terrace after going to the theatre, to kiss a woman under an archway or in the back seat of a taxi, to stop at a bookshop on your way home. And, as chance would have it, he spotted a bookshop on the other side of the street. When he went in, he discovered that it was packed. A woman was crouching down, surrounded by shopping bags, as she looked for a comic book for her granddaughter. An elderly gentleman was leaning on his umbrella, explaining to the bookseller that he wanted to give people classics for Christmas. 'Because everybody loves the classics.' At the till, a young woman in a beige coat was writing a note on the title page of a novel. These sights made Mehdi so happy that he wanted to kiss everyone. He made his way through the aisles. He felt too hot now in his coat and he was sweating inside his fur boots again. He wanted to buy everything he saw: novels, essays, history books, even poetry collections. He imagined a life for himself where he would have time to read all these books, a life with no ambition but to enter the souls of other people, where he could travel the world without moving an inch. That was the problem, he thought: the way he found it impossible to choose an existence and stick to it, this persistent desire for a different kind of life. He found himself in the 'New Releases' section. On a table, he spotted what he was looking for: a pile of copies of *Our Friend the King*, a book about Hassan II that was banned but much debated in Morocco. It was said that the minister of the interior, Driss Basri, had bought hundreds of copies in the hope of making the book unavailable in France, but instead he had helped it become a bestseller. Mehdi picked up three and almost started laughing when he saw the titles of the other books on the same table. To the right, *The Stoning of Soraya M.*; to the right, *The Veil of Silence*; and, behind a sign announcing 'Bestsellers', *Not Without My Daughter*. If only I had a pistol, he thought, and the image of Fernando Rey came back to him.

At the Mohammed V Airport in Casablanca, Mehdi held his passport out to the border guard. On the form he'd filled out, next to 'Occupation', he had written: 'Bank president'.

'Salam khouya, koulchi labess?'

'El Hamdoulilah.'

The policeman straightened his collar, quickly examined the document, then handed it back. Mehdi walked through the baggage claim hall. For an instant he feared that a customs officer was about to signal to him and ask him to open his suitcase, where the forbidden books were hidden. Instead, the man nodded respectfully to this elegant executive in his imported suit, pulling an American suitcase on wheels.

Mustapha was waiting for him in the car park. The chauffeur opened the passenger door and Mehdi asked him how the family was. 'Everyone is well, Monsieur le Président.' One of the technicians at CCM had installed a telephone in Mehdi's Mercedes. 'I want to be available twenty-four-seven.' Mehdi refused to be contradicted by anyone or anything. He hated the idea of being caught out.

He called Aïcha.

'I'll be there in an hour, darling.'

'Tell Mustapha to take it easy. People drive like madmen these days.'

Just before hanging up, Mehdi said: 'Do you remember the name of that Buñuel film that we saw at the Odéon? You know, the one about the ambassador . . .'

'*The Discreet Charm of the Bourgeoisie*?'

'Ah, yes. I'd forgotten the title.'

As soon as he entered the house, the girls threw themselves at him. 'Daddy!' They argued over who would get to take his suitcase. They wanted to pick it up, to weigh it in their arms and guess how many presents he had bought them. He laughed. 'I'm afraid you'll have to wait for Christmas for the presents. But I do have a surprise for you. Come with me.'

The girls followed him into the bedroom and looked questioningly at their mother when Mehdi locked himself in the bathroom. 'Sorry, I don't have a clue what he's up to,' their mother told them. The three of them sat on the bed and waited. They had to wait a long time.

In the bathroom, Mehdi could hear them laughing and asking what was taking him so long. When Aïcha finally knocked at the door and hissed, 'What on earth are you up to?', he told her he would be out in a minute.

At last the door opened but he still didn't appear. They sat up on the bed.

'Are you ready?' Mehdi asked.

'Come on, just show us!'

'Close your eyes. And don't open them until I tell you.'

They obeyed, and when he finally said: 'Okay, now!' they cried out with an emotion that Mehdi could not identify. Was it surprise? Fear? Disgust? Inès laughed nervously. Aïcha kept her hand in front of her open mouth and her eyes – her beautiful eyes – stared at him, wide open. Mia went up to him. She touched his smooth cheek. The skin was paler there than the rest of his face and there were a couple of small razor cuts near the corners of his lips.

'It's weird,' she said. 'You look like someone else.'

'But why did you get rid of your beard?' Inès asked tearfully.

'My beard? Let's just say that it was stolen.'

'Saddam! Ya Habib! Morocco is with you!' For two weeks the Americans had been bombing Baghdad, and in Rabat the crowd was chanting: 'Bush is a murderer! Mitterrand's his dog!' They marched slowly at first, aware of the cameras filming them and the suspiciously peaceful-looking policemen. Huge portraits of Yasser Arafat and Saddam Hussein were carried above their heads. On one side marched the left-wing parties, who believed in Arab solidarity and wanted to show their opposition to the imperialistic powers. Some of them had lived through the 1965 riots in Casablanca and they found it hard to shake the fear that they were about to be shot at, attacked, that the streets would flow with protesters' blood once again. But the policemen didn't lift a finger. They kept their arms crossed, their truncheons hanging from belts. They had been ordered to let the march happen. Let them yell, let them protest, let them vent their anger, because, after all, this is a free country, almost a democracy. Morocco's people were with the Arabs and its rulers with the West. On the other side were bearded men and veiled women waving their copies of the Quran and chanting, 'Allahu Akbar!' What did it matter that Saddam, a hero of the Arab cause, had liquidated left-wingers and Islamists in Iraq? What did it matter? They were here anyway, followed by groups of students whose lecturers had encouraged them to skip their classes. When they reached the parliament building they started shouting as if the people they were addressing were there, behind those ochre walls, and could hear them. They insulted the Western powers and joyously burned the flags of France and Israel. 'Saddam, Ya Habib, destroy Tel Aviv!' Women threw papier-mâché missiles. 'Saddam has Scuds, we have skouts*!'

After the Christmas holidays, the Lycée Descartes did not reopen. There were fears of a terrorist attack, and the school's board of directors advised the teachers to stay in France a little longer. This damn war, thought Mia. This damn war was forcing her to spend a month in Meknes with her little sister and her grandparents. 'You'll be better off over there, in the fresh air,' her mother had told her. But Mia couldn't care less about fresh air. She wanted to see Abla. She wanted to go back to school so she could smoke cigarettes with her friends behind the basketball courts.

'Ah, these teenagers, always sulking,' Mathilde said, shaking her head. In the mornings, she would move the living room furniture out of the way, spread a towel out on the carpet and put on a Jane Fonda tape. However much she made fun of the Daoud girls for being too skinny, Mathilde would have loved to lose all the pounds that made it impossible for her to fit into her summer dresses. Inès stood behind her and said 'That hurts' as she lifted her right leg. In the afternoons they would watch *The Thorn Birds* together and Mathilde would swoon over Father Ralph. At the time, the farm had only one generator, and several times a day a siren would wail to warn them that the power was about to be cut. Once the bombing began,

---

* 'Shut up' in Arabic.

however, Amine gave orders that the generator should be turned on and he spent most of his time in front of the television. This one-time apostle of fresh air now sat for hours in the living room, watching the war.

Sometimes the girls would go into the room and their grandfather wouldn't chase them out. They thought: The war is green and it makes a strange noise. This war was nothing like Amine's war, with the stories he had told them about men facing each other and shooting. No, this was a different kind of war, a war waged by people like Mehdi, people who loved computers. The girls learned the expression 'surgical precision' and one night, on the television news, an American soldier bragged: 'Baghdad is lit up like a Christmas tree.' Amine leapt up from the sofa and yelled insults in Arabic, insults that Mia would never have thought to hear coming from her grandfather's mouth.

Her grandparents were old-fashioned people who lived in accordance with ancient, outdated values. Mathilde criticised ripped jeans and girls with scruffy outfits. She found their music deafening. 'Oh, young people today!' lamented Amine. 'They have no values, no education, no respect. All they think about are drugs and money.' Inès would laugh at this, but Mia would get angry. Yes, they were old-fashioned people who liked to play cards and drink port in the evening, sitting on the garden steps. Mathilde would sew in front of the television and listen to the radio until late at night. She made beds in an old-fashioned way, with woollen blankets that made you itch and sneeze. And she believed in God. Before meals, they would all have to hold hands and recite a naive prayer that Mathilde had invented: 'Some people are hungry and have nothing to eat.

Others have food but aren't hungry. We have food to eat and we are hungry. We thank the Lord for this good food.'

Yes, Mathilde believed in God and in maktub. She believed she was merely the scribe of a much greater writer who adorned the world with magic and gave it depth and mystery. She believed a lot of things, Mathilde. She swore that once, while she had been peeling potatoes, she had seen, through the misted-up window, the ghost of a cousin who had died in the war. She claimed she could communicate with spirits and that we had all lived previous lives. She would look at someone and say: He's an old soul, that one. And the reason she feared knives and mountains was that she had, in another life, died on a snowy peak, and in another life before that been murdered with a sword. She told the girls stories – at night, before they went to sleep, and in the daytime too, to stop them being bored or to distract them if they grazed their knee or if they were upset about something. Sometimes these were true stories, stories about Mathilde 'when she was a little girl', and these stories mentioned the Rhine, which the girls had never seen, and German lessons and a tyrannical teacher. Inès especially liked the story about the old aunt who sold her hair to feed her family, and Mia liked the one about the great-grandmother who laughed herself to death. Amine was a character in these stories too, a character who had killed men, fought with tigers and escaped from a POW camp, like the hero of a film. And then there were the other stories, the ones she invented, the cruel fairy tales that she only told at night, in which a terrible father nailed cabbage leaves to his children's skin. There was that epic tale set in a happy village, isolated from the rest of the world, that was finally conquered by a gang of soldiers. All the inhabitants were killed, even the little girl who was the heroine of the story, and Mathilde insisted that the girl 'died with a smile on her face'. When Mia asked where such ideas came from, Mathilde would shrug and look up at the sky. 'They just come to me. I don't think about it.' She read a lot – books that Mehdi considered unworthy, and which she had bought in bulk from a travelling salesman. Novels, bound in purple leather, that told stories of families and impossible loves. She gave them adventure stories too: *Gulliver's Travels*, a collection of short stories by Selma Lagerlöf and *Little Women* – 'even if you aren't all that little'.

But Mia was busy reading other books. That summer, she devoured novels by Marguerite Duras and James Baldwin. She had found a second-hand copy of *Giovanni's Room* at the bookshop for less than ten dirhams. Certain passages had been underlined. They were not, in Mia's opinion, the most beautiful or poignant passages, but she kept wondering who that previous reader was and what they had thought of the book. Mia spent a large part of January 1991 locked in her bedroom, listening to her Walkman. She kept wondering where Abla was. What is she doing, at this very moment? Is she thinking about me? She kept weaving new tapestries from the threads of her memory, and sometimes she found them wonderful, sometimes disturbing. She called her friend several times, but the maid always said she wasn't home, and one day, in a cold voice, she told Mia that Abla had left town. Mia felt certain she was lying and she wondered if she had done something bad. There was a weight on her chest. She kept seeing Abla's face that morning, the way she had left without a backward glance. 'I've got a headache.' Mia felt guilty. But of what, she wasn't sure. Then she tried to reassure herself. They'd just been playing at butterflies. The things they'd done that night had been childlike, innocent. All girls knew that.

One day, Mia was woken by the banging of shutters. An icy wind was blowing through the trees, making the pipes whistle. She went to the kitchen in her pyjamas and ate a slice of toast with honey. She walked through the corridor. From there, she could hear the sound of her grandmother's typewriter: a rapid, regular clicking. She went into the office and sat in the armchair by the wall. Mathilde didn't notice her and Mia stayed there for almost fifteen minutes, watching her grandmother from behind. Mathilde extracted the pages from the machine, put them on a pile, then added two more blank pages to the typewriter, separated by a sheet of carbon paper. She typed very quickly, using her right hand to move the lever every time she reached the end of a line. Mia admired her dexterity, her concentration. It was soothing to watch her.

'Are you writing a book?' she asked.

Mathilde jumped. 'Ah, it's you. You should put on some slippers – you'll catch a cold.'

But Mia stood up and leaned over the page that Mathilde was attempting to hide with her hand.

'What is it?'

'Nothing. Just stories. Memories. So I don't forget them.'

'Can I read it?'

'Maybe. One day. But please, don't tell your grandfather. This is my time for myself.'

Mathilde was annoyed. Mia had ruined her solitude. It was worth waking up at the crack of dawn, drinking her coffee in the dark so that she could enjoy the silence, so that she would not have to justify herself to her husband, who would tell her she'd be better off using her time to pay bills.

Mia collapsed back into the armchair. She picked up her copy of *The Lover* and declared: 'I want to be a writer too.'

'I'm not a writer,' Mathilde said coldly. 'Besides, that's not the kind of thing you can just decide. You get that pride from your father,' she added, glancing with a frown at the Duras novel. Mathilde had never read anything by Marguerite Duras, but she had seen her on television and thought she was pathetic, disgusting. 'I can't be doing with novels these days. It's just people talking about their lives, revealing intimate details about themselves. But you don't become a writer by looking at yourself in the mirror. A story begins when you go *through* the looking-glass.'

Mia and Mathilde waged a strange little war during the weeks that followed. Mia hid a notebook in the pantry and at every hour of the day, in the living room or the dining room, on the pages with their little squares, she would write letters to Abla. She did this under her grandmother's nose to show her that she was not ashamed, that while she may not have been through a war or a moved to another continent she still had an interesting life that was worth writing about. She developed a taste for this and, sitting on the garden steps, wrapped in a blanket, she would feel tears well in her eyes at some of her own metaphors. If I write to her, she thought, she could get to know me better. She could understand me, forgive me. She hid the notebook under her pillow and dreamed up sentences in her sleep. She imagined Abla drinking in her words, drop by drop, devouring her letters. She thought she was charming her beloved, but it was herself she was hypnotising. She wanted her writing to be beautiful and forgot that it had to be true. She retraced the story of what had happened between them, but writing was very different. It was more intense, and the feelings had time to ripen, to ferment. She used words that were too big for her, words like shirts with sleeves so long that her arms got lost inside them. She didn't admit it to herself, but Abla's absence no longer weighed so heavily upon her. Writing to her was almost better than being with her.

For her first day back at school, Mia wore her white Fruit of the Loom sweatshirt and her jeans. She arrived very early and sat on the steps to wait for Abla. She spotted her a few seconds after the bell rang. She was coming out of the girls' toilets, followed by her little gang of friends. She didn't look at Mia, and Mia was left wondering if she had deliberately ignored her or if she'd just been late for her first class. She had imagined their reunion so many times, like a film that played over and over in her head, but the reality was nothing like that. Abla sat in her old spot at the back of the class, near the radiator, and at the end of the day, when Mia asked her if she wanted to come back to her house so they could do their homework together, Abla raised her eyebrows. 'No, thanks, I'll be fine.' Her coldness hurt Mia so badly that she might easily have started crying in front of everyone, like a child. She wanted to demand an explanation, to grab hold of Abla's arm and force her to talk. But she held herself back. She took the spiral notebook from her schoolbag and handed it to her.

'What's that?'

'I wrote it for you.'

Abla took it, shrugged and turned away.

That afternoon, walking towards the car park where the chauffeur was waiting for her, Mia found it hard to breathe. She didn't understand what was happening. Why had Abla been so mean to her? She remembered the way her friends had all smirked and sniggered. Nobody had said anything to her. Nobody had insulted her or humiliated her, but she felt that she had been sidelined, as if Abla was now surrounded by some invisible forcefield that kept her at a distance. Near the car park, she bumped into Hakim. He held out a bag of sugared mint gums. 'You want one?'

Mia thought he was an idiot. He was just a kid who had no idea what she was going through, who spent his time judging others because he didn't smoke or have sex or drink until he passed out. 'No, I don't,' she said, shoving him away. 'I have to go home.'

She struggled to sleep that week, and in the mornings, when she went to school, her guts and her throat were twisted with anxiety. She failed a maths test and when the teacher expressed surprise at the mediocrity of her results she just shrugged. 'I didn't revise for it.' Over dinner at home, she barely responded to her parents' questions and made no attempt to conceal her boredom at their conversations. She rolled her eyes and thought that adult life was shit, nothing but a series of banalities. 'Oh, stop sulking!' her mother said crossly. Ah yes, of course. If only she was sweet and always smiling, like Inès! If only her walls were covered with posters of Claudia Schiffer and Patrick Swayze, and she still sat in her mother's lap to give her cuddles. Mia wished they would all disappear so she could have the house to herself. Then she could daydream in peace.

By Friday she couldn't stand it any more. During PE she asked Abla if they could talk. The two girls walked away from the rest of the class, to the concrete wall between the athletics field and the eucalyptus forest. Some of the more exhibitionist boys would come here sometimes to slide their dicks into the holes. Abla, in a grey tracksuit, was chewing gum with her arms crossed. Suddenly Mia didn't know what to say. For days she had been longing to be alone with her, but now that the opportunity was here she was too flustered to speak.

Abla said: 'Listen, I'm your friend, but you need to stop acting so weird. Stop calling my parents' house and writing me letters.'

'But you're the one who—'

'I was trying to be kind, that's all.'

'Did you read the notebook?'

'Forget it, okay? I don't want to hurt you, so just let it drop.' She spat out her chewing gum, took a pack of Kent cigarettes from her pocket and lit one.

'You shouldn't smoke here. If the teacher catches you, he'll go crazy.'

'Just mind your own business, okay?'

At five o'clock, Mia walked through the school gates. As happened every Friday, the students hung around a little bit longer in the forecourt outside the school. They talked about their plans for the weekend. Couples snogged, watched lecherously by the pot dealers. Someone was playing a Bob Marley tape. Mia was on the street that led to the car park when she heard Kamel's voice behind her. 'Hey!' She turned around and watched as he moved towards her, smiling. 'So?' he said, slapping her on the back. She was the same height as him and he had acted this way with her for as long as they'd known each other: manly, a bit rough. A car brushed past them. Kamel grabbed Mia's arm and dragged her to the pavement. She noticed then that all his friends were there, leaning against a Renault Espace, watching them. Kamel moved his face towards hers as if he was about to kiss her. He whispered: 'What the fuck is wrong with you? You want me to tell everyone about the filth you wrote to my sister?'

Mia's heart sped up. She was terrified, as if she had been cornered not by a group of skinny, spotty teenage boys but by a pack of starving wolves. She tried to tell them to stay calm, she didn't know what they were talking about. No, she swore she wasn't pretending, she wasn't playing dumb. Kamel continued to glare at her. She took a step backwards and tripped on an uneven paving stone. She fell onto her back and cried out with pain. One of the boys leaned down to help her up, and as she was dusting off her jeans she felt a hand slap her cheek. She almost lost her balance, but she grabbed hold of the car's bonnet. 'So?' Kamel said again. She was going to have to defend herself. She could kick him, or she could run away. She was faster than most boys. When she had fights with her sister, she could sometimes be uncontrollably violent. She had hit Inès with a dictionary once. She had broken her little finger and torn out chunks of her hair. 'You don't know your own strength,' her mother had warned her. 'You'll kill her one day.'

A crowd of other students had gathered around them. Mia could hear them yelling: 'Fight! Fight!' Her heart was pounding now and she felt an intense excitement take hold of her. Suddenly she had turned into an animal. Her field of vision shrank, as if it was caught in a vice, and the entire scene was stained grey. Despite her rage, her legs felt like they were paralysed. Fucking move! she kept telling herself. Move like those boxers she had watched on television with her mother. Move your legs, side to side, back and forth. Put your hands in front of your face. Defend yourself. Hit back. Around them, the students were roaring on the boys. Someone shoved her in the back and she spun around, out of control. Everything was blurry, confused, chaotic. In the distance Bob Marley was singing 'Get Up, Stand Up' and Mia was so nervous she almost laughed. This couldn't be happening. It made no sense, and in a few seconds she would manage to escape this circle that was holding her prisoner and concealing her from the view of passers-by. 'I've never hit a girl,' said Kamel, laughing. 'But you're not really a girl. You think you're a guy? So fight like a guy.' He leapt at Mia, who raised her hands. She felt a fist against her face. The world started to spin. The trees, the pavement, the cars and the sweet vendor's stall all floated through the air. She landed on the tarmac. She put her hand to her cheek. It hurt less than she'd imagined. One of the boys was acting as a lookout while the others bellowed: 'Smash her! Smash her!' Far off, she could hear Kamel's laughter and the sound of his trainers scraping against the ground. Her ears were buzzing. She lost consciousness.

When she came round, Hakim was holding her head under the cold water tap in the girls' bathroom. Her tongue moved around her mouth. She was missing a tooth. She saw trickles of blood in the sink. Inès was there too. She kept asking: 'Are you okay? Are you okay?' and jumping from one foot to the other. Mia couldn't speak or open her right eye.

They took her out to the car park. When Mustapha saw her, he started to wail. 'Lalla Mia, what happened?' He stroked her arm, prayed, said that he would have to call the police and the school's headmaster. He was frightened and he felt guilty. Monsieur le Président would hold him responsible. He would blame Mustapha for dozing in the car park, for chatting with the other chauffeurs when he should have been ensuring his daughters' safety.

Inside the car, Mia didn't think about the pain, or her broken tooth, her swollen lips, her black eye. She thought about Fatima, who would scream, possibly even faint when she saw her like this. About her mother, who would keep asking questions until it got dark outside, who would say: 'I want to know everything.' But Mia knew that wasn't true. Aïcha did not want to hear her confessions.

No, her mother didn't want to know. Her mother would hate it if Mia said the word. The word that named what she was. The word that floated in the air around them. The word that, because it was still unspoken, seemed all the heavier, the more disturbing. Aïcha would have closed her eyes, covered her ears, she would have run away if Mia had started to tell her the details of the love she felt for Abla.

Mia admired her parents. Unlike her friends, who were always complaining about their parents, she tended to emphasise how open-minded hers were, how cultured and intelligent. How interested in other people. How generous. But now she was forced to acknowledge that something was off. Behind those big words, her parents were fearful, conformist, repressed. In the end, Mia realised that she lived between two worlds. The world of home, where her parents appeared modern, eager for their daughters to be free and successful. And the outside world, which was dangerous and incomprehensible. At home it was fine to criticise the veil, to vent your anger at those horrible bearded men who were threatening Salman Rushdie. 'But that's not how it works here.' In the outside world you must not talk, must not be provocative, must pretend to respect the rules of decorum. Her parents were hypocrites and Mia felt humiliated when she realised that they were not free.

Don't talk about Sabah, who lives with a man without being married.

Don't tell anyone that Aïcha doesn't observe Ramadan.

Don't talk about the alcohol we drink, or the pork that Mathilde eats, sometimes even during Muslim holidays.

Don't tell anyone how, one New Year's Eve, Dad dressed up as a woman.

Don't say that we laugh every time we read *Le Matin du Sahara*, that we make fun of royal propaganda and obsequious courtiers.

Don't talk about Selma's lovers.

Don't describe our way of life – what we eat, what we drink, what we say and believe.

Don't tell anyone that Omar shot himself in the mouth a few days after Christmas in 1978, when Mia was four years old.

Don't repeat Selma's jokes about Arabs. Never make jokes about corruption, underdevelopment, bigotry.

Never talk about the king, or rigged elections. Do not utter the name Oufkir or the name of that prison in the south of the country.

Don't tell anyone that Mehdi sometimes doubts the solidity of the regime.

Her parents had accepted this moral confusion as part of their lives, and they had transmitted it to their children. Now Mia knew that they would never be able to help her answer the question: 'Who am I?'

Here, people said: 'Paradise lies beneath the feet of your mother.' Mia loved her mother. She loved her to death – a painful, intense love that sometimes made her wonder if this love was more a kind of hell than a paradise. As a little girl, even before Inès was born, she would sometimes hide inside the house just so she could hear her mother calling for her, so she could hear her name in her mother's mouth and sense her panic when she wasn't able to find her beloved daughter. Yes, Mia could feel her mother's love. She felt it physically at every hour of the day. Of course Aïcha would never say anything terrible, anything despicable. She was not the kind of mother who would insult her child or throw her out of the house for her unnatural desires. Mia could think herself lucky: she would not be locked in an asylum, and the exorcist would not be called in the middle of the night. No, the reality was more insidious than that. Crueller, perhaps. Mia recalled the way Aïcha had reacted when that Charles Aznavour song had played on the radio: 'I'm a homo, as they say,'* he sang, and her mother had quickly turned the knob on the radio to find another station. One day, over dinner, Aïcha had talked about Jean-Marie, the homosexual hairdresser, who had been beaten up in his apartment by a teenage boy. The boy had broken his eye socket with an ashtray, and Aïcha had said: 'Poor guy – people like that are never happy.' Mia never forgot those words. They circled her head constantly until they lost all meaning.

People like that. So she belonged to something. Somewhere, there were other people like her, and she forced herself to forget the implication that what united them was misfortune. People like that. She pretended not to know what her mother meant. Mia never let herself say the word, even in her own head. She told herself: I'm normal and I haven't done anything

---

* Charles Aznavour's 'Comme ils disent' (1972) was one of the first gay-friendly pop songs released in France.

wrong. Her mother wanted her to be happy. Her mother didn't believe she could be happy. She's afraid, thought Mia, that I will be weird, marginalised. A transvestite with AIDS. She would prefer me to be conformist and ordinary. She loves me, but loving someone has nothing to do with words. To love someone means not to ask questions, not to open a closet that the other person has gone to the trouble of locking. Not to dig up buried secrets. To love someone is to be silent, together, to let those unanswered questions float in the air and to realise that they don't matter. To love and to know are two very different things.

People like that . . . Would they know she was one of them? Would they be drawn to her? Would they invite her to join them? Where did they live? She felt sure she'd already seen some. One day, on a hotel terrace during a holiday in Marrakech, she had spent a long time watching two women have lunch together. One of them had started crying. She had blown her nose in a napkin and Mia had known, beyond any doubt, that these women were like her. Now she understood that this secret – this secret that she had not even admitted to herself – was out. Since that day, it seemed to Mia that everything had changed. She felt as if she was naked and the world was watching her. From now on, she would live without armour, vulnerable, deserted. Like a child in a fairy tale, she would move through a cold, dark, mist-wreathed forest. And who knew if she would meet a bear, or a wolf, if she would sleep in a gingerbread house where a witch would try to roast her in an oven. She knew the truth now: she would have to meet these monsters on her own.

A few days after the fight, Mehdi went into his eldest daughter's bedroom. Mia was lying on the bed, facing the wall. He placed a copy of *One Hundred Years of Solitude* on the pink duvet and said: 'Look.'

She sat up, held the thick novel in her hands and flicked through the pages.

'Whatever it is that's making you sad, by the time you finish reading this you'll have forgotten about it.' Before leaving, he kissed her on the forehead.

Mia refused to go back to school. Her lip and her eye were no longer swollen and the dentist had put in a crown, but she claimed she didn't feel ready. She didn't want to see them again, didn't want them to stare at her, mock her, whisper behind her back. She considered suicide. She could slash her wrists in the bathtub. Steal some rat poison from the kitchen cupboard and mix it in a pot of yoghurt. She could hang herself from the white poplar, and tears pricked her eyes as she imagined her mother's grief. She begged her parents to send her to France. 'Let me go to boarding school. I just need to get away.' They told her this was not going to happen. 'Then send me to Meknes. I could work with Grandad. He could teach me how to look after the farm.'

'Oh, be reasonable,' Aïcha said. 'You really want to spend your days dealing with farmworkers? That's no life for someone with a mind as brilliant as yours.'

One night, Inès went into Mia's bedroom and got into bed beside her. 'Budge up.' She rubbed her little feet against her sister's. Outside, the wind was shaking the poplars and they could hear the anxious barking of the local dogs. End-of-the-world weather, Mathilde would have called it, in her Alsatian accent. In a whisper, Inès said to Mia that she had snitched on Kamel to the school's headmaster.

'What? You did what?'

'Hang on, there's no need to get upset. I called from the pay phone at my school. I said Kamel was selling drugs outside Lycée Descartes. I said he had a large quantity of hashish on him.'

'What good will that do? They already know he's a dealer.'

'Exactly. They've just been waiting for an opportunity to get rid of him. They searched his bag and they found a big block of hash. He's been expelled.'

For the first time in weeks, Mia smiled.

'Oh yeah? And where did it come from, this block of hash?'

'You still have friends, you know. Hakim and Adil helped me.' Inès was beaming. 'You are happy, aren't you? Tell me you're happy.'

'But how does a girl your age even come up with an idea like that? And where did you get the hash?'

'Selma gave us a hand. She knows loads of strange people. And you know what she said? There are three things that matter in life: eating well, drinking well, and getting revenge.'

Mia went back to school. Her sole ambition now was to succeed, to have the best possible grades. She became her own torturer, her own prison guard. She gave herself a gruelling schedule, with an early wake-up time and early bedtime, and regular workout sessions. She did press-ups every morning before her shower, and sit-ups in the evening. Three times a week she ran through the Forêt de Hilton to escape her anxieties, which ran alongside her. Sometimes she would turn to the side and see them there.

She stayed close to a small circle of friends at school. Her oldest friends – Hakim, Adil – the oldest of the old, as she called them. She drew up lists of books to read, films to see, dreams to accomplish. During her last year at Lycée Descartes she learned the art of patience. The patience not to participate in a discussion, to stay silent, to be aloof from it all. Mia imagined her future life. She would be so stunningly, so extraordinarily successful that one day she would be able to come back here and throw her success in the faces of the people who'd humiliated her. In January 1992 she announced to her parents that she had enrolled in a preparatory class for business school. They were surprised. They'd always thought their daughter would study literature or philosophy. 'I'm going to be a banker, like Dad,' she declared proudly. She wanted to work as fast as possible, to earn enough money that she would not have to depend on anyone else. Her absurd dreams of being a writer had been buried forever, and at night, when she couldn't sleep, she would think obsessively about that notebook. Where was it? Had Abla shown it to her friends? Had they sat together, laughing at Mia's purple prose, her pretentious quotations, her innermost secrets? Had Abla put it in a drawer somewhere or thrown it in the bin?

In June she took the baccalauréat exams. The essay question for philosophy was: 'Does passion distance us from reality?'

For the first ten minutes she didn't write a word. Legs stretched out under the wooden table, she just sat eating walnuts and raisins. Then she grabbed the pale-pink pages they had been given for the exam and sketched out a rough plan. The essay itself came easily, fluently, and when she left the exam room she was happy. When her parents asked her how it had gone, she replied: 'I said everything I wanted to say.' During that week of exams, she discovered that she was capable of entering an intense state of concentration. After each test, the other students would gather in groups to discuss it. Some of them would cry or compare answers. They would sit on the floor, their bags between their knees, and smoke cigarettes while they moaned and groaned. Mia almost managed not to see them or even hear them. She withdrew into herself, like a snail into its shell. On the day the results were announced, she walked unhurriedly towards the big black gates, where the list of successful candidates had been posted. She had passed with distinction, despite a mediocre score in her Arabic test. School was over. Now her life could begin.

That summer, Mia felt as if she was floating. She was not really here any more but not yet in France, in that land where she would have to look after herself. Now the reality loomed closer, she felt ambivalent about the idea of leaving her homeland. Fatima said irritably: 'Everyone dreams of getting a visa and leaving Morocco, but you're still tied to Mummy's apron strings? You have no idea how lucky you are.' For children like her – the children of the bourgeoisie – everything was prepared in advance, laid out like a train track. But the problem with being on a train was that it went so fast that you didn't even have time to admire the passing landscape.

The computer room at Lycée Descartes had been named after a boy killed by skinheads while he was studying in Eastern Europe. Mia imagined that this could happen to her too. She would be easy enough to spot, with her African features, her frizzy hair, and that surname – Daoud. They would chase her, throw her off a bridge, hold her to the ground and slice her mouth wide open, give her a big smile. That big Arab smile. What did she know of France? In Mathilde's bedroom there was a large, gold-framed black-and-white portrait hung to the right of the bed. Georges and Anne Meyer. Her great-grandparents. Their blood ran through her veins – they were the reason she had a French passport – but she looked nothing like them. If they could see her now, would they recognise her or would they call her a filthy immigrant, Arab scum? She tried to convince herself that it wouldn't be so different, that she would have no trouble finding her place there. She spoke the language, after all, and she knew the codes, the customs. And then there was Paris! Even though she had only visited the city twice, on brief holidays, she felt as if she knew that city as well as she knew her own body. The Saccard mansion in Parc Monceau. The cafés of the Goutte d'Or, where Gervaise grew addicted to absinthe. Aurélien's apartment from Aragon's novel. Then suddenly panic gripped her. Did modern France really have anything to do with Zola, Balzac or Aragon? Besides, in these novels – novels that she loved as much as any books she'd ever read, and which she'd already packed in her suitcase – she had never come across a girl like her. If she did not exist in their books, could she exist in real life?

One afternoon, Mia was lying on the terrace, listening to her Walkman. She didn't hear her father approach. He put his hand on her shoulder and she jumped. He signalled for her to take off her headphones.

'What's that song that you keep listening to all the time?'

'"Losing My Religion".'

His face was terrifying. His eyes were red, with dark rings beneath them, and he stank of alcohol. She could tell he wanted to talk, to tell her something, but Mia had already put her headphones back on and was nodding along to the beat.

Mehdi had been watching her for weeks. The tougher she appeared, the more easily he could see that she was suffering. The more she shone at school and the more muscular her body became, the more he feared she was going to collapse. His daughter with her porcelain heart. Soon she would be gone, like a leaf taken by the wind. Yes, Mia was going to leave. Life with her had gone by so quickly, he'd hardly noticed a thing. If he were put on trial as a father now, he would plead guilty – of being absent, cold, clumsy. Aïcha had taken care of everything. She had gone to Paris three times to visit apartments, each one darker and less salubrious than the last. The landlords had been suspicious. 'But this payslip is in dinars?' 'Listen, nothing against you, but we had a very bad experience with some Algerians.' In the end she'd found a first-floor studio flat near the Tolbiac metro station. Mehdi thought about his daughter, so far away, in that city of endless winter. What would become of her there? Would she turn into a Frenchwoman? He doubted it. He felt sure it wasn't so easy to become French. He would have to harden his heart, to brace himself for the moment when he took her in his arms and said goodbye. He must not let himself succumb to sadness. Nobody would be surprised if Aïcha started crying. All mothers weep when their children leave. But it's different for fathers.

He'd been avoiding the house for weeks, and when he was there he would grow irritated over the slightest thing, speak through gritted teeth. Aïcha had asked him if he was worried about something at work, and he'd told her in a harsh voice to stop asking questions. 'The less you know, the better for you.' Tourism in Morocco had collapsed after the Gulf War. His company's clients had declared bankruptcy one after another, and CCM's debts had grown ever bigger. And then there had been 'The Domain', a huge tourism project that the palace had assigned to him. He'd been told that a Gulf prince had his eye on part of the land, where he intended to have a house built. 'Impossible,' Mehdi had replied coldly, and he'd written a blunt, rational letter to this prince, explaining that royal blood did not give him the ability to do anything he wanted and that he would simply have to give up his dream.

He undressed and got into the shower, and while the hot water ran down his back Mehdi had a vague, distant memory of his father. Mohamed Daoud, in his white djellaba. One day – he must have been about twelve – his father had taken him aside and talked to him about life. You must fear God. Be a good person. Think of others. Had Mehdi ever talked about these things with his daughters? Had he taught them about generosity and consideration? It was time he had a conversation with Mia, father to daughter. He must do his duty: supply her with the weapons she would need to lead her life. He did not want to be comforting or condescending. He must avoid clichés and moralising. His throat tightened and he felt like crying because he knew that he was incapable of following his own advice.

He would talk to her about integrity, about living an intense life, without compromise. He would hide from her his own failures, his doubts. He would resist the desire to make her his confidante so that he could remain, for a little while longer, her hero. He had to prove to her that he respected her, that he held her in high regard. 'I'm proud of you.' He could say that. Yes, he was proud of her – of her intelligence, her culture, of her own pride. He thought about the words that her Year 5 teacher had used – 'Mia will go far' – and suddenly he was struck by the double meaning of that phrase. Struck by it as if by a fist in the stomach. Was distance the condition of success? Aïcha had taken charge of all the practical advice: don't get in a car with someone who's been drinking; don't let others talk you into anything; stay away from drugs. With Mia, there was no need to emphasise the risks of pregnancy or the dangers of falling in love with a man.

Mehdi dried himself, put on a clean T-shirt and a pair of canvas trousers, then rummaged in his bag for the book he had bought for his daughter. He touched the cover reverently and sat down on the bed. Yes, he had to be firm. He could show no sign of weakness. He would suggest to Mia that they go for a walk. He would put his hand on her shoulder, then smile at her and – in his gentlest voice – explain that this was an important step for her, the kind of step that determines an entire life. And, without crying – yes, without shedding a single tear – he would tell her that she must never return. 'Mia, go away and don't come back.' He would tell her about Cortés, the conquistador, who – when he reached the Bay of San Juan – decided to burn all his ships to eliminate the temptation of turning back. 'Swim as far as you can, without worrying about saving your strength for the return journey. I saw it all, you know. I understand. What the others are doing to you, the things they'll say about you. My girl, you must think like a fugitive, because it is always homesickness that is the undoing of a criminal on the run. A birthday, a funeral or just the lure of the past. Homesickness brings them back and they regret it forever after. Don't go back to Ithaca, but find yourself an island like the ones where the Lotus-Eaters live, an island that will make you forget to return, that will anaesthetise your desire to go home.' That was what he had done, after all. He would offer her the same destiny – the destiny of a man with no past. 'Of course people will try to persuade you. You'll think that there's something you should be doing here, that you could be useful to your homeland. But don't believe it. Put wax in your ears, cling to the mast and remember what I've told you. Don't come back. All this rubbish about roots, it's just a way of trying to nail your feet to the ground. So who cares about the past, or home, or objects, or memories. Set fire to your old life and take the fire with you. This is not *au revoir*, my darling, it is *adieu*. I'm pushing you off the cliff. I will let go of the rope and watch you swim. My love, never compromise with freedom. And beware the warmth of home.'

And then he would hand her the book. She would put the wrapped gift in her lap. 'Thank you, Daddy.' Slowly, she would tear the paper off it: *Life Is Elsewhere*.

'You'll like Kundera, I know you will.'

Mia discovered the grey life. Walking along the banks of the Seine in the saddest and most beautiful city in the world. Opening her eyes to the first glimmers of daylight in that freezing bedroom. It was so hard to wake up, she would sometimes fall asleep in class, head buried in the crook of her elbow. No matter what she did to push it away – making her eyes like saucers, stretching her shoulders – sleep would draw her into its depths. She discovered cold mornings and bad coffee sipped by the condensation-covered window of her little studio flat. Alone. Pasta, every day, alone. The supermarkets where, in the first weeks, she felt a childlike excitement at the sight of all those shelves filled with unknown products. She could choose anything she wanted – there was nobody to tell her what to eat – and so she filled her trolley with vacuum-packed sausages, chocolate bars, frozen croque-monsieurs and ready-made salads. She lost money and gained weight.

She lived in a dreary apartment in the thirteenth arrondissement. From the kitchen window she could see the glowing neon sign of a Thai restaurant. In October the pavements were covered with damp leaves, and more than once she almost slipped and fell. Then came November, and the autumn vanished, making way for an endless winter. The days grew shorter and when Mia took the bus in the morning to the Latin Quarter, the sky was still dark. The other passengers all looked tired and sad, but they were willing to fight for a seat. Mia mostly travelled standing up. There was nothing but rain and grey skies, and she could feel the cold seeping through her layers of clothing, chilling her bones, crushing her with fatigue. She walked, hands in the pockets of her brown parka, shoulders hunched, all her muscles tensed. The cold made her melancholy and she feared that this season would last forever, that the light would never return, that her bones would never thaw. She went from her flat to the Lycée Henri IV, then from the prep school to her flat, always following the same itinerary, sitting on the frozen bench at the bus stop and praying that the bus would come as soon as possible, that it would not be too crowded. The few times when she went for a walk, she kept a small map of Paris with a blue cover stuffed deep in her pocket because she was ashamed to look at it in full view of other people.

Paris smelled different to Rabat. There was the smell of cheap, stale wine in the lobby of her apartment building, where a tramp slept every night, a tramp who called her 'Princess'. There was the smell of bakeries, and the smell of cafés too – spilled beer and damp cloths. And then there was the pungent, sickening odour of metro stations. Mia was afraid of the metro and could never remember the numbers of the lines. She was always impressed by the casual way her Parisian classmates would say things like: 'You take the 5 and change at Bastille.' She pictured herself being mugged in those long dark corridors, the thief taking her backpack and with it her class folders, her purse, the keys to her flat. On one of the rare occasions that she rode the famous line 5, she was surprised to find that most of the passengers were Black or North African. They were the ones she feared.

There were about sixty students at Lycée Henri IV preparing for the entrance exams to business schools. Most of them were Parisians, from the best schools – Lycée Carnot, Lycée Fénelon, Lycée Condorcet – or provincials who had studied at the best schools outside of Paris, such as Lycée Kléber in Strasbourg or Lycée Fermat in Toulouse. Mia was the only Moroccan in her class. Most Moroccan students took the science programme and they had a reputation for being brilliant at mathematics. The only foreigners in her class were an Algerian girl, who had escaped the war in Blida, and a girl from Djibouti whose golden skin turned gradually greyer as the winter wore on. All the students cared about were their classes and their results. Mia could sense them sizing each other up, trying to trap each other. In late September she was given her first history grade. 'Three out of twenty, Mademoiselle Daoud. You didn't answer the question.' She was struggling in economics too, but was shining in mathematics and philosophy. In late November the girl from Djibouti gave up. She was depressed and she missed her homeland. She kept saying, 'I'm not going to make it', and nobody contradicted her. Students would often burst into tears after a test. There were rumours about a girl from the first-year literature class who had attempted suicide after being publicly humiliated by her Latin teacher. The teachers kept telling them they were the crème de la crème, the future elite of this country. They told them how lucky they were while cruelly tormenting them. Mia fought against the sadness that was wrapping itself around her heart and against the desire to weep that sometimes overcame her, especially in the evening or early in the morning. Her life seemed to have been stripped of all meaning, and she thought how ridiculous it was that she had ever imagined a great destiny for herself. No, there was no greatness. Everything about her life was small, petty, cramped, stunted. Before going back to her apartment, she would sometimes buy soup from the Chinaman. People talked like that here. The Chinaman. The Arab on the corner. She always ordered the same thing: soup with ravioli and coriander, and the Chinaman, despite seeing her several times a week, never smiled at her or showed the slightest sign of recognition. Mia felt lonely, so lonely she could scream, and on Sundays she would go to a pay phone on Rue de Tolbiac and use a phone card to call her parents. It was usually Fatima who answered. The maid would whoop with joy when she heard Mia's voice, but Mia – watching the balance on the card quickly diminish – would barely answer her questions ('Aren't you cold?'; 'Is it true that Frenchwomen walk around half-naked?'), instead begging her to go and fetch Aïcha. Mia had to force herself not to cry when she heard her mother's gentle voice. She felt an urge to complain – about the cold, her loneliness, her struggles with the classwork, the inhospitable nature of Paris – but she worried that she would make her mother sad or, even worse, hear her say that she should be brave and not expect special treatment. So Mia masked her emotions and reassured her mother. Yes, I'm eating well. Yes, my classmates are nice and I'm working very hard. Yes, I know how lucky I am to live in Paris.

On those nights, she felt her homesickness even more intensely than usual. She thought about the light in Rabat, about the perfect blue skies that hung over even the coldest winter days, about the springtime that would come so quickly, making the flamevines on the garden wall bloom bright orange.

She missed her sister more than she would ever have imagined, and the same was true for her friend Hakim, who had stayed behind in Rabat to study medicine. Her flat was a mess, with piles of dirty laundry all over the floor, and there was a suspicious smell in the kitchen whose source she couldn't track down. She daydreamed of her mother's cooking, of baskets filled with oranges and bouquets of mint. She missed Friday's couscous and the scent of clean sheets and clothes that had dried in the sun. She couldn't take any more of the McDonald's on Rue Soufflot, or cheese-and-ham crêpes, or the rubbery steamed ravioli that she bought from Asian delis. She would have given anything to be back there, with her friends, joking around in Darija, sitting in a beach hut, drinking beer and smoking joints while staring out to sea. That winter, she realised for the first time how much she loved the ability of Moroccans to laugh at anything, the way people were united by their sense of humour. She saw again the toothless smile of the kebab vendor on Avenue de Témara, she heard Fatima's throaty laughter in the kitchen. And she remembered the word 'hanane' – tenderness. She'd had to go away to understand it. Her father had told her: to see an island, you first have to leave it.

In Paris, Mia's classmates were snobbish and over-serious. She felt uncomfortable around them, misunderstood, and she envied the complicity that they seemed to share. They made jokes that she didn't understand and she suspected that they were doing it on purpose, deliberately making references that she couldn't possibly get. Television shows, hip comedians, brands she'd never heard of. She got annoyed when they went on about the comic Smaïn, whom they seemed to assume she would like just because he was of Algerian descent. Above all, Mia thought they were stingy and lacked class. Just before the All Saints holiday, a small girl called Sonia invited a few students to dinner at her apartment. That night, Mia wore her best blouse, which she ironed on the kitchen countertop, and a midnight-blue velvet jacket. She sprayed herself with perfume – a vial of Rocabar that her mother had given her as a leaving present – and, despite her tight budget, bought a bouquet of red roses. Sonia opened the door to her. She was barefoot and wearing the same yellow-and-brown-striped sirwal trousers that she wore all the time. The girl grabbed the bouquet and Mia followed her into the kitchen, where the others were sitting around a wooden table. 'You look very fancy,' said Clémence, a pretty blonde girl who always got the best grades in the class without appearing to make any effort.

'Oh, well, I've just come from another party,' said Mia, suddenly feeling very hot in her velvet jacket.

Sonia ordered some pizzas by phone and sent Jean-Baptiste and Florian to pick them up. 'Oh, and get a bottle of wine from the Arab on the corner. The one on Rue des Écoles, I mean. The other one's a thief. Last time he sold me a carton of orange juice that was past its sell-by date.'

That night, they drank cheap wine, ate pizza and talked about the philosophy teacher who had made them work for more than a month on the first three pages of the *Nicomachean Ethics*.

'He's taking the piss,' repeated Jean-Baptiste.

'The problem is that he doesn't take business students seriously,' said Sonia. 'All he cares about are his lit students.'

At midnight, everyone stood up. They didn't want to miss the last metro. Sonia opened a drawer, took out a pen and made a quick calculation on the back of the pizza box.

'So, with the wine, that's twenty francs each.'

The following Sunday, Mia described this dinner party to Aïcha. 'Can you believe it? They made me pay for what I ate.' She was on holiday and nobody had asked her if she had plans or if her parents were coming to visit her. Mia tried to convince herself that it didn't matter, that she would be better off having time to revise anyway, but her loneliness weighed on her and made her feel ashamed. She was ashamed of her boredom, of all the weekends when she had nothing to do with her time but practise equations and write book synopses. At the end of November strings of lights appeared, covering the trees on Boulevard Saint-Michel. Father Christmases gleamed inside shop windows and the city seemed more hostile than ever. As she walked, she watched other people – people laughing at tables in restaurants, people shopping for clothes in expensive boutiques. These other people who ran up the stairs in metro stations or ran after departing buses because their friends were expecting them and they were going to be late. These other people with lives. In Paris, she had the feeling that even the houses looked down on her or silently mocked her. The apartment buildings had eyes that watched her coldly. Everywhere you went, you needed an entry code to get inside.

Days passed. Classes. Dinners spent revising. The rigid routine that she imposed on herself. What time to wake up, which subjects to study, how long for each course, how long in the bathroom, how many hours of sleep. There was something about this city that resisted all her efforts to belong, as though Paris was surrounded by a fine layer of glass or plastic, invisible at first, against which all those who tried to enter banged their heads. Mia knocked on this barrier with her fist, then pretended she didn't care. She pretended that she didn't want to be part of this world of Claires, Julies, Louises, Thomases and Roberts. This world of country houses in Chartres or Chantilly. The roast chicken served for Sunday lunch. Afternoons at the cinema. Shared memories: 'The first time I went to the Comédie-Française? I must have been about twelve.' This world of television shows she didn't like and comedians who didn't make her laugh. This world where people made jokes about Omar Raddad*, drank coffee out of bowls, listened to the radio in the morning. This world of so many different cheeses whose names she was expected to remember. This world of aperitifs and skiing holidays, of Patrick Bruel and Jean-Jacques Goldman, of junkies in the Gare du Nord and salmon tagliatelle.

During the third term, Mia grew close to Fatna, the Algerian girl. She was very beautiful, with long, straight, dark-brown hair and prominent cheekbones. Her cheeks were hollowed out, as if someone had removed all her teeth. One afternoon in February, Mia found her sitting on the bench at the bus stop and started a conversation.

'So you live in the thirteenth too?'

'Yes, I'm in student housing,' replied Fatna. 'I usually walk home but I'm too tired today. I haven't slept for the past two nights.'

---

* Omar Raddad, an illiterate immigrant from Morocco who worked as a gardener for the wealthy widow Ghislaine Marchal, was arrested for her murder in 1991 and later sentenced to eighteen years in prison. He always maintained his innocence, and the case was highly controversial in France.

'Because of the mock exams? Yeah, I'm stressed out too. I get a stomach ache just thinking about them.'

Fatna smiled but said nothing. Later, Mia would discover that it had not been the mock exams preventing her from falling asleep. At night, Fatna would stare at the blue ceiling and think about her parents in Blida. She knew that, if she closed her eyes, her dreams would be filled with horrific images of massacres. She bought the newspapers every day, not because her economics teacher told her to, but because she was desperate to find out what was happening back in Algeria. She would read the news at lunch and during every break between classes. One morning she read *Libération* on the bus and by the time she got to the classroom her face was covered in black stains. The newspaper ink had run onto her fingers.

Where Fatna was discreet and never mentioned her family or her homeland, Mia was the complete opposite: she talked about Morocco all the time. Whenever she was in a conversation with someone, she would find a way to express the fact that she was not from around here. She was Moroccan, she had spent her whole life there. She was not like the Beurs*. Mia would describe her house, with its luxuriant garden and the pool where she would sometimes swim at lunchtime, the chauffeur who picked her up from school every day. Fatna looked at her strangely when she talked like this. She seemed almost to pity Mia.

In fact, Fatna hated the way her friend tried to sell Morocco as a haven of peace, justice and tolerance. What did she expect to happen? Did she think, just because she was a bourgeois Arab, that people would respect her?

* Second-generation French Moroccans.

Mia was trying to defeat a much stronger enemy. She was attempting, all on her own, to restore the good image of Arabs in France. No, Mia would not lower herself, like those sell-out North African comedians, to tell jokes about how Arabs were thieves who would all rot in prison. Although she did occasionally mimic the Moroccan accent, once she discovered that she could make people laugh this way, or – even better – her grandmother's Alsatian accent when she spoke Arabic. Mia praised Hassan II as a brilliant politician, capable of expressing himself more articulately in French than any Frenchman. She became very angry when her classmates made remarks about glaring inequalities, women being harassed in the streets of Marrakech's medina, or Muslim obscurantism. And especially when they quoted what the king of Morocco had said in a television interview – that 'Moroccans in France will never make good French people', a line that had delighted the far right. 'You don't know anything about it!' Mia would say when anyone challenged her.

She wanted to make people understand that she had somewhere to return to, but the truth was that she was afraid. Afraid of changing. Afraid of forgetting – even betraying – her roots. Afraid of becoming like them. Afraid that the Mia of before would be replaced by another Mia. She sensed that to assimilate meant to dissolve yourself, to erase the past. That the price of integration was a loss of integrity. She was like the Little Mermaid: if she wanted legs, if she wished to walk in the world of these handsome, wonderful human beings, she would have to pay the price. But she couldn't accept the idea of losing her voice.

*

Sometimes Mia and Fatna would eat lunch at the Lebanese place on Rue Blainville or go for a drink at the Pub Saint-Hilaire on Montagne Sainte-Geneviève. Mia liked playing pool there, even though the baize on the table smelled of all the beers that had been spilled on it. The bathroom walls were covered with posters on how to prevent AIDS. One night, Fatna agreed to play a game with her.

'Where did you learn to play?' Mia asked. 'You're not as bad as I expected.'

'My father taught me.'

'What does he do, your father?'

'He's a teacher, like my mother. He teaches history and she teaches law.'

'Were you at a French lycée too?'

'No, I was in a normal school.' Fatna leaned over her cue, closed one eye and missed her shot. 'Your turn.'

Mia wanted to ask her more questions, but Fatna's gentle exterior hid an inner firmness that made it impossible to keep digging. She would not talk about the war or the beauty of Algeria, would not complain about the tough new visa policy implemented by the minister of the interior, Charles Pasqua. She refused to play Mia's little games, like talking Arabic in front of French people or comparing their homelands.

'Don't take this the wrong way,' said Mia one day in a bantering tone, 'but I think everyone knows that Morocco's cuisine is the most refined in North Africa.'

With a tight smile, Fatna replied: 'If you say so.'

In spring the days grew longer again, and one afternoon Mia and Fatna decided to sit on the banks of the Seine to revise for their mock exams. They bought goat's cheese paninis, over which the Indian vendor poured basil olive oil, and they walked under the budding trees. For two hours they took turns questioning each other by the riverside. Then they grew weary of working and they began to look around. They observed couples lying on the ground or leaning against walls, tongues probing as they kissed, hands sliding under blouses. They envied the students who had improvised a picnic with some packets of crisps and a box of rosé. Mia rolled a joint with weed she'd bought from a dealer in Les Olympiades, but Fatna refused to take a drag. She was cold, so Mia handed her the Adidas tracksuit top she was wearing, with blue and white stripes on the shoulders. Night was slowly falling, as if the blue of the sky was being absorbed by the sparkling Seine. Two men passed close by. They had been drinking and one of them – a tall, skinny guy with curly hair and low-cut jeans – turned around several times. At first Mia thought it was because of her joint. Then she imagined that they were going to ask for money or maybe even steal some.

'Let's go,' she said to Fatna, and as they packed up their belongings the tall one came over.

'All right, lezzies, off to lick each other out, are you?' He burst out laughing, and so did his friend.

Mia, in a sudden panic, ran away. Behind her, Fatna yelled: 'Wait!' But Mia was already sprinting up the stairs to the bridge. That was where Fatna caught up with her. She was holding Mia's backpack. 'Don't worry about it, they're just morons. There's no need to be scared.'

Mia refused to talk about it. She took her bag and headed to the metro station. She felt ashamed. Ashamed not of what she was, but of the fear that had overwhelmed her. Fatna had seen her flee like a coward, like a hunted animal. That night, in the corridors of the metro, she kept close to the walls, kept her eyes on her shoes. She wished people would mistake her for a boy, as often happened – 'Excuse me, young man. Oh, sorry, young lady.' In this city, she didn't know how to tell her allies apart from her enemies, and she swore to herself that she would stay on her guard, that she would not forget the fact that, only ten years ago, the police used to raid bars in the Marais. Here, too, God did not love 'people like that'. Here, too, they had to make do with the Days of Desperation organised by ACT UP and with Romane Bohringer's tears when she accepted her César Award. People like me, Mia reminded herself, are never happy.

June 1993

Hi Mia,

I hope you're well. I wanted to thank you for the VHS tapes you gave Mum. I watched the music videos and the episodes of *Beverly Hills* too. Could you record the rest of it for me? I love Dylan and I hate that bitch Kelly. She reminds me of the blonde girl in my class last year. God, she was a total pain in the arse. Nothing new here. Granny came to the house last weekend. She took me to Marjane, the new shopping centre, and she wanted to buy everything. There were loads of people there, whole families walking around looking in shop windows, and Granny filled her trolley and she looked so happy. She talked to a woman in a grey veil and a baggy dress. She asked her: 'Why do you wear this stuff?' I was so embarrassed, and a bit scared too because the woman got angry and started yelling insults at Granny. She called her a filthy Christian and told her to mind her own business. On Sunday, as a treat, she took me to the McDonald's in Casablanca. Like she says, the best stuff is always in Casa. To be honest, though, I didn't like it that much. The burgers were cold and the fries weren't as good as Fatima's.

On Saturday, I invited some friends to the house but when they got here I didn't really know what to do with them. I just felt like staying in my room or having a snack while I watched a film. I asked Mum if we could call their parents and ask them to pick them up. But you know what she's like – she said: 'That kind of thing is just not done.' Oh yeah, and Grandad said something that made me think of you. 'Nothing grows in the shade of a big tree.'

Love,

Inès

PS: Not sure what to say about Dad. Nobody told me anything. All I know is that he came home three weeks ago and he hasn't gone out again since.

INTERMISSION

I landed at the airport in Fes in late August 2022. When I showed my passport to the border guard, he asked me what I did for a living.

'Writer.'

'Journalist?'

'No, writer.'

'And what do you write?'

'Detective novels.'

I walked to the car park. A warm wind enveloped me. The air was full of dust stirred up by cars and mopeds, and I breathed it in deeply. Three men came towards me. 'Big taxi.' They were aggressive. They shoved each other, argued and shouted numbers at me in Arabic that I wasn't sure I fully understood. I didn't want them to know that I always mix up sixteen and sixty, that I can't tell the difference between a hundred and a thousand. I acted annoyed, treating them like little boys whose antics I found boring, then chose the quietest, least insistent one. I told him where I was going. 'The Belhaj farm, on the Route de Meknes.'

He opened the back door of the old white Mercedes for me. I got in and he just stood there.

'What are we waiting for?'

'Other customers.'

I told him I didn't want to share my ride with anyone else

and that I would pay him extra to go on my own. He cleared his throat, then spat on the ground. 'As you like, my girl, as you like.' He looked pleased, like a man who'd caught a big fish. A woman who'd flown in from France, her pockets full of euros. He told me to make myself comfortable. 'You can smoke if you like.' I lit a cigarette as he merged onto the motorway. I didn't really feel like smoking, though. I felt nauseated. I leaned my head against the seat-back, and through the window I saw bay trees shaking in the wind, their branches covered with white flowers. The driver was talkative. He told me he came from Errachidia but that he had settled in this region because of his wife. Life was hard here, he said. They didn't have enough money. And then, in an overexcited voice, he added something I didn't understand. I caught the words 'buying' and 'difficult', but the full meaning escaped me. He turned to face me. I wanted to tell him to keep his eyes on the road, but I could sense that he was waiting for me to agree with him. So I muttered, 'Yeah, you're right', and he slapped the steering wheel triumphantly. I didn't say anything else, though, and I could tell that he was disappointed. My Arabic was like a child's. I had learned it from Fatima. It was the language of someone who wants something to eat or drink and doesn't want to wait. The language of someone whose wishes are commands.

A Taylor Swift song came on the radio. The driver didn't know the words but he nodded along with the beat. There's a motorway going all the way to the farm now. We used to dream of that when we were young and the bumpy track would make us throw up on Dad's brown buckskin seats. A few feet before the exit that leads to the farm, they've built a huge shopping centre. Women with veiled faces pushed trolleys through the car park. Up ahead, I recognised the driveway lined with cypress trees and I pointed the way to the house. As we were getting closer, I spotted some huge blue plastic water slides in the distance and a giant sign spelling out 'AQUALAND'.

An old man was sitting next to the gate marked 'DOMAINE BELHAJ'. I couldn't remember his name, but I knew he was the one who used to take Inès and me on donkey rides in the orange orchard. The one who wept like a child in the pickup truck where Mathilde's body was laid out. The one who found the priest from Benin who agreed to pray beside the imam over my grandmother's grave. I lowered the window. I explained who I was. I apologised for not giving them advance warning. I should have called. He took off his cap and scratched the back of his neck. He didn't recognise me and that seemed to bother him. I paid the taxi driver and walked, behind the old man, along the path that led to the house. He introduced himself – 'Tibari' – and explained that he was the foreman. He was keeping the farm running, and we passed greenhouses where women were crouched, planting seedlings in the earth. He supervised the olive and grape harvests, but he had not been inside the house for a long time. 'Last year, rats gnawed through the pipes and they got into the west wing. They ate the carpets, the curtains. But it could have been worse. I brought some guys over and we killed them all, one by one. They were massive – like *this* big!' I shuddered. I felt ashamed of myself, of this stupid idea. What was I doing here? How had I ever thought I might live here, sleep here, in this remote house? Now I was caught in my own trap. I'd thought I was coming home, but in reality I was just a foreign visitor.

The foreman kept showing me the way, and I wanted to tell him that I already knew it because I used to play here, under this tall, ivy-covered palm tree, listening out for the sound of the generator. He stopped in front of the frosted-glass door and I spotted the doorbell, so high up that Mathilde and I were the only ones who could ring it. Even when Amine and Inès stood on tiptoe it was beyond their reach. Tibari moved around, opening shutters and windows. He seemed ill at ease, as if I was going to stay in his house and I hadn't given him time to prepare things. I wished he would leave. I wanted to be alone to admire an old portrait of Amine taken in front of his olive trees and the agronomy plaques in golden frames that were hung on the wall. I climbed the steps and went into the living room.

It's difficult to believe, difficult to imagine, and yet it's true: nothing has changed. The house is like a sarcophagus, like a place in a fairy tale where a spell has stopped time. My childhood, and all these past lives, are preserved here like something from Pompeii: objects covered in dust and ashes, a whole existence reduced to a fossilised state. In the bathroom off the entrance hall, by the side of the sink, there's a bar of soap, cracked and mouldy. Mathilde's dressing gown still hangs behind the door. I open the cupboard – the one full of special treats that my grandmother always kept locked, the key hidden in her bra. Tins of beans and cans of fizzy drinks have exploded, spreading their contents all over the shelves. The Alsatian plates are still in their place on the dresser. The white cups, the ones decorated with orange flowers, are on the table. I think about Pip's arrival at Satis House. About poor Miss Havisham in her yellowed lace.

It is hard to believe that there was ever life here. Hard to remember that I used to sleep on the tiled floor as a child, to cool myself off in the afternoon heat. This living room once echoed with shouting voices. Through that door, we would bring in the gigantic Christmas trees that Mathilde, even in her dotage, would decorate with childlike glee. Little golden angels. Silver birds that she would attach to the branches with clothes pegs. Arguments once raged around this table, where the dinners always went on too long and where men grew infuriated by their children's insolence. I look at the crumbling walls, the empty swimming pool, the burned grass, and I see, as if superimposed over these images, the house as it was before. Behind this silence, I hear the sound of conversation. There is what I see and what I imagine, what I remember and what I observe, and it all blurs together until I can no longer trace the border between past and present, between truth and invention.

That night, I couldn't sleep. I went to my grandmother's bedroom, and I lay on her bed and stared for hours at the portrait of Georges and Anne Meyer. I thought about my father. Did he actually speak to me before my departure? Did he tell me not to come back? I do not have any precise memory of a conversation, but I think, yes, I think that's what he said to me. Don't come back. If you return, you'll get in trouble. He said something about me being too free or talking too much. Something about me not being made for my own country. One thing's for sure: he wanted me to write.

A few years ago, I tried to write about him. I tried to get hold of documents, but they were nowhere to be found. I had taken notes after a conversation with my mother, but I couldn't find them in any of my notebooks. I leafed through them, page after page, but all I saw were invented stories, characters that I had created and almost instantly doomed. There were letters too, letters that my father received in prison but which had been lost. I couldn't have dreamed those letters. All these documents existed and now they are conspiring against me. They are vanishing to drive me mad, to stop me giving this story a sense of reality. Something is seeking to elude me. On the other hand, I know what doesn't exist. I have no copy of my father's handwriting. He never wrote to me. Not even a brief note or a birthday card. It wasn't me who lost these notes – it was he who never wrote them. There are also no photographs of my grandparents, Farida and Mohamed. It's as if my father gave birth to himself, the first of his line. I have never seen a photo of him as a child.

I did not bring any books with me. I don't read any more. I don't write any more either. It has been weeks since I turned on my computer. I am writing these words in one of my old notebooks. There's a red one, a blue one, an aqua one. I cling to them, and to the hope that they will help me reconstruct the course of events, that they are the tools I will need to be an archaeologist of my own past. In these notebooks I mentioned names that mean nothing to me now, events of which I have not the slightest memory. Obviously, this isn't helped by the drugs or the alcohol. Yes, we laugh, we talk a lot, we dance and we do stupid things. Stupid things that make us ashamed, and that is why we forget them. So we don't have to drag around this cortège of shame, so we don't have to carry the heavy burden of clumsily chosen words, sad gestures. Are people who forget still alive? What happens to you when you lose your memory? Your life before exists like the images of a film, flashing by without anyone knowing whose story this is. Conversations are inaudible, or just meaningless noise. My body dives then floats in the icy water. My body which I am starving, and I am happy because I feel almost nothing. I have disappeared. I have lost track of myself and, when I look back, I see only a valley of mist. You might think that, by writing, I have cleansed the sky, arranged my memories, brought order to the past. You might think that I have let light into my soul. But the opposite is true. I feel like giving it all up. I have started to hate them, these books that have kept me at a distance from life. From love. That have walled me up in words. The books that I have read, in which my father wrote his initials – M.D., the same as mine. And the other books, mine, the ones I wrote. My books are crushing me, suffocating me. They are strangers to me. Sometimes I have the feeling that they are like children – unknown children with pale faces and wide eyes. 'Take them, they're yours,' someone will say, pushing these children towards me. 'You're their mother, you must take care of them.' But I want to abandon them in the middle of a forest and run for my life, as fast and as far as I can.

And yet it is my books that have set me on his trail. Several times people have come to me during literary conferences or bookshop signings, strangers wanting to talk to me about my father. One man had known him in the 1950s in Fes, and in the letter he passed to me across the table of a bookshop in Strasbourg he told me about the afternoons he used to spend with my father at his family home. A home that I have never seen. Once, someone left an envelope beside me. I didn't see the person's face, because I was leaning over a book at the time, signing my name. Inside the envelope was a photograph of Mehdi, sitting behind a large wooden desk. He, too, was leaning over something. A file of some kind. And then there was that woman who was waiting for me in the street one day. She put her hand on my arm and told me that, just like my father, she had lived above the Rex cinema, in an apartment whose bathroom overlooked the big screen. 'Incredible, isn't it?' And yet I felt sure I had invented that apartment.

One night in May 1993, my father came home and said: 'There, it's done.' The kind of thing a paid assassin might say. People had complained to the king about him. I know these people's names, but I will stay silent about that. 'We're having problems with the CCM president.' To which the king replied: 'Get rid of him for me.' It only took a minute or two, the duration of a brief phone call, and then my father packed up his things and went home. The next day, the police came: they confiscated his computer and the phone from his car. Over the years, I have tried to understand. The people I questioned just shook their heads and said mysteriously: 'Someone was settling scores. Your poor father was just the victim.' I tried digging deeper, but all I found were some articles written in Arabic. I didn't understand. Perhaps there was nothing *to* understand. No logic, no rational explanation. Only the arbitrary logic of ambitious courtiers, malicious rumours. He had made enemies, and one day he was removed from power. A few weeks before my father was fired, Pierre Bérégovoy, who had once been prime minister of France, committed suicide, and I remember thinking: Good thing my father doesn't own a revolver.

*

Yesterday I walked in the garden, overgrown with nettles so high that they came up to my waist. The slide under the orange trees has rusted and nothing remains of the geranium beds or the amaryllis-lined paths that Mathilde nurtured so lovingly. I walked to the barn where my mother stored all the crates after she left the house on the Route des Zaërs. She says she has no attachment to any material objects. Like all the other members of this family, she is afraid of heirlooms and belongings. She is wary of anything tied to the past. So she tidied away my childhood in cardboard boxes, my photographs of Marilyn and my corduroy trousers, my cassette tapes and my school exercise books. Tibari opened the door to the barn. It smelled musty in there. Tibari stood in the doorway while I pulled out boxes. I found some books, and just by looking at their covers I could recall the precise moment when I had read them. Of the stories within, though, I had no memory. I took a green dress patterned with birds and one of my father's jackets. As I was digging around at the bottom of a crate, I felt something move. I cried out and the foreman came running. He told me to be careful. Some snakes had made their nests in my mother's old clothes.

II

A grey parrot, sparsely feathered, was walking across the grass. It went past the pool and approached the wall. Its claws gripped the branches of the bougainvillea as it climbed before disappearing between purple leaves. 'We had its wings clipped,' Mehdi had explained to his daughters when he gave them the bird as a present. They had never really taken to the parrot and it lived, free and neglected, in the vast garden. It started squawking 'Fatima!' and the maid, who was the only one to take care of the bird, yelled at it to shut up. Fatima fed it just as she fed the dog that spent its days sleeping outside the kitchen door. She would boil up bones and leftover pasta for Levine, who wolfed them down while grunting with satisfaction.

It was ten in the morning on 14 November 1997. Fatima had to mop the floor before peeling vegetables for lunch. Ten o'clock and the boss was still not up. Fatima went to his bedroom and stood outside the door listening. Perhaps he was getting ready to take his shower? Perhaps he was reading in his bed or performing one of those strange activities that she had never understood. She pressed her ear to the door. Not a sound. She was gripped by anxiety. Never before had Mehdi slept this late. If something had happened to him, she would be the one to get the blame for it. Aïcha would accuse her, the girls would curse her. Everybody would turn against her. She knocked, then waited a few moments, but nothing happened. So she knocked again, harder. She called out: 'Sidi?'

At last she heard Mehdi's voice. 'What is it?'

Fatima bit her lip. He was going to get angry. He was going to reproach her for being overfamiliar, for acting as if she was in her own home. 'They've come to deliver the garden chairs. They have to be paid, Sidi, and Madame didn't leave any money.'

Mehdi came to so suddenly that he didn't know where he was. Once his head had cleared, he looked around for a long time at the enormous bedroom and the glass door opposite the bed. To his left there was a sofa strewn with some of Aïcha's dresses, and to his right the door to the bathroom and the door to the sauna that he had insisted on having built, although he had only used it twice. He knew this room by heart: every knick-knack, every scratch on the drawers of the bedside table. He knew this house so intimately it made him feel sick. He looked for his watch. It was past ten already. He felt ashamed. Until now he had always managed to pretend, to keep up appearances. In four years of unemployment he had always woken at the same time as his wife and his daughter. He would sit with them at the breakfast table, freshly showered and shaved, and behave like a man with a full day's work ahead of him. He would butter their slices of toast even though they never ate more than a single bite. He would make a remark about Inès's clothes: 'That skirt is too short. Go and get changed.' He felt sure she was hiding make-up in her schoolbag. Perhaps she even rolled up the miniskirts that he forbade her to wear and hid them in there too. He knew she called him 'The Ayatollah' behind his back. Aïcha and Inès were always running late, and he would watch them get ready. The two of them spoke a language that he didn't understand, and while they were leaving the house he would listen to the sounds of their voices, like the noises that birds make in the countryside at daybreak. Then Fatima would bring him a Thermos of hot coffee. She knew that Mehdi would stay here for a while, in the beautiful conservatory with its view of the garden. Rather than observing the flowers or the branches of the orange tree sagging under the weight of its fruit, though, he would stare at the trace of lipstick on the edge of Aïcha's cup. And, with his fingertip, wipe it off.

Today, though, he hadn't woken up. And yet nothing in particular had happened last night. He hadn't drunk more than usual, he hadn't gone to bed late. They had watched a film and, as always, Aïcha had fallen asleep in the middle of it. Then she had gone to the children's wing of the house.

'I'm coming!' yelled Mehdi, and he heard Fatima's slippers shuffling along the floor. That idiot's spying on me now, he thought. Who the hell does she think she is, waking me up? I'm not some kid she's being paid to raise. He promised himself he would speak to her about it. That he would tell her to concentrate on her duties – cooking and cleaning, in other words – and not to start knocking on his door when he hadn't summoned her. Mehdi sat up, plumped a cushion behind his back and sat there in bed, staring at the curtains. Will they ever leave me in peace? Couldn't I for once just not get out of bed, not take my shower, not pretend that this endless parade of days has some sort of meaning? He felt like lying on his side, his knees pressed to his chest, and staying like that until his wife came home. He imagined her seeing him in the foetal position and shaking his shoulders. 'What's wrong with you?'

He would respond with silence. Perhaps he would even let himself cry. What was the point in concealing his sadness, after all?

He lifted the blanket and put his feet on the cold floor. A shiver ran down his spine. His body felt weak and it crossed his mind that he might be coming down with something. He had never felt so exhausted in his life. He dragged himself to the bathroom. He took a hot shower and opened his mouth wide under the jet of water. He dried himself without bothering to wipe the steam from the mirrors, without once seeing his reflection, and then he trudged, naked, to the walk-in wardrobe. He took a pair of cords and a polo shirt from one of the shelves. He bent down and grabbed a pair of socks and some clean underwear. When he tried to close the wardrobe door, a tie got stuck in it. There were dozens of ties hanging from hooks on both sides of the wardrobe. The architect who had built this house had told Mehdi that this was the height of fashion in Europe. Mehdi stared at these lengths of fabric, and at first he wanted to laugh, so ridiculous did this accessory appear to him. This pathetic strip of cloth that's tied around the neck like the rope of someone committing suicide. He looked at them, then picked one out. An old-fashioned, rather ugly tie, decorated with colourful flowers. Had he really worn this? He wrapped it around his collar and began to tie it into a knot. 'It's like riding a bike,' he told himself. 'You never forget how.' And his fingers moved. The knot was perfect. He had learned how to do this on his own and would never pass the knowledge on to anyone else. Because his father used to wear djellabas and Mehdi himself had produced only daughters.

If he really tried, would he be able to remember the circumstances in which he had worn this flower-patterned tie? Mehdi never used to pay attention to that kind of thing; it was Aïcha who picked out his clothes for him every morning. She used to lay them on the sofa: a suit, a shirt, a tie. Why had he kept all these ties? He had the feeling now that they were taunting him, laughing at him, just like the pairs of leather shoes that he hadn't worn for years. He was seized by a sudden, uncontrollable rage. He wanted to tear the doors off their hinges, to punch the wall so hard that the whole house collapsed on top of him. He went to the bathroom and grabbed a large pair of pink scissors. One by one, he cut the ties to pieces. Some of them – the crocheted ones, or the ones made of thick wool – were harder to slice through and he ended up ripping them apart with his bare hands. Cloth confetti covered the floor around his feet. Next, he attacked the suit jackets, mutilating them with malicious joy, and then the trousers, sometimes cutting the crotch and sometimes the backside. He could already hear what Aïcha would say when she discovered the massacre. 'We could have given them to people who needed them.' She wouldn't talk about sadness or frustration. She would ignore his anger and treat him like some spoiled, selfish child. Suddenly he found himself naked, in his walk-in wardrobe, the floor carpeted with lacerated clothes. Shit. What would he tell Fatima now? What would she think when she came in to clean his room? He put on a polo shirt. A shapeless old blue polo shirt, way too big for him. He hadn't just lost weight, he thought: he was actually disappearing. His muscles and his bones had melted away. He felt sure he must have shrunk by several inches.

He left the bedroom and, with what remained of his strength and dignity, he went to pay the delivery men. A few days ago, Aïcha had got angry with him because he never helped her, left her to take care of everything. 'The garden chairs are broken. Would it really kill you to go to the shop and buy some new ones?' He sat in his usual spot, on the right-hand corner of the sofa, where the fabric had been stained black by the smoke from his pipes and cigarettes. But what if the delivery men saw him sitting here, doing nothing? What would they think of him? Would they start gossiping with the maids and the caretaker, making fun of this fallen banker, this humiliated member of the bourgeoisie who now spent his life sitting around and waiting? If only there were nobody else to worry about. If only, at his age, he didn't feel such shame at having been caught sleeping late.

After all, he could go out and sit at a café terrace, like most unemployed men did in this country; he could order a ness ness* and read the newspaper while furtively observing the people around him. He could accept the role of Man Who Does Nothing, a useless man whose wife provides for his needs, instead of just sitting here, desperately alone, surrounded by piles of books. Fatima came in to mop the living room floor and the air was filled with the smell of soap and chopped coriander. He could hear the voices of servants and he envied them their busyness. Levine plodded into the room. He nuzzled Mehdi's knees and wagged his tail. People sometimes asked him why he had chosen that name for his dog. 'Levine? What does that mean?'

---

* A Moroccan beverage consisting of half milk and half coffee ('ness ness' means literally 'half-half').

Oh, these days were so long. In the middle of the afternoon, when the maids were napping, he would sometimes think how crazy it was, just waiting like this. Life had nothing else to offer him now. The slow passing of hours was driving him half-mad and he scratched inside himself like a dog digging the ground; he scratched in search of the man he used to be, in search of his last reserves of strength. All this time just to think . . . When he had first been sidelined, he'd found some pathetic little hobbies to pass the time. He'd pursued those hobbies with obsessive passion, diving into them, almost drowning in them, leaving him disgusted with himself. During the months that had followed his dismissal – in May 1993 – he'd become interested in Eastern philosophy. He'd read everything he could find on the history of Tibet, the practice of Zazen, and metempsychosis. He'd ordered a black-and-white leather meditation cushion, and for a while he had woken at dawn every morning to meditate in the garden. He would talk to Aïcha and Inès about the perfection of roses and the soothing rustle of the poplar leaves. Sometimes he almost managed to make them believe that he had reached a state of serenity, that he'd been freed from all the vanities of the earthly world. He no longer seemed to worry about his own fate, about the accusations being made against him – mismanagement, embezzlement of public funds, and other crimes. Then he got bored of meditation. After spending too much time within himself, he ended up feeling only anger. He was overcome by an urge to act, to exist. So he got into photography and had a darkroom built in the garage. He dreamed of that lightless refuge, the excuse it would give him to demand that he not be disturbed. But once all the equipment was in place, once the chemicals had been bought, once the ridiculous sums had been spent on importing the latest cutting-edge technology from France and the United States, he lost interest. To be a photographer he would have had to go outside, through the gates of the property and out into the wider world, like Selim. He would have had to feel a genuine curiosity for others that, at that moment, he totally lacked. What could he say to people in the alleys of the medina who claimed that photographs stole the victims' souls? He thought about photographing his daughter, his wife, himself, but the idea of seeing his face appear, day after day, in the developing baths was terrifying.

He considered painting and had canvases and tubes of gouache delivered. The maids carried away the developing trays and the photographic equipment and in their place they set up an easel. For a few months Mehdi would paint diving suits, stormy skies. He painted his wife's face from memory.

When Inès came home from school she would find him sitting in his studio, his hands smeared with different colours, his features tense with doubt. 'What is it?' she would ask, and the question seemed to annoy her father. 'It's beautiful,' she would say, and that was even worse. Mehdi just scowled and shrugged, as if nobody understood him.

Eventually he went back to the book he had abandoned thirty years earlier. He told himself that everything happened for a reason. His dreams had circled back, like a boomerang, to hit him in the face. But now he had the chance to make them come true. This disappointment was a blessing in disguise, a gift from fate, and soon glory would beckon. The maids carried away the canvases and the easel and in place of the artist's studio they installed a trestle table. Mehdi bought a computer and flew into a rage when Aïcha implied that this was a needless expense. He locked himself away for days, for weeks on end. Nobody was allowed to enter his study and Fatima grew frantic at the idea of all the dust gathering on the shelves. 'At least let me empty the ashtrays and open the window,' she begged him. The desk was covered with sheets on which he had scrawled incomprehensible notes. He chain-smoked as he wrote, and by the end of the day he was disgusted by his own prose and his lungs hurt. He wanted to write with a vengeance, to throw his truth in the face of the world. In front of the computer screen, he dreamed of his future fame. He stole fragments of phrases and metaphors from other books, climbing onto the shoulders of authors he admired in the hope that he would find, there, the strength to become a writer himself. He started a novel, then dreamed of being a poet. He blushed as tears welled in his eyes. He discovered his own fragility, his sentimentality, and he realised just how utterly the life of a courtier had damaged his ability to use words. To rekindle the pure flame that had once burned in his heart he would have had to return to his youth, to his childhood – and that was an impossible journey. He slumped in his chair, threw back his head and remembered the books he had read years before. *Martin Eden. The Horseman on the Roof.* He remembered those heroes who had inspired him, and whom he had betrayed. His lips twitched. The encounter between Angelo and Pauline . . . Had he dreamed this, or had there been a cat that slipped between them? His notes piled up. His head was overflowing with ideas but he couldn't connect them, and on certain days, when he reread what he'd written, he wanted to knock over the trestle table, to break it into pieces and set it on fire.

Then he started drinking. Of all his hobbies, this was the most soothing, the one that felt most right. The only one that offered him any real consolation. He devoted himself methodically to this new occupation. He read all morning – history books, political essays, then the newspaper. At lunch, he allowed himself two glasses of white wine, and the early afternoon was set aside for reading a novel. Around four o'clock, when anxiety gripped him, he poured himself his first whisky in a rounded blue glass. Three ice cubes: he liked the sound they made when they clunked against the glass. Whatever the season, alcohol gave him reasons to be happy. In winter, whisky helped him bear the grey skies and the rain that rippled the surface of the swimming pool. In spring, he reacted with childlike wonder to the return of the birds and he had to restrain himself to avoid calling for someone – anyone – to bear witness to the beauty of nature. He drank slowly while smoking cigarettes, greedily inhaling every drag. Then he waited, feigning calm, to pour himself his second glass. The only thing that bothered him, the thing that undermined his happiness, was Aïcha's disapproval. After all, she was the one who bought the bottles, who paid for the cigarettes, and he felt like a thief caught red-handed whenever he heard Fatima listing what needed to be bought, ending with '. . . and Sidi's bottle'. But sorrow and guilt dissolved in the whisky haze. A thousand different lives became possible, a thousand adventures opened up to him, and he laughed, all alone on his corner of the sofa, with Levine's muzzle resting in his lap. When Inès came back from school, about six in the evening, he would hug her and touch her cheek with his yellowed fingers. He would stare at her, a little glassy-eyed, and ask if she wanted to watch television with him.

During those long, viscous afternoons, he would sometimes daydream. Someone was knocking at the door. The telephone was ringing. The announcement came at last: it was all over, he was free again. Apologies were offered and he accepted them with magnanimity. He was given an ambassadorial post in some obscure African country: not the most glorious of appointments, but better than nothing. Finally the wait was over and he was Somebody again. Yes, a hand had been held out and he had climbed back onto the moving train. Everything would be forgotten now. The betrayals, the bitterness, the regrets. Life would follow its natural course once again. There would be no scores to settle. He had waited so long that he had lost even his appetite for vengeance. Every time the telephone rang, he would remain seated, not wanting to make an exhibition of himself. But he couldn't help calling out: 'Who is it?' It was never for him. He grew angry when Inès hogged the line. He would explode with rage at Mathilde, who always called while they were eating dinner. 'I'm expecting a call,' he would say mysteriously.

He daydreamed about his childhood too. About the sunlight on the terrace of his house in Fes. About the scorpion that had hidden in his brother's shoe and almost stung him. He hadn't seen any of his brothers in years. Where were they now? What were their lives like? Were they happy to know that Mehdi, their remote, arrogant sibling, had fallen from the heights to which he'd climbed? He lay down to take a nap, and when he closed his eyes he saw his father's gentle face, his fingernails covered in white patches, his hands that were always cold, his bluish eyelids. His father, of whom he had been ashamed because he couldn't read, couldn't speak

French. His father, who had teeth missing but who laughed anyway, his mouth wide open, at any stupid little joke. His mother had been right. Farida said that Mehdi had become a stranger in his own land, that he would regret his desire to be like the foreigners. He hadn't invited them to his wedding and he had never shared his success with them. Once, years ago, one of his brothers had come to the house in Rabat and Mehdi had told Fatima to say that he wasn't home. From his bedroom window he had watched his brother standing there on the doorstep, with his pot belly and his moustache, clutching a small old leather bag. Later, he found out that his brother had come to tell him about their father's declining health. Then Mohamed had died of lung cancer and Mehdi had not gone to the funeral. He was on a business trip in London at the time. When he thought about this, it seemed impossible, insane. What kind of man doesn't go to his father's funeral? Maybe he was paying the price for his sins now. Maybe what had happened to him was his punishment for having been a bad son, a selfish and ungrateful son. Once he was drunk, Mehdi imagined he could drive there, now, right away. In three hours, maybe less, he would be in Fes. He would go to the Rex cinema and he would climb the two flights of stairs that led to his old apartment and, inside, nothing would have changed. They would all be there, just the way they used to be. His mother yelling with exasperation. His father sitting on the bench, shrugging as if to apologise for his existence. The air would smell of honey and frying oil and his brothers would come hurtling downstairs, laughing and shouting. The woman next door would bang her hand against the wall. It would be just like the good old days. He was submerged by waves of nostalgia. He poured himself another whisky and held tightly, miserably, to the rounded blue glass.

People didn't come to visit any more. To start with, his friends would stop by on their way back from work, for a drink and a chat. They were worried about him and they would ask questions to which Mehdi would offer cryptic answers. Abdellah came after teaching at the university and vented his anger at this corrupt government and the scheming courtiers who had destroyed Mehdi's career. Two years ago, in December 1995, the minister of the interior, Driss Basri, had launched a clean-up campaign targeting corruption, tax evasion and smuggling. Businessmen, bankers, shopkeepers and bureaucrats were arrested and thrown in prison. The palace wanted to remind this economic elite that no dissidence would be permitted and that it owed its good fortune purely to the goodwill of the inner circle. 'I've heard about executives who have their suitcases packed and ready in their office, just on the off-chance that they're arrested,' said Abdellah. 'Even when they haven't done anything wrong, they know that the government could simply make something up.' This campaign of fear, as people called it, was reminiscent of those ancient harkas when the sultan would mount a horse and ride off to restore order among the rebel tribes. 'They let people get away with it for years. And now they want to make sure that nobody spits in the soup,' Abdellah concluded.

A climate of paranoia took over the capital. The telephone no longer rang and Mehdi realised that, if people had stopped coming to see him, it was not solely out of cowardice or malice. Disgrace had an odour all its own. The others could smell it and they sneaked away, withdrawing into the shadows, without even understanding why at first. They would look contrite and uncomfortable, start lying for no reason. They're covering their backsides, he told himself. They think disgrace is contagious and they're afraid that, if they keep visiting me, they'll be dragged into the chasm of misfortune.

In the evenings, Mehdi waited for Aïcha like a dog for its master. As the time of her return grew closer, he would become agitated, nervous. If she was late, he would summon Inès to the living room. 'What time is it?' Yet he had a watch, and his daughter didn't. He would ask her to call the clinic, and when he found out that his wife had already left he would reassure himself. She'll be home soon. Aïcha, breathing loudly, the smell of outside on her skin. She would come home, bringing with her news of the world, the hum of life, the existence of others, and stories, which these days he encountered only in books. She would come, alive with the scents of the street, full of her patients' chatter, the local gossip. She would honk her car's horn and he would hear the sound of the gate opening, her footsteps inside the house. He would have to accept the fact that she didn't rush to look after him straight away. That she would wash her hands, then put on a sweater and a pair of woollen socks because she always felt cold at home. That she would kiss her daughter and ask about her homework. And that when she'd finally done all these things she would come to him and, no doubt to please him, as an act of tenderness, she would say: 'Guess who I saw in the supermarket today? He sends his greetings. He's thinking of you.' Mehdi would smile. So not everybody had disappeared, after all. Because at night he would start to imagine that, beyond the walls of the house, there no longer existed anything that concerned him. With each passing day, the outside world grew stranger and more hostile. It took on an appearance he had never seen before, its logic became ever more unfathomable. Aïcha told him that life went on – ordinary, stupid, wonderful life. She described the health concerns of women they no longer saw socially but who trusted her and her alone whenever they were unwell.

He was The Man Who Waits. Like a sailor's sweetheart, a soldier's wife, a prison visitor, a mother praying for her son's return, a mistress pining for a letter from her lover. Sometimes it occurred to him that, had he been a woman, this fall from grace would have been less painful. He admired women's capacity to fill their days with a thousand little tasks. If he were a woman, he would go shopping, cook dinner, he would spend long afternoons at the hairdressing salon. He would be fully occupied with a project for renovating the living room. Selma was the only one who dared speak the truth to his face. Aïcha treated him like a breakable object, but Selma showed no tact whatsoever when she came to spend the evening at their house. Instead, she tried to make him move, to go out. 'You don't have any friends left? Well, find some new ones.' She offered to introduce him to people and when he refused she became angry. 'Oh, because the people I know aren't good enough for you, is that it?' One month ago, she had taken him aside. 'Do you remember it will be your wife's birthday soon?' He found it hard to believe, but on 16 November 1997, Aïcha would turn fifty. 'Since you don't have anything better to do, maybe you could organise something for her? You could invite some old friends, family, have a party with music. That's the least you owe her.'

Mia was struggling not to laugh. I saw the way she looked at me, at what I was wearing. 'Interesting jeans,' she said with a slightly raised eyebrow, and I pretended that I wasn't hurt, that I wasn't disappointed. Mia isn't a mean person, though, and she seemed to regret it later. She talked more than usual over dinner, about her dream job in London, she kept mentioning 'the bank' and sprinkling English words throughout her conversation. And then she paid for the meal. It was strange, seeing her take a credit card from her pocket and wave at the Vietnamese waitress. 'I'll take this.' She never carries a handbag, Mia – she keeps her purse in her back pocket and her phone in her jacket. But I didn't say anything about her losing her belongings, she can look after herself now – she's twenty-three, she went to HEC business school, she pays for meals at restaurants, she doesn't need to hear me say stuff like that. I won't wear these jeans again. I bought them this morning, they were a bit expensive, I thought they looked good in the fitting room – different, more modern – and the sales girl winked at me, but that's all part of the trick, getting you to buy their gear. I've heard that the mirrors in those fitting rooms make you look better, slimmer, taller than reality. I don't look the same in this mirror. If I'd seen my reflection in this badly lit bathroom I would never have bought these stupid jeans. Thankfully I insisted on getting a hotel room. Tomorrow I'll go to see Mia's apartment, we'll talk about Inès's arrival, we'll get things organised, but in the meantime I have a room to myself, I can take a bath or watch a film, and it's a shame I'm not hungry because I could have ordered room service. Paris, the streets, the cinema, and no obligation to make conversation. Solitude. I'm getting used to it. Acclimatising myself to the idea. Anyway, it's more or less as if Inès has already left. She was sulking on my birthday, and I could tell that she hadn't been involved in choosing the cake or the candles, I'm not even sure she gave me a present. She can't wait to get away from us. I understand that. But then I'll find myself alone with him. Like before, but not like before, because all this time I've been living my life for the girls. It drives Selma crazy when she hears me talk like this, but it's the truth, and I'm not ashamed of it – I lived for them, for my daughters. Mehdi would never say that. It's not that he loves them less than I do, but men don't say that – that they live for something or someone. They're obsessed by an ambition, an objective, a status they want to achieve, but I've never heard any of them say, 'I lived for my children.' Tomorrow I'll go to see the apartment, I hope it's not bad timing, but my belly isn't swollen and I haven't had cramps, so hopefully it'll be okay. Mehdi couldn't believe it when it happened to me, when I started crying at breakfast and talking about the despair I felt and wanting to jump out of the window. He looked panicked, as though he was about to apologise, to ask my forgiveness for making me unhappy, but I didn't let him speak. I said 'the menopause', and I could tell that he was deeply uncomfortable but also relieved. The menopause, and he was happy because it's the perfect excuse. It suits men to think that we're just having a bad day. She's in a bad mood, poor woman, oh don't worry about her, she's a shrew, an animal. 'Ah, okay,' he said, and he wanted me to spare him the details. Nobody wants to talk about that, including me. What was I thinking, asking Mum about it? I just wanted to know what age she was when it happened to her because that's generally a good indicator, or at least that's what I've heard, but anyway she didn't like my question at all. 'I have no idea.' I don't believe her. I don't see how she could possibly have forgotten. At least I'm pretty sure I won't forget what it's like to sweat from my scalp and to wake up in bed, in the middle of the night, convinced that I must have pissed myself. I thought I'd be relieved – I mean, it's a nightmare, isn't it, the cramps, the pads, the tampons, the sheets of toilet paper folded into eight. That's what I tell my patients when they complain: it must be a relief, no? What was it that teacher in Strasbourg used to say about it? Oh yes, he talked about the critical age. Or the dangerous age, maybe, I can't remember, anyway he said stuff about the melancholy of women who found themselves deprived of a future and of a sense of usefulness. The old women who kept their bad blood inside, they were called witches and they were accused of being venomous towards younger women. Oh, that makes me want to throw up, I really wish I wouldn't think about it, but I can't help it, I see them as soon as I shut my eyes, the two dead flies, yes, those two enormous flies in the old Bartoli woman's chignon. Next time I'll hide, I'll tell her it's impossible, that I can't see her. Doesn't she realise how horrible it is watching her get undressed and spread her legs? She should be in an asylum, with her delusions about being pregnant and her claptrap about happy events. 'I can feel it moving, Doctor. I can feel it.'

And I'm too much of a coward to explain that her womb is arid, that nothing will ever move inside it again, and even if Rachid tells me off, even if the secretaries say that I'm as mad as she is, I can't help feeling sorry for her. Oh, how she yelled! Her howling was almost worse than the dead flies. The way old Madame Bartoli howled when I tried to insert the speculum. *Total fusion of the anterior and posterior vaginal walls at approximately 1cm from entrance. Gynaecological examination impossible.* Mehdi would have said something crude about nuns and broomstick handles, he thinks it's funny to mock virgins and frigid women, he's convinced that lack of sex is the reason why Fatima is so crabby, as if only by fucking us can men put us in a better mood. Earlier, at the pharmacy, there was a boy standing near the condom shelves, he was so handsome, I'm sure he was North African, I looked at him and God knows I imagined it all, the sounds, the movements, the beginnings of an affair, even his awkwardness afterwards, and I felt something. I started to sweat. I was so hot I could have stripped naked in the middle of that shop, but it had nothing to do with desire. Quite the opposite – I was terrified. I was thinking about Bartoli, about vaginas closing up, the onset of necrosis, tissue dying, flesh crumbling, about the lives of the sex-starved who will never know what it's like to feel another's hands on your body. I'll never manage to fall asleep at this rate. I won't get the worst of the symptoms tomorrow, but I'll get them soon, and sometimes I think that it's through a woman's sex organs that death insinuates itself, closing up her vagina as if healing a wound. The origin of the world? Give me a break. I've seen enough to know that the Grim Reaper doesn't kiss his victims on the mouth, but on the lips between their legs.

It's not the origin of the world but the scene of its loss. Oh, come on, Aïcha, don't deepen the wrinkles on your face by frowning. Don't weep hot tears over your withered cheeks. That's the last thing you need. Every morning, putting your palms on the sides of your face and pulling the skin back so you look even close to the way you used to look. Every morning, leaning down and counting the grey hairs and wondering how much longer will this last? How can you be a woman now, at this age? I would like to see what it's like inside. The others are obsessed with their crows' feet, their sagging breasts, the white hairs in their eyebrows. And it's not that I'm indifferent to these things, but I would like to see what a stomach looks like after digesting food for fifty years, and this poor heart of mine that has been beating, beating, beating for so long. Lady Di is dead and I kept my short hair. It suits me now, because old ladies don't let their hair grow long, and oh, now I can see those damned flies again and the greenish hue in old Bartoli's chignon. Mehdi didn't understand why I was sobbing so hard – 'You're right, it's sad, and it's true that she was young and beautiful, but I mean, we didn't know her, did we?' But in truth I wasn't crying for Lady Di, I was crying for my children and I was imagining what it would be like if I wasn't here to live for them any more, and I wanted to know – yes, I desperately yearned to know – what their grief would be like.

In September 1997, the day she started her last year at Lycée Descartes, Inès was handed a form by her teacher. First name, last name, date of birth, number of brothers and sisters at the school, interest in the subject matter, occupation of mother and father. To get on the teacher's good side, Inès claimed to have read lots of books about which she only knew the title and the plot because Mia had told her about them. Oh yes, and she should mention Mia in the section on brothers and sisters – that would prompt the usual remarks: 'If you're as brilliant as your elder sister, we're going to have a very good year.' But the section that most worried her was the one for parents' occupation. For her mother, this was easy. She wrote doctor. For her father, on the other hand, she hesitated. She couldn't leave it blank, because that would only pique her teachers' curiosity. They would think that her father was dead or that he'd abandoned them or, perhaps, that he was unemployed. Although that last option would probably be the least plausible, in their eyes. Because while lots of mothers didn't have a job, her classmates' fathers generally had high-profile careers in industry, government, law or commerce. In the end, Inès decided to leave it blank.

In the weeks that followed, she noticed that her teachers were looking at her with sympathetic expressions, even with a hint of tenderness. They didn't dare say anything, but it was as if they were in on her secret. For weeks she tasted the joy of being an orphan, even while her father was alive, and the comfort of the adult compassion that it provoked. But she couldn't keep playing this game for long. 'Truth will out,' Aïcha always said, and this was the curse of all highly imaginative liars. In October 1997 articles about Mehdi were published in the newspapers. Palace-sponsored journalists accused him, in grotesque language, of having embezzled money intended for the construction of luxury hotels in Portugal to buy jewellery for his daughters. In class, the other students taunted Inès for being a liar and the daughter of a liar.

Inès had always had a tendency to bend the truth, but since starting Lycée Descartes this element of her personality had grown. Or rather, it had become more obvious because she was no longer given the benefit of the doubt by her classmates. Before, she'd been forgiven for her fibs and delusions because she was a child and she was pretty. But now her classmates were angry with her for treating them like imbeciles. Like the time she swore she was going to pose for a Benetton ad with other models from all over the world. Yes, she told everyone, people think Arab girls are beautiful now, even the ones with curly hair and thick eyebrows. Like all the girls of her generation, she was obsessed with supermodels – Claudia, Cindy, Naomi – for whom she nurtured a dark envy. She told people that she had a boyfriend in France, an eighteen-year-old she'd met in a nightclub and who had fallen madly in love with her. She forged love letters to herself, trying to transform her handwriting, then showed them off to her horrified friends. 'Stop it, Inès – we know you wrote them.' Rather than admitting the truth or apologising, Inès doubled down on her claim, which just made her appear even more pathetic and dislikeable. She was prepared to do anything to make people believe her, to make them give her the attention she felt she deserved.

One day in November she arrived home earlier than usual. Her father was watching television. Fatima was peeling potatoes on the Formica table. Inès had felt cold in the unheated classrooms so she decided to take a bath. She sank into the hot water, unscrewed the showerhead, aimed the jet of water at her clitoris and masturbated. Once, twice, three times, four times. She came and came until her fingers were wrinkled and her face bright red from the pleasure and the heat. Numbly, she rested her head against the edge of the bathtub and then, without thinking about it, without any premeditation at all, she began banging her cheek against the enamel. She did it again and again, harder and harder, and – to her astonishment – she was able to bear the pain. Next, she pinched her bruised cheek between her finger and thumb to increase the swelling and the discoloration. When Aïcha came home that evening, she flew into a panic. 'What happened to you?' Inès told her a story about getting injured during her PE class and Aïcha couldn't stop gasping: 'You could have died or lost an eye.'

That night, Inès prayed for her cheek to keep swelling, for the bruise to be as dark and impressive as possible, and when she woke the next morning there was a large bluish mark below her left eye. When her classmates spotted this in the playground, they asked her about it and Inès smiled and said, 'Oh, it's nothing', then turned on her heels with the happy certainty that, behind her, the rumours would already have started. Inès was an abused child. It was probably the father, but maybe others were involved too. She was a victim of abuse and that explained all her strange behaviour. So she lied not because she was stupid or duplicitous, but to cover up an immense and unspeakable sadness. Yes, everything would make sense to them now and they would all want to know her, love her, protect her. They would apologise for not having understood before. Inès imagined them feeling sorry for her, then naturally absolving her of all blame. She did not yet know that misfortune does not make you more desirable in other people's eyes.

There were so many reasons to lie. She lied out of boredom. Because life passed slowly and the days were all the same. She lied to stop herself falling asleep on her exercise book during afternoon classes. The English teacher gave them writing assignments, and in response to the ludicrously dull questions, she came up with extravagant fictions. What did you do on your summer holidays? And Inès described a wild week in New York, staying with her uncle Selim, who, in her imagination, hung out with celebrities and took her to a party where he introduced her to Claudia Schiffer and Julia Roberts. What did you do last Sunday? Instead of telling the truth – that she hadn't done anything at all – Inès invented a new group of friends. She lied out of love too, and it was for a boy she liked that she made up the story of the Benetton ad. He was a French boy called Éric who wore check shirts and jeans so oversized that you could see the brand name on his boxer shorts. Éric was tall and blond, and Inès felt sure that he could never love a girl like her, a girl with dark skin whose curly hair smelled of argan oil. She thought about boys all the time, and to make them like her she projected an image of being easy. At seventeen she talked like some experienced thirty-year-old.

'Oh, I love that . . . and I'm good at it too.' She was convinced that boys liked liberated girls such as Madonna and Sharon Stone. Of course, she would never be as blonde or as beautiful as them, but she was perfectly capable of slowly crossing her legs after forgetting to put on any underwear.

And she wasn't ugly, as she reminded herself constantly, feeling boys' eyes on her body. She writhed with excitement at the thought of all the filth that lurked inside men. She had never seen this filth herself yet, but she couldn't wait to discover it. Inès wanted to see naked men. She didn't have a brother or a male cousin or even a friend who she could ask to unzip his jeans and pull down his underwear. It seemed to her that the only way she could be free, the only way she could become herself, was to be defiled. To kill the little girl with puppy-dog eyes who used to sit in a shop window. Her mother often talked about men with Mathilde or Selma. Mostly they complained about them, but all the same they did talk about them a lot. Their eyes shone and their cheeks glowed when they talked about men, their own husbands and other women's, the bastards and the sweethearts. Sometimes they would whisper and one of them would start giggling. They shared secrets and recipes, witches' spells that would punish them or keep them close. Men without whom they would have been happier. Men who had turned the head of this girl and lied to that one. Men were the ones who made decisions. Men drove cars, windows open, their suntanned arms leaning nonchalantly over the door. Men wanted to be free. Men were restless. You must never be demanding with a man, never tell him what to do, never be jealous or clingy. You must never ask him: 'When will I see you again?' This is what Selma had told her, and Inès believed her.

The maids talked about men in the scullery. They wept for their nephews, who had failed an exam or been drowned crossing 'the river', as they called the Strait of Gibraltar. Men were always leaving, Inès understood. Men left Morocco for another country, another continent. They left the countryside for the city, their wives for mistresses. In her nightmares she imagined a world where only women remained. Streets where the only people walking were young women tottering on high heels and old women with tattooed chins. She pictured her grandparents' farm without any shepherds, without the guy driving the tractor and the guy selling poultry. She saw empty apartments in which women sat, condemned to wait and to hope.

Inès thought it would change everything to be loved by a man, to be chosen by him. The older she got, the more the mystery of maleness deepened. In their presence, she acted like an idiot. When they sat down, Inès would stare at their crotch. She would observe the bulge in their trousers with a mixture of fear and gluttony and wonder what it looked like. What colour was it? What did it feel like? Was it beautiful? Her father would glare at her sometimes. Did he suspect something? Perhaps he remembered that night – Inès must have been six or seven – when she had sneaked into the conjugal bed. The weak light of dawn was filtering through a gap between the curtains and she had seen her parents' naked bodies, bathed in a dim bluish halo. Her father's legs were covered by a sheet. Slowly, Inès moved closer. She clambered over her mother's body: Aïcha was sleeping deeply, one hand resting on her breast. Inès lay facing her father, and as she tried, with little movements of her feet, to push away the sheet that was covering him, Mehdi woke up. He opened his dark eyes and stared at her so severely that she wanted to cry. 'Aïcha!' Mehdi shook his wife's shoulder. 'Your daughter is in our bed. Get her out.' From that day on, the bedroom door was always kept locked.

Once a year, at the end of May, the students at Lycée Descartes put on a play at the Théâtre Mohammed V. It was a major event and all the students' parents attended. The previous year, Inès had gone to a performance of *A Streetcar Named Desire* with her mother, and that had been one of the most beautiful and heart-rending nights of her young life. She was transfixed. That streetcar. That sad, lost city. Those two sisters, who could have been her and Mia. She fell a little bit in love with the boy who was playing Stanley, an olive-skinned Moroccan boy with purple lips, whose biceps bulged inside a skintight T-shirt. The set was kitsch, the secondary roles unconvincing. One of the actors forgot his lines and there was a problem with a chandelier. But the actress who played Blanche was breathtaking, and her performance had the whole audience eating out of her hand. Her face would sometimes disappear behind her long, curly hair and she would shake her head, stare into the distance, put her hands over her chest and start to laugh. At school she was a quiet girl who always wore glasses and baggy, pilled sweaters. But there, on the stage, she was no longer the same girl; her face was radiant and you got the feeling that she had lived other lives before this one. The curtain fell, there was a thunder of applause and the actress took her bow. 'Bravo!' yelled the spectators, and a little girl got up on stage to hand her a bouquet of flowers.

Seventeen-year-old Inès wanted that. From that day on, what she yearned for more than anything else was for people to look at her, for the director to kiss her on the forehead as if she was a gift to the entire world.

The auditions took place in January. The director, Éric Baillard, was preparing an adaptation of *My Fair Lady* and each student had to perform a song. Monsieur Baillard, the literature teacher, was a well-known figure at the school, easily recognisable in his brightly coloured jackets and his ties with their childish designs. Inès had heard that he sometimes gave his classes in the garden. For days she had been practising in front of the bathroom mirror. She chose the Dalida song 'Il venait d'avoir 18 ans'*, and when she sang the lines 'I brushed my hair' and 'put a little more kohl on my eyes' she made sweeping, melancholic gestures. She also practised in front of her mother, who watched her with the same blissful expression she had worn when Inès, as a little girl, used to recite stupid nursery rhymes. At the audition, her turn came after two boys who had gone on stage as a joke, bawling 'Frère Jacques', their eyes reddened by the joint they'd smoked in the playground. Inès walked across the stage. She had pins and needles in her legs and her throat was so dry that she feared she wouldn't be able to make a sound. 'Come closer,' Monsieur Baillard told her. She stood with her feet at the edge of the stage. 'Whenever you're ready.'

She did not have a particularly nice voice but she could sing in tune, and with a little bit of work she might be a useful addition. This was what the director said that afternoon, when he called out the names of the chosen students.

* 'He Had Just Turned 18'

From that day on, Monsieur Baillard was all Inès thought about. In the mornings, she dressed for him. In her bag she hid skirts and shorts that she knew her father would never let her wear, and she stole a tube of lipstick from her mother. In class she worked harder than she'd ever worked before. She wanted him to see her, to be moved by her presence. For him, she wanted something to emerge from her. She dreamed of blossoming, of rising far above the mass of sniggering, stupid students. In the evenings, when she got home, she locked herself in her bedroom and thought about him. She would put on a tape by Eros Ramazzotti or Céline Dion, she would remember scenes from her favourite films (*Ghost*, *Pretty Woman*) and she would dream that he was kissing her neck, running his hands through her hair. She would squeeze her legs together, tense her vagina, put her hand down her knickers, rewind the tape and listen to it again. In a notebook she would write him letters, trying clumsily to explain how she felt about him. She never imagined sending them to him. She wasn't so naive as to think he might actually be interested in her. At times, when she surrendered to her fantasies, she felt ashamed of herself and started trying to find fault with him. She observed him, examined him, hoping to spot something that might disappoint or, even better, disgust her and forever break the spell that he had cast over her.

One Saturday afternoon, she let some of the boys in her class convince her to skip a rehearsal. There was nothing unusual about their suggestion – going for a ride in a car, to smoke joints and drink beers at a car park near the beach with some older boys – but she told herself that it would be good to find some age-appropriate distractions, to take her mind off this man who haunted her every waking thought. The following Monday, during her French class, Monsieur Baillard was cold and surly. Everything seemed to get on his nerves, and he sent one of the girls to the headmaster just because she'd forgotten her book. At the end of the class he told Inès to stay. Standing beside the teacher's desk, she waited for the other students to leave. Her classmates all gurned at her. 'Trying to be teacher's pet again?'

In the empty classroom, Monsieur Baillard stared at his desk as he slowly put his class notes back into his bag. 'You weren't at the rehearsal on Saturday.'

'I was ill.'

'It was a very important rehearsal, and when you're not there we can't make any progress.'

'I know, but I was ill.'

'That's not true. You weren't ill. You decided you would rather have fun with your friends instead. I'm very disappointed in you, Inès. I thought you cared about this play.'

'I do care about it! Honestly. I promise. I care a lot, and if you want, I'll do extra rehearsals this week.'

'It's not just that.'

Inès looked at her teacher, but he kept his eyes lowered. She felt an urge to touch his arm, to get down on her knees and swear that she would never let him down again. For a few seconds, as he stayed silent, she imagined a thousand different scenarios. He was going to take the part away from her and choose another girl, someone more talented and beautiful than her. Or he would keep her in the role but he wouldn't trust her any more, and he would never again give her those tender looks or sweet gestures that sent her into raptures and made her dream up romantic films in which Inès and Monsieur Baillard were the main characters.

'It's not just that,' he repeated, looking up at her. Had his face turned pale? His eyes seemed full of a sadness that she didn't understand. How could such a small, simple event – a single missed rehearsal, and a white lie about the reason for it – send him into a state like this? 'You see, Inès, there's the heart and then there's reason, and sometimes the two are in conflict because they don't want the same thing. Do you understand what I'm saying?'

Inès nodded. Yes, she understood. She understood exactly what he was saying, and her heart was pounding so fast that she found it hard to keep her composure. She sensed that she was living through the kind of moment that she would want to remember, later, in perfect detail. She focused her mind fully on the words he was using, on the way his long fingers looked as they rested on the desk.

'I shouldn't be telling you this. But I'm losing my mind, you see. You're driving me crazy. It's all I think about, and I know it's not right. I know it makes no sense, but I just can't . . .'

Inès put her hand on his arm. She stepped forward and pressed her body against his. She didn't say anything, but she breathed him in, her nose touching his white shirt. How is this possible? she thought. She wanted to laugh, to scream with joy. How did this man, this grown-up, this teacher, even see me? So it wasn't only in books or films that this sort of thing could happen. Men you imagined to be completely out of your league could secretly be in love with you. Selma was right. Your desire could influence the world around you. If you really wanted something, you could make it bend to your will.

He held her tightly, then gently picked her up and put her on the desk. She closed her eyes then opened them again. She watched this strange scene as if from above. Monsieur Baillard leaned towards her. His lips touched hers. What a strange way of kissing. Was this how adults did it? His kisses were so serious and sombre. He kissed her as if he would never kiss anyone again.

Thus began, for the two of them, a life of secrets, lies and subterfuge. A life where they expressed their feelings in a single look during a class, a rehearsal or as they were passing in a school corridor. Inès didn't lose her head. Quite the opposite, in fact. During the weeks that followed, she was so proud at having finally become an adult that she forced herself to behave like one. She began wearing jackets and blouses and begged her mother to buy her a pair of high heels. Goth and grunge were the predominant styles among the students – it was fashionable to wear torn jeans and black lipstick – but Inès did her best to look like a 1950s secretary. She worked even harder than usual, because she didn't want to disappoint this man that she adored. He was her teacher, after all. He kissed her, he caressed her breasts, he stuck his middle finger up her vagina, and then he corrected her essays and discussed her grades with the other teachers. Sometimes he could be scathing towards her, as when he doubted that she would emulate her sister by getting the best possible mark on her baccalauréat. He forbade her to cut her hair and he often made fun of her naivety, her lack of culture. Strangely, she liked this. The way he would rebuff her or criticise her. The occasionally condescending way he would speak to her. Things like 'What would you know about it?' or 'You'll understand when you're older.' She didn't get annoyed by these remarks, she didn't sulk. She wanted to react like a woman, and during conversations of this kind, she felt as if they were playing at mummies and daddies. She wasn't just a kid any more, because a man – a man much older than her – was interested in her. Monsieur Baillard was thirty-seven and she had no idea what that meant. What sort of things have you lived through by the time you're thirty-seven?

The teacher took certain risks to see his mistress. He'd acquired a floor plan of the school, showing all the different classrooms, and he would tell her to meet him in one of the empty rooms with a door that could be locked with a key. They would lie on the floor, so that nobody could spot them through the window, and force themselves to be as quiet as possible. Monsieur Baillard would unbutton Inès's blouse, he would take off her skirt. He would pull down her knickers and stuff them in his pocket. 'So we don't lose them,' he always said. The first time he licked her, she burst out laughing. She was terribly embarrassed and didn't know what to do with her hands or her legs. Should she keep them where they were or spread them wide or wrap them around Monsieur Baillard's head? His hands were cupping Inès's buttocks and soon she lost the desire to laugh. She opened her mouth and started panting like a woman giving birth. She sunk her fingers into Monsieur Baillard's hair. She wanted to hurt him, wanted him deep inside her. She came and when she opened her eyes, he was there, above her, his eyes shining, his face wet.

Sex drove him mad. Each time they did it his desire was even more urgent, more passionate. Sometimes he even found it hard to talk until he had taken off her knickers and put his hand between her legs. Inès found it extraordinary, wildly improbable, that she was experiencing all this. It seemed like a miracle, and it never occurred to her that Monsieur Baillard felt the same way about kissing the breasts and thighs of a seventeen-year-old girl. She was flattered that he couldn't 'hold himself in', and the urgency of his desire seemed to her irrefutable proof that he loved her. It turned her on to watch his face when they had sex, to see him grimace when he came. She often found that sex lasted too long, that it hurt.

Sometimes her lover appeared sombre and anxious; he would jump at the slightest sound, imagine enemies all around. She did not seem as affected as he did by the obstacles that confronted them. She couldn't understand. She was too young and didn't know what it was to be married with two children. He put his head in his hands and tore at his hair: he couldn't stand any more of these brief encounters. In the winter they went to the beach several times. Monsieur Baillard would park his car on a deserted path and turn the heating on. And on sunny days they would walk on the sand. If they encountered someone else, they thought, they could just dive into the cold water and swim far out to sea. Another time, exasperated by their clandestine meetings at the school, Monsieur Baillard had the idea of renting a room in a hotel close to the train station. Inès was afraid. For the first time she felt anxious and she opened up to him. No, of course she wasn't talking about her fear of getting pregnant or catching one of those horrible diseases that she had seen photographs of in a medical journal of her mother's. But she pointed out that in Morocco it was against the law for an unmarried couple to get a hotel room together. Even she knew that, and she didn't want to end up in the back of a police van, which is what had happened to several of her friends. Monsieur Baillard reassured her: he'd given the receptionist some money to ensure his discretion. He would go up to the room first and she would join him; nobody would notice a thing. And that afternoon, lying in bed at the Ibis Hotel, she thought she'd been right to listen to him and that there was nothing more wonderful than white sheets, a bed, shutters that could be closed and a warm naked body that she could lie next to while she took a nap.

She wished she could talk to someone about all this. If only she had a male friend like Mia's Hakim, a confidant with whom she could share her discoveries. She would have liked to tell someone about the time that had passed before that first kiss. It had only been a few seconds, but she had so much to say about those few seconds. Those seconds had changed her life and she could have talked about them for hours.

One day, when he had to drive her home after a rehearsal – 'Remember to thank him nicely,' Aïcha had told her beforehand – Monsieur Baillard decided to steal a few extra minutes of love, so he took her to the forest on the edge of the Dar Es Salam golf club. Inside the car, he took off her bra, kissed her neck and told her how beautiful she was. Inès put her hand between Monsieur Baillard's legs and caressed his balls through the fabric of his trousers. With her thumb and her middle finger, she took hold of his penis, then wrapped her palm around the shaft and slowly moved it up and down until it grew hard. Under the flesh of her fingertips, she felt the blood beat in the glans. In that moment she wished the world were totally silent, a world without words. A world where nothing existed any more except the body and the sounds it made.

He liked to lightly pinch her nipple until she closed her eyes and started to moan. He was doing this now, when she heard someone knock on the car window. She instantly recognised the policeman's uniform and read the words painted on the car that was parked under a nearby tree: 'GENDARMERIE ROYALE'. She buttoned up her blouse, gasping, 'Oh my God, oh my God', and Monsieur Baillard, equally panicked, kept his hands on the steering wheel. Finally he opened the window.

'Papers.' The cop was a man in his early fifties, slim and dark-skinned. Like his colleague, who had remained inside the police car, he had a thick moustache.

Monsieur Baillard opened the glove compartment, taking care not to touch Inès's bare legs. He handed his papers to the policeman and Inès heard a voice she didn't recognise. A child's voice, trembling and obsequious: 'Here you are, monsieur.'

The policeman went back to his car and Inès and Monsieur Baillard waited for him in silence. Inès was blushing hotly. The policeman returned with the papers.

'What are the two of you doing here?' The policeman spoke French with a strong accent.

'She's my student. We were rehearsing a play, and I was driving her home.'

The policeman looked at Inès. He examined her legs, then the bra lying on the floor of the car.

'Are you Moroccan?' he asked Inès in Arabic. 'What the hell are you doing with this old French guy? You don't look like a whore.'

'He's my teacher. We were rehearsing a play . . .'

'The girl's papers.'

'Listen, we didn't do anything wrong and we'll get going now. I'm sure we can come to an arrangement.' Monsieur Baillard was shaking.

'No arrangements,' the policeman said coldly. He turned to his colleague, who was standing in front of the car, talking into the radio. 'We're going to take you to the station. What you're doing is forbidden in Morocco, monsieur. This isn't Sweden.'

Then he walked away, as if he wanted to give them time to think. Inès begged her lover to bribe them. Monsieur Baillard opened the door and got out. She watched him walk away with the policeman. They stood talking under a cork oak tree. Inès thought: They're talking about me. They're haggling over me. Those two men will decide my fate. She started to cry. She imagined her parents receiving the call from the police. Her mother's disappointment, her father's rage. She pictured herself, like someone in a film, lying on a bench in a prison cell, surrounded by whores and thugs. Monsieur Baillard got back in the car. He put the key in the ignition and turned on the engine. His fingers were trembling, but he forced himself to smile at the policeman and hold up his hand as he drove away.

'Did you pay him?'

He didn't reply.

In June of that year, Inès's performance in *My Fair Lady* was a triumph. Even Mehdi overcame his shame, and his fear of being seen by Rabat's elite, to watch his daughter act. 'You have a queenly bearing,' he told her afterwards. That night, Inès went out with some friends to celebrate. Monsieur Baillard made a big scene about this. He told her she should go to bed early, and that he was talking to her as her director, not her lover. But Inès just rolled her eyes. More and more now, he bored her. She was tired of his presence, of being tethered to him. Everyone knew about their relationship, and one day someone slipped a threatening letter under a classroom door. Inès's fear, which had fuelled her excitement for months, became a gnawing anxiety. The spell was broken and it was as if Monsieur Baillard was suddenly exposed in a glaring light that made all his flaws repugnant. She decided to dump him. There was no generosity in the love that this man felt for her. She felt sure he didn't want her to succeed because that would mean her moving away from him.

She had chosen to go to medical school and everyone seemed to think she was following some sort of family vocation. The truth was that she didn't know what else to do. She admired people with convictions, ideas, principles. Nothing impressed her more than pure souls who refused to compromise. But she knew she was easily swayed. She always believed the last person to speak and she often found herself repeating things that Monsieur Baillard had said to her, without even knowing what they meant. To Inès, everything seemed blurred, and she found it impossible to trace the borders between right and wrong, between what was permitted and what forbidden.

'Medicine?' one of her classmates said to her. 'I could never do that – I'm too afraid of blood.' Inès thought this was stupid. Why would she be afraid of blood? No, what scared her were not bodies, wounds or the sight of glistening organs, but tears. She found out that nothing made her more afraid than a man who wept. She made this discovery at the Agdal, in Monsieur Baillard's apartment, when he sat on the edge of the bed and sobbed. He wasn't wearing socks or shoes and, for minutes on end, all she could do was stare at his hairy feet, his long toenails. Her lover's pain left her paralysed, and she just repeated the same useless words: 'I'm sorry.' She had always thought that there was nothing more difficult than telling someone 'I love you', but now she realised that it was far more painful and took far more courage to admit: 'I don't love you any more.' Their relationship had no future, and she – a seventeen-year-old girl – had to explain this to him, a thirty-seven-year-old man. 'I'll be leaving for Paris soon. I'll meet people my own age. You understand, don't you?'

But he didn't understand. 'I can't live without you,' her former teacher said between sobs. 'My heart is broken.' Sob. 'Don't you realise everything I did for you?' Sob. 'You're just a bitch.' Sob. 'You're a whore.'

She left his apartment and took a taxi to Avenue de Témara. She didn't feel anything, not even guilt. She was empty and cold inside. So that was a man? She thought about her father, always sitting in the same spot, his breath stinking of alcohol. She saw Amine, the patriarch, staring into space, convinced that there was a ghost sitting on the edge of his bed. So that was a man? This old guy yelling to be carried to the shower, to the toilet, to the window so he could look at the trees he had planted even though he was no longer capable of remembering their names. Inès had always heard that women want to possess and men to flee, but she was no longer sure that this was true.

Selma had given her a copy of the keys to her flat, and after knocking twice Inès let herself in. 'Oh, you're here?' Inès heard her great-aunt's voice coming from the end of the hallway. Selma was lying on the bed, her bad leg propped on a cushion. She was wearing thick, clear-rimmed glasses. Around her were a selection of women's magazines and travel guides. Scotland, Florida, Southern Italy. She would sometimes spend whole afternoons looking through them. Selma read travel guides the way other people masturbate, with a mixture of shame and delight, and sometimes she would fall asleep and dream, dry-mouthed, of wandering the streets of Edinburgh or taking a train in Peru.

Inès lay beside her. This place was a refuge from her home, where an oppressive silence reigned. Ever since her father had stopped working at CCM, nobody had explained anything to her. Her mother worked even longer hours than before – someone had to pay the bills and Mia's tuition fees – and Inès was left to drag her boredom around the empty house. A month from now, she would be gone. Her first term at medical school did not start until late September, but she'd convinced her parents to let her spend the summer in Paris. She wanted to have fun with her sister, who in late August would be moving to London, where she'd found a job at a prestigious investment bank.

'So?' asked Selma.

'He cried.'

'He'll get over it.'

'Whatever. I couldn't stand him any more. The way he always wanted to keep me to himself. It made me sick.'

Inès picked up the guide to Italy. She looked at the image on the cover. A high wall with orange bougainvillea growing on it, and a woman astride a Vespa.

'I wish I'd already left. I've had it up to here with school and my parents and Morocco. Mum reminds me of Blanche DuBois. *A Streetcar Named Desire*. She smiles as if everything's fine, but I know she's just pretending. I'd rather see her cry.'

'You shouldn't be so hard on her.' Selma stood up and headed towards the cupboard. 'Everyone pretends, you know. We pretend to come, so it'll be over more quickly. We pretend to laugh, so they don't think we're oversensitive or hysterical. We pretend we're not in pain,' she added, handing Inès a pair of high heels. 'We say we're not hungry and we order a side salad when the truth is we're dreaming of a plate of chips or a bowl of cream. It's one of the first things a woman learns to do, pretending.' She placed a black silk dress on the bed, fluid, with slender straps.

Inès shrugged. 'What about my father? Why does he stay here? If I was him, I'd have escaped, even if it meant crawling through the sewers. He keeps saying that he believes in his country's justice system. But what justice system is he talking about? The one that would put Mia and me behind bars for our loose morals? What more would it take for him to understand?'

'All right, calm down. Try on this dress, and these shoes. I've always loved these shoes.'

Inès undressed. Watching her, Selma understood what it was that drove men mad. She was touchingly slim. Her ribs showed through her skin. Her perfectly rounded buttocks were each small enough to fit in a man's hand. Her hips looked so fragile. And yet all of this was coupled with a smouldering sensuality. As if Inès was some kind of half-starved cat, a creature of the night. She turned to Selma, standing tall in her high heels. She was ravishing.

'Perfect. You can put them in that bag. All this is for you. You'll have a whole armoury to take with you.'

Selma had taught her that looking good was the best way to conceal her unease, to make up for the impression that she was a little girl lost in a dark forest. With the right image, you could create a character and any sadness you felt would be that character's rather than your own.

Selma fell back on the bed and lit a cigarette. 'You'll leave and you'll get your revenge. But promise me that one day you'll come back and rescue me. Nobody my age can make a new life for themselves, but I could help you with yours.'

'I promise. Cross my heart and hope to die.'

Mia was smoking a cigarette on the pavement. She waved her arms and called out: 'Inès! Over here! Hang on, I'll help you with your bags . . .' She opened the back door of the taxi. She was wearing jeans, a white T-shirt and a pair of flip-flops that showed off her suntanned feet. She went up to the driver, a Haitian guy who had spent the whole trip listening to French radio, and handed him some cash. Inès had been so afraid that she wouldn't have enough money. After leaving the airport, they'd become snarled up in traffic jams. She hadn't even looked out the window because she'd been staring so fixedly at the meter as the numbers mounted in time with her anxiety. But Mia was here now and Mia had no money problems at all. She had finished business school, having spent the last year working for the Consulting Club, carrying out surveys and marketing studies and earning a very good salary. Ever since Mehdi had lost his job she'd made it her ambition not to be a burden on anyone.

The apartment was located at 25 Boulevard de Sébastopol. Mia rolled the two suitcases across the cobblestones of a large interior courtyard, then the two of them climbed four flights of stairs. The wooden steps were varnished to such a shine that Inès almost slipped twice. 'This is the living room.' It was small but filled with light that poured through the two large windows, which offered a view of the Fontaine des Innocents. Trees swayed behind the glass panes and in the distance you could make out the Saint-Eustache Church and part of the Forum des Halles. Between the two windows stood a round table and four chairs. To the right, against the wall, was the couch. 'I'll sleep here, on the sofa bed,' said Mia. 'The kitchen is through there, but be careful – the fridge door doesn't shut properly. And this is your bedroom. If you need some drawers or hangers, let me know. Okay?'

Inès pulled her suitcases into the bedroom, which had a view of the square. She could hear water running in the fountain below. She started to unpack. Selma's dresses, the new underwear that her mother had bought for her and woolly jumpers for winter. Mehdi hadn't come to the airport. Two months ago, he'd received a letter informing him that he was no longer allowed to leave Moroccan territory. An official had come to confiscate his passport and make him sign some documents. 'You don't have any other nationalities?' 'No,' Mehdi had replied, before adding stupidly: 'I have faith in my country's justice system.' So Mehdi hadn't dared to accompany his daughter to the departure lounge. Perhaps he was afraid that some overzealous official would make a remark, or perhaps he was afraid that, seeing his youngest child fly the nest, he would feel such overpowering sadness that he would not be able to stop himself crying. Aïcha had cried, of course. She had hugged Inès tightly, told her to be careful and asked her to promise not to drink too much, not to put herself in danger, not to get in trouble.

Mia came into the bedroom. She sat on the bed and stroked the fabric of a purple printed dress. 'Okay, well, we don't have time for this. It's the match today. Let's go.' It was 12 July 1998 and for the past month France had been in a state of World Cup fever. In the streets of Paris, football was all anybody talked about. In all the cafés, bars and bistros of the city, a television was always on and the customers would discuss line-ups, results and tactics. The windows of restaurants were decorated with flags of every colour. That summer, beer sales were at a record high, and by early morning all the city's fountains were yellow with piss. They walked along the boulevard and Inès struggled to keep up with her sister. She was dazzled by the agitation on the streets, the beauty of the people she saw, the relaxed atmosphere. She stopped in front of the window of a shop selling wedge heels and second-hand clothes. A few boys were leaning against some railings, smoking joints. Mia told her: 'Never go through the Jardin des Halles on your own. If someone asks you for a cigarette, tell them you don't smoke.' Inès kept wanting to ask lots of questions, mostly 'Where are we?' and 'Where are we going?' She looked at a couple holding a piece of cardboard with 'Need tickets' written on it. Mia signalled at her to hurry up – 'It's over there' – and she rang a doorbell on Rue Beauregard. The apartment was on the ground floor and Inès followed her sister, who appeared to know exactly where she was going. Two boys and a girl were sitting on a sofa in a large living room, facing a television screen. To the right hung a hammock, and Mia climbed into this after grabbing a bottle of beer. 'Arthur, Tiago, Sarah, this is my sister Inès. Inès, these are my friends.'

'Hey, little sis.' Inès wasn't sure if this was Tiago or Arthur. Whoever it was, he seemed to be the owner of the apartment because he got up and opened the fridge. 'Beer okay?'

'Yes, very good.'

When she was nervous, Inès had a tendency to say stuff that made her sound stupid. Shut up if you don't have anything to say, she reminded herself as she stroked the bottle's neck with the tip of her thumb. The boy who had given her the beer – this was Arthur, it turned out, and he shared the apartment with the other two – waved his arms around when he spoke and exaggerated everything to make the others laugh. His midnight-blue shirt was unbuttoned and Inès stared at his hairless, golden-skinned torso. Tiago, for his part, seemed more interested in the match that was about to start. He was Portuguese and he was wearing a Brazil shirt.

'Our father brought us some shirts like that after he went to Rio,' said Inès. The others turned to look at her. She was afraid she had said something stupid again, but Mia looked up from her hammock and said: 'You remember that story he used to tell us all the time?'

'About the Maracanã?'

'Yeah, he got in a taxi, started talking about Maradona, and—'

'The taxi driver threw him out.'

'He found himself all alone in the middle of a favela.'

'In the middle of a favela – that's what he said.'

They laughed. The others turned to look at the television. Well, they were sisters, after all. They'd grown up together, they shared their own language, they shared codes and secrets that nobody else could understand. For the next hour they all drank beers and talked about the geopolitics of sport and the tactics of the game. Mia was both the most passionate and the most knowledgeable, and the others looked serious and nodded when they listened to her. Sarah, who had enormous thighs and the face of a Madonna, rolled joints with the aid of a little machine that made them look like ordinary cigarettes. 'Okay, here we go!' But it wasn't yet the start of the match. The pitch was covered with a vast sky-blue cloth. The music began – Ravel's *Boléro* – and some women started to parade past. The most beautiful women in the world: the supermodels that Inès had admired so much when she was younger, whose photographs had been plastered all over the walls of her bedroom. 'Carla! Karen!' yelled Arthur, and Inès felt a surge of gratitude towards him. He, too, liked gold high heels and he knew all Yves Saint Laurent's iconic dresses. Inès felt like Paris was winking at her, as if this pre-match show was its way of welcoming her among these women in armour. Maybe it was the beer or the joint, but she couldn't help seeing this as a good omen.

By the time the match began, Inès was already drunk. At first she found it hard to concentrate on the action. She stared at the thousands of red, white and blue cards that had been handed out to the spectators and the way the sunlight reflected off them. She observed the tense, concentrated expression on her sister's face and the way Arthur kept biting his lip, tearing little bits of skin off with his teeth. Then she slowly surrendered to the euphoria and the tension, and she surprised herself by lusting for a French victory as if her life depended on it. At one point Mia got up to go to the toilet and when she came back she stood just behind Inès with her hands on her shoulders. Mia's hands were heavy and warm, and Inès wished her sister would keep them there forever. Zinedine Zidane scored the first goal with a header. A huge roar arose in the living room, and Inès could hear it echoed in the apartment building above, in the streets outside, a roar that seemed to unfurl endlessly throughout the city. Mia couldn't keep still any more. Sarah kept saying, 'I can't watch, I can't watch', and several times she disappeared to the kitchen or the bathroom. She was eating a peach when Zidane scored the second goal.

During half-time, Tiago found himself outnumbered. He kept saying, 'It's not over yet', and the others got annoyed. They were in France, after all: it would be classier of him to show some solidarity. The match restarted and Mia sat on the arm of the sofa, her hands clasped together. Her right leg was shaking. When Desailly was sent off, she yelled 'Fuck!' and buried her head in her hands. Does she know how much she resembles Mehdi? Inès wondered. From outside came the blare of car horns, and through the open window she could hear people shouting, the hum of conversation. The whole city was drunk, the whole city was holding its breath as the final minutes ticked down, the growing relief, the possibility of victory. And then the third goal was scored – Vieira . . . Petit! – and the city exploded. Arthur hugged Inès and Sarah burst into tears. 'We're the champions! Fucking hell, we're the champions of the world!'

From that moment on, Inès felt as if she was caught in a sort of dream, swept away by an ecstatic crowd, like that line in an Édith Piaf song. Mia kissed her on the mouth. The neighbours ran out into the courtyard, hugging each other and kicking dustbins.

'I don't believe it!'

'I told you!'

They decided to get the metro to the Champs-Élysées. All around them, in the station and on the train, families, couples, groups of friends were jumping up and down, chanting 'One–nil two–nil three–nil yeah!' The train driver yelled into his microphone: 'We are the champions, we are the champions!' They got out underneath the most beautiful avenue in the world and, emerging from the metro station, found themselves sucked into the middle of a tightly packed crowd. People were shoving each other and Mia took Inès by the hand. 'Stay close to me.' But Inès couldn't hear a thing. Mia's voice was drowned out by the sound of darbukas and trumpets, by shouting and singing. Inès could never have imagined this many people in a single place. There were thousands of them, hundreds of thousands, and she was here, in the middle of this sea of red, white and blue shirts, wigs, flags. Above all, there were men, tens of thousands of men, white men, Black men, Arab men, and – right there in front of her – a boy who looked like the one who worked at the Berber corner shop in the Agdal, wearing a Phrygian cap. Some of the men had their faces painted, and there were children asking to be carried on their shoulders. The people she passed all smiled at her. In a side street she saw some young men climbing on the roofs of cars. She didn't know if they were lowlife criminals or high-spirited bourgeois kids, but they were running on top of these vehicles that some idiots had left parked in the wrong place. There were young men hanging from lampposts or bus shelters to get a better view of Zidane's face when it was projected onto the Arc de Triomphe. 'Zidane for president!' someone yelled, and the crowd began singing 'La Marseillaise'. Algerian and Palestinian flags were waved on the Champs-Élysées and the people sang, in a single voice, '*Aux armes, citoyens!*' Mia shouted in her ear: 'The magic of football!' and Inès realised that this was the first time in her life that she'd ever taken part in a collective event, the first time she'd been in the middle of a crowd. In Rabat, her mother always avoided gatherings and protest marches. When unemployed graduates assembled outside the parliament building, Aïcha worried that the crowds would make her late for work. Thinking about it now, Inès had never understood what it was that the unemployed graduates were protesting against.

Having lost Arthur and Tiago, the two of them withdrew to a pub, where the barman was pouring beer after beer and handing them out left, right and centre. Nobody was paying – drinks were on the house. Inès didn't object when a boy picked her up by the waist and lifted her onto the bar. She said to him: 'I was born during a football match, you know.'

But the boy – handsome, dark-haired, early twenties – made a sign with his arm. 'It's too noisy, I can't hear you.'

Then he kissed her: a long, wonderful kiss that meant nothing at all.

Mia, who was drunk too, was talking with a group of North African men. 'Good thing we had some Arabs on the team. When we score goals, everyone loves us!'

'Algerian, not Arab,' replied a guy with receding gums. 'Zidane is Algerian.'

They danced to 'I Will Survive', went to two or three different bars, and Inès spent a long time in conversation with a girl. (The next day, she would not remember the girl's face or what they had talked about.) Eventually, Mia signalled for her to follow. 'I need to piss.' She crouched down between two cars, and afterwards they walked home. It was a warm night and the pavements were littered with flags and empty bottles. Their ears were buzzing and they held each other round the waist so they wouldn't fall over.

'I bet Dad will be happy,' Mia shouted. 'What a fucking match!' The sky was growing light by the time they reached Boulevard de Sébastopol. Someone had vomited in the gutter. They collapsed onto Inès's bed and fell asleep next to each other, without even taking off their shoes.

The next day, Inès put her clothes in the wardrobe. Then, still hung over, she took a nap. 'I'm never getting drunk on beer again,' swore Mia, whose chest was convulsing as if she was about to throw up. They spent the whole day at the apartment. Mia smoked cigarettes on the balcony and cut her toenails on the couch. They watched television in silence and Mia went to Pizza Pino to grab dinner and came back with two tubs of Häagen-Dazs. She gave Inès her little guide to Paris, the one with the blue cover, but her sister didn't use it that summer. She just followed Mia wherever she went. It was a summer of celebration, the most beautiful summer she had ever known. She admired and envied her sister's poise, her ability to charm people and make them laugh. She was no longer the brooding, suspicious Mia who had left home all those years ago, but a flamboyant, self-assured young woman who made dirty jokes and drank tequila shots. Around four every afternoon, Mia and her friends would meet up for a drink on the terrace of Café Beaubourg, then they would go out to dinner, although they never ate much because of the lines of coke they sniffed in the toilet. The waiter would come over several times to ask if they'd finished their meal. It didn't bother them to send back a barely touched roast chicken or a bowl of soup with a skin on its surface. Often they would hang around the apartment or at Arthur's place. Tiago was an actor, Arthur created accessories for Dior and Paco Rabanne and Sarah sold ice creams at a cinema in the Grands Boulevards. They would buy alcohol, packets of crisps and taramasalata from the local corner shop, and when the neighbours came to knock on their door at one in the morning to complain about the noise, they would offer them a drink or a drag on their joint. Inès didn't want to embarrass Mia, to be a burden or the butt of her friends' jokes. She knew she had to get into the swing of things. She had to prove to them that she, too, knew how to have fun, how to get wasted. How to make herself feel like shit the next day.

Mia looked after her. She took her to buy a yellow Nokia and went with her to the bank to open an account. She showed her how to use the launderette and introduced her to the Tunisian guy from Djerba who ran the local twenty-four-hour corner shop. 'Tunisians don't say "shukran", we say "ayshek" – funny, right?'

Inès discovered the joys of happy-hour five-franc beers and the gay clubbing scene. She sniffed poppers and for fifteen seconds she felt herself leave her body and got very hot. She clung to the nets above the dancefloor at Le Queen and ended up with her hands covered in blood. One day, she saw Björk and Alexander McQueen in a second-hand clothes shop. When she told Mia this, her sister replied: 'Well, I saw Naomi Campbell at Les Bains.' One night she watched two girls have a fight outside Le Pulp, and she also saw a well-known comedian get drunk in a booth at Club Banana.

They spent a lot of time in the Marais district. Her sister read *Têtu* magazine and bought her books at Mots à la Bouche, but she refused to play the role of the resident dyke. One day, while they were sitting at a terrace on Rue Vieille-du-Temple, she explained: 'I hate *Priscilla, Queen of the Desert* and shit like that. I hate anything that makes us look like a bunch of weirdos. I don't want to be a militant or a circus freak. And I really can't be arsed attending meetings about women oppressed by the patriarchy, you know?' Arthur rolled his eyes at this. That night, Mia introduced Inès to her current girlfriend, Margaux, a pretty brunette who had left her boyfriend to be with Mia. She had long straight hair and wore a top so short that you could see the diamond sparkling in her belly button. She sat opposite Mia, and for the first time Inès saw her sister kiss another woman. A wet, noisy, languorous kiss. Mia's hand slid slowly up Margaux's thigh. Inès tried to imagine their lovemaking. What was it like? She pictured her sister's face between Margaux's thighs, and she thought she would like some of that herself – long kisses, romantic walks along the Seine, a tongue inside her vagina – but her sister kept a close watch over her.

Mia had noticed the way that boys looked at Inès. Her sister exuded sex appeal and this made her uncomfortable: Inès's natural charm, her animal grace. Inès didn't have to do anything in particular, she wasn't even trying to draw attention to herself, and that was the worst thing about it. It was her innocence that men lusted after. In the street, they would wink at her or turn around to watch her walk away. Once, a guy had jumped onto their bus at the last moment and handed Inès a note. 'What did he write?' Mia asked.

'"Can I see you again?"'

'Dickhead,' said Mia, and tossed the piece of paper out of the window.

'She's really pretty, your sister,' Arthur remarked once, as though amazed that Mia could be related by blood to this graceful, doll-like beauty.

When Inès had arrived in Paris, she'd thought she was discovering freedom. For the first time in her life she had an apartment of her own in a city where she could walk down the street, look at boys and have them look at her. But everywhere she went, the shadow of her sister loomed over her. Mia was constantly asking her where she was going, what she was doing. She would give her orders too: 'Today you're coming with me.'

At night, when they went out to clubs or bars together, Mia worried that Inès would get drunk. She didn't want men buying her sister drinks, and she would rudely rebuff anyone who tried to chat her up. She couldn't help thinking about all the men she'd known. The things she'd heard them say, the things she'd seen them do. In Morocco, men would fuck whores and maids; they were coarse and stupid. But French guys weren't much better. At business school, during student nights at clubs, she'd seen them drink themselves into a coma and make bets about who would be the first one to screw a girl up the arse in the bathroom.

Arthur made fun of her. 'You're like some macho boyfriend. Why don't you just leave her in peace? You'll be in London soon anyway, and she's got her own life to lead.' At the apartment, the atmosphere between them grew increasingly tense. Inès didn't say anything, but she made no attempt to hide her irritation. She would lock herself in the bathroom for hours. She and Sarah would whisper together, and when Mia asked what they were talking about, Inès would say:

'Nothing.' Mia loved her sister, in a clumsy, anxious sort of way. She always felt as if she were walking a tightrope, as if one word or gesture out of place might destroy the strange complicity between them.

In the middle of August, Mia accepted Margaux's invitation to spend two days at her house in the country. The Parisians had left Paris: all the best shops were closed, and the prospect of going skinny-dipping together was enticing. What did it matter if Margaux was only doing this to piss off her parents or her ex-boyfriend? What did it matter if she treated Mia like she was a guy? What did it matter if all she really wanted was to slum it with a girl, a real lesbian, a dyke? During those two days in Avignon, Mia didn't think about Inès. She was obsessed by her lover's body, her dark-nippled breasts, her belly, those thighs that she could caress for hours. She made love to her on the kitchen table and Margaux screamed. She said something like 'I've never felt that before.' Her pussy had the sweet taste and even the consistency of the thick-skinned yellow melons that Mia used to eat during summers in Morocco. They only went swimming at night, because of the swarms of bees that flew over the pool during the day, and in the afternoons they took a nap together in the bedroom with the shutters closed. On the train that took her back to Paris, Mia drifted into a daydream. She relived every gesture, every scene, in exquisite detail, and for a moment she even thought about going to the tiny bathroom to masturbate. She sent Inès a message letting her know what time she expected to arrive. Her sister didn't respond. She must still be sulking, thought Mia. She swore she would make an effort when she got back. Maybe the two of them could go somewhere. A change of scenery. Sure, why not? She could suggest a weekend in Amsterdam, for instance. 'We'll smoke joints and have a laugh together.'

On Boulevard de Sébastopol, two tourists were staring at a big map of Paris. They wanted to visit Notre-Dame and Mia showed them how to get there. Inside the apartment, just as she was about to call out 'Inès!', she heard a noise. A moan, barely perceptible, as if someone was asleep and having a very nice dream. Then she heard panting, like an animal, and the sound of an unfamiliar voice. She stood, frozen, bag in hand, in the middle of the living room. Her heart sped up and she didn't know if her dominant emotion was disgust, shame or anger. There was another sound – not a moan this time, but a cry, a disgusting, vulgar cry like the ones the girls made in the porn films she used to watch with her schoolfriends. She put down her bag and balled her fists. Her first thought was to play some music very loudly on the stereo. But it wasn't only the sounds that bothered her. The door was closed and yet she felt that she could see them, their ridiculous bodies intertwined, and that she could even smell the hot, sickening odour of their copulation. She didn't put the stereo on. She could just have gone outside and sat on the terrace to wait until it was over, but rage made her lose her head. Hate flowed hotly down her throat and into her belly, like neat vodka. She yelled: 'Inès!', and after a few seconds her sister appeared in the doorway, her hair mussed, her cheeks bright pink, holding her dress in front of her naked body. That odour – that wet, oppressive odour – assailed Mia's nostrils. The bedroom was dark. Mia grabbed her sister by the arm and, after dragging her over to the naked, disconcerted boy, she slapped her.

That night, Mia packed her suitcase. The next morning, she caught a train to London.

One morning in April 1999, Amine crashed his car into the big palm tree. Tibari, the foreman, heard the crunch of metal and came running. Amine wasn't injured, but he was sitting behind the wheel, wild-eyed, hands shaking. 'Boss, are you okay?' Tibari asked anxiously. For an instant Amine looked like a child caught red-handed. At eighty-two he was no longer allowed to drive, or even to walk around the property on his own. His doctors had diagnosed advanced dementia. They'd warned Mathilde: 'There's nothing you can do. Just try to be patient.'

Tibari helped Amine out of the car. He murmured some reassuring words, put his arm under the boss's arm, and together they walked back to the house. 'He called me Mourad again,' the foreman told Mathilde. 'He was telling me something about the war.'

Mathilde didn't mention the accident to Aïcha. Her daughter would have told her off. She would have insisted that her father should travel to Rabat for a thorough examination. She would have suggested new protocols, stronger medications, maybe even a stay in hospital. But Mathilde was certain it wouldn't do any good. She knew this man better than she knew herself. They had celebrated their fiftieth wedding anniversary: half a century living under the same roof, watching each other grow old, accumulating worries and memories, sharing triumphs and happiness. Amine was disappearing. Every day, Mathilde could tell, her husband was slipping away from her. He was a man out of time, drawn irresistibly back towards the past. In the evening she would sit down to watch television and he would ask her: 'Are the children home yet? I'd like to eat dinner now.' He would worry about the absence of their friend Dragan, who had died of cancer twenty years ago, and for the first time in her life Mathilde heard her husband use swear words and laugh about it. Sometimes Amine would become, once again, the young man she'd fallen in love with. Behind his wrinkled face, his low forehead, his grey hair, would gleam the ghost of youth. When that happened, she would lie down beside him and they would laugh together.

It was during this period that Mathilde officially took charge of the Belhaj farm. She had no trouble imposing her authority on the workers, who all trusted her and were respectful and grateful towards her. Mathilde had watched her husband work, and – like him – she courted clients, oversaw harvests and deliveries, dealt with the bank and the payment of wages. She negotiated prices, sometimes helped by Tibari, and complained about being squeezed by the competition from Chinese almonds and those bastards in the retail sector. But Mathilde also decided to change a few things. She had a retention pond built to collect rainwater. 'Water is our lifeblood,' she often told Tibari. She was interested in new, more environmentally friendly farming methods, and had acres of vines planted opposite the quince fields. She never touched her husband's desk. Amine would sit there sometimes and stare at the portrait of the king or the press cuttings about the Belhaj farm, which Mathilde had had framed and hung on the wall. She had a small table brought in, barely big enough for her typewriter, the telephone and a large notepad. It was here that she wrote invoices and went through the books. Here, too, that she organised the visit of a Libyan delegation who wanted to buy thousands of olive seedlings.

Today, Mathilde had a meal prepared that she would serve in the garden. A méchoui, some Moroccan salads and mint tea to help digest the mutton fat. She knew that delegations of this kind disapproved of the presence of women at the table, and that was a relief. She wouldn't have to watch them stuffing themselves, and when their bellies were full she would take them for a tour of the property and tell them about the exceptional qualities of the Belhaj olive tree variety. At eleven that morning, as the pressure cooker was whistling in the kitchen and the embroidered doilies were being laid out on the tables, she went to fetch Amine. She entered his bedroom, with its scent of camphor and medicine. Her husband wasn't there. Nor was he in the office or in the garden, where he sometimes liked to drink coffee and listen to the radio. She asked Thamo, the cook, and Tibari, but nobody had seen him.

The Libyan delegation arrived. Mathilde opened the door to them and made an effort not to take offence at their disappointed, contemptuous expressions. Who was this old white woman? Surely she wasn't the boss? She spoke to them in classical Arabic, and the oldest among them, a man with the square face of an Aztec king, held her hand for a long time. She took them to visit the office. They noticed the photographs of the king, of Amine, and the press cuttings. There were no photographs of her. She led them into the garden, then ran to the kitchen. Through the open window she asked Thamo: 'Still no sign of him?' The cook shook her head sadly.

Amine heard the Libyans' car, and rather than walking along the wide dirt path he slipped between the trees. He started laughing because he'd escaped them. It was a game, even if he didn't know who he was playing with. The air was pleasant in the shade of the olive trees. Nasturtium bushes and blood-red poppies grew around the base of the trunks. He walked towards the greenhouses and then, after a while, he no longer knew where he was going. In fact, he wasn't entirely sure who he was any more. What was his name? He tapped frantically on his forehead with the tip of his index finger, as if trying to drill a hole through his own skull. Birds flew from one tree to another and he looked up to watch them. Tonight he would take little Aïcha from her bedroom and he would show her, by the light of his torch, the flight of the birds in the darkness. He walked across fields. From the greenhouses came the smell of damp earth, the sweetest smell in the world. In every part of his body – in his hands, in the flesh of his fingertips – he could feel the vibration of the seeds slowly growing underground. Yes, he could feel all of that: the magic of life contained within these plants, within these buds, in the thick roots of the rubber tree. He thought he could even hear sap flowing through the trees' veins. He had spent his life listening to their secrets, and now he could understand their rugged, mysterious language. A sensation of warmth filled his chest and he took a deep breath. The olive press was on the other side of the path, and some women were sitting on the ground, sorting through the fruit. They were singing an ancient song that, season after season, had been sung during olive, almond and peach harvests. He wished he could sing it too, but he was finding it hard to open his mouth, to move his jaw. In the distance he saw the Zerhoun. The mountain resembled a man lying on his side. A wise man taking a rest, savouring the beauty of spring.

Across from him, the low wall around the cemetery, freshly whitewashed, shone in the sunlight. He passed the orchard with its golden paths. The birds had devoured the skin on the fruit of the lemon trees, stripping them down to the white rind. The poor lemons looked naked and Amine felt a rush of shame, as if he were the one hanging from those branches. He felt sickened, as when someone you love says something cruel or ugly. We should plant more trees, he thought. We should plant thousands of blossoming almond trees to make Mathilde think it's winter and that the farm is covered in snow. Mathilde . . . He missed her, and he turned back in search of the house. He and Mathilde had always told the children: 'If you get lost, stay where you are. We'll come and find you.' So he didn't move. A confusion of images crowded his mind. He was in Germany, in that frozen field where he'd taken refuge after escaping from the camp, and he saw again the face of that peasant who hadn't denounced him. The smell of his mother's hands came back to him and the sound of Selma's laughter when she greeted him from the terrace of the house in Berrima. His head ached and he felt as if something was blocking his field of vision. He could no longer see the cemetery wall or the mountain. He felt like he was standing on a boat, swaying from side to side in choppy waters, and he feared he would be thrown into the cold dark water at any moment. He put his hands to his head and collapsed to the ground. Some of the women came running. They'd seen him fall. They crouched around him. His eyes were half-closed. His hands rested in the gravel. 'Forgive me,' he whispered. 'Forgive me.'

In the garden, the Libyans were noisily eating and greedily washing down the food with the sugary mint tea that Mathilde had prepared for them. They seemed to have completely forgotten the reason they were here. One of them tore open a half-roll of bread and filled it with meat and shakshuka. Mathilde was cutting up slices of lamb when she spotted Tibari running towards the wrought-iron gate to the swimming pool. He was waving his arms and she knew instantly. She calmly walked to the big palm tree, where she saw her husband's body lying in the back of the pickup truck. Women stood in tears around the vehicle, all of them talking at the same time, and Mathilde didn't understand a word they were saying. 'Give me the keys,' she told Tibari.

'Lalla, I'll come with you.'

'Sit in the back, beside him. Talk to him. Whatever you do, don't stop talking.'

She sat behind the wheel and sped along the road to Rabat.

After two days in hospital, Amine opened his eyes. Mathilde was asleep in a chair next to his bed. He tried to say something but all that came out was a grunt.

Mathilde woke up and heard voices coming from the corridor: her daughter talking with some other doctors. She could guess exactly what they were saying. It was over: he was done for, he would never recover from this. They were saying 'He's a vegetable' and Mathilde wanted to shout: 'No, he's a tree!

Look at his hands, callused and misshapen, like the roots of a magnolia. Look at his legs, like the branches of an olive tree.' At that instant, sitting in the fake-leather armchair, she remembered what Amine had told her once, when they were in Alsace, lying on the banks of the Rhine. He had claimed that trees didn't die, at least not in the way that human beings or animals die. 'A tree,' he'd explained, 'can continue to grow for decades, even centuries. And if nothing stops its growth, if it isn't hit by lightning or eaten by a parasite, it will continue to grow and to bloom.'

In the months that followed, Mathilde took care of him like a baby that would never grow up. She brought him back to the farm, where she put him in the master bedroom, the one with high windows overlooking the cypress-lined driveway. She taught Tibari to carry him to the blue-enamelled bathtub and wash him. She showed him how to cut his fingernails and toenails with a pair of small metal clippers. She gave Thamo the task of feeding him with mashed fruit or vegetables or pots of yoghurt. Whenever anyone came to visit, she made sure that the baby was changed, clean, scented. She sat him in a wheelchair, with a cool towel on his forehead, then rolled him into the living room. She protected him and made a fuss of him, but occasionally, when she was tired or dejected, she would think about the past and she would be seized with a desire to avenge herself on him. Amine was a baby, yes, but he was a baby who had lived with her for fifty years and who had hurt her. A baby who had cheated on her and lied to her.

She lied to him too. Or rather, she didn't tell him about the death of Hassan II on 23 July 1999. That day, she confiscated his radio – 'I'm going to fix it' – and chose the television show they were going to watch. It was the second time a king had died since she'd moved to Morocco, and she could remember, as if it were yesterday, the funeral held for Mohammed V in 1961. At the time, she'd been appalled by the scenes of mass hysteria, the women who clawed at their own faces and screamed until they lost their voices. She'd made fun of these women, who arched their backs, their eyes bulging, like the madwomen in Dr Charcot's photographs. Back then she hadn't understood the fervour that took hold of people, and she'd doubted the sincerity of their grief. But everything was different now, and she wept too, in front of the television. She sobbed real tears – noisily, wetly – not like the miserly little moans and tiny tears that trickled down the cheeks of her cousins during funerals in Alsace. She wept as she watched images of the coffin covered with a gold-embroidered shroud and followed by heads of state from all over the world. She felt proud and called for Tibari and Thamo, who came into the room but remained standing. 'That man,' she said, 'the small one holding the coffin, is Bouteflika, the president of Algeria. And that is Ben Ali, the Tunisian president.' She pointed out Clinton, Chirac, Prince Philip, old Yasser Arafat, being supported by Ben Ali, and the Israeli leader Ehud Barak. Thamo and Tiberi nodded and murmured 'Ah, ah', as if the greatness of their king, even now he was dead, continued to make a big impression on them. Some important men were burying an important man, and the whole world had come to Rabat for the ceremony. The French commentator, who seemed to miss the pomp of monarchy, explained how the people had walked all night to see the cortège and to bid farewell to their beloved sovereign. The prayer began. Tibari and Thamo lowered their eyes. They started to chant, and Mathilde joined in too. She knew the Fatiha by heart and shared their faith. 'All is in the hands of God, He sees us and one day he will reward us for our goodness and our devotion.'

When Aïcha was a child, she used to talk about death all the time. About her own death and other people's. One day, she'd asked her mother: 'When you die, will you be buried in Alsace?' At the time, Mathilde had not taken the question seriously. 'I don't know,' she'd replied casually, before adding: 'Anyway, I'm not ready to die just yet.' But now, at seventy-three, she wondered what Alsace was for her. At what point does your homeland stop being home? Of course she would still think longingly, nostalgically about it, especially in winter, when mist wreathed the countryside and she remembered Christmases by the fire, the taste of mulled wine. But as the years had passed she'd gradually realised how attached she had become to Morocco. She was no longer the girl who'd grown up on the banks of the Rhine amid blue spruces and Vosges mountain streams, because the landscape that had truly formed her was the sandy earth here, and the elements that had shaped her were the burning sun and the dry southern wind. Her face was craggy, and her feet – always bare – had grown so wide that they would no longer fit in women's shoes. Mathilde felt like a stranger to her own childhood, as if it had been merely a recurring dream, a vague memory. She had lived in Morocco, in this house on the hill, for the whole of her adult life. She had grown used to this country's climate, its landscapes, even its food. She knew the customs here, and often, when she was around foreigners, she would forget that she wasn't Moroccan. Yes, this had become her homeland, and she thought there was no better place to grow old. In Morocco, old people were not locked away in retirement homes or abandoned in hospices to be looked after by strangers who felt no appreciation or affection towards them. For a woman, growing old was the greatest sort of vengeance because you were finally treated with respect. People kissed you on the shoulder and blessed you. Once your breasts and your vagina dried out, once your face was ravaged by worry lines, you were accepted at last, taken seriously. In the sunset of your life, people realised that it was true: you had given so much, you had shown great endurance and showered your children with love, and now they had grown up and had children of their own. Age gave you the power that you'd always lacked, the respectability to which you'd aspired. Old women could be tyrannical, autocratic, queens of all they surveyed. They could use their canes to beat and scold others. They could yell and be demanding, and nobody dared to contradict them.

She would be buried here, in the little cemetery. She would talk to Tibari about it tomorrow: a simple grave, next to her husband's. The foreman would have to take care of it and pick up any rubbish that the farmworkers might leave there. For her funeral she wanted a priest and an imam, and before Tibari could object she told him: 'That's just the way it is. You'll find a solution.' She admitted to him that she feared she would die before Amine. She was old too, after all. She had survived kidney surgery and a hip replacement. She had a pacemaker. 'I'm tough,' she said, 'but I'm not immortal.'

No matter what she did, no matter how she tried to reason with herself, Inès was afraid of the police. In Paris, she never broke the law: she didn't buy drugs in the street and she resisted the desire to steal earrings at Monoprix. She refused to join her fellow medical students on a protest march that ended with some of them in custody. She sometimes wondered if it was because of what had happened with Monsieur Baillard and the policemen in the forest. Or if it was because her father lived under the constant threat of a trial that she knew nothing about. Whatever the reason, any time Inès found herself face to face with a representative of law and order, she started to tremble. In France, when she handed her passport to the border guard, she smiled stupidly and deliberately used formal language so that they would respect her. She had French papers, she was allowed to travel anywhere she wanted, but she lived in fear of not being believed, of being thought an impostor, of someone saying: 'Wait a minute, I have to check something.' She would have confessed to crimes she hadn't committed, would have got down on her knees and begged for forgiveness, if only they would leave her in peace.

In 2000, Ramadan occurred at the same time as the Christmas holidays. Aïcha had warned her daughter before she came back to Rabat: 'Whatever you do, don't chew gum at the airport and don't light a cigarette.' During the holy month everyone became suddenly devout. It was like a contest to see who could be the most pious, whose face was the palest, whose eyes had the darkest bags under them. Men who normally wore three-piece suits in hotel bars were now to be seen only in djellabas and taqiyahs. Women stopped wearing perfume and make-up and declared that it was forbidden to brush your teeth.

Inès showed her French passport to a policeman – 'Inès . . . You're from Morocco originally?' – and just as she was about to walk out of the airport a customs official called her over. There was a large brown zebiba* in the middle of his forehead. 'Open your suitcase.' Slowly, the customs official lifted up the piles of T-shirts and trousers, pushed aside the underwear and bras. Inès knew perfectly well that there was nothing forbidden inside her suitcase and yet she felt almost paralysed with anxiety. She could already see herself in handcuffs, accused of smuggling drugs or arms. Her shirt was drenched with sweat.

'And what are these?' asked the official, pointing to two packets covered in red-and-green wrapping paper.

'Those? They're Christmas presents,' she said, her voice too shrill.

'There is no Christmas here.'

The customs official sighed and Inès bit her lip.

'Put it away. You can go.'

Inès did not tell her parents about this incident. They would have thought that she'd been stupid and reckless, and she didn't want to ruin their festive reunion. It had been more

---

* A mark on the forehead caused by repeated prostration during prayer.

than two years since her departure, and in her memory that time was a blur of hard, exhausting work, long evenings spent memorising her anatomy and biochemistry lessons. But she had passed her exam and, as she kissed her mother in the airport arrivals lounge, she thought that soon she would be a doctor too. A doctor, just like Mum. Except that she would never specialise in anything as disgusting as gynaecology. No, her heart was set on cardiology.

The streets of Rabat were empty. It was almost time for fasting to end and Aïcha drove very slowly, leaning forward over the steering wheel. Inès barely had time to greet her father and put her luggage in her bedroom before she heard the call to prayer. Fatima appeared, looking much older – 'Hello, benti' – then went back to the kitchen and turned up the volume of the radio, which was broadcasting a recital from the Quran.

They sat at the table together. There was a tureen of harira, some hard-boiled eggs, pastries with honey, and curds. Mehdi was wearing his old cords and a shapeless sweater. Three days earlier, he had quit smoking. But he was so happy to see his daughter again that he felt like celebrating, so he decided to allow himself a cigarette, just one, and sat on the sofa to light it. Hassan II had died a year ago and there was a feeling of optimism in the country. People were talking about the Moroccan Movida, freedom of speech and the fight against inequality under the reign of the new monarch, known as the 'king of the poor'. All summer long there had been rumours that a vast deposit of oil and gas had been found in the highlands. 'But I don't know if that's good news,' Mehdi told his daughter. 'Oil has always brought the Arabs misfortune.'

Mohammed VI had also raised hope among women, because he'd promised to review their status by reforming the family code, the Mudawana. The country, though, was divided. In March, Islamists had paraded through the streets of Casablanca, while 'modernists' had demonstrated in the capital. Inès had seen pictures in the newspapers of thousands of veiled women railing against the 'Westernised elites' and demanding 'respect for the values of Islam'. She'd found it hard to understand how women could be opposed to more equality. 'But what do you know about what's good for me? You think because you live in France now that you know everything?' Fatima had said while they were talking about this in the kitchen. Inès stared at the maid's back as she hunched over a cooking pot, and she thought: I slept on that back. I blew my nose on her apron. And she felt ashamed of herself for lecturing Fatima about freedom. The maid always said that God loved those who were submissive and obedient, those who did not ask pointless questions, like Abraham who had even been willing to sacrifice his son. Fatima turned around, holding a wooden spoon, and said: 'This isn't Sweden. If people don't like their country's values, they can live somewhere else.'

Inès would have liked to tell her what it was like to live in France, in a country where you didn't risk arrest for eating a snack in the street during Ramadan or being homosexual. She would have liked to tell her about the secular state, but she didn't know how to explain the word 'secular', which didn't exist in Arabic. She could have mentioned underage marriage, or the fact that two-thirds of Moroccan women were illiterate, or the violence of repudiation. If she'd been able to find the words, she would have told her the story that had just popped into her memory – about the woman who used to stand outside her primary school, trying to get a glimpse of her children through the railings around the playground. The woman would watch them play and sometimes, unable to bear it any more, she would say something, call out their names, and finally the people who ran the school would react. The truth was that they felt sorry for her, and it broke their hearts, but they still approached her and told her to pull herself together. 'I understand,' the teacher would repeat. 'I swear I do. But your presence here only upsets the children.' Inès would have liked to tell Fatima all that, but she couldn't. She couldn't speak her own language well enough to communicate something like that, and it crossed her mind that perhaps Fatima was right. Inès was just an impious woman, a stranger in her own land, and infidels like her ought to keep their mouths shut. What was their place here? Her parents, her sister, Inès herself . . . Were they doing something wrong? If they spent their time lying and hiding, it must be because they were guilty of something.

With age, Fatima was becoming touchy and cantankerous. Mehdi called her 'Mars, God of War' and he had to restrain himself from giving her a piece of his mind after she told him that she would no longer touch his bottles of alcohol, that he would have to wash his own whisky glass. 'It's your problem if you want to go to hell.'

Fatima would often regret such outbursts, accusing herself of ingratitude. Are the Daouds my family? she would ask herself. Because what can anyone count on, other than God and family? She loved the children in particular, the little girls she had cuddled, carried around on her back, fed couscous with her fingers. The girls she had washed and dressed, whose hair she had brushed, whom she had called 'my children, my darlings'. She also knew she could count on Aïcha, that Aïcha would take care of her, just as Fatima swore that – if it one day became necessary – she would wipe her boss's arse and even carry her around on her back. There were times, though, when she felt revolted by the Daouds' manners, their lifestyle, the freedom to which their money entitled them. She judged their morals and, after listening to the sermons of preachers on television or the radio vilifying Jews and Westerners and homosexuals, she started to hate them. One day, Aïcha had told her she was intelligent. She could write, a little bit. 'Li bouli' for the chicken (*le poulet*) she was starting to defrost. 'Sosse toumat' for tomato sauce. Fatima regretted not having gone to school, but at the same time she had heard terrible things about schools: the strikes, the arrests, the dreams that turned to dust. When she went back to her own neighbourhood she wondered what she was still doing in this part of the world. Fatima brought new habits back to the *bidonville*. She copied Aïcha's recipes. 'A pear tart?' her nieces said, grimacing with disgust. She repeated phrases she'd heard or rumours that only rich people could know about. She made fun of members of her family who put a bowl of salted water on the electric meter to make it turn more slowly, who hung an old couscous steamer on the television aerial. She didn't belong here any more, but she would never belong there either. All she did was smuggle money from one world to another.

A few months before this, during the summer, she had thought her life might finally be about to change. A man had asked to marry her, and that Sunday, when Fatima had arrived at her mother's house in the *bidonville*, her mother had smiled at her enthusiastically. A meeting was arranged, in a café with red plastic chairs. The man was not good-looking. He barely spoke at all, saying a few words and then falling silent. She let the silence stretch out before drinking a mouthful of tea and asking a question. The man was a widower with three children, and Fatima quickly understood that he was simply looking for someone to look after his house and watch his kids. He wanted a maid. A maid he wouldn't have to pay. That night, Fatima went back to the Daouds' house without stopping at her own, and when she reached the Ambassadors she got in her bed and slept a deep, heavy sleep full of hate. In this country, only money mattered. There was no place for feelings.

They didn't drink champagne at Christmas, but on New Year's Eve the Daouds went to visit Abdellah, who continued to proclaim that God was dead and who liked to recite Rumi's poems celebrating drunkenness. 'Fuck it, I'll do what I want with my life!' the philosophy teacher roared when Aïcha asked him if it wasn't dangerous to open a bottle of wine so soon after the end of Ramadan. 'Alcohol makes me love other people.' Aïcha advised him to hide the bottles in a brown bag and to drive a few miles before throwing them away. She'd heard that there were militias in the neighbourhood who were cracking down on alcoholics, non-conformists and hashish smokers. She herself had suffered the humiliation of a man refusing to shake her hand, and one of her colleagues had denounced an underage mother to the police. Hakim, who was studying medicine in Rabat, nodded. 'Just come to the lecture hall and you'll see. It's become almost normal for men and women not to sit together. As for the lecturers, some are brilliant but others are basically religious fanatics who are paid to teach us science but intone "inshallah" at the end of every sentence.'

Inès's parents, relaxed by the wine, talked about their youth in the supposedly halcyon days of the 1970s, when religion had been less overpowering, when girls could smoke on benches at the university and when they would sometimes eat during Ramadan without feeling judged. Hakim, irritated by this orgy of nostalgia, dragged Inès out to the balcony. He was even more handsome than before, having had his hair cut very short, and she felt intimidated in his presence.

'So you're a doctor too?' he asked.

She nodded.

'What do you want to specialise in?'

'Maybe cardiology. Abdellah told me you've chosen neurology.'

'Yeah, I'm thinking about doing my specialisation in France.'

The apartment was located in the city centre, above a Lebanese restaurant. From the balcony they could see Place Pietri and, in the distance, the archways of the flower market.

'The little girl in the shop window.'

'What?'

'The little girl in the shop window. That was you, wasn't it? I used to spy on you sometimes on Saturdays. I'd stand on the balcony and watch you.'

Inès laughed. 'You never told me that before.'

'Well, I didn't tell your sister, that's for sure. Mia was always very protective of you. She wouldn't have liked me looking at you like that.'

And he looked at her. Like that. In a way he'd never looked at her before. He looked at her the way Amine looked at his trees, with respect and wonder, with no other hope than to see them bloom.

Until the end of her days, Mathilde would feel a fierce, savage, inextinguishable hate for Osama bin Laden. Some would even say that it was this hate that gave her the strength to stay alive for so long, many years after the terrorist had been killed. Her bitterness had nothing to do with the fact that bin Laden was a murderer, a madman or a misogynist. A religious fanatic, a criminal responsible for the deaths of thousands of innocent people. No, this Islamist, this 'bearded bastard', as she called him, had stolen what was most precious to her at the time: her grief for the love of her life.

She was supervising the cooking of the turnip tagines for dinner on the third day when she heard shouts coming from the dining room. Mehdi kept repeating: 'Oh my God!' and 'I don't believe it!' and 'Selim, come here!' For days the only sounds in the house had been whispers. Everyone had been speaking in low voices because Amine was dying and then because he was dead, so Mathilde jumped when she heard these exclamations, like someone startled awake after a long sleep. She wiped her hands on a dish towel – she was worried about staining her white djellaba with the turmeric she had just added to the vegetables – then walked through the hallway. They were all sitting in front of the television: Mehdi, Aïcha, Selma and Selim. Suddenly indifferent to her sorrow, forgetful of all decorum, they signalled her to sit down with them. 'Look at this,' said Mehdi. 'Two planes have just crashed into the World Trade Center. They think it's probably the Palestinians.'

Mathilde did not sit down. She leaned against the wall and almost absent-mindedly turned to face the screen. An aeroplane smashed into a building and she could hear the screams of the crowd below, a sort of mass gasp. 'I don't know if there will be enough tagines for everyone,' she said. 'Maybe I should roast a couple of chickens.' But the others were deep in discussion now. About what this would mean for the future of the world. War, war, war . . .

Mathilde went back to the kitchen. Thamo was sitting at the table, peeling turnips. 'They're full of fibres,' she said, shaking her head. 'It's been too hot lately.' In the backyard, about twenty farmworkers were sitting on the steps or on the ground. They had come from afar to pay one last tribute to the boss, silently drinking their mint tea. The previous day, when Amine's body had been taken in a pickup truck to the cemetery, the workers had lined up either side of the driveway to salute him. Mathilde, who was not allowed to attend the burial since she was a woman, had watched them, and she had felt her pride swell, soothing her heartache a little. Now they were sipping their tea and wiping the sweat from their foreheads and their necks with their large peasant hands. September had brought no respite: it was even hotter than August had been. When Amine had begun to sink into a coma, the air outside had grown dark with thunderbugs. These black insects were tiny, but there were so many of them and they flew into people's nostrils and ears. The wind had dropped and the tree branches had grown so still that it felt as if time had stopped. The closer Amine came to death, the closer his soul approached to God, the higher the temperature rose. In the bedroom, on the edge of their father's bed, the children had appeared exhausted by the heatwave. They had sat in silence, sweating even from their eyelids. Now, in the dining room with its open windows, they were arguing, turning up the volume on the television, and Mathilde felt ashamed because the farmworkers would hear them. They would know that these children from the city were not weeping over the soul of the departed.

Mathilde took two chickens from the fridge. She slathered them in olive oil and butter. She sprinkled them with minced garlic and thyme, told Thamo to roast them, then went through the hallway. A hideous ammonia smell came from her husband's bedroom. The mattress was still damp, and so was the rug, which the cleaners hadn't rolled up to protect it from stains. They had closed the door and hadn't let anyone in, apart from Tibari who helped them undress the dead man. They had refused to allow Mathilde to watch this ritual, and she'd almost laughed at the stupidity of it all. She knew all about her husband's body, and it had nothing to do with sex. No, sex was ancient history. Over the years, she'd seen Amine's nails grow as hard and thick as stone, his eyes take on a milky hue that gave him a disturbing appearance. She'd wiped his scrawny arse; by the end, his poor buttocks were not much more than folds. She went into his bedroom, lay down on the bed and closed her eyes. She waited for someone to come, to spare a thought for the poor widow who was, after all, an old woman too, worn down by the years and her grief. But nobody came and she drifted into a dreamless sleep.

When she woke, the pillow was soaked with saliva and her white djellaba was creased. She was afraid she had slept too long, afraid that the tagine had burned, and that a crowd of visitors was waiting for her in the office or the living room. She went back to the kitchen and lifted the lid of the casserole dish. The vegetables were all shrunken, but the sauce . . . The sauce was perfect, reduced, almost caramelised, and she felt a great satisfaction at that. In the dining room, they were all sitting in the same places, and the ashtray on the table was overflowing with cigarette stubs. Selim looked pale. He was holding his head in his hands and Aïcha was stroking his back. Mathilde would have liked to believe she was consoling him, that they were connected in that moment by a shared grief, a grief that was theirs alone, but she could hear the reporter's voice on the television saying: 'If you're just joining us, it's six p.m. and the United States has just been hit with the worst terrorist attack in the country's history.'

A guest expert explained: 'Only a group without roots could have done something like this. A terrorist group, not a state.'

Mathilde was filled with a black, blind fury and she stalked off to the backyard, yelling: 'Tibari!'

The foreman came running and he saw his boss take off her djellaba and climb up the ladder that led to the roof. He followed her without a word: she might have gone mad with grief, he thought, and he'd always been taught not to argue with mad people. When he caught up with her, standing next to the large grey satellite dish, she said: 'Help me.'

'What is it, Lalla? Isn't it working?'

'It is working – that's the problem. Help me tear it out.'

She put her hands on the edge of the dish and began to pull.

'Wait, wait,' said Tibari gently. 'Just pull out this wire.' And she did.

As she was going back down the ladder, she heard cries of irritation coming from the dining room and she felt a cruel pleasure. It was her house, it was her grief, and she expected everyone to respect that.

'The TV's stopped working,' her son lamented. He was standing in the kitchen, his face as pale as the turnips that Thamo was peeling.

Mathilde wanted to laugh or to bite him, but instead she looked sad and took his hand in hers. 'It's such a shame you couldn't come earlier. He wouldn't have been able to speak, of course, but he would have been happy to see you.'

The visitors arrived, but there were fewer of them than Mathilde had expected and in the end they didn't serve the roast chickens. They sat around tables covered with white cloths – the bourgeoisie of Meknes, some old friends, other local property owners – but Mathilde felt incapable of making conversation. This was due not only to her tiredness or her emotion, but also to the fact that she was staring at all the empty chairs in a rage, as if she'd failed to keep a promise she'd made to her husband. Hamza, the widower, sat to her right, and facing them was his new girlfriend, wearing a Hermès scarf over her djellaba, her designer handbag hanging from the back of her chair. Hamza put his hand on Mathilde's arm.

'He was an honest man. The most honest man I ever met. A hard worker.'

She nodded. 'When we arrived here, there was nothing but stones and doum palm trees. And not a drop of water. He worked like a slave, for me and for his children.'

His children, sitting at the table that overlooked the garden, his children who were still talking about New York as if it was the centre of their lives, as if, even tonight, in this sweltering patch of countryside, the outside world had to continue existing. Of course, it wasn't a tragedy. It was sad but not a tragedy: an eighty-five-year-old man had died. But he'd been *her* eighty-five-year-old man, and she might have hoped for a few tears instead of this indifference, or even this relief. 'It was the best thing that could have happened,' people kept telling her.

Aïcha got up to talk to her daughters on the phone. Mia was stuck in London, where she was working for a bank, and Inès had just started a cardiology rotation. Aïcha kept saying: 'Anything might happen now. We'll never be at peace again.'

The dentist was talking with Mehdi. He was convinced that the Arabs could not have organised this on their own. 'The CIA is behind this. It wouldn't have been possible otherwise.'

'And why would the CIA do that?' Selim snapped angrily. 'It makes no sense.'

'Oh, because you know what the CIA is up to?'

'May God welcome those innocent victims,' cut in Rachid, who had a vineyard a few miles away. 'Those poor souls are paying for America's arrogance. You cannot despise and humiliate people with impunity.'

'Anyone who gloats is a fool,' Selma warned them. Her fingernails were stained dark yellow from the turmeric sauce. 'It's the Arabs who will pay for this.'

Mathilde felt like standing up and telling them all to shut up, as she used to do when they were still children. She could smack them on the backs of their heads or pinch their shoulders, but she didn't move. She pushed the turnip tagine towards Hamza's mistress. 'Have some. Eat.' This was all that was left for her to do: be a good hostess to these ingrates. Only the farmworkers were truly in mourning. They were sitting further away, around tables in the garden. They alone could understand. Not that they were ignorant of what had happened in New York. They knew all about that. They'd watched television too. They'd talked on the phone to a brother or a cousin. Some said that in the quarries of Casablanca people were going to slaughter a sheep or a calf in celebration. Cries of joy had been heard. 'Allahu Akbar!' A famous preacher had proclaimed that this was a blessed day.

Selim left the table. He lit a cigarette, sat behind the desk and, for the fifth or sixth time that day, tried to call Cynthia. He heard two beeps, and then nothing. He couldn't even leave a message, couldn't even say that he was thinking about them. Yesterday he'd had a long conversation with Cynthia. She'd asked how the funeral had been; she'd wanted to know all the details. 'No coffin, really? Is it true that widows wear white there?' And she'd insisted on talking to Mathilde, to offer her condolences. 'Barrett and I are with you, with all our heart.'

Where were they now? Where had they been when the first plane crashed? When the first tower collapsed? That afternoon, as he stared at the television screen, Selim had been constantly on the lookout for them. He'd imagined Cynthia covered in ash. He'd pictured Thomas running northward along Fifth Avenue. Aïcha had stroked his shoulder. 'I'm so glad you're here,' she'd said. 'You're better off here, with us.' Was she a complete idiot? he wondered. How could she think he was better off here, in the middle of nowhere, than at home in Manhattan?

He went out into the garden and walked around the big palm tree. The sky was flecked with stars and he could see the moon, tiny, between two palm leaves. Ever since he'd got here the heat had been so bad that day and night felt like the same thing and he'd lost all sense of time. He felt an intense anger. Towards his mother, for tearing out the wires of the satellite dish. Towards Mehdi, who felt entitled to spout his theories about Islamism and American geopolitics just because he'd read a few books. But above all he was angry at his father, as if Amine had planned this, as if, when his soul made its way up to heaven, the apocalypse had been his last wish. His father had trapped him here, with no possibility of escape. All flights had been cancelled, all airports and borders closed. The United States had become an island, and he had been excommunicated. No, he wasn't better off here, with them, but he couldn't possibly have explained to his sister what he was going through. The frustration he felt at the idea of being excluded at this moment, this unique and seminal moment, this moment that would, he felt certain, still be talked about in ten or twenty years. People would ask: 'Where were you when it happened?' His New York friends would tell their stories. The fear, the frantic race northward, the tears and the sense of communion with strangers, passers-by weeping in your arms. He would have nothing to say, and people would tell him: 'You weren't there. You don't know what it was like.' Yes, Selim had suffered with grief as he sat watching television: grief and an all-consuming envy of that woman, her face grey with dust, who was answering a reporter's questions. He also envied the cameraman who had filmed the images of the first tower falling, and those anonymous men and women who had handed out food and water to the firefighters.

Yesterday, when his father's body was carried out of the house, he had not wept. He had gone with the men to the little cemetery; they were mostly peasant farmers, and they had patted him on the shoulder, as if he was their boss now. 'The man of the family,' they said. The heir, who would receive twice the inheritance of his sister – 'It's Muslim law,' Mathilde had explained sadly – and Selim felt doomed to dishonour. For three days he'd been trying to understand how this made him feel. Not his father's death – that was just part of life – but his father's house, land, fields, trees, and his father's workers, who took off their hats when they saw him. He thought about those illegal immigrants who burned their papers when they arrived so they couldn't be sent back home. The 'harragas' who gave themselves invented identities. Like them, he wanted to live free from father and God, free from this land under which Amine's corpse was buried. 'Leave your daughters in peace,' Mehdi had told Aïcha earlier. 'They're fine where they are.' If only my father had felt the same way, thought Selim. If only he'd been the kind of father who wants his children to get away instead of being the kind that waits for them to return.

Through the window he could see his mother in her white djellaba and Mehdi, who was smoking a cigarette. Selma was smoking too, sitting in the red velvet armchair. Now that her brother was dead she no longer felt any need to hide. He stepped back and thought how perfect the composition was. Why did nobody ever take photographs during funerals? There was always a photographer present for birthdays, weddings and baptisms, so why wouldn't people want a souvenir of a funeral? Selim had got into photography by chance. After a spell in Ibiza, where he'd met Thomas Barrett, he had moved to a small studio flat in the Lower East Side. He hadn't known what to do with himself, so he'd spent his days roaming the streets and taking photographs. He'd kept the camera that he'd stolen in Essaouira, a Leica that he still had in a drawer somewhere. What a camera that was. In the streets of New York, he photographed the strangeness. Two men kissing. A group of very thin girls in extravagant dresses and red high-heeled boots. An old lady softly pulling her dog's ear on a bench in Central Park. A Black guy climbing over the subway turnstiles. Back then he could barely speak a word of English and the camera offered him the possibility of another language. Sometimes passers-by would smile at him. They would strike a pose. Some girls tried hitting on him and they looked disappointed when he retreated, walking backwards, eyes lowered. He got his photographs developed wherever he could. An old Armenian man, who ran a local pharmacy and a corner shop, gave him a discount in exchange for a series of portraits of his family: an obese wife and two daughters with matching moustaches. With Thomas's help, he was hired as an assistant by a fashion photographer: a horribly skinny guy whose extremely long fingers were almost translucent. At the time, Selim had felt numbed by the city's immensity, its filthiness, its violence. In his neighbourhood all the walls were covered with obscene graffiti. New York sometimes left him so exhausted that he could hardly believe there were any old people living here, that the city had not killed them. But Americans were tough. He learned that over time and came to admire their cool self-assurance. He always found their patriotism a bit ridiculous, but he kept that to himself. His first exhibition took place in the mid-1980s at a shabby little bar-gallery. It was entitled *Don't Be a Stranger*.

When he'd first moved to the US, nobody had heard of his homeland. They didn't understand. Selim would repeat

'Morocco' and they would frown or smile uncertainly and say: 'Oh, you mean Monaco?' Some of them thought Morocco was in Asia, some got it mixed up with Turkey or Oman. After a few years he chose the simplest option: he told people he came from France. That always impressed them. They automatically assumed that he must be refined and insolent, cultivated and arrogant. In the world of fashion, that 'French touch' was very helpful, and he never confessed to anyone that he had never lived in France, that he'd only ever visited Paris as a tourist. There weren't any Moroccans in his circle of acquaintances, so there was no risk of getting caught in his lie. He enjoyed these shifting identities, which he reworked as and when he needed.

But as he got older – and he had just turned fifty, after all – he was surprised to discover a certain nostalgia within himself, a desire, probably a somewhat childish desire, to reconnect with his origins. He found a Moroccan hairdresser in the Astoria neighbourhood, where there was a large Arab community. The hairdresser's name was Bilal and he had won his green card in the lottery. He came from Khemisset. On the windows of his salon there were photographs of the Kutubiyya Mosque and Moulay Idriss, and that was what made Selim go inside. The hairdresser complimented him on his hair, so blond and so soft. He seemed surprised that an elegant, athletic man like Selim should come to his shabby little salon where a small radio was broadcasting a recital from the Quran. Selim sat in an old leather chair. While the hairdresser grabbed a small pink plastic brush – exactly the same kind as the one Amine used to have – Selim asked him how he'd learned to cut hair. Bilal shrugged. 'I just learned like that. On the job, you know. I left school at thirteen. When I got here I didn't know how to do anything. But I had a cousin – well, in Morocco everyone's a cousin – anyway, he gave me a chance, I watched him, and there you go.' He began roughly massaging Selim's scalp. Strangely, it was not unpleasant. He twisted Selim's head from side to side, making his neck crack. 'Don't try that at home – you could kill your wife!' he said, before laughing loudly.

Selim went back to Astoria on a regular basis. Sometimes he would go to a café to eat a msemmen covered with honey, or a chicken tagine. He would walk in the streets, where a halal butcher's stood next to an Egyptian café or a corner shop run by Yemenites. He liked chatting with Bilal. The hairdresser had a lively intelligence and his English, although far from fluent, sounded very beautiful. He complained about the stress and the noise and the Chinese guys who smoked and spat on the pavements. 'They talk so loud that sometimes I want to bang their heads together.' Selim never admitted that he was Moroccan too. One day, he asked Bilal if he ever got homesick or thought about going back there. The hairdresser pulled a face. 'It is shameful to go back. The ones who go back are losers. If you don't go back, they think you are a big success and that makes them happy.'

Selim handed him a ten-dollar bill, put his jacket back on and, before leaving, asked him if it would be okay to photograph him in his salon one day. 'I work for a magazine and I think they might like it.'

But Bilal looked alarmed. He had left Morocco during the Years of Lead, and in a high-pitched voice he protested: 'I don't want any trouble. I'm not interested in politics.'

That night, before falling asleep, Selim thought about Bilal: You're not interested in politics, but soon politics will be interested in you. There would come a time when people like Bilal would have to choose, to prove their loyalty, to hang a flag outside their home. They were doomed to live in a sort of purgatory, caught in a vice between the hatred of Islamists and the ignorance of Westerners. Is it possible to love a country that doesn't love us back? he wondered. Is it possible to be from here and, at the same time, from there?

One night in October 2002, Aïcha bumped into her friend Oumaïma outside the clinic. The lawyer was wearing a fitted beige skirt suit and an enormous pearl necklace that she kept touching as if afraid it was going to strangle her. She had brown skin, dark lips and ever-deeper frown lines.

'Are you looking for Rachid?' Aïcha asked. 'I think he's performing a C-section.'

'No, it's you I came to see.'

She took Aïcha by the arm and led her into the small room that served as their staff lounge. She closed the door and whispered: 'I heard Mehdi received a summons.'

'Yes, he told me that. He has a meeting with the judge tomorrow morning in Casablanca.'

Oumaïma looked anxious but said nothing.

'What's the matter? Should I be worried?'

'Well, you know what it's like here. There are all sorts of rumours. But it's not impossible that the meeting with the judge will last a little longer than you expect. What I mean is . . . I think they're going to put Mehdi in prison.' Before Aïcha could say a word, before she had to be reassured or consoled, Oumaïma added: 'Don't tell him. There's no point upsetting him. Just don't let him go there empty-handed. Make sure he has plenty of cigarettes. Something to eat.'

Oumaïma took out her pack of Marlboro Reds and lit one. 'I

don't deal with this kind of case, but I'll find someone for you. As for your husband, he needs to swallow his pride and start defending himself.' She stubbed out her cigarette and kissed Aïcha on the cheek, a lingering kiss, before closing the door behind her.

Aïcha stopped at the supermarket on her way home. She wandered through the aisles with her empty trolley. Please don't let me see anyone I know, she prayed, before finding herself face to face with a patient. She politely made conversation, but her thoughts were elsewhere. She wanted to buy something for Mehdi, but at the same time she feared that such an act might bring bad luck. If she could just forget what Oumaïma had said, if she could tell herself that it was nothing but malicious gossip, maybe nothing bad would happen. The cashier, who saw her practically every day and for whom Aïcha had recently prescribed the pill, looked surprised. 'Is that all you're getting, Doctor?' On the checkout belt between them there was only a bar of chocolate and a box of Kiri cheese wedges.

That night, they ate dinner while watching an American action film that Mehdi had chosen, and for once Aïcha did not criticise the acting or the script. She made no remark about the cigarettes that he chain-smoked, and she was the one who offered to pour him another whisky when his glass was empty. Then she stood up, wished him goodnight, walked through the long hallway and went to bed in Inès's room. For an instant Aïcha thought about going back to the master bedroom. She could lie down beside her husband, put her head on his shoulder and express all the tenderness that she felt for him in her heart at that moment. But she also knew that this might cause a misunderstanding. Perhaps he would think she wanted to make love. Or, worse, he would realise that she was frightened. She didn't sleep that night. When the sun rose she made some coffee and toasted a few slices of bread. Mehdi appeared. He was wearing one of his old suits – one of the few to have survived the great cull – and it looked far too big on him. They drank their coffee standing up in the kitchen. 'I should get going,' he said. And Aïcha, without looking at him, her throat tightening with a sob, handed him a plastic bag. 'Here,' she mumbled, before walking away.

At the clinic, nobody noticed anything amiss. Aïcha arrived on time, in a beige linen suit and high heels. She put on her white coat and picked up the patient files, then washed her hands, for a long time, in the flow of hot water. She wanted the day to go by as fast as possible, and she felt a stab of shame at wishing that her patients could have serious, complicated diseases that might occupy her mind, forcing her to think about something else. She wanted to feel useful. At three o'clock, a woman entered her office. Aïcha had been seeing her for a long time and had delivered both of her children. The woman undressed behind the screen while she told Aïcha about her sons – 'They grow up so fast!' – and complained about the hot flushes she kept having. She lay naked on the examining table and Aïcha, sitting on a small white stool on wheels, moved between her legs. She was about to grab the speculum when the telephone rang. She jumped.

'Excuse me, I'll just be a second.'

She picked up the receiver. 'It's your husband, Doctor. I'll put you through to him now.'

Aïcha turned away from her patient and heard Mehdi's voice in her ear. 'It's me.' He paused. 'I've just come out of the judge's office. He informed me that I'm being indicted and will be imprisoned with immediate effect. They're taking me to Salé in a police van.' Aïcha swallowed. 'Don't wait up for me tonight.' Mehdi's voice broke into sobs. He hung up. Aïcha put the telephone back on her desk, turned around and wheeled her stool back into position. She picked up the speculum and inserted it into the patient's vagina. For what felt like a long time, she remained like that, staring at the woman's crotch without doing anything, terrified at the idea that the patient would see the tears pouring down her face. She put her cold hands on the woman's thighs and the woman shivered. Then Aïcha stared at her vagina as if this was the first time she had seen one.

'What's going on, Doctor? Is there something wrong?' The patient sounded worried.

Aïcha had to force herself not to rest her head on the woman's belly and wail: 'Yes, there's something very wrong.' Instead, she wiped her snot and tears on the sleeve of her coat and went back to her desk. 'No, nothing to worry about. Everything's fine.'

How was she going to face her secretaries, her patients, her friends, her neighbours, her relatives? She felt sure that everyone knew. She grabbed the phone and called Oumaïma. It rang three or four times before the lawyer finally answered. She sighed when she heard the catch in Aïcha's voice. 'The lawyer I mentioned is going to get in touch with you. Go home as soon as you can. Don't stay there.'

Aïcha obeyed this command. She tossed her white coat on the examining table, picked up her handbag and left the clinic without a word to anyone. On the way home she was crying so hard that she could barely see the cars coming in the opposite direction. Perhaps it wouldn't be the worst thing in the world if I crashed into a tree, she thought fleetingly. She didn't really understand what was happening or what the consequences might be. Everything still seemed up in the air, but her most pressing concern was her children. Should she tell them or could she hide it from them? Perhaps this incarceration was just a sick joke, a mistake that would be quickly resolved before anyone found out.

Back at home, she locked herself in the bedroom. She sat on the bed, her handbag slung over her shoulder, still wearing her high heels, and waited. For half an hour, maybe longer, she sat without moving, without speaking, without a single coherent thought forming inside her head. She was in a state of shock, unable to function. Then the telephone rang. 'Do you have a pen and paper to hand?' It was the lawyer, the man that Oumaïma had told her about. Aïcha grabbed a pencil from the bedside table. 'Write this down. Your husband's incarceration number: 13121. His cell number: 16.' The lawyer said he was going to visit his client as soon as possible.

Aïcha had so many questions, but she was incapable of gathering them into words. In the end, all she managed to say was: 'He didn't take much with him. Could you get some things to him?'

'Of course,' the man replied. 'Pack a suitcase and I'll give it to him. He'll need some warm clothes.'

At last she had something to focus on. A task to accomplish. Aïcha stood up and ran to her car. She drove at top speed to Marjane and found two trunks at the far end of the shop. She also bought some woollen blankets, socks and underwear,

Tupperware boxes, packs of tissues and toilet paper, a pack of lighters in various colours, instant coffee, exercise books, a Thermos, a radio, dry shampoo and vanilla-scented soap, packs of chewing gum and mints. She went home and, watched by the open-mouthed Fatima, emptied the boot of the car. She took the maid aside and, in a harsh voice – a voice that mingled anguish with menace – told her what had happened.

Fatima grabbed Aïcha's hands and clicked her tongue against her palate. 'Ah moussiba, Sidi meskine.' When she realised that Aïcha was weeping, she tried to reassure her: 'Don't worry, it'll be okay. My nephew has been in prison for six months because he rode a moped without insurance. Poor kid couldn't take his baccalauréat exams because of that. My cousin Hanane's husband is in prison too. It happens.'

No, Fatima, thought Aïcha. It doesn't happen.

Together, they packed the two trunks, and as Fatima was going to bed the doorbell rang. It was the lawyer. When he saw the two trunks he looked surprised, almost amused. 'Are you kidding? I said a few things, just to make sure he doesn't get cold. For the rest of the stuff, we'll see later.' He took a blanket, the toilet paper and the instant coffee. He explained what would happen next and promised to update Aïcha as soon as possible. 'There's no reason to keep him in prison. He's not a danger to society, and he's always made himself available to the police. Given his age and his reputation, I'm sure we'll be able to resolve this very quickly.'

That evening, Aïcha didn't eat dinner. She drank the remains of the bottle of wine that Mehdi had opened the night before and she lay on her bed. She stared at the ceiling and thought about chocolate, about the benefits of magnesium.

She wondered if Mehdi had smiled or wept when he looked inside the little bag she had handed him that morning. Had he been comforted at all as he bit into the chocolate bar? She imagined him sitting in his cell and breaking the bar into pieces. Mehdi, her love, her tormentor, the father of her children. Mehdi, the best friend she'd ever had, the man to whom she had whispered secrets in the hush of the night. Mehdi, who knew everything about her. Mehdi, who was capable, with a single gesture, of making her heart swell with love or breaking it in two. Mehdi, whom she didn't understand, whom she had lived with as if with an enigma, because she respected his mysteriousness, or perhaps just because she was a coward. Mehdi, to whom she had offered her body, on every continent, in every climate. Mehdi, with whom she had grown older. She regretted now all the moments when she had not paid attention to him, when she had been insensitive to his needs. She wished she could repent, make things better. She would give anything, do anything, to get him out of there. That chocolate bar . . . Perhaps he hadn't even eaten it? He'd probably shared it with the men who had become, in an instant, his companions in misfortune. She imagined the chocolate she had chosen for him, melting inside those strangers' mouths.

Soon, everybody knew. Mathilde screamed hysterically down the phone. 'I'm on my way!' she announced, but Aïcha begged her to stay at the farm.

Selma, by contrast, remained calm and pragmatic. She had been to the Salé prison a few times before, to visit a friend who had murdered her husband with an iron. She offered to go with her to the first visiting session, but Aïcha refused. 'I'd rather go on my own the first time. After that, we'll see.'

All night long, Aïcha cooked. A tagine of chicken with olives. A cheese omelette. Meat briouats. Semolina with raisins and caramelised onions. She had seen the lawyer yesterday and he'd sounded less optimistic. He hadn't wanted to go into the details of the case, and Aïcha – who had long ago got used to not asking questions – had accepted his cursory explanations. He'd told her that prison food was vile, and if possible she should take her husband a basket of provisions every two or three days.

It was raining that morning, on the day of her first prison visit. She drove through Bouregreg, entered Salé, then got lost. Two teenage boys were taking shelter in a doorway. She lowered the window and beckoned them over. They ran to the car, covering their heads with a piece of cardboard.

'Yes, madame?'

'Do you know where the prison is?'

She heard herself speak these words, and it was as if someone else were talking for her, someone who had usurped her identity and was living this strange destiny of hers. One of the boys told her she'd just driven past it. 'It's right there, behind you.' She turned around and saw the immense grey building. She parked outside it. It was raining so hard that there were enormous puddles in the car park. She got out of the car and, even though she was quickly soaked to the bone, even though she had to hold the basket of sheets and food against her body, she was glad that it was winter. This would have been unbearable in spring. And with a surge of dread she imagined Mehdi still being here, behind bars, when the Bouregreg Valley was covered with poppies, when storks were flying low above the houses. He might still be here when the jacarandas and the flame trees were blooming, when the first hot days sent people rushing to the beaches of Salé and Oudayas.

Numb with fear, she joined the queue of women. As they were pushed forward by the brutal guards, two of the women grabbed hold of each other and started spitting insults, showing off their gold teeth. Aïcha observed them from behind, their clothes, their henna-stained fingernails, the headscarves covering their dirty hair. Most of the women in line were carrying a single plastic bag containing mandarins, pears, bread rolls and packets of black olives. Aïcha looked down, her cheeks burning with shame. Suddenly everything she had done struck her as absurd, derisory. Those brand-new Tupperware boxes she'd bought, those little paper napkins that she'd carefully folded, the great care she'd taken in cooking these meals. She'd even scolded Fatima because the cutlery didn't match. This basket now seemed to her the saddest and most pathetic thing in the world. Everyone was going to stare at her, with her clean basket, her flannel trousers, her expensive coat. She felt ridiculous.

The rain was coming down thickly, the way it does in arid countries. The queue wasn't moving, but from time to time a woman would get out of line and be let inside. Aïcha overheard a conversation between two other visitors. One of them was there to see her husband. His crime, she said, was stealing a bull.

'All right, my lovely, who are you here to see?'
'My husband.'

'And what did he do, your husband?'

'He's a political prisoner.'

'Yeah, sure, political,' repeated the female guard, mocking Aïcha's bourgeois accent. She burst out laughing, shaking her head from side to side like an actress in a Turkish soap opera. Aïcha would never forget this round, puffy face, coarsened by too much alcohol. The guard had badly dyed blonde hair, cut short, and was wearing a pair of combat trousers that were too small for her. Aïcha guessed that the woman must use a skin-lightening cream, because there were lots of little pinkish stains on her temples. 'Open the basket, my lovely.' The other women, complicit and silent, watched as Aïcha put the basket on the floor and opened it. 'Open the boxes. Come on, hurry up. All of them.' The guard grabbed her dirty truncheon and shoved it into each meal. She smashed up the pieces of meat and crushed the omelette, spilling half the food on the ground. Kneeling in front of her, Aïcha tried to repair the damage. 'And what's this?' High on her own authority, the guard had taken from the basket the carton of Marlboro cigarettes, the ten lighters and a medicine kit. 'Sorry, honey, but you're going to have to pay for these.'

Aïcha put her hand in her pocket and felt the reassuring thickness of a wad of banknotes against her thigh. She knew she was going to hand over too much money, that everyone was going to laugh at her. She would have to negotiate if she wanted to do this again next time.

'I'll pay for the cigarettes, but not for the medicine. He needs it. He has high blood pressure.'

Metal bars. A door. The sound of a truncheon hitting a wall, three times. More metal bars, then another door, and – in the distance – the sound of the sea. Waves crashing against the rocks, a storm raging over the freezing coast. It was like putting a large shell to her ear. Aïcha went into the visiting room. It was vast, its ceiling so swollen with rain and mud and mould that it looked on the verge of collapse. There were some women holding babies, and some young boys leaning against one of the walls. All of them were waiting. Aïcha looked around. She listened. Crying babies, wailing women, the hum of murmured conversations, the guards' yelled orders . . . All of it came together to create a hubbub of noise that Aïcha found unbearable. She couldn't think, couldn't feel. The basket's handle was hurting her hands and she didn't know what to do with herself. Then the doors opened and she saw the prisoners enter, in single file. She had been expecting to see scowling faces, scarred cheeks, sinister looks. But these men were not frightening at all. Most of them moved forward with their eyes lowered, hands in pockets. Mehdi wasn't among them. Mehdi wasn't there and now almost all the tables were taken. The room contained tables but no chairs. At last she glimpsed her husband. Her husband in his suit, holding a plastic stool. He saw her too. She met his gaze and tried to smile, but she had no idea what the expression on his face meant. She raised her hand. And Mehdi disappeared.

When Aïcha got home that evening, it was dark. She sent Fatima to bed – 'I'm not hungry' – and sat on the living room sofa, in Mehdi's spot. She didn't know what to do. Watch television? Tidy the cupboards? Wash her hair? Feed the dog? She no longer knew what would be an *appropriate* thing to do. This was how she had always lived her life: perform the next appropriate action. Levine came up and sat facing her. The dog stared at her as if expecting to be comforted, as if wondering: Where is my master? What are you doing in his spot? She stared back at the animal and felt like getting down on all fours.

I'm Mehdi's dog now, she thought, and I am going to bite. I'm not going to stay here, waiting for him to come back so I can nuzzle my wet nose against his knees. I'm not going to whine, tail between my legs, and go back to my kennel. Get out of here, dog, get out. Everything has exploded, all the rules have been blown to pieces. I don't know what the appropriate thing to do is any more – there's no logic now, no propriety. I need to become brutal. I have to prove I can be another kind of woman. This morning, the smell in the corridor, and his face, from a distance, looking so sad, and I wanted him to come over so I could touch him and we could weep together. No, I don't blame him for running away, for not wanting to see me. I'm not in his place – what do I know about it? No, nothing is the way it used to be. There are no more rules, no more decorum. What would be the point in always doing the right thing? I want to scream, kick the dog, strip naked, laugh at beggars, eat with my hands behind my back and my face in the food. I want to go mad and forget everything – yes, mad not sad, as mad as those people who walk down the street yelling insults, dragging around a plastic bag full of shit. I need to concentrate on deciding *what* to do. I can't think. It's as if normal life feels strange now, the life when I would eat dinner without wondering if Mehdi was eating dinner, the life when I would cover my feet with a blanket without wondering if Mehdi was cold. I'm not stupid, I know everyone is looking at me, and I couldn't, earlier, at the supermarket. I just couldn't, it was the first time that's happened to me, I couldn't see clearly any more, and it's true, I would have laughed if a patient had described those symptoms to me. A panic attack, obviously: you're hysterical and you have no dignity, that's what I would have thought. Well, good for me. They must have laughed, those people who saw me crying in front of the courgettes. It's been so long since I smoked a cigarette. I'm going to start again, I'm going to become a smoker again, and that'll help me calm down. I wonder how you steal a bull. Did the guy go into a neighbour's field? Did he tie a rope around its neck and drag it back to his own field? There was a film like that, a film I saw when I was young, but it wasn't a bull, it was a cow, and now I think about it I'm not sure the cow was stolen. Oh, what am I supposed to do now? In this house that has grown emptier and emptier until it has lost all its meaning. I'm going to sit in a corner, I'm going to lock the doors or maybe I'm going to go outside, dig a hole in the garden with my bare hands. I can't think in this house, it's like the walls are closing in on me and that brings back memories. I should have said that to Fatima, I should have told her to remove all the memories, but she wouldn't have understood. I don't want to remember, I mustn't be distracted. Stay focused on the present, on the emergency. Aïcha the martyr. And me complaining about everything I had to do. I would give anything, Mehdi, I would give anything to go back to a world where I had to make dinner for the children and help them with their homework and buy them clothes and change their sheets and give orders to Fatima and go to their dance recitals and look after them when they have the flu and organise our holidays. You always told me that I was lucky, that I had no idea what it would be like to have nothing to do. Wait, that can't be me. There must be a problem with the mirror because I don't look like that. It's ridiculous – my neck has never been that long and I've never had those bags under my eyes, or wait, maybe that's why Mehdi left and I just didn't understand, as usual. I need to understand. I need to know, I need to stop being such an idiot. What am I supposed to do now that he won't let me into his office? I'm going in and I'm going to look through the drawers even if it makes me ashamed, even if it reminds me of Mathilde going through Dad's pockets, sniffing his shirts, clearing out the glove compartment in his car, and how she once wrote 'BASTARD' in lipstick on the windscreen and I almost died of embarrassment for her.

She went into his office. She emptied drawers that were filled with photographs of her and the children. She didn't know what she was looking for. An answer, perhaps. A logical explanation for this crazy situation. She opened CCM files, attempting to make sense of the graphs and the lists of figures. But she had no idea what any of it meant, and she felt like banging her head against the cedar bookshelves. 'What did you do? What did you do?' she kept saying out loud. In a large manila clasp envelope she found a letter on World Bank headed notepaper, signed by a certain Curtis O'Hare. The letter was two pages long, and Mr O'Hare saluted Mehdi's admirable management, acknowledging the combination of difficult circumstances that CCM had faced. There were tears in her eyes, and if this Curtis guy had been here, this Curtis guy she had never seen in her life, she would have wrapped her arms around him. She folded the envelope and promised herself she would take it to the lawyer's office first thing tomorrow. She was about to leave the room when she spotted, on top of a pile of books, a small Clairefontaine notebook with a purple cover. She opened it and on the first page she saw Mehdi's tortured handwriting.

Mehdi Daoud: My Moroccan Destiny
Born in Fes. Traditional family. Marxist activist.
The choice.
— *Stay on the margins, protesting, die without being sure that things can ever change.*
— *Move into the public sphere, believing that it's possible to transform the system from within (also a personal choice: admirable wife, two daughters, wants to make them happy and give them a future).*
He will choose entryism.

It was the beginning of a book.

Aïcha had called three times. She'd left a message on the answering machine. 'Call me, darling. It's important.' Mia hid her BlackBerry under a folder. She didn't trust her mother's judgement when it came to what was or wasn't important. Or rather, she knew what was important in Aïcha's eyes: 'Are you eating properly? Are you getting enough rest? You shouldn't work so hard.' Mia felt as if she'd been having the same conversation with her mother for years. A banal, pointless conversation about nothing of substance, only trivial concerns. Mia was twenty-eight and she kept her love life secret from her mother. Well, Aïcha spared *her* the grisly details about her worries and her sorrows, didn't she? Her phone started to vibrate. Aïcha wasn't giving up. Mia thought then that perhaps something terrible had happened – an accident, a terrorist attack. 1994, Marrakech; 1995, Saint-Michel; 1999, the bomb at the Admiral Duncan pub to kill queers. And then 9/11, of course. And the suicide bombings in Israel, Pakistan, Tunisia. Yes, perhaps something terrible had happened. And if it hadn't, she would cut short the conversation.

She answered the phone and whispered: 'I'm at work.'

Aïcha started whispering too: 'I just wanted to check you were okay. I'm not bothering you, am I?'

'What do you want, Mum?'

'Why don't you answer? Why don't you answer the phone even when I tell you it's important?' Her mother was angry now. Her voice sounded different, as if she'd been crying or yelling at someone. As if she'd been drinking. From the other side of the open-plan office, one of Mia's colleagues smiled at her. She smiled back.

'Mum, just tell me what you want. What's happened?'

It was hard to understand exactly what Aïcha was saying, but Mia realised that it was about her father.

'Wait, wait, I don't understand. Who came? Where did he go?'

Aïcha hissed: 'To prison. They took him to prison.'

Mia started to laugh. She knew this was no joke, but it was as if the news was so tragic that it became incongruous. Mehdi in prison? It made no sense. She would have understood if her mother had told her there'd been a car accident, or a cancer diagnosis, or if her father had run off with a twenty-year-old girl, even if he'd just vanished after claiming he was going out to buy cigarettes. Any of these events would have been plausible. Dramatic, sure, but plausible. Mia stood up. 'Hang on a second. I'm going somewhere quieter.' She looked around. There was nowhere to hide. In this office everyone was permanently visible. Even the computer screens were filmed to make sure the employees were not watching porn when they should be filling out Excel spreadsheets. She went to the bathroom and locked herself in a cubicle.

'What prison? What are you talking about? What did he do?'

Before her mother could even reply, she thought: He must have run somebody over. He killed a pedestrian and he'll have to pay off the family and the police, it'll be okay. He'll be shaken up, he's so sensitive and proud, but it'll be okay.

'You know what this is about,' replied Aïcha in a thick voice, as if she was being bugged. 'We're not going to talk about it on the telephone. I need to tell your sister too. I don't know how I'm going to break the news to her.'

Later, Mia would wonder what had got into her, why she had responded: 'I'll go. I'll tell her. I'll take the train to Paris this afternoon.'

Mia went back to her desk. She shut down her computer, put her desk diary in her backpack and – without thinking anything, her head totally empty – left the open-plan office. She heard someone call out 'Daoud!' but she pressed the lift button anyway, and as she got out on the ground floor she knew this was the last time she would ever walk across the lobby of Goodman Partners bank.

She walked to her apartment at 93 Lexham Gardens. It was eleven in the morning but she felt like she was drunk or high as a kite. She was making strange movements with her mouth. She closed her eyes, balled her fists. The image of her father flashed into her mind and she shook her head quickly to rid herself of it, as if she feared that the image would make her heart explode. She wanted to remain rational. She needed to think. The news was so huge that it had completely numbed her. She walked across Hyde Park. A woman was walking a dog with a limp. Some Asian nannies were holding hands with white children, and a very pretty woman was reading a book on a bench. In other circumstances Mia would have sat down next to her. She would have asked her what book she was reading, and told her that she, too, loved sitting alone on a park bench and reading. Mia felt good in London. The city was not as elegant or heart-rendingly beautiful as Paris, but Mia enjoyed the openness of London's parks, the charm of its buildings, the warmth of its pubs. It was a hard-working, cheerful city that lured young people from all over the world. It was also one of the freest places on the planet. Where else could you see girls in miniskirts at midnight on a freezing-cold night and follow them to clubs that stayed open until dawn? It was a city where everyone was free to think and say whatever they liked, to stand on a plastic crate and tell people that Martians were real or the apocalypse was coming. And even if Osama bin Laden had mentioned the United Kingdom as an ally of the American Satan, naming it as a target for jihad, Londoners were not about to lose their famously stiff upper lip. They kept calm and they carried on. When people asked her if she wasn't tired of the rain and grey skies, she replied that they had a false idea of the English climate. In fact, she enjoyed the windy afternoons and the way evening turned to night. Here, in this city so spread out that it seemed impossible ever to know it in its entirety, she loved to get lost, to wander aimlessly. She loved shopping at a Jamaican corner shop and seeing crow women* on the Edgware Road. She couldn't care less that she wasn't English; in fact, the idea struck her as incongruous, because here it wasn't necessary to belong in order to be happy. She'd been expecting the people to be cold and distant, so she was continually surprised whenever a taxi driver called her 'Darling' or a cashier smiled at her and said: 'Have a nice day, my love.' And she adored speaking English. It was a relief to

---

* Women in black niqabs that hide their bodies and their faces.

have left behind not only her mother tongue but her father tongue too, in favour of a third, more neutral language that she wanted to make her own. To start with she'd found it infuriating that nobody seemed to understand her. In a local pub she'd asked for an 'American coffee' and the waitress had said: 'A bacon cheeseburger?' Another time, she'd spent the afternoon trying to correctly pronounce the word 'plunger' because her shower was blocked.

She arrived back at her flat. It was on the first floor and she shared it with two dancers – two young women who left their clothes lying all over the place but always knew the best places to go out at night. There was Elvira, a Venezuelan with high cheekbones who shaved her eyebrows and wore a multitude of small silver earrings in her lobes. And there was Chris, who dreamed of Paris and the Crazy Horse. Mia spent very little time here. She only came home to get changed, take showers and sleep for a few hours. She could just as easily have lived in a hotel. Her life revolved wholly around work. When she'd started at Goodman, in 1998, her manager, an Angolan guy in his early thirties, had gathered all the new recruits in a top-floor room and given each of them an assignment in his sing-song voice: 'You're going to work your arses off, but you'll also have a good laugh.' Mia liked José. He was demanding but fair, capable of explaining the mistake you'd made without shouting at you. He'd grown up as part of a wealthy family in Luanda and had studied at Oxford. He'd told Mia that he was planning to quit the bank soon so he could return to Angola and become a politician. One day, as they were eating salads, standing up in a Pret a Manger, they'd talked about their childhoods in Africa. Both of them had gone to private schools. They'd had chauffeurs and servants and had grown ignorant of or, worse, indifferent to the poverty all around them. They'd read the books of others, in preparation for living in the country of others, but while Mia considered this a source of shame José saw it as a reason to be proud. Across from them a group of young traders were eating sandwiches. Their cheeks were covered in freckles and their hair was as fine as a newborn's. José put his hand on Mia's shoulder and whispered into her ear: 'You know, it's us, the children of their former colonies, who are the truly cosmopolitan ones. When you think about it, we know much more about the world than those little blond boys do. We could live anywhere.' In Mia's team, there was Jilali, another Moroccan, and Michel, a Lebanese man who had grown up in a poor part of Tripoli. A few months ago, Jilali had bought a Maserati. He'd offered to take them all for a ride, and Mia had agreed in the end, even though she found fast cars boring. 'At least London is not like Paris. An Arab can drive a luxury car here without the cops assuming you must be a dealer.'

When she'd first started working at Goodman, the company had been about seventy-five per cent male, and most of the women who worked there had fathers who were bankers or lawyers. Four years later, ninety per cent of the employees were male. The men said it was because women couldn't handle the pace, that they were 'physically' incapable of working until midnight every day, going out partying, sleeping two hours, then going back to work the next day. No, girls were simply not 'physically' up to it, and the reason they kept quitting was that they were exhausted. It didn't seem to occur to these men that the reason women kept quitting was because of the coarse remarks, the guys who felt you up in lifts or boasted over lunch about being sucked off in Deauville by an Estonian prostitute. Nor did it cross their minds that the women who quit might think that a life without friends, without family, without rest – a life where nothing mattered but money – was not a life worth living.

At twenty-eight, Mia earned more money than her parents. She made about three hundred thousand euros per year, and after a while she started to believe what José had told her: 'You deserve it, because you're making lots of money for other people.' She understood, now, that money was a world in itself. A world where race and gender are dissolved in the number of zeroes. Money was a world where people don't think about money. Where everybody feels at home. Where you can spend ten pounds on a peach in winter, where you can go everywhere by taxi without worrying about the cost. A world where you no longer encounter any ordinary people, where you have no idea how they live. She had discovered yachting holidays in Ibiza, where her Black Card opened every door and where she used it to cut lines of coke in the toilets of private clubs. She ate in restaurants without even bothering to check the prices on the menu. She took her mistresses to luxury boutiques where you didn't waste time trying to find a saleswoman, where they always had your size and offered you a glass of champagne. José had asked her if she often went back to Rabat, but Mia had said she preferred to spend a weekend in Beirut and dance with beautiful rich girls who were not scared of anything and who considered impunity a form of emancipation. 'Do you know who I am?' they liked to ask. She very quickly became habituated to this lifestyle. Now she had her suits made to measure by a Savile Row tailor, and sometimes, when she wore her wool and cashmere jackets, she would think about the girl she used to be, roaming the streets of Paris in her brown parka. These memories would bring back a feeling of loneliness and the hurtful impression of being a foreigner who didn't understand anything about the world around her. She was no longer the girl who would walk with shoulders hunched along Boulevard Saint-Michel, thinking that she would never get used to the cold. She knew now that the colder it got, the more you had to relax your shoulders and stand straight. Winter didn't frighten her any more. She liked the rain and the cold mornings.

Mia packed her suitcase – two pairs of jeans, three Pink blouses, some white T-shirts and a pair of Westons – then hailed a taxi on Marloes Road and ran through the corridors of the train station to catch the next Eurostar. It was only when she was sitting on the train, legs crossed, head leaning against the seat-back, that she let herself think about Mehdi. Her father was in prison. As she looked around, she wondered how she would ever be able to say those words aloud. 'Dad's in prison,' she would say, soon, to Inès, and her first reaction was pure incredulity. Her father was in prison, and prison was where criminals were locked up. Was Mehdi guilty of something? She knew that where there was money there was the possibility of a crime, and she remembered that day, as a child, when she had got in bed with her sister and whispered: 'Daddy looks after money.' How many times had she heard stories about bankers who used company money to rent private jets? How many people did she know who'd been arrested for insider trading? Last year a Goodman employee had been fired for buying shares because he knew the price was about to rocket. The guy was an imbecile, thought Mia. And my father is not an imbecile. Although he's not a saint either. She wasn't naive or ignorant enough to believe that it was possible to be completely honest in a country like Morocco. She wanted to call her mother. Now that she was calm and alone, now that she felt capable of thinking clearly, she would be able to ask questions, demand details.

She bought a bottle of beer at the onboard café and drank it slowly while she watched the landscape flash past the window. José had left her two messages. She'd run out of the office on a sudden impulse and she felt no anxiety about it, no regret. In fact, what she felt was a sort of exaltation, as if she'd finally come to the crucial part of the story. For the first time in her life a crack had appeared in the shell that she'd been living inside. She realised the shell was an egg and she was hatching. Everything that had happened before would forever be seen in the light of this moment. Through the cracks in the eggshell, she could see the real world. The perfect, boring world of her childhood lay in pieces at her feet. The spoiled, lucky little girl she had been was dead. Something was finally happening. Misfortune, at last!

Misfortune! At last!

On his first night, Mehdi thought about alcohol. A whisky on the rocks. An ice-cold beer. A sip of Saint-Estèphe. He sat on the edge of his bed, chain-smoking. He was wearing his grey flannel suit and his cellmates were giving him strange looks. Nobody had spoken to him since he arrived. He counted them. There were four other men in the cell and none of them had done more than grunt when they saw him. They're going to eat me alive, he kept thinking. I'm like a Christian in the lions' den. Where did that image come from – *Quo Vadis*? What was the author's name again? Something Polish and complicated. He remembered seeing it one day on a plaque in Rue de Rome. But the name wouldn't come to him. He tried to concentrate on recalling a poem sunk somewhere deep inside him, like a shipwreck. If he could recite poems, he told himself, that would protect him.

And as one mounts the steps of worldly fame . . .
A sound of dead illusions, vain regrets

For two days Mehdi was lost in a state of vast confusion. He didn't know what to do with himself. He was afraid to speak, sleep, move. He was even afraid to look around the tiny cell or at the faces of his companions. The room was dirty and cluttered with plastic bags, piles of clothes and old utensils tossed in bowls. He refused to eat or go out to the exercise yard. Instead he tried to remember his meditation lessons. What he wanted was for his soul to escape the confines of his body and wander free, far from this filthy straw mattress.

On Wednesday he went to the visiting room along with the other prisoners. He didn't pay attention to them because he was so focused on what he would say to Aïcha, the things he would ask her to do for him. All night long he'd been torn between a deep dejection and the determination to fight. As they descended the stairs, a guard shouted, 'Come on, keep moving!' and when Mehdi spotted Aïcha and her all-seeing eyes, Aïcha and the basket she was holding, he recoiled. He didn't even wave at her, he just fled without a word of explanation, and an hour later one of the guards brought the basket to his cell. Mehdi was lying on the bed because he didn't want anyone to see him crying, but a prisoner tapped him on the back. 'Aren't you going to share?'

They're going to eat me alive, thought Mehdi again, staring at the mould on the wall.

'Take what you want,' he said without turning around. 'Help yourself.'

'We share everything here. Come on, boss, get up and let's see what fate has brought us in this beautiful basket.'

Yes, the basket was beautiful and Mehdi couldn't help smiling when he saw the elegant paper napkins, the cutlery, the new Tupperware boxes filled with home-cooked food. He smiled as he listened to the comments of a boy with a spotty face whose hands were like an old man's hands: large and red, the skin peeling, as if they'd been exposed to chemical products year after year. The boy made all the others laugh with his language of the street, and Mehdi smiled, hearing those forgotten words. It was beautiful, more beautiful than poetry.

'She can cook, your missus. You're lucky, boss. And we're lucky too, sharing a cell with a rich guy.'

Mehdi shared his cigarettes and the air grew thick with smoke. They rolled enormous cone-shaped joints with a Marlboro Red filter at the end. His eyes stung, but he didn't dare complain. He was careful. While his cellmates wolfed down the omelette and the chicken tagine, Mehdi watched them. Tawfiq, the boy with the old man's hands, was obviously the leader. Then there was Mamoun, who always sat with his ear to the door, as though expecting someone to arrive. The guy who slept on the bed opposite Mehdi's was known as Rasputin, but Mehdi didn't ask why. He'd realised that questions were better unasked in prison, especially 'Why are you here?' Even so, he was curious about the crimes these men had committed. What had poor skinny Mohamed done, for instance? The others all called him 'El Afrit' – the devil – and he spent his time fingering his prayer beads and praying to Allah. Would they, like him, protest their innocence? Were they, in turn, wondering what Mehdi had done? They probably imagined he was a thief, like the rest of the bourgeoisie. A guy who'd milked the system before the system turned on him.

Mehdi was afraid, and it didn't reassure him in the slightest to know that he was in what the prison authorities called the 'European quarter' due to the high number of foreign prisoners. In this wing, the cells were opened between eight in the morning and six in the evening, and the prisoners were allowed to practise sport in the exercise yard or to play endless games of cards or draughts. It was a far cry from the part of the prison where the real criminals were kept, or – even worse – the part reserved for Islamists. That was a seriously violent place, Tawfiq told him one day. It was like another world, with its own rules and traditions and pecking order. On the lowest rung were the poor and the mad, who cooked the meals and washed the clothes of those at the top of the ladder. They smuggled drugs into the prison, dealing karkoubi, hashish and alcohol to the different cells. And if they were caught they never denounced their bosses. The European quarter was home to government employees, corporate executives, military officers, corrupt bureaucrats and a large number of bankers, who had been targeted by successive clean-up campaigns. These high-society types now shared their everyday life with Spanish and Dutch drug dealers or young surfers who'd naively agreed to carry suspect parcels in their van. There were also men who were here to pay for the crimes of others. Mehdi learned later that Tawfiq was a bricklayer, and Mamoun a cart driver whose job was to transport cement, and that they both worked for a corrupt mayor who'd sold land for illegal construction.

Tawfiq turned on the radio. A football match. Mehdi risked a few comments, and the others nodded. Mehdi would never have believed it possible, but he actually felt fine. Misfortune, at last! Real misfortune, with a setting and secondary characters to match. Not the fake misfortune that he had lamented, year after year, in his vast mansion.

Aïcha came once a week. At first he'd refused to see her. He'd instructed his lawyer to tell her that he didn't want any visitors. Especially not his children. The shame was too much. The lawyer was one of Oumaïma's friends, a competent guy who smoked as much as Mehdi did and whose black humour he would end up enjoying. The first time they met, the lawyer addressed him in Arabic, but this made him uncomfortable so he asked the man to speak French. 'I'm not sure my Arabic is good enough for me to understand legal terms.' The lawyer nodded and went on in French. He had a strong accent and he rolled his rs. He spoke quite harshly to Mehdi, and without any particular deference. He said he didn't want Mehdi feeling sorry for himself. Above all, he told him, there was no point seeking explanations or trying to respond rationally to an inherently irrational situation. 'Justice, injustice . . . doesn't matter. You know how it is: once you've made an enemy here, it's like being bitten by a dog that won't let go.' He told Mehdi to work. 'Write letters. To ministers, deputies, and of course to His Majesty.' But Mehdi couldn't bring himself to do it. Every Wednesday, in the visiting room, Aïcha would tell him off. She was knocking on every door, fighting to get him out of there, and she couldn't understand why her husband was passive, so jaded. But it was as if all those years of waiting had sapped his fighting spirit, his ability to bounce back, to believe in a better future. Day after day he felt like he was being dragged towards a pit of misery, and at night, face turned to the wall, he saw himself slipping into an ever-deeper solitude. Sometimes he would weep, not at the injustice but at the stupidity of his situation. His rage was not directed at anyone in particular; it was born from his inability to find a meaning, a reason for what was happening. It was over. Afterwards, after prison, there would be nothing. He was incapable of writing that part of the story – he wouldn't have the strength, and he knew it. He wouldn't have the strength to look at them, to pretend, to keep going. There would be no happy ending, no return to normality, nothing that could erase the stain on his life. Until now, with the aid of whisky and his illusions, he had believed. He'd imagined going off to battle, proving his innocence, but all that was over. Nothing remained but to stay here and look at these faces, the terrifying faces of the men he lived with now. It was written and there was nothing he could do to change it. A great writer, a truly great writer, might have been able to reword his destiny. But Mehdi was no writer.

These walls held him captive but they also protected him, and the outside world became more abstract with each passing day. Prison is to free men what the land of the dead is to the living. Invisible, unfathomable. Mehdi was like a child screaming, unheard, behind a thick pane of glass. But he wasn't going to weep, to kick and hit at the glass, to wail like a kid: 'It wasn't me, I didn't do anything wrong.' Over time he'd learned not to trust the stories the other prisoners told. They claimed to be innocent and seemed to believe what they were saying. But the truth was that nobody was innocent, nobody except animals and children. Not once during his six months behind bars had he thought about trying to escape. This fact disturbed him. Surely anyone would think about escape: it ought to be the imprisoned man's natural reaction. The reason cages exist is that everyone – every animal – possesses the desire to run away. But he was a domesticated man, stripped of all his wild instincts. He missed his dog. He remembered how stupidly satisfied he felt when, after yelling at Levine, he would watch the dog trudge back to its kennel, hind legs bowed, tail lowered in submission. All the people he'd ever known – all the men and women he'd encountered in his life – accepted, and sometimes even justified, their humiliations. Prison extended much further than he could possibly have imagined.

He had time to think, but not in the way he used to at home. Here, silence and solitude were impossible. You had to put up with the sounds of men's bodies, their coughs and farts, their sniffs and throat-clearings. You had to live with the sickening sight of bodies deformed by incarceration. The greenish swellings on their skin, the lank hair infested with nits, the boils and the long fingernails, the whitish sores at the corners of their lips. He asked Aïcha to bring him a bedsheet and some clothes pegs and he tried to create a screen between his bed and the rest of the cell. But every time he went out into the exercise yard the pegs would disappear. He thought about the inner life of a man, about what it was in him that was inaccessible to others, to humiliation. He thought about the fire inside, the force that resists, and he tried – with what little strength remained to him – to keep this fire alive. Even if it was not a blaze but merely a small flame, he had to keep it burning. He was like a dead man watching his life flash before his eyes, judging his own successes and failures with all the detachment and irony of the dead. Aïcha always said that she lived for their daughters. And he was forced to acknowledge, or rather he was proud to realise, that they were his greatest success. His wife and his daughters. Oh, how he missed them. For more than twenty years he'd lived surrounded by women, and it was not only their gentleness that he yearned for but their élan vital. The sounds of their conversations about ordinary life. Their laughter and their love.

On Wednesdays, Aïcha would bring him books, food, clean clothes and sheets. She picked up his dirty laundry and returned it washed. It was very cold in the cell and he wore several layers. When Aïcha worried about him, he told her he would rather be too cold than too hot. 'I'm dreading the summer. It'll be like an oven in here.' In November, Mehdi caught bronchitis – he was smoking two packs a day and the cell walls were covered with mould – and he wasn't able to go to the visiting room. He was bedridden with fever and he felt so exhausted that he thought he could sleep the rest of his life away. He passed on a message to Aïcha, who sent him some medicine and a letter in which she said she was taking flying lessons. 'I'm begging you: find something to hold on to and don't let go, no matter what.'

Mehdi no longer feared his cellmates. As the weeks passed he was surprised to notice that life inside the prison mirrored the same social hierarchies as in the outside world. The others called him 'Boss' and were so respectful towards him that it made him uncomfortable. They watched as he read books by foreigners and filed his nails. They were grateful to him for sharing his meals and cigarettes. Mehdi wanted to thank them, in his way, for not having eaten him alive. In the mornings, when he stretched his legs in the exercise yard, he tried to motivate the ones who were sinking into despair. 'Come on,' he said to Mamoun one day, 'come and walk around with me. Don't let the bastards grind you down.' For the first time in years he felt useful. He was fascinated by the people around him, and even if he missed his wife, even if he longed for his daughters, and his home, for the comfort of his bedroom and the smell of the books piled up near the sofa, something held him here – something less solid, less palpable than the walls of the prison. This place had brought him face to face with the kind of men he would never have encountered in his previous life. Men who, had he passed them in one of the capital's dark alleys, would probably have beaten or robbed him. In the eyes of these prisoners he discovered essential truths. Who was I really working for? he wondered. He'd thought he was working for the country, for the people, but in reality he'd never been anything more than a puppet of the ruling classes. He laughed at himself, at his hypocrisy, at the vanity of his choices. In the past, people had suggested he should leave Morocco. But to do what? To be an old immigrant in a cold European city? A fugitive and a coward in the country of others? He recalled a line from Kundera's *Immortality*: 'The ally of his own gravediggers.' Yes, that's what he was.

Because he was bourgeois and educated, the other prisoners asked for his advice and his cell became a sort of office where he would receive patients every afternoon. Most of them were on remand, and some weren't even sure what had brought them here. They'd lost all sense of time and rarely heard any news from outside. Their wives didn't have time to visit them because they had to work every hour of the day to pay for lawyers who didn't turn up to hearings and for intermediaries who claimed to know people at the Ministry of the Interior or the palace. These men held out folded sheets of paper to Mehdi because they were incapable of reading what was written on them. A police report. A debt collection letter. A report of seized contraband. Mehdi took a particular interest in the case of Mamoun, who'd been subjected to the most absurd, revolting treatment. The poor man had found himself on trial at the

Special Court as a civil servant when the truth was that he'd done nothing more than transport building materials on his cart. He often wept over his donkey, which had been taken away by the police when he was arrested. 'God only knows where he is or what they've done with him. As God is my witness, I never hurt an animal. My donkey is the only thing I ever owned.' Mehdi asked Aïcha to bring him his purple notebook. 'It's a small Clairefontaine notebook. You'll find it in my office, on one of the shelves.' And every day he would write down the stories he heard.

As Christmas approached, his bronchitis worsened. He had a hacking cough that kept him awake all night and annoyed the others. His fever would not go down and Tawfiq grew concerned. 'You need to see a doctor, boss. There's one here, you know – the guy with the head like a light bulb and those little weasel eyes.' Mehdi started to laugh, which set off another coughing fit. That evening, the doctor turned up at their cell. He was a prisoner who treated the guards in return for them getting his prescriptions filled and supplying him with equipment – stethoscope, head mirror, cardboard tongue depressors.

After examining Mehdi, he gave his diagnosis: 'It's a pulmonary infection. You could make a request to be taken to hospital, but that won't do any good here. I once waited two days for a biro. It's not my specialty, but I would say that a good dose of antibiotics should be enough to get you back on your feet.'

'What is your specialty?' Mehdi asked.

'Oh, you don't know? I'm a gynaecologist. That's why I'm here.' He rolled his eyes and gave a deep sigh. 'Abortion.'

Dr Zouheir was right: a week later Mehdi felt much better. He was still short of breath and he hadn't got rid of his cough, but his fever had gone and his appetite had returned. The doctor dropped by every day to check on him. Mehdi told him that his wife was a gynaecologist too, and this was probably what led Dr Zouheir to confide in him. He'd been in prison for two years and up until now he had carefully avoided making friends. He was wary of everybody and spent his time reading or listening to Middle Eastern music. One afternoon, when Mehdi's cellmates were engaged in a furious game of dominoes ('I don't like to play,' the banker always told them), Dr Zouheir told him his story.

'I was caught red-handed in the operating room. I was still wearing my white coat, my mask and gloves when they threw me in the back of the police van. The judge was a lunatic. He yelled at me: "We know all about people like you. You take babies out of women and you kill them!" He sentenced me to ten years. Reduced to four on appeal. That judge was less fanatical, but he was corrupt. He kept sending me messages on my mobile, trying to get money out of me. As I'm sure you know, we don't perform abortions for the pleasure of it. Some women need them, and it's far less dangerous if a competent doctor does it. I'm not a militant or an intellectual. It just happened by chance. The first time, a women came to my office. She was very pale and she was wearing an old-fashioned headscarf and djellaba. She told me she'd had an abortion and that she hadn't stopped bleeding since. She didn't hide her occupation: she was a prostitute, you see, and she had a child. But if she never stopped bleeding, she wouldn't be able to work any more. And she didn't have a penny. As I said before, I don't judge people. What they do with their bodies is not my concern. I diagnosed intrauterine retention and performed a revision. The guy who'd operated on her was a real butcher – he could have killed her. The girl kissed my hands and my shoulder. She blessed me and promised she would save enough money to pay me. She came back a few weeks later. She was so elegantly dressed that I didn't recognise her. She gave me a thousand dirhams. After that, all the prostitutes came to see me. I also treated students, the daughters of doctors and lawyers, even girls as young as thirteen, disabled children impregnated by an uncle or a father. You can't imagine the things I've seen.' He slid his hand over his face, from his forehead to his mouth, as if trying to wipe away the memories imprinted on his retinas. 'I'm not going to lie to you – I was attracted by the money. Your wife must know this, right? Childbirth and cancer pay much less than abortions. When it comes to abortion, there's no haggling. Either you pay up or you can forget it. I earned good money. I paid off the mortgage on my office and, two years ago, I decided to stop doing abortions. I'd heard about someone who was arrested for performing abortions near Beni Mellal. I'd already made the decision, I swear, but someone denounced me. They sent letters to the Order of Doctors, to the police, to the public prosecutor. And I was arrested.' He nodded slowly, as if still unable to believe that such a thing could have happened to him.

Nobody wants to hear about vaginas, thought Mehdi. Aïcha could have been here instead of him. Aïcha the saint. Aïcha the martyr.

Aïcha, meanwhile, was busy running around, making calls. She had long ago swallowed the last mouthfuls of her pride and now she was begging, pestering, spending hours sitting around in waiting rooms. The blood in her veins had been replaced by molten lava, and she felt ready to bite people, to hit them. Everybody pleaded with her to be patient. 'They just want to reassure the people, show them that they're tough on corruption. But don't worry, things will clear up soon,' a former minister of justice told her. She couldn't eat or sleep any more, and Fatima kept begging her to get some rest. Mathilde came to stay with her in Rabat, despite her daughter telling her to stay at the farm. Mathilde did the shopping and cooked meals. Selma joined them too. She slept in Inès's bedroom and in the evenings she would invite some of her acquaintances to the house: former cops, criminals, anyone who might provide them with information. They all said the same thing: 'You're going to have to pay.' One evening, when Aïcha came back from the clinic, Mathilde and Selma made her sit on the sofa and handed her a flight ticket. 'You're leaving for Paris tomorrow,' her mother told her. 'Don't start arguing – you're going, and that's that. Selma and I will take care of the baskets. Mehdi will have everything he needs. It'll do you good to spend a few days with your daughters.'

Aïcha obeyed her mother. She pulled clothes off their hangers and threw them in a suitcase. She landed at Orly at six the following evening. As she leaned back in the speeding taxi, she felt an intense relief – and an immense gratitude towards Mathilde and Selma. She hadn't thought it would be possible, but being here, she felt far from the prison, from the misfortune and anxiety of her daily life. The avenues were all lit up for Christmas and people were walking around with shopping bags full of gifts: life went on. Her daughters had been waiting, and they went down to the lobby to welcome her. There, without a single word being spoken except for 'Mum', they hugged one another. For a long, long time.

How grown-up they were, these children of hers! They'd decorated the apartment – 'It was a nightmare getting the tree up here,' admitted Mia – and filled the fridge. Aïcha offered to cook Christmas dinner, but everything was different here. She couldn't find the spices she needed, and the kitchen was too small and poorly equipped. She felt lost without Fatima; she didn't know where to start. In the end, she burned the guinea fowl and the green beans were oversalted. 'It's impossible to cook well when you're not hungry,' she concluded. So, instead of eating, they drank champagne. The girls didn't dare ask her about the 'situation'. Mathilde had told them that Aïcha needed to take her mind off it, so they forced themselves to talk of more cheerful things. They were opening a bottle of wine when Aïcha's phone rang. She always kept it on her, just in case there was news about Mehdi.

'I don't know this number,' she said. 'But I'm going to answer it anyway – it might be important.' She went out into the hallway. 'Hello?' And she heard her husband's deep, cavernous, beautiful voice. 'Aïcha, it's me. I can't talk for long. Someone lent me a mobile, I'll tell you about it later. Are the girls with you?' Aïcha leaned back against the wall. The look on her face must have been quite a sight, because Inès and Mia were staring at her anxiously. 'Yes, they're here beside me.'

'Tell them to come closer so I can speak to them. Hello, my darlings. I wanted to wish you a merry Christmas.'

27 December 2002

Dear Dad,

Mum will bring you this letter. Because, sadly, she'll be leaving us soon. I'm going to try to keep my handwriting legible because Mum told me that you had trouble reading my last letter.

I think about you all the time. I almost didn't want to tell you that, because I was afraid it might worry you or make you suffer. But my thoughts for you aren't sad or morbid. You live inside me. You come with me wherever I go. Perhaps I should make small talk, but I'm not very good at that. I know Mum doesn't want us to talk about the 'situation'. I understand that. There's no point feeling sorry for ourselves or crying ourselves to sleep at night.

I think constantly about all the things you can't do any more, and I try to live my life even more, even better, to make up for it. I don't sleep much, but I read a lot. I'm learning things that you already know. I watch football matches with Mia and I've recorded your Sunday morning shows for you. I went to see an action movie – I hated it, but I know you would have liked it.

I feel like the seconds are denser, the hours heavier than before. Everything I do and say is for you, and sometimes I feel ashamed of the use I make of my freedom, the banality of my actions and my thoughts. On the bus, on a café terrace, during the commute to the hospital, I try to imagine what it would be like, a life without movement, with no horizon. When I sleep, the warmth of my bed is for you. All my meagre joys are for you. You're like a phantom limb, Dad.

I hope you know how much we're thinking of you – Mia, Mum and me – and how much we love you. I understand that you don't want to see us, but I promise, if you ever change your mind, I will be strong enough.

Your daughter, Inès

It started with her hands. Little white marks appeared around her fingers, on her palms. Mia showed them to Inès, who shrugged and said: 'Dermatology's not really my thing. It could be a fungus, I guess.' Then the marks spread to her elbows, her knees, even her belly. The girls she slept with examined her body like children trying to see creatures in the clouds. Geographically inclined lovers traced the coastline of Africa with a fingertip. Poetic mistresses discerned birds, unicorns and mermaids on her skin.

In the end, she went to see a doctor, who diagnosed vitiligo. It was an autoimmune disorder, he explained. 'Your body is fighting against itself.' He asked her if anything had happened in her life recently, a particularly stressful event that might have triggered the malady. 'It happens, you know.'

Mia pretended to muse on this before telling him: 'No, I can't think of anything.'

She had done nothing since leaving London. Well, nothing except walking and reading, going to the cinema and taking shelter in churches when it got too cold. At first she read Wilde, Kafka, Dostoevsky, driven by the absurd desire to understand what her father was going through, to embrace his suffering. Then she bought poetry collections and devoured American novels, especially William Styron and Carson McCullers. She read everywhere, all the time. At the bus stop, in a queue at the supermarket, in restaurants where she ate lunch alone. The books protected her, saved her from the shame of solitude. Sometimes she felt as if Paris sympathised with her sorrow, understood it. She walked on bridges and thought about throwing herself into the Seine or getting drunk in the yellow light of a brasserie, numbed by the hubbub of conversation, the clink of cutlery, plates and glasses. She drank to drain her rage, to silence the voices that screamed inside her head. The night she'd returned to Paris, she had stopped at a bar before going to see her sister. Before telling her. Through the window of a small bistro where she was sitting, she saw a billboard ad at a bus stop: 'Morocco, the most beautiful country in the world.' That night, she waited on the landing outside Inès's door for a long time before her sister appeared, even lovelier and slimmer than the last time she had seen her. Mia, not knowing how to break the news, said: 'Do you have anything to drink?' It was only after the first glass, or maybe the second, that she was able to say the words. 'Dad's in prison.' Through the half-open window she could hear the water in the Fontaine des Innocents. Inès tilted her head and smiled sadly. Images, too clichéd to share, came to their minds – of handcuffs and iron bars, a ball and chain attached to an ankle, the rattle of mess tins, wails of despair. A man in a cage. Their father in a cage. The bird with clipped wings. Their memories of that night would be hazy. They drank a lot and laughed as they talked about their childhood, clinging to the past so they wouldn't have to endure the present. For a long time Mia would say that Inès had slept on the floor, and Inès would say that her sister had cried out in her sleep, a shrill cry like the siren of a departing ship.

*

'Don't come,' Aïcha told them, and from that day on they waited. As calm and obedient as Levine. Down, girl. Sit. Stay. They didn't want to stir up trouble, to make a scene. What was worse – their mother's suffering or their father's? And which of them was the most admirable? Not that it mattered, because they knew they were powerless anyway. They didn't ask questions – 'Innocent or guilty? And of what?' – and when they talked on the phone with their mother they spoke in code, convinced that their calls were being monitored. They respected Aïcha's desire to spare them. It was then – in the long hours of that night and in the days that followed, spent wandering the streets of Paris – that Mia felt her old desire to write rising inside her again, like a drowned man floating back up to the surface. She was haunted by her father's solitude, not only the solitude of his prison cell but the solitude of almost ten years spent rattling around that mansion in the Ambassadors, and she sentenced herself to the same punishment. There was only one way of escaping injustice, she told herself, and that was solitude. She made herself a mask, like an actor in a Noh drama, a mask of inscrutability. To escape injustice you must take nothing and give nothing. You must write, in absolute secrecy.

Inès worked constantly, shift after shift, and when she was home all she talked about was Jérôme. She'd met him at medical school. He lived at the bottom of Rue Soufflot and for a month he'd had white roses delivered to her every Friday. With Jérôme, she talked constantly about Mia. She told him how formidable and funny and courageous her sister was. 'Mia's read everything and she's travelled all over the world . . . Mia's not afraid of anything.' Jérôme would roll his eyes whenever Inès praised her elder sister. Sometimes it bothered her, the way he spoke about women or homosexuals or international politics. 'Oh, don't say anything like that in front of Mia!' Hearing this, Jérôme had less and less desire to meet her. He hadn't made a fuss like this when he invited her to dinner with his parents.

At the time, he and Inès had been together almost a year, and she had been sleeping with him practically every night in his attic room above his parents' apartment. Inès had been nervous about the encounter. Instead of roses she'd bought them a rose bush, and she'd felt a bit ridiculous standing there with the big pot in her hands when Jérôme's mother opened the door to her. 'How kind, really, you shouldn't have.' His mother had been wearing a navy-blue cardigan with orange trim and Inès had admired her elegance. She'd followed this woman into a living room with windows overlooking the Jardin du Luxembourg. The decor was drab and old-fashioned, and the old armchairs looked terribly threadbare. Later, she would discover that they were Louis XV, and that the long wooden table had been won after a fierce battle over a legacy.

The mother – Catherine – had smiled at her, but it was the father who'd done all the talking. He had long hairs growing out of his ears, and his nose and forehead were dotted with crater-like pores. He wrote books and seemed very proud of the fact – books published by university presses. He knew lots of people in publishing and was currently working on a novel. 'Morocco? Ah, very good.' He had travelled through Algeria in the 1970s – yes, after independence. He'd wanted to help. 'You can't imagine how poor people were. It brought me to tears once. They couldn't even afford a carton of milk for their children.'

'And there's Saadia too,' the mother added. 'She's Moroccan, isn't she?'

Yes, Saadia, their cleaning lady, who had practically raised Jérôme and his sister, and who had worked for them for more than twenty years. It was regretful the way it had come to an end, but best not to rake over all that again. They thought they were being polite, telling her again and again how hospitable and tolerant Morocco was.

Sitting, legs crossed, in her uncomfortable chair, Inès just smiled and nodded. She wanted to tell them the truth about other aspects of her homeland – the parts that annoyed her and made her angry – but she didn't dare. She didn't know whether to betray her country or betray herself. She didn't mention her father. Since his imprisonment she'd started inventing different stories about him. To a friend at medical school she claimed he was an opposition leader, a martyr, a brilliant intellectual incarcerated for his ideas. To other people she implied that Mehdi was a criminal, a sort of mafioso. But she wasn't sure which lie to tell Jérôme's parents, so she just kept quiet about him.

It was often like this when she told people she was Moroccan. People felt obliged to show their interest, their open-mindedness. They wanted to prove that they didn't tar all Arabs with the same brush, that they were not the type of people who sank to the level of stereotypes. Whenever a raï song came on at a club, she would find herself pushed onto the dancefloor. People were surprised that she ate pork and drank alcohol, and they were thrilled when she told them that her sister was gay. 'That's wonderful!' And then there were those who felt sorry for her, who thought it admirable that she had got this far in life, given her background. They were convinced that she must have crawled out of some gutter, and for these people she described the gutter in great detail, making it as dark and stinking as they imagined it. She never lost her temper or expressed any irritation.

Jérôme's parents seemed to find her charming. 'And pretty too,' Jérôme's father would tell him later, 'very pretty', as though he was proud of his son for netting such a beauty. At the table, Catherine served them a bland, stodgy quiche. Inès observed this couple and couldn't help thinking that she hated them. She felt certain that Jérôme's father had cheated on his wife, frequently, and perhaps that he had beaten her too. A slap in the face when she got on his nerves. As he carved the chicken, she imagined him raising his right hand, brows furrowed with rage, like a father trying to scare a child. There was a sadness, a bitterness in the air of this apartment. Melancholy seemed to seep from Catherine in particular. When Inès had asked her boyfriend about his mother's job, he'd replied: 'She looked after us.' Inès had found this strange, although she knew better than to say so. She and her sister had been taught never to be dependent on a man.

But Jérôme was handsome, he was perfect. He was at ease everywhere in Paris, and he had childhood friends and memories on every street in the sixteenth arrondissement. He played rugby, and once a week he would go on a boys' night out, coming home completely wrecked. He always knew about the hip new restaurants. He took Inès on weekends to the Normandy coast or to his friends' country house. Once, he announced to everyone: 'Inès is going to make us a couscous.' His friends were all thrilled, and Inès spent the whole morning sweating in the kitchen. Jérôme spent summers in Corsica, at his family's second home, and he promised her that one day he would teach his beautiful African girlfriend to ski, even though she didn't like the cold. He loved her hair, the density of her curls, and it turned him on to grab a handful when they had sex. Sometimes she wished he would be less prudish, less polite, when he took her. She was too shy to tell him, but she wanted him to insult her, to talk dirty, to get rough with her. He lost his temper once because she started stroking her clitoris while he was inside her. He sat naked on the edge of the bed and sulked. 'It's like you don't even need me.'

Soon he would be a great doctor, a famous professor, and Inès thought how wonderful it would be to have a husband like him, a French husband with a French surname, a husband from here who had grown up near the Jardin du Luxembourg. She told her mother all about Jérôme, and she felt sure that Aïcha was happy and reassured to know that her youngest daughter was boxed off, that she had someone. Inès felt safe with Jérôme: there was nothing mysterious or elusive about him. She was sure he would never end up in prison like her father. He was a worrier who was always reminding her that it was important to keep her papers in order, and a conscientious boyfriend who helped her fill out the necessary paperwork. Inès told her mother all this. She thought she was being very grown-up, but in reality she was still thinking like a child. She wanted to love this man to make her mum happy.

When it came to Jérôme and Mia, it was a whole other story. For weeks Inès had been finding excuses to postpone their meeting. All her life she had been afraid of her sister, of her violence, and now she was afraid of Jérôme. She felt sure that he was much more intelligent and cultivated than her and she admired the way he had an opinion on everything. They would argue sometimes, and he would make cruel, cutting remarks. One day, he made fun of Muslims' annoying tendency to say 'inshallah' all the time. He considered it cowardly and irresponsible to always leave things up to God, and said that all this talk about destiny was bullshit. He had strong viewpoints on the monarchy and on bourgeois Moroccan families like Inès's, who employed slaves – 'yes, slaves' – and exploited the lower classes. 'And if everybody leaves your homeland, even the richest people who own everything, who will be left to develop the country?' He thought it perfectly understandable that people should flee war or famine. 'But why bother coming to France, a country where – let's be honest – lots of people don't want you?' She was with him on election night in 2002 and he started crying when Jean-Marie Le Pen's face appeared on the television screen. She didn't admit that she'd never voted in her life and that all she knew about French politics was what she had learned from the satirical TV show *Les Guignols*. She asked him why he was so upset. What difference could it make to a man like him if the Front National were elected? 'But don't you see?' he told her. 'I'm crying for you.'

While Mia liked to lose herself among the crowds in Barbès and try to follow conversations in Arabic, Inès had turned her back on her homeland. I feel French, she told herself repeatedly. Of course I'm French. One day in March 2003, coming out of a restaurant carrying shopping bags, she bumped into a couple on Rue du Renard. She was on the phone with Aïcha. Mehdi was increasingly ill and there was a chance he would soon be granted medical parole. 'Medical parole my eye!' her mother said, growing heated. 'They just want him to die at home.' As Inès continued walking towards Beaubourg, she heard someone shout: *'Racaille!'* The man yelled it several times, and in the end she turned around, but not for a second did it cross her mind that the man might be yelling at *her*. That wasn't possible. The insult couldn't be aimed at her because she was invisible. She wasn't scum. She wasn't like the others. She wasn't that kind of Arab. But when she looked back, she saw a man in his fifties glaring at her while his wife stared at the ground, ashamed of her husband's rage. Slowly, Inès walked towards them and, in a soft voice, asked if they were talking to her. The man responded by shouting that she had pushed over his wife, who'd almost broken her hip on the pavement, and that it was typical of people like her. Illegals. Criminals. Inès kept smiling. Perhaps she should have tied up her hair, but she'd just finished her shift and that was why she looked a little dishevelled at that moment. Without losing her composure, she apologised profusely, even asking the woman if she'd been hurt. 'I'm a doctor . . . Well, actually a medical student. Could I buy you a coffee? We could find somewhere for you to sit down, so you could rest . . .' The woman stared at her with big, pale, sad eyes. Inès was desperate to please her, to apologise for the mix-up, to apologise for all the real Arab scum, the ones who committed crimes and stole people's jobs, because she wasn't one of them. She explained that she was not a criminal or an illegal immigrant, just an overworked medical student who'd been in a rush. She was just a woman, like her, who'd eaten a quick dinner and was talking on the phone to her mother.

'Yes, yes,' the woman said.

Her husband, looking sheepish, muttered: 'But you could have said sorry.'

Inès nodded. 'Yes, monsieur, you're absolutely right. I should have said sorry.'

'All right, let's go,' said the woman, deeply embarrassed by the whole situation, and she held on to her husband's arm. Inès watched them go, and in that moment she felt proud of herself. As she walked towards Boulevard de Sébastopol, she thought what a good job she'd done of shutting them up, making them look petty and ridiculous with her perfect manners and her pretty smile.

In the days after this, she thought about the incident more and more, but her pride gradually faded and was replaced with regret. She played the scene over and over in her mind, but now she got angry, she gave them the finger, she told them to fuck off. She daydreamed about seeing them again, by chance, and taking back the apology she'd offered. She didn't tell Mia or Jérôme about what had happened. She was disgusted with herself. She'd acted like a child, like a little people-pleaser, desperate to reassure them: 'I'm like you, not like them.' She'd abased herself, humiliated herself. And what if I'd spoken with an accent? she wondered. What if I'd been wearing a veil? What if I'd got angry? What would have happened then? She wondered if she was guilty of betraying her people. Then she wondered: Who are my people?

'Don't come,' Aïcha told her daughters again in the spring. 'He needs to rest and recuperate.' Medical parole or not, Mehdi was released from prison. One morning, a guard told him to pack his stuff and put his flannel suit back on. It was far too big for him now. As on his first day in the cell, he sat on the edge of his mattress and waited. He didn't want to get his hopes up too high; he feared being disappointed again. It had happened once or twice already since he'd been here. But this time the guard returned and said: 'Daoud, let's go.' Mehdi, whose complexion was the ashen grey of the very ill, shook his cellmates' hands. 'May God watch over you,' they said to him, and Mehdi thought: Please, no, I don't want Him to watch over me. May He have the decency to leave me in peace.

Aïcha was waiting for him in the car park. He got in the car, her husband in his grey suit with his grey face, smelling faintly stale and mouldy. Back at home, Mathilde and Selma were waiting and they threw themselves at him, as clumsy and sincere as Levine, who pissed on the living room carpet.

'What would you like to do?' asked Mathilde.

'Anything you want,' added Selma.

Mehdi smiled at them. 'All I want is a whisky and a steak.'

Selma took charge of the alcohol and Mathilde went to the butcher's. By the time they got back, Mehdi was asleep on the sofa, sitting in his spot, where the armrest was black from cigarette smoke. He looked like one of those giraffe women after their neck rings have been removed: head thrown back, like a dead swan.

What Mia would later recall from this period were, above all, the unspoken words. One evening, she overheard her sister talking on the phone with Hakim. She heard the words 'oncologist' and 'protocol', and Inès kept repeating the expression 'such bad luck'. What she knew about cancer – the mere word made her shiver – Mia had learned from films with heart-rending titles: *Terms of Endearment*, *Dying Young* with Julia Roberts, stories of bald people vomiting into toilet bowls, farewell scenes around hospital beds, howls of rage against the injustice of it all. Those films always ended badly.

One morning, Levine vanished. Fatima was cooking his breakfast. She stood in the kitchen doorway and shouted the dog's name, which she found difficult to pronounce. She looked for it in its kennel and in the garden. She opened the gate and gazed up the deserted driveway. Levine was nowhere to be seen. Fatima never wanted to talk about what happened that morning. 'Too sad,' she would tell the girls when they pestered her with questions. 'Heartbreaking.' Yes, it was true, she had seen it all – Aïcha's frantic attempts to revive her husband – and she'd heard the screams, but as God was her witness, she did not want to talk about it.

'You need to come,' Aïcha told Inès one morning in June 2003. Inès tried to get in touch with Mia, but her sister wasn't answering her phone. Of all the days to let her phone battery die . . . Inès went into all the bars and cafés in the neighbourhood. 'She's very tall, short brown hair, with white stains on her hands.' She went back to the apartment and bought two flight tickets, and when Mia came home, pupils dilated from the joint she'd smoked on the quays of the Seine, Inès yelled at her. 'And on top of everything else, you're stoned. Dad's dead and you're off your fucking head!'

Inès had been trying to pack her suitcase for the last hour but couldn't find anything suitable to wear. Not the black dress with spaghetti straps. Not the cream-coloured blouse that she only wore on special occasions. Mia, meanwhile, was rummaging through the pile of books she'd had brought over from London. 'What the hell are you doing with those stupid books?' Inès demanded.

Mia said she wanted another drink, just one before the taxi came. 'What difference can it make? I don't care what they think of me.'

In the taxi Mia was almost cheerful, on the verge of laughter, which was presumably what made the airline employee at Orly ask them if they were going somewhere sunny on their holidays as he smiled a little flirtatiously at Inès.

'Yeah, that's right,' Mia replied sarcastically. 'And I hope you get to enjoy the same sort of holiday one day very soon, monsieur.'

The flight was delayed, which was no bad thing. Mia bought a beer and a sandwich that she didn't take out of its packaging. 'Passengers for the Royal Air Maroc flight to . . .' She repacked her bag, crushed the Heineken can in one hand and headed towards the gate. That was when she saw Inès, standing in the middle of the duty-free shop. Inès, staring into a mirror and frantically applying gold eyeshadow with her index finger. Inès turned around and Mia saw that she was crying. She looked like a peacock, black tears running down her cheeks, as if all the colour was bleeding from her beautiful dark irises and pupils. Mia rushed over and hugged her. She held her hand and didn't let go of it for the rest of the journey, and this made them laugh, the two of them holding hands like that, like a pair of six-year-old girls in the school playground. They didn't feel like eating their vile-looking in-flight meals anyway, so neither of them needed more than one hand.

There were no tears at the house. Not even from Fatima and Mathilde, who normally wept so easily but whom Aïcha must have lectured beforehand. Aïcha's face was as expressionless as marble, and she looked younger, her wrinkles erased, as if rejuvenated by grief. Her eyes were as dry as stone, and a little frightening in the way they never seemed to blink. No tears were shed until it was time to see the body. Mehdi was there, laid out in the master bedroom, facing the patio door. At this point it became impossible to hold back. Aïcha had told them to go in alone, one by one, and she guarded the door like some one-headed Cerberus. Standing in front of their father's emaciated body, though, staring at his gaunt cheeks and bald head, Mia and Inès each found it impossible to maintain their self-control. His lips were purple, as if he'd drunk too much red wine, and his immense bulging forehead was so cold under their fingertips. Poor Mehdi, eroded by sickness and sorrow until he was little more than a bag of bones. That night, all five women slept in the same room, as far away from the corpse as they could, at the very end of the children's wing of the mansion. Mathilde, Selma, Aïcha and the two young women whom they continued to call 'the girls'. They lay on mattresses. It was over. They had outlived the last man. That night, Inès had her old nightmare about cities bereft of all male presence, cities where the women waited for a return that would never happen. Aïcha slept deeply, and she snored. There was a measure of relief mixed in with their grief. At last, Mehdi's torments were over. At last, they would be able to talk about something else, recite other prayers, nurture new dreams. They were like little girls who'd been caught in a game of

Grandmother's Footsteps and were finally able, free from Mehdi's staring eyes, to unfreeze and start running around the playground again.

At dawn, the masters of ceremonies made their appearance. Three men: one in a burnous and babouche slippers, the other two in suits and sunglasses. They looked deeply distressed as they greeted the widow and the daughters. They were professionals. The eldest man lowered the hood of his djellaba and clicked his tongue against his palate. He held out his hand to Mia and said something incomprehensible in Arabic.

'You must say "Amen", my girl.'

'Amen.'

What they lacked was not courage but vocabulary. Inès asked Selma: 'What are we supposed to say when people offer us their condolences? What's the accepted phrasing?' But no matter how many times Selma repeated it to them, they couldn't remember it and in the end they just nodded or sniffed in response to the other mourners. 'Our Father, who art in heaven': that was the only prayer that Mia knew. She'd read it in so many books. Heard it in so many films. She buried her father following rites that she knew nothing about, in the name of a god that she didn't believe in, in a language that she didn't understand. She thought about the stories her grandmother used to tell her when she was a child. About the world before Babel, when all men were close to God and misunderstandings did not exist.

They were dressed in the white djellabas that Selma had found at the last minute, cheap djellabas made from the same poor-quality fabric as the caterer's tablecloths. Mehdi's body was brought to the middle of the living room, wrapped in a shroud. They laid it on the cold floor. The men sat cross-legged and began to sing. The tallest man, the one in a grey suit, had a very beautiful voice. Aïcha twisted her headscarf between her fingers; she was upset by the absence of a coffin and kept thinking: He wouldn't have liked that. He wouldn't have liked it at all. She would have preferred other rites, a deep grave dug in the earth, a boat sailing towards the kingdom of the dead. A jackal-faced god weighing her husband's heart. How much did Mehdi's heart weigh? More or less than a feather? She remembered a story she'd heard about corpses being burned by the banks of the Ganges in India. It was said that the dead people who'd suffered, those whose lives had been marked by anguish and conflict, took longer to burn and their pyres had to be constantly fed with more fuel.

The five women were there, dressed in white, hair wrapped in headscarves. No perfume, no make-up. They were there, like a five-headed Hydra, a mythological figure that could never be slain. A clan. Faced with this assembly all praying to the same god, it seemed that these women too were connected by a common dogma, a shared faith, a mystical urge that gave them the feeling that their body was the extension of another's. Aïcha sat in Mehdi's spot on the sofa and the others squeezed together next to her. They were there, silent, complicit, and they stood up when the crowd began to arrive. Two buses had been chartered by CCM and Mehdi's former employees came to pay him one last tribute. Their faces disfigured by perspiration and sadness, they offered each of the women a comforting word, a happy memory. Wafa, more blonde than ever, her eyes puffy with tears. Hicham Benomar, Farid and the whole IT team took the girls' hands in theirs. 'A great man, truly. He didn't deserve what happened to him.'

It was as if time had stopped, or rather as if past and present had merged and the long parenthesis of isolation and degradation had never existed. The living room and the conservatory were packed with mourners. Old friends, acquaintances, former colleagues. The funeral was a society event. An elegant old man who had never left the alleys of the medina stood chatting with a general. A Jewish doctor, now living in Canada, told Mia that he'd known her father in Fes in the 1950s. 'He was a real champion, Mehdi, always top of the class.'

Mia instantly recognised Professor Slimane. His hair and moustache had turned white and he'd put on a little weight, but his features were the same as ever: gentle and harmonious. Her former Arabic teacher stood shyly in a corner, unsure what to say or do. Mia walked over to him. 'Thank you for coming.'

He put his hand on Mia's shoulder. 'Your father was very proud of you, you know. He told me that every time I saw him.'

Yes, the past was coming back in waves and she saw some old school friends among the crowd. Girls she had once thought beautiful and who now had two children, fat ankles and a drinking problem.

An ambulance driver entered the living room and stood beside the officiants. He kept glancing at the screen of his mobile phone, as though he had somewhere else to be. The crowd responded to the incantations, chorusing 'Amen', left hands raised. 'They're accompanying the angels,' Selma explained to Inès. 'Look, the soul is flying away.' The angels? But where had they been, these angels, through all those years? Inès was sweating inside her horrible synthetic djellaba and that made her angry. She wished she could have worn a pretty black dress, a hat with a veil, high-heeled shoes. She watched as women sobbed, hands covering their eyes, and thought about her break-up from Jérôme a week ago. The way he'd kept repeating: 'I don't understand, it's so unfair.' She had replied: 'There's nothing to understand. It is what it is.'

The ambulance driver looked relieved. At last, they were about to leave. The men lifted the body and escorted the dead man to the seaside cemetery opposite the kasbah in Oudayas. By two o'clock only the women were left in the house. The sole sound was the shuffling of sandals, djellabas being folded and picked up. The other women – friends, secretaries, former servants, distant cousins whose names they'd forgotten – were slumped around tables, their collars yellowed by foundation. They dipped their bread in melted butter, spooned honey over it and nodded sombrely.

Aïcha took refuge in the garden. She sat in a plastic chair under the jacaranda and lit a cigarette. She would have liked to enjoy being alone for a while, but Kaoutar, a tall, elegant brunette with aesthetically altered lips, sat beside her. Kaoutar was a doctor too and Aïcha could smell the alcohol on her breath. Gin, she guessed, or possibly vodka. Kaoutar took off her shoes and Aïcha observed her friend's swollen, purplish feet.

'We don't spend enough time in our gardens,' said Kaoutar.

'That's true,' said Aïcha with a smile. She didn't feel like talking.

'Do you remember, the year that Mia was born? I was pregnant with a boy and I had a miscarriage. Well, I buried the baby under our pergola. Youssef never understood that. He held it against me. But I found it comforting, a sort of consolation. In fact, I think it made me love my garden a little bit more.' She took a beige leather flask from the pocket of her djellaba. 'You know, it's not so terrible, being a widow. Of course, you'll be haunted by your memories to start with. You'll feel a pang of sadness when you go through his clothes. And you won't be able to eat the food he loved any more. When Youssef died, I didn't eat endives for at least two years. Now I adore them again. What did Mehdi love?'

Aïcha gestured at the flask and said: 'He loved that.'

Kaoutar slept on the sofa that night. She was too drunk to go home and Selma hid her car keys. It was already dark outside when a man came to the door. He insisted on seeing Aïcha, and when Fatima asked him his name, he said: 'They call me Rasputin.' The maid went to fetch Aïcha, who came to the entrance hall, accompanied by Selma. The man waited, hands in pockets, intrigued by the paintings hung on the wall. His face was covered by a thick black beard and he had tangled, greasy hair. He was tall, very thin, and despite his badly cut clothes there was something stylish about him.

He pointed at a painting. 'Did the boss do that?'

Aïcha nodded.

'My condolences. The boss was a great man. We met at Salé. He helped me. So I just wanted to say, if you ever need something, you can count on me. Anything.' And, with his thumb, Rasputin made a throat-slitting gesture.

Epilogue

When I left the farm, I didn't bring anything with me. At first I'd thought I might take a few knick-knacks, souvenirs, a book or a photograph album, but in the end I decided against it. The more time passed, the less I felt like opening drawers or cupboards, acting like a grave robber. The objects around me gave me bad dreams, and at night I was assailed by images of corpses. I was afraid of unearthing secrets, resurrecting former lovers, discovering some disgusting habit or pathetic obsession. I didn't find my father's notebook, the one with the purple cover, nor my grandmother's typewritten stories. I told Tibari to set fire to all the cardboard boxes. I hate novels where the protagonist finds a lost manuscript, cassette tapes containing the dead man's confessions, the vestiges of a life unlived. It's too easy. Life isn't like that. And time does not uncover secrets, only more mysteries. 'The less you know, the better for you,' my father used to say, and in the end I decided he was right. The truth should be left to families with no imagination. When Mathilde and Mehdi dreamed of being writers, perhaps they had started to crack the world's armour. Perhaps they thought that they could mend something, that writing would give their existence soul, meaning, a sense of accomplishment. What did they lack? Time, talent, courage? Mathilde thought she'd led an interesting life, that it might make a good story, but for Mehdi it was different. I suspect he wanted to write because he knew he was incapable of giving anything up, of being content with what he had, and now it is up to me to confront his opacity. I cannot say anything definitive about him: every time I make a statement about my father, it seems as if I could also affirm the exact opposite. Yes, I was the one who had to tell this story, and I think about the Painted Lady butterflies that make the epic voyage from Africa to the Arctic Circle, guided only by the sun. These migratory butterflies are tiny – they weigh barely a quarter of a gram – and it is never the butterfly that leaves Africa that reaches its destination, but its distant descendant. These eternal fugitives brave the sun that burns their wings and the cold that freezes them. Blindly, they await the winds of night to carry them across seas.

I always saw my father as a character in a novel. Or rather, he became so mixed up in my mind with the books he gave me to read that his tracks have been well and truly covered. I don't believe that he wanted to prevent me getting to know him. On the contrary, he gave me the key to another part of him, at once the most secret and the most essential: his fantasies, his self-image, the flame that burned deep inside him. Gone was the CEO in his tenth-floor office, and I was left with the memory of his tears when he watched Inès sing 'Le Blues du Businessman'. He was an actor without a stage, imprisoned within himself, forced to make the long march to humility, and he died out of politeness. Enough of this. It's gone on too long.

My neurologist told me to write down my memories. 'Your cognitive resources must be emptied so that they can be reallocated to something else.' In other words, I need to learn to forget, to jettison this burden of the past, so as soon as something comes to me – a memory or a lie – I scrawl it on a Post-it note. The walls of my bedroom are covered in them. Mathilde's picnics at the cemetery. The apartment above the Rex cinema. The sauerkraut that my mother served to the minister of industry. Sometimes I feel as if I'm finding my way out of the woods like Hansel and Gretel, following a trail of white pebbles, and at other times the ground gives way beneath my feet and I feel lost again: this story's meaning eludes me. I close my eyes and try to recall the sound of poplar leaves rustling in the wind, the taste of the misty air coming back from a day at the beach, the feel of Fatima's callused fingers on my back. I wish I'd managed to write more evocatively of happiness. Like the night my mother took us to sleep on the beach so we could admire the moon. The way my grandmother would mess around while driving, almost killing us all. The scent of the geranium petals that Inès stuck to her dolls' eyelids. It's not true that people only leave when they no longer feel any love.

My mother is angry with me. She didn't like me spending the summer at the farm, profaning her past. She can't stand the beasts that dwell within me. She wants me to recuperate, to get better. It's important to her that I am happy. She asks me lots of questions about the book I'm writing. She knows it's about our family and that bothers her. She's like her father: she dislikes these fables of the 'romantic soldier'; she refuses to let her life be wrung out to disgorge stories. She thinks it's not good for me, stirring up the past like this, picking at old wounds. She believes we should drink from the waters of Lethe, forget everything. Not make the same mistake as certain poets, lured by pride or madness into visiting the kingdom of the dead. She says: 'I wish you were done with this novel.'

And: 'I forbid you to get inside my head.' I also wish I was done with it, and at the same time I wish it would never end. If only I could never talk again, just live inside my book as if it were a house, weave it every day and unravel it every night, like Penelope's shroud, never letting anyone read it. But sometimes I look outside, I go for a walk, and I feel the desire to live. To be done with this room, this desk, this paper, these annotated books, this life lived only to be written, this terror of conversation. Ghosts. I imagine a day when I will no longer need to put books between myself and life, when I'll be able to linger, to pass unnoticed, to be in stories instead of telling them. Perhaps that's why I'm losing my memory. I can no longer cage or tame the woman inside me.

Hakim wrote me a message: 'I'm so happy. You realise this is the first time in twenty years that there's been good news about Muslims?' I didn't respond. That night, he would watch the World Cup semi-final between France and Morocco in his Parisian apartment, and he and Inès would paint their children's faces – on one side with the green star of the kingdom and on the other with the French cockerel. They would say: 'May the best team win. We're happy whatever happens.' They're afraid things will get out of hand, afraid of racist attacks and Arabs burning cars. Afraid that people will doubt their loyalties. Journalists keep leaving me messages. They want to know who I'm supporting. An American writer sent me his congratulations. Even my mother won't stop talking about it. 'Have you seen how good they are? How proud they make us? Did you know that most of them weren't born in Morocco, and they don't even speak Arabic?' She sent me the video of Boufal dancing on the pitch with his mother. They all seem convinced that if Morocco wins this match everything will be made right, that justice will be done and Goliath defeated. A new world order will open up for all the damned of the earth and the time of humiliation will be over. Yeah, sure. 'It's no better or worse here than it is over there.'

My father and I used to play a game: we had to say whether this or that country, this sea, that mountain, was a man or a woman. Morocco? A man with a moustache. France? A woman who smokes cigarettes. The Atlantic was a man, the Mediterranean a woman. None of us say it, but it's him we're thinking about. Mehdi, who would be sitting on the edge of the sofa, his eyes ablaze with pride and joy. He's always present in my mind: the way his hand trembled when he smoked, the way he used to crush the cigarette stub afterwards, the way he sat, the sound when he turned the pages of a book. His smile. My father, who was so naive he believed that all the walls in the world would fall and we would build tunnels. That tunnel does not exist. Or, if it does, it's a cold, dark place through which I am crawling like some blind, obstinate creature. Since he's dead, this match is futile and it will give me no joy. What was the point in trying to work out where I belonged, which country was mine, when I didn't even know who I was? What is identity without memory? I'm not talking about the memory of a people – I don't really care about that – but the stories my grandmother told me, the fables that my father invented, those intimate *once upon a time*s of which I am made and with which I am covering the walls. When people ask me where I'm from, I never know what to say. I become like a stutterer, unable to get the word out, and finally, exhausted, give up trying. My father, the great pretender, liked to make out he was something he wasn't, and – like him – I have become my own counterfeiter, a poor copy of a masterpiece, a forged banknote that is worthless to all but the most gullible fools, those who deserve to be ripped off.

In one of Aragon's poems, he wrote about 'the malice of the drowning man', but I think my father would have been a gentle, docile drowner, smiling in the face of misfortune. A small man in a cage, a deposed lord entrenched behind the citadel he had built from piles of books. At one point he was offered the chance to leave the country. Others had done it before him: corrupt businessmen, senior officials who had jet-skied to Spain. It could have been a real adventure, a great escape, like something from *Papillon*. My dad might have enjoyed that, but he didn't want to do it. He never left, and yet I always knew that he was in a kind of exile. Eight years after his death, my father was cleared of all charges. There was an official apology. But the shame remained, and so did the fear. What is the point in being proclaimed innocent once you're dead? Innocence only exists in books.

Acknowledgements

My thanks to the team at Villa Albertine in New York – Gaëtan Bruel, Louise Quantin, Judith Roze, Anne and Raphaël Bourgois – for their kindness and the help they gave me in my research. My thanks to the Dom Luis I Foundation who welcomed me to the beautiful town of Cascais so I could work there. I am grateful to Nuno Costa Santos and Sara Leal for introducing me to the Azores, as part of the Arquipélago de Escritores festival. I often go back there to write. To Emmanuel Delavenne, thank you for the 'room of one's own' and the pretty desk.

I would like to warmly express my gratitude to Abdellah Labraiki, Moulay Arafa Alaoui, Said Boufaim, Azzedine El Mountassir and Ghislaine Benkirane for sharing with me their happy and sometimes painful memories of my father. Thank you to Dominique Lons, to Chafik Chraïbi and to Professor Jacques Hughon for having so generously shared their medical knowledge with me. Thank you to Guillaume Badoual, my former philosophy teacher and my friend, for sharing his memories of Lycée Descartes in the 1990s. To Reda Allali, Hicham Houdaifa, Abdellah Tourabi, thank you for describing your adolescent years and your passion for football with such humour and subtlety. And lastly, thank you to all those whose names I can't mention, my lifelong friends, who have no choice but to keep their sexuality secret. This book is for you. I owe you so much and your fire burns inside me forever.